PRAISE FOR DiANN MILLS

BURDEN OF PROOF

"DiAnn Mills never disappoints. From characters to fall in love with to those who need to be behind bars, this story is one that will tug on every emotion and wring you dry— while making you love every minute. Put on a fresh pot of coffee before you start this one because you're not going to want to sleep until the suspense ride is over. You might want to grab a safety harness while you're at it—you're going to need it!"

LYNETTE EASON, bestselling, award-winning author of the Elite Guardians and Blue Justice series

"In *Burden of Proof*, DiAnn Mills pairs a traumatized FBI agent with a desperate father to create a suspense-packed story that will keep readers captivated until the very last page."

NANCY MEHL, author of the Defenders of Justice series

"DiAnn Mills has raised the bar for romantic suspense yet again. *Burden of Proof* will hover in your mind until you finish it and are sad there is no more. Good thing she continues to write such powerful novels."

LAURAINE SNELLING, author of the Under Northern Lights series

"In this third book in Mills's action-packed FBI Task Force series, the stakes are higher than ever. Compelling characters and a riveting plot that fits seamlessly with current events make this novel impossible to put down. Readers can count on being glued to the pages late into the night—as 'just one more chapter' turns into 'can't stop now.'"
    ROMANTIC TIMES

"Mills has brought cultural and spiritual differences to life. Her characters, along with their real-life struggles, will bring an instant connection to readers. Her expertise in story development guarantees *High Treason* will end up as a favorite."
    CHRISTIAN MARKET MAGAZINE

"This suspenseful novel will appeal to Christian readers looking for a tidy, uplifting tale."
    PUBLISHERS WEEKLY

"The action-packed, romantic suspense includes the FBI, the CIA, a Saudi prince, and foreign intrigue wrapped in a mystery that keeps readers guessing until the last page is turned. . . . Fans of clean read suspense, without explicit sexual content and bad language, will enjoy the romantic chemistry, the suspense, and the conclusion."
    MIDWEST BOOK REVIEW

DEEP EXTRACTION

"A harrowing police procedural [that] . . . Mills's many fans will devour."

LIBRARY JOURNAL

"Few characters in Mills's latest novel are who they appear to be at first glance. . . . Combined with intense action and stunning twists, this search for the truth keeps readers on the edges of their favorite reading chairs. . . . The crime is tightly plotted, and the message of faith is authentic and sincere."

ROMANTIC TIMES, 4½-star review, Top Pick

DEADLY ENCOUNTER

"Crackling dialogue and heart-stopping plotlines are the hallmarks of Mills's thrillers, and this series launch won't disappoint her many fans. Dealing with issues of murder, domestic terrorism, and airport security, it eerily echoes current events."

LIBRARY JOURNAL

"[Mills] has the ability to sweep you off your feet and into the middle of an adventure in a matter of paragraphs. . . . If you are looking for a little bit of action, romance, intrigue, and domestic terrorism (and a happily ever after!), then this is the book for you."

Radiant Lit

"Fans of clean romantic suspense will enjoy this well-plotted winner."

PUBLISHERS WEEKLY

"From the first paragraph until the last, this story is a nail-biter, promising to delight readers who enjoy a well-written adventure."

CHRISTIAN MARKET MAGAZINE

"Steady pacing and solid characterization make this latest from DiAnn Mills a sure favorite among FBI procedural fans. . . . The well-crafted case takes several twists and turns along the way and keeps the pace and tension high."

ROMANTIC TIMES

DEADLOCK

"DiAnn Mills brings us another magnificent, inspirational thriller in her FBI: Houston series. *Deadlock* is a riveting, fast-paced adventure that will hold you captive from the opening pages to the closing epilogue."

FRESH FICTION

"Mills's newest installment in the FBI: Houston series will keep readers on the edge of their seats. For those who love a good 'who-done-it,' *Deadlock* delivers."

CBA RETAILERS + RESOURCES

"Mills does a superb job building the relationship between the two polar opposite detectives. With some faith overtones, *Deadlock* is an excellent police drama that even mainstream readers would enjoy."

ROMANTIC TIMES

DOUBLE CROSS

"DiAnn Mills always gives us a good thriller, filled with inspirational thoughts, and *Double Cross* is another great one!"

FRESH FICTION

"Tension explodes at every corner within these pages. . . . Mills's writing is transparently crisp, backed up with solid research, filled with believable characters and sparks of romantic chemistry."

NOVELCROSSING.COM

"For the romantic suspense fan, there is plenty of action and twists present. For the inspirational reader, the faith elements fit nicely into the context of the story. . . . The romance is tenderly beautiful, and the ending bittersweet."

ROMANTIC TIMES

FIREWALL

"Mills takes readers on an explosive ride. . . . A story as romantic as it is exciting, *Firewall* will appeal to fans of Dee Henderson's romantic suspense stories."

BOOKLIST

"With an intricate plot involving domestic terrorism that could have been ripped from the headlines, Mills's romantic thriller makes for compelling reading."

"A fast-moving, intricately plotted thriller."

"Mills once again demonstrates her spectacular writing skills in her latest action-packed work. . . . The story moves at a fast pace that will keep readers riveted until the climactic end."

FATAL STRIKE

FATAL
STRIKE

Tyndale House Publishers, Inc., Carol Stream, Illinois

DiANN
MILLS

Visit Tyndale online at www.tyndale.com.

Visit DiAnn Mills at www.diannmills.com.

TYNDALE and Tyndale's quill logo are registered trademarks of Tyndale House Publishers, Inc.

Fatal Strike

Designed by Dean H. Renninger

Edited by Erin E. Smith

Published in association with the literary agency of Books & Such Literary Management, 52 Mission Circle, Suite 122, PMB 170, Santa Rosa, CA 95409.

Fatal Strike is a work of fiction. Where real people, events, establishments, organizations, or locales appear, they are used fictitiously. All other elements of the novel are drawn from the author's imagination.

For information about special discounts for bulk purchases, please contact Tyndale House Publishers at csresponse@tyndale.com or call 1-800-323-9400.

Library of Congress Cataloging-in-Publication Data
Names: Mills, DiAnn, author.
Title: Fatal strike / DiAnn Mills.
Description: Carol Stream, Illinois : Tyndale House Publishers, Inc., [2019]
Identifiers: LCCN 2019012319| ISBN 9781496427090 (hc) | ISBN 9781496427106 (sc)
Subjects: | GSAFD: Suspense fiction. | Christian fiction.
Classification: LCC PS3613.I567 F38 2019 | DDC 813/.6—dc23 LC record available at
    https://lccn.loc.gov/2019012319

Printed in the United States of America

25	24	23	22	21	20	19
7	6	5	4	3	2	1

Dedicated to Tony and Cathy Barrett,
my brother and sister-in-love. Thank you for
your support and believing in my stories.

ACKNOWLEDGMENTS

MY SINCERE GRATITUDE to all who helped me during the writing of *Fatal Strike*. I appreciate your wisdom and encouragement.

Todd Allen—You are the super-critiquer. Thanks for never holding back.

Lynette Eason—Love our brainstorming sessions. We are sister-plotters!

Guy Gourley—Thank you for taking the time to explain the psychology of my characters. Your suggestions always make my stories stronger.

Karl Harroff—Thank you for never refusing to help me figure out weapons and ammo!

Heather Kreke—You were my go-to person to understand Father Gabriel and Silvia. Thank you!

Mark Lanier—Your teachings in the biblical literacy class give me insight to the spiritual growth of my characters. Thank you!

Pastor Averri LeMalle—Your life lessons helped me all the way through this book.

Richard Mabry—The mention of medical terminology and treatment is spot-on because of you. Thanks!

Edie Melson—Thanks for always encouraging me and giving me tips on steampunk decor. You are amazing.

Many thanks to the FBI for their willingness to answer my questions and help me work through plot points.

1

SPECIAL AGENT LEAH RIESEL scanned the headlines on her phone. A prosecutor from Galveston had been found murdered behind a construction site, the second apparent victim of gang violence in two days. Both deaths were caused by rattlesnake venom injections to the heart. Before she could pull up additional reports on the woman's untimely death, Leah's phone rang.

"Riesel, hostage situation in Galveston," the SWAT commander said. "Grab your gear. The chopper takes off in five."

"On it." She took a last lingering look at the half-eaten blueberry donut and coffee on her cubicle's desk.

Could this have anything to do with the two murders in Galveston?

Before most of the city began the workday, Leah boarded a

Little Bird helicopter beneath whirling blades and the pressure of a critical operation. Dressed in full camo and shouldering her sniper gear, she inhaled the rising temps. Feverish Houston. With the familiar air transport sounds ushering in memories of past missions, her adrenaline kicked in.

A pilot from the tactical helicopter unit lifted the chopper into the air for the twenty-minute ride to Galveston. She recognized him from previous assignments involving aircraft used to deliver SWAT and the elite hostage rescue teams to crisis incidents. This morning her focus eliminated any chitchat.

Leah grabbed sound-canceling headphones and contacted the SWAT commander already on the ground. "Riesel here. Special Agent in Charge Thomas briefed me on a home invasion that's turned violent."

The SAC would be watching the operation at the Crisis Management Operations Center.

"Negotiations have gotten us nowhere." The SWAT commander's voice rose above the chopper's blade-snap. "Two unidentified men are holding two women and three children at gunpoint. Galveston PD estimates they've been inside the home for at least an hour. Demanding we leave the area after giving them five hundred grand and a gassed-up speedboat. Clock is ticking with forty minutes max. We've backed off as far as they know."

Leah swiped through pics taken with telephoto lenses and sent to her phone. Each ski-masked man held a child as a shield. Leah detested the savagery and the horrific emotions the hostages must be feeling.

"We're located on San Luis Pass Road on the western section of the island. Nearest house is five hundred yards away. Owners are in Europe. We're in contact with the agency managing it."

She didn't need a key to access the home.

The SWAT commander continued. "One of the hostages is the owner of the home, Amanda Barton."

"Is there a Mr. Barton in the picture?"

"Divorced. Lives in California."

Unlikely the ex-husband was behind this.

"Agent Jon Colbert will be on scene shortly," the commander said. "He had a deposition early this morning in Texas City and drove on to Galveston. Over the weekend, his SWAT partner had emergency knee surgery. Out for six weeks."

And Leah's partner had left the city yesterday on vacation. The luck of the draw meant she and Jon would be working together. "I'll contact you as soon as we land."

Jon Colbert, a sniper who had excellent marksmanship and a stellar reputation, also worked organized crime. But she and Jon had never worked together. The idea of teaming up with an agent she barely knew made her uneasy. If a sniper mission required a partner, she preferred an established relationship where she would know how the person processed information.

Shoving aside her doubts, she narrowed her thoughts on what lay ahead. The precarious situation and local law enforcement's inability to negotiate added up to why she and Jon had been assigned to the case.

She grasped her backpack, lighter than usual with only a spotting scope, ammo, water, communication equipment, extra batteries, granola bar, and a handheld radio. Her Glock, as comfortable in her right hand as a toothbrush, found its spot in her back waistband. She touched her H-S Precision heavy tactical rifle.

The sooner she got to Galveston, the sooner she could provide intelligence and help neutralize the circumstances. Her priority was seeing the women and children freed from these ruthless men.

Jon received a text from Special Agent in Charge Thomas that Leah Riesel had left the Houston FBI office and was en route to Galveston. He'd met her a few times, and they'd qualified together. Attractive woman—dark-brown hair, light-olive skin, New Yorker with the accent to prove it. Her professionalism in the violent crime division wavered between exceptional and extraordinary. A touch of toughness. Jon had heard not to make her mad—she had earned the nickname Panther for a reason. He remembered her stats—number three in the US for distance shots. Good thing he wasn't easily intimidated.

Once the chopper landed, Leah would be transported in an unmarked car to a vacant house more than a quarter of a mile away from the Barton home. No point in making the two men more trigger-happy when they'd warned law enforcement to back off.

The SWAT commander spoke through Jon's radio attached to his collar. "Thermal imaging confirms four adults and three children inside the Barton home. The men claim they'll kill the children first. We have fifteen minutes."

In Galveston, Jon stopped at Broadway and Sixty-First Street. Tourists persisted in the middle of the thoroughfare, pushing strollers, riding surrey bikes, and enjoying the day. Some were dressed for the beach and others clutched what they needed for their excursion. All hindered his turn. Obstacles in his mission. If they knew the situation not far from them, they'd grab their loved ones and speed home. Each moment delayed his shot and shoved the hostages closer to death. A chilling composure took over his emotional, mental, and physical reactions.

The busy street finally cleared. Jon turned west onto Seawall Boulevard and drove on to San Luis Pass Road. The hostage site was four and a half miles beyond there.

Were the two men inside the Barton home wannabes looking to make a name for themselves? Strung out on drugs? Was this a personal vendetta? No matter how this ended—either a surrender or he'd be instructed to take a shot—their moment in history would likely be the lead story on tonight's news.

His phone alerted him to an incoming call. He responded before the first ring ended. "Colbert." The chopper's rhythmic whir reverberated through his phone.

"Riesel here. Landing in five at Galveston Island State Park. SWAT commander has given me a location on the west side of the Barton home."

"I'll be on foot by then. Taking a position on the east, beach side."

"I'll need seven minutes to get into place," she said.

"Okay." No need to remind her of the ticking clock.

He touched End and whipped his truck onto a beach-access road where police officers had instructed residents to shelter in place. He switched off the engine. Grabbing his gear, he bolted down the beach. A Galveston police officer stopped him, and Jon handed him his ID. Seconds later, he moved toward his site. A sultry breeze blew across the water, and he recalculated his shot.

Crouching low, he moved past police SWAT standing guard. FBI SWAT held the position Riesel was headed for. They were racing against time, a commodity that stopped for nothing or no one. At any moment, one of the armed men could pull the trigger on those inside the Barton home.

Restraint.

Control.

Tense muscles relaxed.

His heartbeat slowed.

A clear head laid out the steps before the kill shot.

No mistakes.

Precision.

Accuracy.

A chance for the women and children to live another day.

Near a sand dune, he tuned out the occasional seagull and the waves rushing against the shore. After wiping the sweat from his hands on his pants, Jon set up his rifle and scope, activated his radio, and spoke to the SWAT commander and Leah Riesel.

2

LEAH HOPED THE ARMED INTRUDERS didn't lose patience. Fat chance the hostages would be released alive when they wore short-sleeved shirts with identifiable tats. On the western side of the empty house, she assembled her rifle while a member of the FBI SWAT team held an H&K submachine gun and surveyed the area. She pried open a window and climbed through. He handed her the rest of her gear. They worked mechanically, like always.

She and the SWAT member, a man she respected, moved through the house to an eastern window where she'd have full view of the Barton home. After opening the window, she cradled her rifle and adjusted the scope to line up with the man wielding a gun in one hand and holding a small, screaming boy in front of his face. The little guy squirmed and twisted. What a coward to use a defenseless toddler. The man closest to Jon waved a gun and wrestled with a little girl.

Leah's sympathies wrapped around the women and children. If only she could send a message that trained people were in place to help.

Time ticked.

Was she doing the right thing? Had the negotiator exhausted all means of talking the two men down? A sniper's actions were often described as both personal and impersonal. The men inside the Barton home, no matter how savage their behavior, had family and friends who loved them. Perhaps mothers who held them in their hearts and would grieve their deaths. Leah was about to end any thoughts of their rehabilitation.

She wondered if the same questions darted through Jon's mind. That's who they were—intelligent and caring people who chose to stop killers when all negotiations failed. Someone put her out of her misery if she ever became impervious to taking a life, when squeezing the trigger stopped being a regret. These were human beings, not targets. All the training, mastering skill sets, and psychological hints and helps pointed to her making mental adjustments to survive.

One day, she wanted to be a mother, but she had no idea how she'd explain her FBI roles to loved ones. How did a woman justify such a controversial calling? Her conviction, her life mission to keep people safe, ran through her veins as sure as oxygen.

Leah drew in a few deep breaths and embraced the familiar control of her body. Shoving aside the pressure to free the hostages, she slowed her heart rate and relaxed her body. Expelled all thoughts from her mind. Lined up the shot. Nothing pressed her but the mission.

"Agents Riesel and Colbert, take your shot," the SWAT commander said. This was what she and Jon needed: assurance of their backstop, that no one was behind the targets who might be harmed.

The man at the other end of her scope turned slightly. Clearly he had no intentions of lining up for the perfect kill shot.

She spoke into the microphone to Jon and the SWAT commander. "Ready?"

"Yes." Jon's voice resonated firm.

They needed immediate incapacitation. Some claimed a sniper pulled the trigger between heartbeats. Maybe so. She fired when her mind registered the right moment.

A feeling of *now* suspended. She gently pulled the trigger back.

The explosion. Then impact.

The familiar kickback shook her body.

The man went down, releasing the small boy.

Jon's man also slumped onto the floor, and the little girl he'd been holding broke free. Leah reached for her binoculars. SWAT raced toward the Barton home. She panned her scope to the women, who drew their children close, covering them in tears laced with terror and joy. An intimate moment not meant for Leah's eyes, but if she were there, she'd hold them tightly. She pulled away from viewing the crime scene.

While relief flowed through her body, there was no celebration for two men's deaths. A critical situation had been neutralized.

Scrutinizing the outside area, she spoke into the mic again. "Looks like the hostages are okay. Can you confirm?"

"Affirmative," the SWAT commander's low voice responded. "Riesel, Colbert, SAC Thomas will contact you within fifteen minutes."

"Riesel, I'm heading your way," Jon said.

After packing her gear, she texted SAC Thomas, her normal

protocol upon completing an assignment. She left the house, this time through the front door, noting the airy beach decor. A relaxed atmosphere for those who needed a getaway. Leah walked toward the SWAT team at the Barton home. Her gear weighed her down in the heat, and right now it felt twice as heavy.

Jon ambled her way. His stride and erect shoulders exuded confidence. Danger drew him like a magnet. She bore the same chemicals in her brain.

A trait they needed to stay alive.

Jon's responsibilities in the FBI organized crime division, specifically gangs, kept him busy when he wasn't working directly with the SWAT team.

He filed this morning's mission into a part of his brain labeled "process later." There was value in trekking through every moment of a sniper mission. This part of analyzing himself had more to do with ensuring he remained mentally strong than providing an explanation or justification for his actions.

To the bureau, the mission's success was critical, and the actions would be reviewed later. To Jon, success meant his ability to emotionally detach and then reel in his human instincts. When the job turned him into a machine—or an animal—he'd resign.

Leah Riesel approached him. "Can you give me a ride back to Houston? My chopper left me."

"Sure. I assume the after-action review will be mid- to late afternoon."

They'd both go through the debrief later in Houston. Part of the job. If they'd failed at the Barton home, SWAT would determine what went wrong on-site there and repeat in Houston.

Ambulances shrieked closer to the crime scene. Galveston police stopped a KHOU TV van before it drove into the Barton driveway. The van backed up and parked on the side of the road. Three newspeople emerged with equipment and broadcast lights, signaling they were going live.

"Here come the reporters." Leah's tone avoided condescension. Simply a fact.

"At times, I'd like to eliminate the police radios in the newsroom."

"And deny media the fun?"

Jon detected her slight smile. So she did have a sense of humor, contrary to popular reports that her attitude gave stoics a run for their money.

One of the reporters rushed toward them. "We have what appears to be FBI SWAT. Can we have a word?"

Jon surveyed the beach and flatland around them. "Not at this time."

The man was not deterred. "This must have been quite an ordeal for the hostages. Who's the other woman with Mrs. Barton? Did you take the kill shots?" The reporter pressed a mic to Jon's mouth. "When will the FBI make a statement?"

Leah and Jon ignored the reporter and walked toward Jon's truck.

Once there, he started up the engine and waited for the cool blast of AC. Their phones, like appendages, alerted them to a text. They both focused on the message from SAC Thomas.

Don't leave Galveston. New case for both of you. Will do action review at 6 p.m. today. Call me.

Jon set his phone on the dashboard, pressed in SAC Thomas's number, and tapped Speaker. One mission over and a new one beginning.

3

THE AIR-CONDITIONING IN JON'S TRUCK bathed Leah's face, but the cool air failed to relax her. Had Galveston PD contacted the FBI for an assist in the two recent murders? Why else would SAC Thomas brief her and Jon on a new case on the heels of a sniper mission? A few miles' run always helped her body and mind calm. Those were the times she imagined Central Park in late April and early May and envisioned white-petaled bloodroot and golden Alexanders, red maple and Virginia bluebells. For now, self-talk would have to do. Guilt scraped her conscience for the momentary reprieve while other law enforcement sweated buckets in the heat.

"In the past two days, Galveston has lost two people dedicated to preserving the law—Police Officer Ian Greer and Prosecuting Attorney Marcia Trevelle," SAC Thomas said.

"The police department is working around the clock to find the killers. No arrests or suspects. Yesterday afternoon, Galveston Police Chief Zachary Everson requested the FBI's assistance in finding whoever is responsible for the death of Officer Greer. Then Attorney Trevelle's body was found."

Leah briefly wondered if the delay in getting FBI agents on the ground might have cost the woman her life.

SAC Thomas continued. "We suspect the Venenos are behind the murders. And unfortunately it appears they've struck again. This morning at 4:30, Judge Nicolás Mendez left his home for a run. When he didn't return by 6 a.m., his wife assumed he stopped to have breakfast. When he hadn't returned by 7:30, she called his cell phone, but he didn't pick up. She contacted his office and learned his staff hadn't heard from him either. She immediately called Chief Everson. A search ensued. Meanwhile, Father Gabriel of St. Peter's in Galveston received a call around 8 a.m. from a man who identified himself as a Veneno and took responsibility for the judge's death."

"Oh no," Leah whispered. What was going on?

SAC Thomas continued. "The judge's body was found outside the rear doors of the church. He appears to have received an injection of venom to the heart, an identical execution as the other two victims. And a dead rattler lay over the body."

She chilled, thinking about her snake phobia. The Veneno—Venom—gang was demonstrating a pattern.

"From the cuts and bruises, he was beaten. The medical examiner will disclose the origin of blood, type, and pinpoint what killed him. We assume it was rattlesnake venom." He took a deep breath. "The governor requested the FBI form a task force with GPD to not only find the killers but also bring down this gang. I let him know we were on it."

A task force made incredible sense. Law enforcement in and around Houston had been kept in the loop with the gang's activities, but Leah wanted the reports now, including evidence. The use of venom as a weapon meant no bullets or guns to trace. When finished, the gang slithered away.

On remote missions, she controlled her phobia with her mind. In and out, get the job done. She would handle it with this case, too, and no one would learn the truth.

SAC Thomas gave them additional information while she made mental notes.

"I want you two to take the lead on investigating the judge's death. We'll have other teams assigned to the police officer's and prosecutor's cases. Coordinate with Galveston Police Chief Everson. He's already received a solid lead from a male resident who reported at 6 a.m. that two men left the rear of the church and drove off in a late-model car. I'm sending the lead's name, number, and a full report of the crime to your phones. GPD has his statement and is securing the crime scene for now. I'm also forwarding contact information for Rachel Mendez and Father Gabriel. She told GPD her husband had so many enemies that she wouldn't know where to begin. She's on her way home now to compile a list of potential suspects."

"We'll talk to Mrs. Mendez, then contact the lead." Jon glanced at Leah and she nodded. Since the witness had already made a statement, talking to him could wait.

"Good. Make sure you two interview Father Gabriel today," the SAC said. "Find out what he knows."

After reminding them he'd see them both in his office at 6 p.m., the SAC ended the call. Leah looked at Jon, forming where to begin their discussion. Although Leah wasn't a part of the FBI's multiagency gang task force like Jon, many times the violent crime division was involved with agents in organized crime, and she was no stranger to the depravity of evil minds.

"The Veneno gang has a presence in San Antonio, Austin, and Dallas," Jon said, seeming to read her mind. "In the past year, we've seen a handful of murders that sound similar to the ones here in Galveston—but three deaths in three days suggests something big is going on."

"Do we have any idea who or what's behind them?" Leah said.

"No. TAG suspects drugs and human trafficking. Unconfirmed." He turned the air-conditioning in the truck lower. "Venenos usually have a rallying cry of *reconquista*—they want to reclaim Texas as part of Mexico. And they haven't been shy about targeting anyone who gets in their way."

How frustrating to admit few leads and no motive.

Jon crossed his arms over his chest. "I'd like the security cam footage for Judge Mendez's home and office."

"I'm sure the SAC will send it to us. Do you know anything about the judge?"

"My partner's wife used to work for him, and they have tremendous respect for his personal convictions and integrity. There are two types of judges—those who uphold the law by viewing it as right and just, and those with a more liberal attitude. Judge Mendez advocated the conservative approach." Jon paused. "No one charged with a crime, especially a violent one, wanted to go before him. He spoke openly about gang activities, and he gave members the maximum sentence."

"Someone took vengeance—and not just against him."

He tapped his steering wheel. "What are they doing besides murdering those who oppose their *reconquista* views?"

"Million-dollar question. What do you think of the *recon-quista* mantra?"

"My guess is it's a means to recruit Hispanics."

Jon stared out at the ocean, and she did the same. The water glistened in the midmorning sun. In the distance a shrimp boat bobbed on the horizon. Peaceful, unlike the turmoil around them.

Leah pushed aside thoughts about this morning's violence. "Beautiful, isn't it? Like diamonds."

"Hope you hadn't planned on catching up on sleep soon."

"Or beach time." A gust of wind picked up a swirl of sand and playfully danced across the shore.

"Can we investigate this case without killing each other?" he said. "Haven't worked an investigation with another sniper."

Jon didn't say a woman. A point for his side. "Me either. We might have similar ways of analyzing evidence."

"We can work smart, be aware of the tendency."

The Venenos believed they were impregnable, but a cocky attitude would be their downfall.

4

WHILE JON DROVE to the Mendez residence on the west side of Galveston Island, Leah read through SAC Thomas's report and information online.

"Did you know Rachel Mendez was a former attorney?" she said.

Jon lifted his chin. "She's a smart woman and reportedly active in the judge's affairs."

Leah paused to focus on what little she knew of the woman—age forty-two, fourteen years younger than the judge. Questions mounted.

"Do we know the ages of the children? Hold on, I'll look." Leah scrolled through her phone. "Their oldest child is a girl, age five. And a baby boy. Nix the idea of the kids offering a testimony."

Leah spotted the Mendez home—a three-story beach structure painted mint green and erected on stilts disguised with white latticework. A photographer's dream view of the ocean. The kind of home Pinterest users drool over and pin to a board titled Perfect Vacation Spot. Palm trees swayed and boats dipped in the water like kids bobbing in a pool. This morning's sunlight held stage over jewel-studded water, peaceful and breathtaking, except for the reason she and Jon were there.

Jon rang the doorbell, and a police officer opened the door. After Jon and Leah identified themselves and displayed their creds, the officer stepped aside for them to enter a light-filled living area with a rear wall of glass facing the bay. A cream-colored sofa and turquoise-and-cream chairs were positioned with views of the water. Wall hangings and accents picked up the colors and beach theme.

The police officer disappeared to speak to Mrs. Mendez. Leah would be the primary in the questioning unless the woman preferred talking to Jon.

Within a few minutes, Rachel Mendez emerged dressed in stylish torn jeans, a white shirt, and gold sandals. Leah recognized her from online pics. She'd been a model before turning lawyer, and it was no surprise Judge Mendez had fallen in love. Her features were airbrush perfect—light-brown, shoulder-length hair and huge blue eyes. She carried a toddler boy, and a little girl held an older woman's hand. Both children resembled their father's roots and had their mother's delicate features.

Jon introduced himself and Leah, and each presented their card to her.

"Agents Colbert and Riesel, please sit down." With red-rimmed eyes, Mrs. Mendez pointed to the seating area. She introduced her mother. "If you'll excuse me, I'll be right with you. We just returned from the hospital. My children are clingy, and neither want to stay with their *abuela*. They're too young to comprehend what has happened, but they sense something is terribly wrong."

The two women disappeared with the children. From another room, the cries of unhappy little ones met her and Jon's ears. Leah spotted a family portrait on a nearby distressed-wood credenza. Judge Mendez and his family smiled into the camera. Nothing would ever be the same for this family struck by tragedy.

Mrs. Mendez returned and sat opposite them. "My mother has been a wonderful help. I'm fortunate she lives on the island. She's always been there for me, a saint like my dear husband."

"We are very sorry for your loss." Leah allowed sympathy to lace her words. "We promise to find whoever's responsible for your husband's death."

She shook her head. "You can't promise anything, Agent Riesel. We can only pool our thoughts and resources to bring these tragedies to an end." She breathed in deeply, no doubt for control, and resumed her poised stance. "I want my husband's killers found and prosecuted."

A take-charge woman. "You're a brave woman." Leah added compassion to her tone. "Do we have your permission to record our conversation?"

She met Leah's gaze. "My background and the judge's voice whispering in my ear tells me to have an attorney present, but I am an attorney. Record it. I don't want to go through the interview again."

Jon pulled out his phone and laid it on the table between the women.

"Agent Colbert and I will be asking questions, but for now

we need to hear from you exactly what happened prior to learning about your husband's death. We respect your pain. Don't feel like you must hide your emotions."

Rachel stared at her hands folded in her lap. "Thank you. I'll do my best. I must be strong for my children and those around me." She blinked back a tear, and the mask of a sophisticated woman lifted to reveal grief.

"Take your time, Mrs. Mendez."

Mrs. Mendez closed her eyes. "The judge ran weekday mornings. He claimed exercise gave him energy for the day. This morning he kissed me good-bye while I was still in bed and said to have the coffee ready." She sighed and bit back a sob. "He said the same thing every morning he ran, his way of saying he loved me. We treasured our early mornings together, sharing coffee and greeting our children as they wakened. When he didn't return, I thought he'd stopped for breakfast, which he does on occasion."

Rachel glanced out onto the waters, then back to Leah. "Father Gabriel contacted me, but when he said he and Nicolás were at the church, I knew something was wrong. My husband would have called me, not Father Gabriel. I had no idea that when my husband kissed me, it would be our last time together." She blinked back tears.

"Has there been anything unusual about his behavior?" Leah said.

"I'm not sure how to appropriately answer. Yesterday, after the police found Marcia Trevelle's body, Nicolás received a phone call. He tried to record the conversation, but the man hung up."

"What was said?" Leah observed the woman nibbling her lip.

"All I know is the man spoke in English. According to

Nicolás, he was high or drunk, and he claimed my husband would be the next to die by the Venenos."

"How many times had this happened?"

"Only once."

Leah wondered if Judge Mendez had received other threats that he'd not told his wife.

"Mrs. Mendez," Jon said, "did your husband report the threat?"

"Yes, sir, directly to Chief of Police Zachary Everson, who said he'd contacted the FBI for assistance. Chief Everson recommended immediate protection, which neither of us wanted. My husband refused to cower to bullies. Both the judge and I carry weapons and are trained to use them. I see now we were foolish, which is why I requested police assistance until this is over." She gripped her hands. "Nothing stops fear for my children."

Leah had talked to distraught people, and each time it strengthened her belief in her job. "Were you friends with the other two victims?"

"Everyone knows everyone else here on the island. Marcia Trevelle and I were close. At one time, we worked for the same legal firm. Stayed friends. The judge was more acquainted with Officer Ian Greer."

"Did you and your husband discuss their deaths?"

"We were heartbroken and angry. This has all been so incredibly sudden. Last night, my husband renewed his commitment to rid Galveston of the Venenos and all violent crime."

"Judge Mendez is to be commended for his position." Leah hoped her words sounded as sincere as she intended them to be.

Tiny lines fanned from Mrs. Mendez's eyes. "I appreciate it."

"Were there any conversations we should be aware of regarding the other deaths?"

The woman tilted her head as though contemplating her reply. "Nothing substantial. I suggest having a conversation with Chief of Police Everson. My husband valued his dedication to the police department."

The tension in the room escalated, and Leah wondered if Rachel Mendez opposed Everson. A door slammed, and the little girl burst into the room in tears.

"Mama." The child ran to her. "Let me stay with you. I'll be quiet."

Rachel pulled her daughter onto her lap and kissed her cheek. "This is a grown-up conversation," she whispered.

"Daddy says I'll be grown soon enough."

Leah's heart seemed to melt at the tender sight. She smiled into the little girl's large brown eyes. "Hey, I'm Leah. What's your name?"

The girl leaned into Rachel's embrace. "Ella."

"Beautiful name. I bet you're going to school soon."

"Yes, ma'am. Kindergarten."

The grandmother appeared, holding a fussing baby. "Ella, please come with me so Mama can talk to these people."

"I like this lady." Ella reached out her hand, and Leah took it.

"I like you too," Leah said. "When I was a little girl, my mama always wanted me to be obedient."

Ella turned to look at her mother, who nodded. The girl then smiled shyly at Leah. "Okay. Will you tell me bye before you leave?"

"If it's okay with your mom," Leah said.

Ella slipped from her mother's lap and followed her grandmother from the room.

Rachel whispered her thanks. "Parenting is more difficult than I ever imagined." She took a breath. "Back to helping you and Agent Colbert. I need to compile a list of those who opposed my husband, and I apologize for not having it this morning. He had many enemies, and someone is guilty. If you'll check back tomorrow, I'll have it ready for you."

"We'll be here all day," Leah said. "The list is critical for the investigation. Are there any names that rise to the surface?"

Rachel's chin trembled. "I suggest looking at all of his cases. Have you filed search warrants for our home and my husband's office?"

"Do we need them?" Leah said.

"My attorney would not approve of what I'm about to say, but I want to help find my husband's killer. For his professional office, I require a search warrant. For here at home, I give you permission to search through his desk drawers, any storage folders in the closet and credenza, and image his computer and other mobile devices. I have his passwords. He had his phone with him, and Chief of Police Everson has it. I assume he's run prints. You can obtain a copy of his calls from him."

"We appreciate your cooperation. An FBI team will be assigned to the sweep here and later at the courthouse when the warrant is in place. In the meantime, Agent Colbert and I would like to look at the judge's office."

"I'll show you where he worked."

5

IN THEIR BRIEF SEARCH of Judge Mendez's office, Jon and Leah didn't turn up anything of note. Jon contacted Houston FBI for a team to image the computer, sweep the room, and request a search warrant for the judge's courthouse office. He hoped the FBI team had better luck.

In his truck with Leah beside him, Jon drove down Thirty-Second Street toward the home of Edgar Whitson, the witness to this morning's crime. Leah had called him as a courtesy to make sure he was home.

GPD officers surrounded St. Peter's on the corner. Jon parked half a block away from the church near the Whitson home, a freshly painted white bungalow facing seaward and backing up to the church. With residences lining only one side of the street, the chances of neighbors having cameras that might have picked up those who'd dumped the judge's body decreased.

An elderly man with a full head of snow-white hair stepped out of the house onto a porch bordered with yellow roses as thick as dandelions in spring. An American flag waved from one porch post, and a Texas flag saluted them on the other. As Jon and Leah approached the porch, the man introduced himself. Jon reached out and shook his hand. "I'm Agent Colbert, and this is my partner, Agent Riesel."

She grasped his hand. "We appreciate your willingness to talk to us."

"I fought in the Punchbowl in 1951, the Korean War." He nodded. "The families here on the island who've been hurt need to see justice served." Mr. Whitson returned her smile. "Miss, the FBI's doing a great job of recruiting pretty gals."

"Thank you."

"The wife's lying down. Feeling a bit puny today. The older we get, sleeping comes full circle like we're babies again."

"I'm sorry," she said. "We won't be long."

"Whatever y'all need. Come on inside, where it's cooler." He opened the door to a living room bright with sunlight. Usually older people lived in the dark, at least in Jon's experience. The scent of freshly brewed coffee met his nostrils.

Mr. Whitson led the way into the kitchen. "Made a new pot a few minutes ago. Want a cup?"

"A jolt of caffeine sounds wonderful," Leah said.

"You, sir?"

"Never met a cup of coffee I didn't like." The three filled their cups, rich and dark like Jon preferred. He picked up a framed wedding photograph near the coffeemaker. A much younger Edgar, dressed in his Marines uniform, stood erect beside a lovely petite woman.

"That's me and the missus some sixty-five years ago. The war was over, and we were ready to put it behind us."

Jon handed it to Leah. "What a beautiful couple." She glanced up. "Mr. Whitson, you're still the same size as you were then."

He laughed. "I'll be sure to tell the missus. She complains about my middle. Our granddaughter's an interior decorator, and she says pictures don't go in the kitchen. But I don't care."

"Me, either." Leah peered at the vintage photo. "Looks perfect here."

"Mr. Whitson, we'd like to record your testimony." Jon held up his cell phone. "Are you okay with that?"

The older man hesitated. "But can you keep my name out of it for the missus's sake? The Venenos won't take kindly to me talking to you folks."

"We'll keep your name from the media," Jon said. "In fact, we'll be knocking on your neighbors' doors too. If your information leads to an arrest and the case goes to court, we'll make sure you and your wife are protected."

"Good." Mr. Whitson nodded. "Let's take our coffee out back. Been thinking about the view from there, and you might want to take a few pictures."

"Mr. Whitson, you're a smart man," Jon said. "Might need to recruit you."

Leah held up her phone to Jon. "I'll take the pics if you'll record."

Outside, humidity dripped from plants and flowers. Jon complimented him on his vegetable garden. Huge red tomatoes, green and red bell peppers, and two varieties of lettuce. Jon gazed about sixty feet over the five-foot-tall bush line to the rear door of St. Peter's. "What happened this morning?"

"I woke early, before 6 a.m., and thought I'd pick a fresh tomato from the garden. Me and the wife like 'em for breakfast. I went outside and heard a commotion at the back of the church, like a thump. I peered over there and saw two men at the rear door. They walked down the steps to a car parked real close. One of them slammed the trunk. Drove off. Didn't think much about it until I saw the police show up around 8:30. I went over and learned a body had been found at the church. I told an officer I needed to talk to whoever was in charge. They connected me to Chief of Police Everson. He told me the FBI had been called in to work the case. Before you two got here, I heard on the news about Judge Mendez's body left at St. Peter's back door."

"Are you sure of what you saw?" Leah said. "It's still dark then."

"There's a light pole in the church's parking lot, and I have one mounted back here on my garage." Mr. Whitson pointed to both. "The lights showed me the man's face who shut the trunk. He looked familiar, but I didn't place him until Agent Riesel called me about your visit." He yanked a weed shooting up from a bottlebrush. "Thought I got all them boogers."

Jon wanted to be that spry one day. "Can you give us a name?"

"Hate to accuse a man of a vicious crime. But why were those men back there unless they were up to no good? The man was Dylan Ortega. He and his mother belong to St. Peter's, like me and my wife. Well, his mom attends regular, and he's there at Christmas, Easter, and Mother's Day. You know, a holiday Christian."

"And you're sure his name is Dylan Ortega?"

"Yes, sir. When he was younger, he'd help me pull weeds in

my flower beds and keep the yard looking good. Great kid then. I speak to him when he comes to church. He's changed in his looks—longer hair and an earring. Not judging those things, only noticing a difference. Sorry to say he did time for burglary a while back."

Jon jotted down the need for a background on Ortega. "Can you describe the second person?"

"Similar build. Wore a baseball cap over his eyes."

"Make of car?"

"When it backed out under the pole light, I caught sight of the hood. Looked like a Mustang. Dark color."

"Dylan Ortega might have a legitimate reason for being at the church."

"There isn't Mass then, and even in my day young people didn't go to confession at 6 a.m." The older man was blunt and spot-on.

"Anything else?"

"Don't think so."

"We appreciate your coming forward. If you think of anything you've missed, please contact us." Jon gave him his business card.

"If what I saw brings justice in the judge's death or either of those other victims, I'm glad I spoke up." He arched his shoulders. "Oorah."

6

LEAH LEFT THE WHITSON HOME with her mind on the dear retired Marine who wasn't afraid to speak the truth. "Mr. Whitson reinforced my belief in the American people."

"Bet he marches in every parade, and his uniform still fits," Jon said.

She laughed, and it felt good. "Married for sixty-five years? Loved the photo of him and his wife on their wedding day. My belief in marriage rose several notches."

"Depends on the commitment, I guess."

Leah shook away any thoughts of her own parents' forty-year marriage. Back to business. She stopped at the passenger door of Jon's truck. "I'll pull up Ortega's address. Finding him takes precedence over talking to Father Gabriel or the other neighbors."

"Would you contact Chief of Police Everson to see if he has additional information about Dylan Ortega?"

She pressed in the number, and Everson answered on the first ring. She explained the conversation with Edgar Whitson. "We're heading to his address now."

"He hasn't had an issue with us since his arrest for armed robbery," Everson said. "Keep me posted."

"Thanks." Leah laid her phone on her lap. "Let's hold off on a BOLO until we have a chance to question him."

Like Jon, Leah believed a be-on-the-lookout alert might work against them if Ortega panicked or ran. She held up a finger. "I have the address, and I'll send a request for his background." When she finished typing, she slipped her phone into her pocket. "I took enough pics to get an idea of what Mr. Whitson saw." She lifted her head and stretched her shoulders. A good workout would help her body fight the aches of stress.

In Jon's truck, a text landed in her phone. "Here's what we have on Dylan Ortega," she said. "He's twenty-one years old. Lives with his mother, Silvia Ortega. He's employed at the Hotel Galvez. Works days in the maintenance department. Two years ago he was convicted of a second-degree felony, armed robbery, and Judge Mendez sentenced him to eleven months in jail, then released him on parole. Been clean since with no arrests, and not a suspect in any outstanding crimes." She glanced up. "I'll see if he's at work. We might luck out." She pressed in the Hotel Galvez's number and requested the manager.

"Dylan Ortega hasn't reported to work or called in the past three days. Hold on a moment." The creak of a shutting door, then the manager spoke again. "Dylan's no longer considered an employee of the Hotel Galvez. I'm disappointed. He was a good worker."

"What was his prior record?"

"Outstanding, but we have a strict policy on reporting to work. Why is the FBI interested?"

"We have a few questions. If he makes contact, please notify the FBI immediately. Here's my number." She finished the conversation and huffed. "Let's hope Ortega isn't on the run."

"Fired?"

"That happens when you don't show up to work."

While Jon drove to the Ortega residence, she pondered. What were the odds of a young man dumping a body at a church where he was a member? Not a smart move. But it was all they had.

How did Ortega spend his spare time? Who were his friends? What were his values? How had prison affected him? Her mind continued to flood with questions.

Her phone sounded a news update. "Media found out about Dylan Ortega."

"If he's not already on the run, he will be now. Time to request a BOLO for Dylan Ortega."

"According to Mr. Whitson, Dylan wasn't alone. I'm hoping Dylan's at home and has no idea he was identified this morning. If he's not there, do you mind if I take the lead with his mother?"

"Go for it. A single mom may feel more comfortable with another woman. Considering her son's past record, she'll be real nervous about the FBI wanting to question him."

Leah stared out the passenger window. "If she warms up to me, I can sympathize with her. We'll learn soon enough if she's a law-and-order type." A thought occurred to her. "Edgar Whitson said she and Dylan are members of St. Peter's. Is Judge Mendez? Do we know for sure?"

"Should be in his background."

She navigated her phone and discovered what she'd suspected. "Judge Mendez, our witness, and the suspect are church members. Odd, don't you think?"

Jon nodded. "Connections are what we want. Check on the church affiliation for the other two victims."

The search didn't take Leah long. "Neither Officer Greer nor Attorney Trevelle belonged to St. Peter's. Both are recorded as Protestants and members of separate denominations."

"Shove that into a mental file because we might need that later." Jon pulled into a middle-class neighborhood.

"Do you think Father Gabriel might have information?"

"Little early to say since the other two victims were found in separate locations. Plus, priests take a vow not to reveal anything said to them during confession."

"Even when a church member is killed?"

"Right." Jon shook his head. "The killers could be using him, a pawn in their game. Look at the way they've crawled into other Texas cities. They select one Catholic church and a particular priest. Then they beat up somebody and leave the poor soul at the church door and call the priest to check out their deposit. All we can pinpoint is the similar scenario."

Jon stopped at the curb in front of the Ortega home. Leah took in the neighborhood. Most of the houses displayed pride with well-kept yards. The two-story Ortega home boasted fresh white paint trimmed in blue. Modest and neat.

"What do we have on the mother?" he said.

"Forty-three years old. Works as a dental hygienist. Never married. I'm curious about how she instilled values and respect."

"Anything else?"

"Only child. Her father worked as a dentist in Mexico City.

Entered the country legally when Silvia was four. They settled on Galveston Island. Several years ago, her parents died within a few months of each other. The father passed of a heart attack and the mother of a blood disorder."

"So Dylan is her only family."

Leah frowned, thinking about her own mother. "Is she a mama-bear type who believes her son is a perfect specimen of mankind? Or does she see faults and weaknesses?"

"Only one way to find out."

7

FROM AN UPSTAIRS WINDOW of her home, Silvia studied the black Ford pickup parked at the curb. If a family hadn't canceled her last three cleaning appointments, she'd still be at the dental office.

A woman and a man exited and studied the area. What did they want, or who were they looking for? Both were dressed in camouflage pants and black T-shirts. She tasted acid rising in her throat. Holstered guns were attached to their belts.

The strangers spoke and pointed to her door. No mistake they were there to see her. Surely nothing about Dylan. He hadn't come home last night, and he must have forgotten to call or text. He and Elena could be together. Silvia didn't approve. God warned people about such things. Her scattered thoughts refused to pull together.

Dear God, don't let my son be in trouble again.

She crept down the steps to the landing, holding her ample middle. The porch steps squeaked with the familiar sound of someone approaching the door. Pounding caused Silvia to jump.

Ignore them? Oh, she wanted to. The unknown always shook her to the core. Why would armed people be at her front door unless they had bad news?

A second round of pounding.

If the two people really wanted inside, all they had to do was break down the door. She unlocked the dead bolt, squeezed the knob, and turned it to reveal those on her doorstep.

The woman with large eyes, like copper pennies, and dark, wavy hair greeted her. "Ms. Ortega, I'm Special Agent Leah Riesel from the FBI, and this is Special Agent Jon Colbert."

The man had short, dark hair and wide shoulders. Silvia sealed them both in memory. They displayed their identifications. Silvia had no idea what FBI credentials were supposed to look like, but she examined each one and hoped the two were official.

"Why are you here?" Silvia did her best to hide the trembling.

"We'd like to talk to your son, Dylan," Agent Riesel said. "Is he home?"

A sensation like a sledgehammer battered against her chest. "Not right now. Why?"

"We'd like to ask him a few questions about this morning. When do you expect him?"

Silvia bit into her lip. "I'm not sure."

"Was he home last night?" Agent Riesel's persistence both frightened and angered her.

"No."

"Do you know where he stayed?"

Silvia dug her fingers into her palm. "No."

"When was the last time you spoke to your son?"

"Last night around 8 p.m. Right now he's at work." She dipped her chin to punctuate her words.

"Ms. Ortega," the woman said, "his employer at the Hotel Galvez says your son hasn't been to work in three days."

Silvia had washed his uniform and laid it on his bed, but she hadn't looked to see if he'd returned for it. "There must be a mistake."

"May we come in and talk?" Agent Riesel said.

Silvia shook her head. "Explain to me what this is about."

A bead of sweat rolled down Agent Riesel's face. "Judge Nicolás Mendez was killed this morning. Agent Colbert and I are assigned to the investigation."

Silvia had heard the tragic news at the dentist office earlier. "I don't understand. Of course I'm sick about what happened. But I barely know Judge Mendez and his family."

Agent Riesel tucked a strand of hair behind her ear. "A witness claims to have seen Dylan at St. Peter's early this morning about the same time police believe Judge Mendez's body was left at the church. That's why we need to talk to him."

Her stomach soured. "This is a bit overwhelming. Come in and we'll straighten it out." She stepped aside and allowed the two agents to enter. The aroma of a vanilla candle filled her home. Normally the scent gave her peace. She pointed to the living room. "Please, sit down."

Silvia's attention settled on her sacred wall and shelf across the room. In the middle was a shrine to Mary, and on each side were photos of Dylan—Little League, first Communion, football, school, soccer, and three from his high school graduation. Constant reminders of her dear son.

Agent Colbert took a chair, and Agent Riesel sat on the sofa, leaving the other end open.

"Would you like something to drink?" Silvia said. "Coffee? Tea? Lemonade?"

They declined. They weren't there to socialize, and she was only prolonging the inevitable. She moved a chair beside a small table that held more Dylan photos and her rosary. Nightmare emotions flooded her, like the last time Dylan broke the law. "You say this is about Judge Mendez's death? I'm confused. My son is a good boy." But she understood perfectly why the agents were there.

"I'm sure he is," the woman said. "But he's a person of interest."

"What does that mean?"

"It means we need to talk to him."

Silvia wished she hadn't opened the door to the FBI agents. "How can I convince you he's not a part of Judge Mendez's death? Someone has lied to you. My son is innocent."

"Ms. Ortega," Agent Riesel said, her voice kind, but Silvia doubted she meant it, "I can only imagine how you must feel—"

Silvia's worst fear screamed across her mind. "Unless you have a child, then you have no idea."

"You're right. I have no concept of your angst. But not being able to talk to your son forces us to secure a search warrant. In the meantime, authorities will be looking for Dylan."

Agent Riesel's words pierced Silvia's heart. She gathered up the rosary from the table beside her and silently prayed while caressing each bead. She struggled for a clear mind. "He loves his mother. Was brought up in church. Talk to our priest, Father Gabriel at St. Peter's. He knows my son." Sadness dripped into her words.

"Take a deep breath." Agent Riesel spoke as though they were friends. "I know you want to help. Has he contacted you?"

She refused to sink into a panic attack and breathed in deeply as Agent Riesel suggested. "He went for a walk around 8 p.m. but never returned. His motorcycle is still in the garage. Usually he calls or texts. We're very close, always have been. I'm worried he might be hurt. And now you people accuse him of murder."

"We haven't accused him of anything." Agent Riesel gave a sad smile as if it would help Silvia feel better. "We have questions pertaining to his whereabouts at the time of the crime. What's his cell phone number?"

As Silvia gave the number, Agent Colbert pressed each digit into his cell phone. She waited, begging God to make things right.

Agent Colbert placed the phone back into his pant pocket. "It rang four times and stopped. No voice mail."

Silvia blinked back the tears. Had Dylan tossed his phone, or was he afraid to answer a strange number? "Try texting him and explain who you are." She'd texted him twice early this morning before his shift, but he hadn't responded.

Agent Colbert did as she requested. Again they waited.

"Dylan often loses his phone." Silvia gripped the rosary beads tighter. "He misplaces them." She wanted to say more, that Dylan was going to school and had a wonderful future planned. "Agent Riesel, my son respected the judge. When he needed a job, I spoke to Father Gabriel. He put the two in touch. Dylan worked for the judge off and on, maintenance things at his office and rental property." She noted the look the agents exchanged with each other.

"When did this occur?" Agent Riesel said.

"About six months before going to work full-time at the Hotel Galvez."

Agent Riesel pulled a pen and notepad from her pocket and jotted down something. "Does Dylan know Mrs. Mendez?"

"He may have met her." She worried about how much to say.

"Does he know anyone in the Veneno gang, agree with their beliefs?"

"No. Never." Silvia arched her back. "They murder people with their misconstrued justice. My son doesn't agree with their actions."

Agent Riesel nodded. "What about their views?"

"Are you twisting my words?"

"Ms. Ortega, I'm sorry to upset you, but my intentions are to clarify answers."

Silvia stared at the framed photographs of her son. "Dylan didn't approve of anything about the Venenos. Not the *reconquista* slogan either. How else do you want me to say it?"

Agent Colbert cleared his throat. "We'd like a list of his friends. He could be with them now and have no idea the authorities are looking for him."

She wavered between trusting the agents completely and wondering if this was all a ploy to pin a crime on her son. "I don't know any of his friends."

"But you do." Agent Colbert's firm voice competed with the tick of a mantel clock. "You care about your son, reared him by yourself. Made sacrifices for him. He spent over eleven months in jail for armed robbery, and you'll do anything to make sure it never happens again. You're involved with every part of his life. You invite his friends here. Make sure there's plenty of food. You give them space. You even slid a pack of cigarettes into the cushion of the chair, and now you're second-guessing yourself."

"They don't belong to Dylan." The cigarettes would stay where she stuffed them. "He doesn't smoke. Naturally, I can't give you what isn't his." Silvia's voice rose. "He paid his debt to society." She stopped speaking to regain emotional stability and search for words. "He learned from his mistake and will never break the law again."

"Agent Riesel and I hope so for your sake." Agent Colbert seemed all businesslike. "It's apparent you love him. Help him by helping us. Who are his friends?"

She stared at the rosary beads. Sharing information with the FBI agents might lead to bad feelings between Dylan and his friends. "I suppose I can give you the name of a young man Dylan went to high school with. He's a fine boy. I'll get his contact information for you." She laid the rosary on the table and slipped the cigarettes into her pocket.

"I'll join you." Agent Riesel followed her into the kitchen for her address book and then back into the living room. Silvia read off Aaron Michaels's name and cell phone number.

Agent Colbert spoke up. "This makes it easier for all of us, Ms. Ortega. We need your full cooperation to find the truth."

"You're the ones making this difficult. I'm afraid for my son."

"Does Dylan have a girlfriend?"

She gazed into the male agent's face. What should she say?

"May I have her name?"

She hastily rid her eyes of tears. "Her name is Elena James. She's very pretty. Sweet and generous. Brings me flowers and compliments my cooking." Silvia allowed a bit of pride to calm her racing thoughts. Food—feeding her family—was her love language. Would she ever get to prepare a special meal for Dylan again?

Agent Riesel took over the conversation. "We understand

your heartache. May I have her phone number? She and Dylan could be together now, safe and innocent of any wrongdoing. We want the truth about this morning. Don't you?"

"Yes, ma'am." She recited Elena's phone number, and Agent Riesel wrote the information down on her notepad.

"Would you mind giving us Elena's address?" The female agent waited.

Silvia gave the information. Later she'd phone Elena and apologize.

"Thank you," Agent Riesel said. "There've been two other victims killed by the same method, Officer Ian Greer and Attorney Marcia Trevelle. Did you know either of them?"

"No, ma'am." Her fear spiraled.

"Is there anything you'd like to ask us?"

"Will you find my son before someone hurts him?"

"We'll do our best," Agent Riesel said. "I'm so sorry you're going through this."

Silvia stood and walked to the tables displaying Dylan's photos. She traced her finger over frames and faces, lingering and praying. Gathering up her Bible, she presented it to Agent Riesel. "From the time Dylan was six years old, he gave me flowers for Mother's Day. I kept one of each and pressed them into this book. These are not the actions of a killer. God will show you my son is innocent."

8

LEAH AND JON WALKED from the Ortega home to the curb where the truck was parked. Leah admired the simple beauty of purple and white petunias framing the front of the porch.

Once they talked to Father Gabriel, Jon would drive them back to Houston in time for the debrief with SAC Thomas and the SWAT team.

They'd left Silvia somewhat hostile and in tears. She truly believed in Dylan's innocence—or she performed well. The woman's final words accused law enforcement of believing the worst about her son without evidence.

Midway to the truck, Jon coughed into his fist. "We're being watched at our ten o'clock—two men outside a garage. Could be nothing but curiosity." His Glock was tucked securely in the back waist of his tactical pants within easy reach.

Leah wrapped her fingers around her weapon. "At two o'clock, a man's leaning against a late-model Ford pickup parked in the driveway. A second man is in the same position on the opposite side of the truck." She took a mental snapshot of the first man at her two o'clock . . . sleeveless shirt, mustache, early thirties. She slid into the passenger side of Jon's truck.

Jon opened his door and started the engine. "They're taking notes. Keep your eyes open. Your brain engaged. And your hand close to your firearm."

"Hard to miss us dressed like snipers. You have the organized gang training. What does your gut say?"

"We're the main attraction, and from the looks of those guys, they don't live in this neighborhood."

He drove past a group of small girls huddled together on porch steps with their dolls. A boy rode his bike in front of Jon's truck, and he swerved to miss the kid, who never looked.

Once they left the area with no incidents, Leah replayed the interview with Silvia Ortega, reexamining body language and evaluating words. She learned a long time ago people were driven by what they thought about the most. Whatever surfaced each morning when they opened their eyes ruled their hearts. Good. Evil. Love. Hate. Benevolence. Sex. Greed. For Silvia Ortega, love for Dylan occupied every breath and most likely her heart.

"Analyzing?" Jon's voice broke her silent interlude.

"Not sure if I should feel sorry for Silvia Ortega or shake her for naiveté. She's blinded by love."

"Love takes many forms," Jon said. "Like you, I want Dylan to be exonerated for her sake. But her motherly feelings don't negate his possible guilt, not only in the death of Judge Mendez but the other two victims as well. When she stuffed the pack of

Marlboros into the chair cushion, I assumed they belonged to him. When she claimed they didn't, I knew she'd lie, do anything to protect him."

"Doubt she'll ask him to contact us."

Jon blew out obvious frustration. "Was he there hiding and listening to our conversation?"

She'd considered the same thing. Without a search warrant, they had no jurisdiction to check each room. Leah doubted the BOLO would produce the man they were looking for anytime soon.

"We also need a search warrant and a surveillance team assigned to monitor Silvia Ortega's activities."

Leah sent the text and checked her phone. "From what Edgar Whitson told us about Dylan helping him as a boy, makes me wonder when things went downhill."

"Peer pressure and not having the right man in his life," Jon said. "Hits all income brackets."

She despised seeing people destroy their lives. "Dylan's record makes him a repeat offender, and I'm sure his mother knows the stats. If he's guilty, he has to accept responsibility for his own actions."

"We all do. Sounds like your parents instilled strong values."

"They did." Too bad she didn't understand their actions at the time. She needed to get past this subject before he asked another question. "I'd like to dig deeper into Dylan's background, talk to those who know him." Behavior analysts at Quantico had been assigned to develop the Veneno profile, but despite the urgency of this case, their evaluation and recommendations could take weeks.

"Why don't you try the girlfriend first?"

Leah pressed in the number Silvia had given her for Elena

James. A young woman answered on the second ring with a perky response. "Elena, this is FBI Special Agent Leah Riesel. We're looking for Dylan Ortega."

"The FBI? Seriously?"

"Yes. Do you know where Dylan is?"

"I haven't seen him for over a week. We broke up."

"I'm sorry."

"It's okay," Elena said.

"What happened?"

"Doesn't matter. We're done."

Had she broken up with Dylan or lied for him? "Do you know any of his friends or where he hangs out?"

"You'd have to ask his mother."

"We talked to her. She gave us your number."

Elena sighed. "Dylan and I met secretly. My parents wouldn't have approved."

"It's urgent that we talk to him," Leah said. "Can you think of any place he might be now?"

The girl drew in an audible breath. "Even if I could tell you where he was, I wouldn't. I know why you want to talk to him, but he would never do anything to harm someone else." She hung up.

"How did it go?" Jon kept his eyes on the road.

"Not good. We need an interview. I'll add a subpoena for her phone records and run a background. Once word gets around that Dylan is wanted as a person of interest, he'll be smart enough not to use his cell phone to contact Elena or his mother. But he might pick up another phone."

9

GALVESTON POLICE AND an unmarked car blocked the rear parking lot of St. Peter's. Jon studied the church building, gray stones that had weathered hurricanes and dissension. A cross pointed up to a dreary sky. Crime scene tape at the back door marked where the body of Judge Mendez had been found with a dead rattler poised across his chest and an injection of most likely venom to his heart. The gang had branding down to a deadly template.

Jon and Leah exited the truck and presented their IDs to a police officer, a rail-thin man in his midthirties. While he ran a report on their creds, Jon recognized Rex, an agent from the Houston office, who came up to the officer.

"These two are ours. Ignore how they're dressed." Rex wiped the sweat dripping down his square face. "Both can be a pain."

Jon shook his hand. "I resemble that, but Leah's a crack shot, and I don't want to cross her."

She pointed a finger at him. "Don't forget it."

"You both are scary with a sniper rifle." Rex introduced Jon and Leah to the officer. "We're covering every inch of the steps and landing, including where we believe the car was parked." The agent pointed to two other officers and a second agent sweeping the area.

The officer returned Leah's and Jon's IDs. "Saw the news report identifying Dylan Ortega as a person of interest in this case." He shook his head. "Too bad the witness didn't get a license plate number."

"The witness thinks they were driving a Mustang. And we have a BOLO out for Ortega now." Jon fumed over the leak to the media. "Would you know how the news got wind of the suspect's name?"

The officer held up his palm. "Not me. Whoever tipped off the media was an idiot."

Jon believed the officer. Too late anyway. The damage had been done.

The officer's radio alerted him to a call, and he took it, moving to a secluded corner of the church's parking lot.

Jon glanced over the bottlebrush bushes to the Whitson home, then back to Rex. "Have you found anything?"

"Hard to say," the agent said. "Is the witness reliable?"

"No reason to doubt him."

Leah walked to the tape line and bent to the pavement where the car most likely had been parked. She snapped a pic and looked up at Rex. "I'm sure you and these officers have plenty of tread mark images, but one more won't hurt. We could get lucky and find a match among hundreds of other vehicles." She straightened. "Paint chips would be a gift. But all I see is sand, which sticks to every vehicle in Galveston."

Jon stood approximately where the trunk would have been. The judge was muscular, would have required more than one man to lift him from the trunk. Jon searched the concrete. A button, clothing fibers, blood, anything with DNA to help find the killers.

Rex lifted a bottle of water to his lips. "We have a few things to bag: a beer can, potato chip and gum wrappers, and several cigarette butts. Must be the disposal spot before entering the church."

"Get everything you can find," Jon said. Half of a Marlboro cigarette wrapper lay at the edge of the concrete. Someone who'd been in the Ortega home smoked the same brand. And their DNA might be in the system. "Would you expedite an analysis on the cigarettes?"

"Sure." Rex pointed to the side of the church. "There's Father Gabriel. I imagine you two need to talk to him. Good luck. I have work to do."

A man in black pants and a shirt with a white tab collar approached Jon and Leah. "Father Xavier Gabriel." The priest extended his hand. "Are you police or FBI?"

Jon and Leah displayed their IDs, and Jon got right to the point. "We'd like to talk in private."

The priest frowned. "Nothing's changed since I talked to GPD's Chief of Police Everson. Can't we eliminate a second statement?"

"I'm sorry. We need a separate interview. The suspect is a member of this church."

"I heard the news." Father Gabriel's forehead beaded in the blistering sun. "Come inside."

Jon and Leah followed the priest to the sidewalk and around the church. Jon looked for debris, anything leading back to the killers. The priest gestured them through richly carved wooden doors.

"First, let me show you our sanctuary," he said.

Jon hadn't been in a Catholic church, only a nondenominational one with his old friend Hanson. Eerily quiet. Not a single sound met his ears. Reverent. Hanson would have taken a front pew and studied the altar.

A statue of Jesus on the cross and another of the Virgin Mary in lifelike form caught his attention. Both left no doubt in his mind of the holiness penetrating and swirling throughout the massive area, and Jon wasn't a man who focused on beauty and art—only facts. He expected the organ to break into an ancient hymn. "Beautiful, Father Gabriel." In different circumstances, he'd opt for sitting awhile in the sanctuary.

"God's presence, even in the midst of tragedy. I encourage both of you to return for prayer and worship." He led them down a wood-paneled hallway to a well-lit office. Huge corner windows allowed natural light to spill in.

Jon and Leah sat in dark-brown leather chairs facing his desk. A wide-screen monitor sat on the left side of the oak desk, and a Bible lay open with a pen and a highlighter in the fold. To the right of the Bible was a photo of a smiling young man, the only item indicative of the priest's personal life. A crucifix was centered on the wall behind his desk, and below it was a bookshelf filled with volumes of books. Uncluttered. Largely impersonal.

"May we record our conversation?" Jon said.

"I'm sorry. It's not in my best interest or those within my church who seek me for confession."

10

SEATED IN FATHER GABRIEL'S OFFICE, Leah observed Jon's face tighten with the priest's refusal to record their interview. She wasn't pleased either, but he had a right to say no—unless an interview took place at the FBI office. And that had her vote. A twinge of misgivings about the priest swirled through her mind. She understood confidentiality of information. Did the priest harbor information and claim his religious convictions to cover it?

Father Gabriel folded his hands on the desk, giving him an authoritative demeanor. Leah didn't fault him. This church and office were his domain. The priest continued. "Normally my duties here take precedence over everything else, but not in the matter of a murder. I want to help."

Jon moved toward the purpose of the interview. "What happened this morning?"

Father Gabriel rubbed his palms together. "I received a call on the church's landline shortly before 8 a.m. from a man who claimed to be a Veneno. I'm here most mornings before five for prayer, and today was no exception. The man told me to check outside the church's rear doors. He said I'd find a Veneno enemy, and the people of Texas needed to pay attention to the future of their state. He also said the gang was watching me. His final word was *reconquista*. When I looked, I found Judge Mendez. His eyes were open, and he had no pulse. I contacted 911 on my cell phone."

"Your details will help law enforcement put together the case. What language did the caller use?"

"English."

"Why would they be watching you?"

"I don't know, unless they think I know who's responsible."

"Do you?"

"No, sir."

"What did you do while you waited for an ambulance?"

"I prayed for Judge Mendez and his family."

"Rachel Mendez told us she received a call from you. Did you contact his wife?"

He nodded. "I told her the judge was with me. I didn't tell her he'd already passed or the police were on their way. She wanted to drive to the church, but I suggested she meet me at John Sealy Hospital. The ambulance and the police arrived before we ended the conversation. I told the police I planned to meet Mrs. Mendez at the hospital. They allowed me to drive and interviewed me there and here again."

"Did anyone at the hospital look suspicious?"

"My attention was on Mrs. Mendez."

"When did you return to church?" Jon said.

"Shortly after Mrs. Mendez's mother arrived and took her and the children to the Mendez home. I'll meet with Mrs. Mendez later to discuss the services." He paused. "Silvia Ortega contacted me. She expressed concern about a warrant issued for Dylan's arrest and your disbelief in his innocence in the murder of Judge Mendez."

"As we told Ms. Ortega, her son is wanted for questioning as a person of interest. We have a BOLO out, but there's no warrant for his arrest. We just need to talk to him." Jon's words settled before he spoke again. "If she knows where her son is, then she needs to inform us or persuade him to contact law enforcement."

"The news reported Dylan was seen outside the church's rear doors early this morning," Father Gabriel said.

"Correct."

"She believes he was here to pray."

"Did you see or hear him?" Jon said.

Father Gabriel shook his head. "Prayer is of the heart, not necessarily audible."

Jon nodded. "The front door creaked when we came in. Do the back doors?"

"I can't recall. I've been here many years, and noises are commonplace."

Was the priest avoiding Jon's question or responding candidly?

Father Gabriel eased back in his chair. "Dylan needs someone to champion him. But I agree he should talk to law enforcement about this morning."

"Do you think his mother knows his whereabouts?"

Father Gabriel studied them before answering. "Maybe. I'll talk to her, encourage her to cooperate with you."

"What can you tell us about Dylan?" Jon said.

"In the years I've been at St. Peter's, we've talked twice privately."

"Do those times include confession?"

"My vows preclude me from answering your question."

"So he's attended confession?"

"I've spoken with him at his mother's home and here in my office."

A clever evasion, Leah noted.

"What were the discussions about?"

"Sports, church activities, and part-time employment for Judge Mendez."

"Ms. Ortega told us you helped Dylan by recommending him for the job."

"I did. And I've thought about it all day." His mouth drooped as though emotion might overtake him.

"How long were the talks?" Jon said.

"Ten minutes at the most."

"So after a total of twenty minutes' conversation with Dylan, you went to Judge Mendez and recommended a man who'd done eleven months for armed robbery? Or was this a favor to Ms. Ortega?"

Leah scrutinized the priest in hopes of discerning the mixed emotional messages she was getting from him. Would Dylan kill a man who gave him a job?

"Yes, to both questions. Like God, I believe in second, third, and as many chances as it takes to help a person find the way to righteousness. It was the judge's decision to hire Dylan."

"I believe in helping others," Jon said. "But Dylan has been identified by a credible witness, and Judge Mendez is the third victim of violence this week."

"Eyewitnesses can be mistaken."

Jon moved ahead. "If the witness made an error, where is Dylan?"

"If I knew, I'd be persuading him to talk to you."

Silence swirled around the room, and Leah picked up the conversation. "Unfortunately, we're unable to work the case effectively until we find Dylan Ortega. These killers who call themselves the Venenos must be apprehended."

"Stopped. Rehabilitated. Shown God's love and forgiveness," Father Gabriel added. "Agent Riesel, I'm not sure Dylan is guilty."

"Why?" Leah said.

"If he was here early this morning in a possible criminal capacity, he may have been compelled by the killers."

11

JON WAITED FOR LEAH'S RESPONSE to Father Gabriel.

"What makes you think the gang might have forced him?" Leah maintained an impassive look on her face.

"Rumors. And I have no verification either way."

"Where did you hear about the coercion?"

Father Gabriel hesitated. "My responsibilities take me to many areas," he said. "God's work doesn't keep one away from dangerous places. I've heard the gang forces young men to join by threatening family and loved ones. Unfortunately, most gangs require the initiation of blood in, and the member's blood to get out. I want to avoid any more deaths. And to the best of my knowledge, I don't know any Venenos."

"Unless the information was revealed in confession," Leah said, her tone beginning to show her frustration.

He held up his hand. "Then I'd encourage the person to turn himself in."

That made Jon feel slightly better.

"Why do you think the gang singled you and your church out in the death of Judge Mendez?" Leah said.

"I wish I had an answer. I understand churches and priests in other cities are also faced with Veneno crimes."

"Were you acquainted with the other two victims—Ian Greer and Marcia Trevelle?"

"No, ma'am."

"Tell us about your relationship with Judge Mendez," she said.

"We played golf once a week." Father Gabriel sighed. "I lost a good friend today."

"I'm sorry."

Jon wondered if her sympathy would cause the priest to reveal more than he was willing to share or if he would see it as an insincere gesture.

"I can only forgive the killer, not only for the judge but the other two who died as well," Father Gabriel continued. "I neither condone murder nor excuse breaking the law, but the church stands for mercy and embraces the sinner."

"Murder is not a slap-your-hand offense."

"The church is in the business of saving souls by bringing all men into communion with God through Jesus Christ."

Jon stepped in before the steadily rising tension between Father Gabriel and Leah could boil over.

"Regarding the Veneno presence in the other cities," Jon said, "what have the priests of these churches involved relayed to you? The—"

"Before you go any further, I haven't talked to those priests,"

Father Gabriel said. "I recognize their names, but I haven't been to those churches. We don't belong to a club."

Jon was getting frustrated himself. "The church helps people draw the line between right and wrong," he said. "'You shall not murder' is one of the Ten Commandments as well as 'You shall not bear false witness.'"

Father Gabriel's face reddened. "Agent Colbert, you're speaking to a man who has the commandments memorized. I live them, breathe them, pray them, and teach them."

Jon reached for civility and spoke calmness into his words. "My apologies. When was the last time you saw or spoke to Dylan?"

"About a month ago from a distance. No words were exchanged." Father Gabriel sat back in his chair. "Other than reviewing questions for the Galveston Police Department and avoiding media, my day's been a juggle of one crisis after another. Rachel Mendez is grieving the loss of her husband and the father to their children. Silvia Ortega is heartbroken because of one person's accusation. A prayer service and a funeral need to be planned."

Leah spoke up, noticeably calmer. "We understand your stress and the overwhelming burdens. I can't imagine how you are dealing with this."

"My God supplies all my needs." He shook his head as if regretting the automatic response. "God's provision doesn't mean my job or yours is easy."

"Then you must see how Agent Colbert and I have a job to do, to end the rising fear regarding the deaths of three highly respected people."

Father Gabriel nodded. "Law enforcement work never ends, just like mine. But while I choose to embrace lives, I fear you have a different perspective."

"Law enforcement's role is to protect the innocent."

"And using violence to combat violence won't eliminate the problem. If I can talk to these men, I can influence them to end the violence and turn themselves in. Not only the Venenos but all gangs."

"I commend your aspirations," Leah said. "But many people on the island are afraid of who could be targeted next."

"Then I must seek out gang members before another death occurs."

Jon stifled a sigh. The Venenos were terrorists, and no one in their right mind negotiated with killers.

12

LEAH CHECKED HER PHONE for the time and status of late-afternoon traffic while Jon drove the stretch of I-45 north to Houston. They'd make their meeting with SAC Thomas and the SWAT team if traffic didn't bottleneck. Being late didn't match a sniper's DNA.

"I should have asked for a Coke before we left Galveston." She yawned.

"I can pull over."

"I'm okay."

"But I'm not." He moved into the right lane and exited at the next feeder where a Whataburger saluted them with an orange *W*.

After a jaunt through the drive-through for a Diet Coke for her and a Dr Pepper for him, they were back on the road again

59

like a Willie Nelson song. She wanted to discuss the investigation, but her mind needed to analyze findings and body language. Edgar Whitson was a hero in her eyes, and she hadn't detected anything but honesty from him. As much as Leah wanted Silvia Ortega's heart to be at peace, Leah recognized the woman's fierce protectiveness regarding Dylan . . . possibly to the extent of breaking the law. Elena James might have lied—it was hard to tell from their brief phone conversation. Had they really broken up, or was she covering for him? Father Gabriel's stand seemed illogical. He had the vow and faith thing going, which she failed to understand. But the man wanted the murders stopped and claimed he'd help. In her opinion, he'd walk into danger to save a man's soul. A threat on his life hadn't lessened his zeal.

She reached for her phone. "I'll type our notes. Then we can prioritize them and make a list for tomorrow."

"They'll change after we talk to the SAC. My guess is our meeting will be short, a debrief from this morning's shootings, and then we'll catch the SAC up to speed on Judge Mendez's case. Possibly there's new intel in the deaths of Greer and Trevelle."

"Wish we could have finished out the day in Galveston and talked to more people." She shrugged, regretting how they'd left Silvia Ortega. "Hated we weren't able to gain Silvia's confidence."

"She may be afraid to provide intel. Death by lethal venom injection isn't a great way to go."

"And this isn't her first rodeo, as you Texans say."

"How long have you been in Houston?"

"Eight years. Four previously in Dallas. Anyway, reality can be paralyzing. How does Silvia feel about learning her son may be part of a gang?" How had her own mother felt about Leah's behavior? Although she'd never broken any laws, she'd given her parents plenty of sleepless nights. Mom and Dad had tried to talk to her about responsibility until Leah ran. "Her faith will be her strength or weakness."

"We may see both before this is over." He tapped the steering wheel.

"Unload your thoughts."

"I want to discover the Venenos' endgame." Jon hammered in a good point. "Time isn't an ally. Right now, we have nothing but a rising body count."

Like Jon, she wanted solid answers. "Okay, here's my best shot." She shook her head. "Poor choice of words. We're compiling questions. On our agenda for tomorrow, I have another meeting with Rachel Mendez, Elena James—who came up clean on her background—Judge Mendez's staff, Chief of Police Zachary Everson, and Dylan's high school bud Aaron Michaels."

"Add researching known persons in southeast Texas who milk poisonous snakes."

"Rattlesnake farms." She hadn't considered the rare business of wranglers. No reason to mention her phobia. Her blood pressure shot straight up at the thought of one snake, always been that way. "I'm adding the Hotel Galvez manager."

"At the Galvez, we can check if Dylan had any visitors or mentioned where he spent his spare time. If we're lucky, we'll be given access to security footage and won't have to wait for a warrant." Jon kept his attention on the road. "Regardless of when Dylan's found, my guess is his employer, coworkers, and girlfriend know a different man than his mother or the priest."

She typed with her forefingers and thumbs. "The island's going to feel an economic pinch with the murders. Business owners will be concerned about the tourist trade taking a nosedive."

"A press release about GPD and the FBI working 24-7 should help on that front. The public needs to know law enforcement is on their side."

She lifted her fingers from her phone. "And who knows? Father Gabriel might remember something useful."

"He's putting himself in danger by wanting to bring the bad guys to God, and he believes it's noble to his faith. The hardest thing to do is persuade a man who's ruled by his convictions." Jon changed lanes and pressed the gas. "He reminds me of someone."

"Another priest?"

"Not exactly." Jon chuckled.

"Clue me in so I can find some humor in today."

"Father Gabriel reminds me of my father. Both are opinionated to a fault. Their beliefs are a religion."

She studied him. "I'm waiting."

Jon sighed. "My dad insists I resign from the FBI. Hightail it back to Oklahoma and work for the Chickasaw Nation. My plans for the future don't play into his. I'm extremely proud of my heritage, treasure it. Except my career is with the FBI."

Jon must value his dad's approval, and their relationship sounded messy. "What exactly does he want you to do there?"

"Use my criminal justice degree to get involved in the tribal governing body."

"Sounds like a desk job."

"Tell me about it."

"You two don't get along?" she said.

"Dad's taught me a lot, and we have a respectful relationship. I love him but not his notions about what's best for me."

He pointed to her phone. "Add Father Gabriel's background, his community outreach, the names of his biggest contributors, a list of St. Peter's members who have records, and the dates and names of his prison and jail visits."

"Slow down. Are you always this keyed up after a day like ours?"

He nodded. "Dylan Ortega fooled his mother—maybe. He no longer has a girlfriend—maybe. Good chance of him being a member of a deadly gang. His priest has been threatened and reminds me of a mule."

"I don't think Father Gabriel would cover for a gang member, especially when he's been threatened. But he may inadvertently know a Veneno, and that's why he was threatened."

"Makes me wonder if the gang recruits members according to church affiliation."

"Morbid thought." Leah turned to another question. "What if the cry of *reconquista* is just an excuse to commit crimes and frighten people? The three deaths were those who enforced the law, not anti-*reconquista* supporters."

"The mantra is certainly being used to cause panic," Jon said. "But I want to know what their moneymaker is. This says sophistication to me. By following the money trail, we'll have a better idea of why our victims faced execution."

Leah wasn't sure she agreed. They had a solid lead—he was just hiding. "Anything else for tomorrow's agenda?" She glanced at her notes. "We need to examine the death reports for Ian Greer and Marcia Trevelle—see how far the task force has gotten with interviews and the investigations." She took a long drink of the Diet Coke, no longer dragging from the day's activities. "Your energy level is rubbing off on me."

"Not a bad thing considering how much sleep we won't get

until this is over," he said. "Include the staging of the bodies. Photos of the three victims. Medical examiner's initial reports."

She ceased typing. "I'll send some of these questions to the FIG's expertise." The Field Intelligence Group had the technology to research and provide the information they needed.

"Before our attention turns to the action review, what time do I pick you up in the morning?"

"I can drive. You've been behind the wheel all day."

Jon frowned, and reality hit her.

"You're the alpha who has to be in control."

"I am." He moaned, then tossed her a grin. "So are you."

"I'll concede this time. The FBI office at 5:30?"

"Works for me. We can grab breakfast at a little café in Galveston that I know about. Great food and coffee."

13

JON AND LEAH ENTERED an FBI conference room where the SWAT team, SAC Thomas, the ASAC, and a counselor from the employee assistance program all sat around a long table. She'd been through the drill before but regretted being the last ones to report in. Although summer usually meant less traffic, the drive into town had been brutal, putting them back at FBI headquarters with less than five minutes to spare.

SAC Thomas stood, an impressive figure with massive shoulders pointing to his Baylor football days. He welcomed the agents and gave them paper copies of the mission report before turning the meeting over to the SWAT commander. A discussion about the morning's mission ensued with the typical what went right, what went wrong, and lessons learned. Since snipers were employed to neutralize the situation, the mission qualified as stressful.

Leah typed the men's names who'd been killed into her phone.

Jon, also busy with his phone, was probably doing the same. Neither man had a previous record. They were both single, in their late twenties, products of drug addiction and poor decisions.

The EAP counselor waved. "Any of you need to speak to me, I'm here, or send an email."

Leah had been through a psych eval three months ago after a high-risk confrontation on the northeast side of Houston. She believed the key to managing stress came from living a low-key life when not involved with SWAT, on a lone sniper mission, or working violent crime. Easy for her to do since she chose a private life.

When the meeting ended, SAC Thomas asked for her and Jon to stay behind. "We have the new case to discuss—Judge Mendez's murder and the Venenos' activities in Galveston."

The room emptied. The SAC closed the conference door and clicked on a screen at the front of the room. "This debriefing won't take long." He sat across from Leah and Jon. "Are you okay to work the gang-related homicide? Leah?"

"I'm fine, sir."

"Jon?"

"Me too. My partner's wife used to work for the judge. I know that has no legal bearing on me working the case, but I wanted you to be aware."

"Thanks. We're good there. Do either of you feel the other is not psychologically fit to work these homicides?"

Neither of them had objections. Strange question to ask with both present.

"Get the paperwork done about this morning. I don't want it to interfere with the homicides."

Leah despised that part of her job. Had to be completed, no way around it.

The SAC aimed the remote and clicked to an image of Judge Mendez's body at the rear of St. Peter's church taken by GPD before an ambulance transported the body to the hospital. The dead rattler lay across his chest. "Initial signs indicate all three victims died of a venom injection to the heart." He advanced to a photo of Ian Greer, whose body lay in an identical manner to Judge Mendez's. Marcia Trevelle's body matched the other two.

"Back up to the judge's body," Jon said. "Zoom in on his face and neck." When the image was enlarged, Jon walked to the monitor and pointed to the judge's upper torso. "Earlier you reported the judge had been beaten, which is unlike the other two victims."

Leah studied the massive bruising and cuts. "He put up a fight."

"We're analyzing hair and clothing particles," the SAC said. "We'll know soon when the full ME report is released. Where are we regarding initial interviews?"

Leah outlined Rachel Mendez's statement, Edgar Whitson's, Silvia Ortega's, Father Gabriel's, and the brief phone call to Elena James, concluding with "We requested surveillance on Silvia Ortega. She's insistent her son is innocent."

"While he remains at large. Electronic billboards will be going up all over Houston, Galveston, and the surrounding area to enlist community support." The SAC held his pen over a legal pad. "Stay on Silvia Ortega, the ex-girlfriend, and any other women linked to these homicides, because the Venenos in other cities use women to pass on messages."

For the past few years, the governor's Criminal Justice Division had provided funds for an ongoing Texas Antigang Center in Houston—TAG. The Venenos had no idea how many law enforcement specialists were on this.

"What's TAG saying after their initial response this morning?" Jon said.

"Word on the street is the Venenos are recruiting members as young as fourteen. We suspect they're trafficking illegal drugs, but since the Venenos don't have any distinguishing tats or use gang signs, it's hard to prove who belongs or what they're doing. A TAG meeting is scheduled for Friday at 9 a.m. I'll be there in your place. Need you on the case. I'll contact both of you afterward." He turned off the monitor. "Tell me about Father Gabriel."

Jon shook his head. "He has this grandiose idea of stopping the gang single-handedly. This morning's caller told Father Gabriel he was being watched. While he claimed not to know why, I think he's holding out on information."

"Your take?" the SAC said to Leah.

She sighed. "Regular stuff—no detection of nervousness in his body language. The victim and a suspect are members of his church, and Father Gabriel was shaken today. I think he's scared he'll be the next victim."

"We've learned more about him this afternoon," SAC Thomas said. "It explains his quest to convert criminals. He lost a nephew in a gang firefight in 2012. The death started his prison and community work. He's on a one-man campaign to rehabilitate every fugitive in Galveston." SAC Thomas lifted his chin. "My experience with priests tells me Father Gabriel most likely puts the church at the forefront. He wants the killings stopped, and he will do all he can to make sure that happens. But it won't necessarily be on our terms."

Jon nodded. "We'll see if he offers solid intel. I need to work harder at gaining his confidence."

And Leah needed a fast-track course on how Jon processed info.

14

JON'S BODY REQUIRED ONLY a few hours' sleep to function, and not all at the same time. Sniper missions and working organized crime were easier to accomplish with his erratic sleep pattern. As a kid, his sleep habits drove his parents crazy. To keep him inside the house, they added a lock at his dad's height—until Jon used a chair to reach it at 3 a.m. one night.

Tonight, after he finished his mental moment-by-moment replay of the hostage situation, he sat at the kitchen table of his farmhouse and pored over the ongoing reports of the three murders. The victims were too closely connected to be random, but how did they fit into the Venenos' operation? While Jon considered theorizing for the rest of the night, he needed more intel to understand a gang that used a precise method to kill three distinct people who'd sworn to uphold the law.

What did the three-day span mean? A tactic to frighten the people of Galveston? Had the victims stumbled onto something that got them killed? Were more at risk? The three victims had been alone when abducted, obviously stalked before execution. Premeditated murder.

He logged into the FBI secure site and studied Ian Greer's file. Married with two children. Active in the community. Outstanding officer with several commendations. Greer wasn't a member of St. Peter's, but he and Judge Mendez had gone to high school and college together. His body had been found Sunday morning by fishermen on the east side of the island.

Marcia Trevelle had an excellent record as a prosecuting attorney. Single, lived alone. Mentored at-risk middle grade girls. From her home alarm data, she'd left work on Monday and never returned. Her body was found at a construction site by the GPD in response to an anonymous call. Her car hadn't been located.

Jon reviewed Judge Nicolás Mendez's file. Nothing new in the investigation since the meeting at the FBI office. Jon skimmed rulings and cases for the past eighteen months in search of names, charges, convictions, sentences, and common-alities. The judge's strict interpretation of the law made defense attorneys cringe and set him up as a target for offenders, but were other law enforcement and judicial persons who worked tirelessly to protect citizens on a kill list? Would other officials back off and subsequent rulings show leniency until the Venenos were stopped? Did the killers think they had their bases covered?

Finding Dylan Ortega would be a boost for their side. So would locating the Mustang or getting a lead through DNA left behind. Maybe test results would show the blood on the judge's knuckles wasn't his own but his assailant's.

Jon dug deeper for information about Father Gabriel and his community work. The man had been a positive influence in many lives, and Jon commended him for his sacrificial efforts. Prison ministries, rehabilitation programs, health needs, and family counseling contributed to channeling lawbreakers in the right direction. But did he realize gang members could offer lip service to God while their lifestyle was still full of toxins?

Father Gabriel arranged for those assigned to court-ordered community service from Judge Mendez's office to work off their hours at St. Peter's. A little more research and Dylan's name popped up. Judge Mendez had instructed him to complete 150 hours of community service on top of his jail time. Jon sent a request to the FIG and copied Leah. In addition to all members with a record, Jon wanted a list of every person from Mendez's court who had done community service at St. Peter's church.

An email from earlier in the day garnered his attention, and he noted the sender. He'd rather hit Delete than dive into personal stuff. The message was from the widow of a good friend . . . Hanson. Hard memories refused to let him go, and just when he thought he'd licked it, bits of Hanson and Chip plodded across his mind and heart.

Face it. The truth will never let you go.

He clicked on the email.

Jon,

It's late but I wanted to thank you for little Jon's birthday present, except he's not so little anymore. At eleven years old, he's shooting up like a cornstalk in summer. You were far too generous, and he loves the drone. As you recommended in his birthday card, he spent hours reading the instructions and watching the recommended YouTube clips for more information.

He asked to send you a thank-you email, but I need your permission first.

Hope all goes well with you. We're good here. School starts for me in one week, and little Jon starts the next.

I'm seeing a man from my church. He's a widower. It's getting a little serious. We're both scared and stepping out in faith. Jon adores him—almost as much as he loves you.

And you? Are you saving lives by risking your own? My dear Jon and Hanson. True heroes.

We miss you and pray for you. When will you be in Illinois?

Love,
Claire

Jon scrolled down through the email to a pic of Jon, his namesake. The red-haired, freckle-faced boy held up the assembled drone and grinned into the camera. Looking at the familiar dark-blue eyes, so dark they looked black, and the thick red hair brought back images of Hanson. The man looked at life and laughed. Preacher Hanson, the others called him. The one man who'd shown Jon what faith in God meant by living it. No matter what knocked him to his knees, he got back up. Defied danger. Except for the last time.

Jon shoved aside the acid roiling in his stomach. If Claire could take a bold step, he could too.

Hi Claire,

Thanks for the birthday pic of Jon. Hanson lives on in your son. Please give little Jon my email address. He can write anytime he wants.

Claire, I'm no hero, but I am fulfilled with my role in the organized gang division and as a SWAT sniper. Lives are saved. I've never told you what my job involves, but it's more about gathering information and observing situations so a problem can be solved without loss of life. I wouldn't want little Jon to think I shoot people for a living.

Glad you're looking to the future. I need to meet this guy. :) I'm on a mission, but as soon as it's over, I'll plan a trip your way.

I'm not seeing anyone. Well, my new partner is a woman. But two snipers? Two type A personalities? I think we'd kill each other. I can hear Hanson making fun of me.

Thanks for your prayers.

Jon

He stole a look at the time: 12:45 a.m. He should get a little sleep soon. Leah had most likely been in bed for hours. He liked her. Today he'd seen a professional woman who had a compassionate side. Earlier when they completed the paperwork from the SWAT mission and then requested reports for the new case, night had crested. Dark circles under her striking copper-colored eyes and exhaustion in her voice said the day had been long enough. Morning was soon enough to bring her up to speed.

15

THE ALARM SOUNDED AT 4 A.M., much too early for Leah, but the hour came with the job. At least she'd managed to sleep in her own bed and breathe in the comforts of home and she wasn't in some remote spot waiting for orders to shoot. After a hot shower, she blew her hair dry, watching the time. With Houston's traffic, Jon's suggestion of leaving the office at 5:30 was a good idea. She'd rather avoid bumper-to-bumper madness and drive into Galveston early.

With nine minutes to spare, she brought her laptop to life. Intel was her lifeblood, and she craved information like a toddler whimpered for cookies. She scrolled through her in-box and clicked on a message from Jon sent around 2 a.m. Why hadn't he been sleeping? They needed to have their heads in the game.

She read while her electric toothbrush did its job. Dylan's

friend Aaron Michaels was enrolled at the University of Houston. He'd contacted Galveston police to offer information after the BOLO went public. A little odd in her opinion. Maybe Michaels didn't want to be implicated in a crime. He hadn't seen Dylan since December. Their friendship had deteriorated several months ago, but no explanation was given. Michaels had a clean record. Still he'd be talking to the chief of police today and perhaps to her and Jon.

Grabbing her backpack, she set the home alarm and hurried to her Camaro for the fifteen-minute drive to the office.

Leah pulled into the employee parking lot at FBI headquarters and discovered Jon's truck idling. Interesting. Agent Colbert played the always-early game. So much for demonstrating control in this new partnership. She'd remember this for the future. The moment she opened his truck door and slipped her backpack behind the seat, she smelled the amazing aroma of coffee, and like a warm blanket enveloping her, her ruffled personality was soothed.

"Good morning." She pointed to the cups in the console. "The coffee smells wonderful. You're about to be my fave agent."

"Are you saying if I hadn't brought you coffee, then I'd be your least favorite?"

"Give or take." She buckled her seat belt and hid a grin. They both had the navy-blue pants and blazer going . . . FBI typical.

"Are you perky in the mornings?" He pulled through the gate and onto Highway 290.

"Once I have a few swallows of coffee, I'll be jabbering." She peeled back the plastic tab on the coffee cup and blew into it before taking a sip. "I read your email. What time did you go to bed?"

"Shortly after three. And you?"

"I worked until eleven, specifically on the police reports regarding Ian Greer's and Marcia Trevelle's deaths. But you received those?" When Jon nodded, she placed the coffee back into the console. Too hot to drink.

"Did you notice a discrepancy in the way the bodies were staged and the Veneno pattern in other cities?" Jon said.

"What am I missing?"

"Aside from Galveston, all the bodies were left at the entrance of a church, not the rear like Judge Mendez. And Ian Greer's and Marcia Trevelle's bodies weren't found anywhere near a church."

She recalled the reports from the previous night. "Neither did all the victims have a dead rattler draped across their chest. Wonder why the Venenos switched up their mode of operation?"

Jon shook his head. "Has to mean something, but what?"

"Chief of Police Everson could have insight." Leah shifted gears to the other issue that had been nagging her after reviewing the reports. "It's odd that Rachel Mendez didn't mention how the judge and Greer were schoolmates." She noted Jon's nod, then said, "Maybe in her grief, she forgot to mention it. Definitely want to talk to her about that today. We have a full schedule. I assume we'll also interview Judge Mendez's staff at his office, and I have questions for Aaron Michaels. Plus those we listed yesterday."

"Let's start with breakfast at the Sunflower Cafe," Jon said. "I think you'll like it. Great local food."

Leah was used to coffee and a bagel for breakfast, carryover from being a New York City gal, and she was picky when it came to food. If she'd take the time to eat, she'd have more of a shape than a fence post—a true Texan expression.

Jon continued. "Why don't you call Father Gabriel and ask him to join us?"

Leah pressed in the priest's number, and he answered on the second ring.

"Agent Colbert and I are en route to Galveston. We'd like you to join us at the Sunflower Cafe at 7 a.m. for breakfast and to discuss the case."

"Eggs and interrogation on the menu?" he said.

She glanced at Jon. "The only thing Agent Colbert and I eat early in the morning." She was relieved when he agreed and ended the call. "Father Gabriel might have found a surge of cooperation."

"Or a stab of guilt?"

"We'll find out." She tried her coffee again, and like Goldilocks's, the temperature was perfect. "I honestly understand how he wants to help and push us away at the same time. Losing his nephew to a gang means the death affected him, or he wouldn't have chosen to rehabilitate others."

"His thinking is a bit skewed."

"I intended to research Catholicism and priestly vows last night, but it never happened. I'm pretty clueless when it comes to religion."

"Everyone believes in something." Jon shot her a look, then returned his focus to the road. "In short, a priest doesn't betray those who seek his confidence," he said. "Wonder if the nephew was caught in cross fire or if he was a gang member?"

"I'll request it." She typed a quick note to the FIG. "In your email, you mentioned wanting to talk about our partnership."

"Yep. My partner fell while rock climbing with his kids. Had emergency surgery and will be out for six weeks."

"Now you're stuck with me. We're working well together . . .

so far. Do you have family? Other than your dad, who reminds you of Father Gabriel?"

"Mom teaches political science on a collegiate level. Active in promoting literacy. Three sisters who are older, married, and with kids in high school."

"Ever been married?"

"Nope. What about you?"

She took another delicious drink of coffee. "Haven't found a man who wanted to take on my temperament or my job." Truth was she'd like to one day find a husband, but then she'd have to be honest about her past.

"Parents? Brothers? Sisters?"

She hadn't seen any of them in years. How did she respond? "I'd rather not discuss my family. I'm a one-woman show."

"Hey, we all have things we want left alone. What have you heard about me? I'm sure I need to explain some rumors."

She thought through the bits and pieces of info filtering through her brain. Jon was incredibly good-looking, but she'd not mention it. "Crack shot. Intense. Likable. Doesn't talk a lot about himself. Okay, turnabout is fair play."

"Don't make her mad." He lifted his brows, an exaggerated expression. "Stoic. New Yorker. Full of surprises. Outstanding marksmanship as your reputation proves. Can't think of anything else."

"I'm stubborn, particularly when I know I'm right." She paused, running through the nicknames she'd been given. "What does New Yorker mean?"

"Beats me."

"Cold? Unfeeling? Blunt? I fall into all three."

"I think the accent," he said.

"What about Panther?"

He took a breath. "I plead the Fifth."

"Actually I don't mind that one. Keeps the come-on boys away."

"I'll remember those words of wisdom. Here's another question." Traffic slid to a snail's pace. "Is there anything about the way I handled the SWAT mission and later the preliminaries of Judge Mendez's death that hindered our working relationship?"

"Ah, yes."

"Bring it on."

"I feel out of control with you driving."

He laughed. "Can't even picture myself sitting on the passenger side with you at the wheel."

"Are you saying you can't handle a woman driving?"

"I'd rather not discuss my obsessive fears."

He'd succeeded in making her smile. Again. She didn't see any problems in their working arrangement yet. "If you make me crazy, I'll let you know. And feel free to reciprocate." She sipped her coffee, and her mind went straight to the case. "What's really going on here? Judge Mendez sentenced Dylan Ortega to eleven months for armed robbery. Later he assigned Dylan to Father Gabriel for community service. Then Judge Mendez gave him a job. Why would he kill a man who tried to help?"

Jon turned onto Fourteenth Street toward the café meeting place. "Definitive answers are in the making with our breakfast, optimistically speaking."

"You're sure of yourself," she said. "Maybe Father Gabriel's just worried about the status of your soul."

"Mine's in good shape. No need for him to waste his prayers."

16

JON AND LEAH WALKED INSIDE the Sunflower Cafe and inhaled the mouthwatering smells of bacon, coffee, and cinnamon rolls. Jon spotted Father Gabriel at a table on the left side, his back facing the entrance. Not smart for a man who'd been threatened. A handful of people sat around the tables. None appeared suspicious.

He and Leah wove around the tables to the priest. A tea bag was steeping in his mug. If Jon were to stereotype a priest, the choice of caffeine in a bag fit. Father Gabriel stood, his black shirt and white collar giving him a distinguished look against his white hair and beard. Dark circles beneath his eyes indicated a lack of sleep.

What kept you up last night? Were you wrestling with your conscience or unable to rest because of the turmoil in your church and community? Or both?

The three shook hands and eased onto chairs that gave him and Leah full view of those entering and leaving the restaurant. After a waitress filled Jon's and Leah's cups with coffee, they gave their food orders—shrimp omelet for Leah, eggs Benedict for Father Gabriel, and smoked chicken hash for Jon.

Once the waitress disappeared, Father Gabriel folded his arms on the table. "I'd like to apologize for what may appear to be a lack of assistance in the investigation of three murders. I assure you, I'm deeply troubled by the deaths, and I want the senseless violence stopped. The island is filled with people who are scared and grieving. They need to see God in my words and actions."

"What's changed since our last conversation?" Jon was in no way interested in starting an argument at 7 a.m.

"I want my cooperation clarified. How do you think I feel about my church used as a transfer station for a violent gang's crime?"

"Angry? Distressed?"

Father Gabriel breathed in deeply. "Add mourning."

"In the event Dylan or a criminal makes confession, would you encourage them to contact law enforcement?"

"I assume their efforts to that effect would be termed as cooperation?"

"It's always better for suspects to turn themselves in. Is there a reason you neglected to tell us about St. Peter's being a community service organization for those under Judge Mendez's court, specifically Dylan Ortega?"

Not a muscle moved on Father Gabriel's face. "I apologize for omitting the information." He held up his hand as though to stop Jon from saying more. "Yesterday I spoke the truth. I haven't talked to Dylan but twice. He came to the church, completed his responsibilities, and left. He checked in and out with my secretary."

"What were his duties?"

"To keep the grounds clean and make any small repairs deemed necessary. If there was a matter needing his attention, then I left instructions with my secretary."

The priest's hands-off attitude didn't seem like the actions of a man who wanted to rehabilitate those assigned to community service. "You didn't try to strike up a conversation? Try to get to know him better? Draw him into church?"

"He wasn't interested. I approached him many times, but a conversation takes two people. Dylan is resentful of God, has no use for our Lord."

"We'd like a list of those persons who've completed community service at your church, male or female, and dates."

"All right." Father Gabriel pulled out his phone and typed. "You'll have the information before noon." He laid the device beside his knife.

Jon turned to Leah. "Agent Riesel, what questions do you have?"

"You mentioned a church secretary. We didn't see anyone in your office yesterday."

"She's on vacation this week. I've been handling the clerical responsibilities myself."

"We'd like her name and contact information." Leah positioned her hand over her phone's keypad.

"Lucinda Serrano." Father Gabriel gave the phone number.

"What can you tell us about her?"

He removed the tea bag from his cup. Looked like coffee. "In her early fifties. Married. Grown daughters. Lucinda never forgets a face."

"Did she know Greer or Trevelle?" Leah said.

Their breakfast was set before them, and Father Gabriel

asked God to bless their food and their time together. He crossed himself. "You asked if Lucinda was acquainted with the other victims, and I'm not sure."

While the three ate breakfast, Jon's thoughts centered on how to stop a string of deaths . . . and where Father Gabriel's new information would take them.

The priest laid down his fork. "Agent Colbert, you're honest and to the point. I'm a man of God above all things. My vow of obedience means the church comes before anything else in my life. Serving my members and the community is my priority. I'm responsible to spiritually guide those within my flock, and I will denounce this violence from the pulpit. I'll contact the local newspaper and a Houston TV station with a plea for anyone who has information to step forward. I want people to know all are welcome at St. Peter's, Catholic or otherwise, to have absolution of their sins through the sacrament of confession."

"Thank you." Jon toyed with the handle of his coffee cup. "I commend you for your devotion. I understand forgiveness, but have you forgotten the threat on your life?"

"I'm offering God's grace. I encourage forgiveness, mercy, and an opportunity to secure lasting peace with our heavenly Father. I'm a priest, not a member of law enforcement or the judicial community. God will render His justice to those responsible."

The conversation stepped close to mirroring yesterday's, but Jon understood distancing himself from the priest wasn't wise. "If you're made aware of a name or a possible dangerous situation outside your vows, will you help us?"

"I'll do my best."

Jon filed the conversation in his memory bank. Would be interesting to see how the chief of police viewed the priest's style of cooperation.

17

JON AND LEAH SAID THEIR GOOD-BYES to Father Gabriel and left the Sunflower Cafe to talk in his truck. Their discussion needed to be in private.

"Glad we had an opportunity to talk to Father Gabriel," she said.

"Thoughts?" Now that they didn't have an audience, Jon was eager to get Leah's take on the man.

"I'm weighing his words and attempting to balance them with my lack of understanding of Catholicism. Regardless of how we feel about him or his odd means of stopping crime, he has agreed to help."

"Which makes his position dangerous," Jon said. "He's walking too close to the middle of the road where neither law enforcement nor the gang can fully trust him. He'll assist us while wanting to talk down a killer first."

"Solo takedowns normally have bad results. And I doubt he carries a weapon."

"I don't want him dead. He's a shepherd to his community." Jon tapped the steering wheel. "If he follows the gang's instructions, he's not supposed to talk to cops. If they're keeping tabs on him, they're aware of where he was this morning. I should have considered that my invitation to join us exposed him to danger. Not my intention. I hate to think he has a confirmed death sentence—all for a venture of spreading love like a sixties flower child and helping us at the same time. Bet a steak dinner he's trying to locate Dylan on his own."

"GPD hasn't put a surveillance team on him, but we can," she said. "Might keep him alive or lead us in the right direction."

"I'll request surveillance if you'll check for updates," he said.

They had plenty of time before meeting Chief of Police Everson at 11:00. Until then, they needed to clarify a few things with Rachel Mendez. Leah called her and paved the way for a second interview.

Jon backed out of the parking spot at the café. "I'm beginning to wonder what the Venenos are all about. The lack of gang markings and online activity bothered me right from the start."

"Are you thinking more about my idea that the *reconquista* mantra is a cover-up?"

"Strong possibility. Worth digging deeper and keeping our eyes open. The men watching us at Silvia Ortega's stood where I couldn't identify them."

"I didn't see all of them clearly either. I assumed."

"We might have profiled the Venenos without evidence," he said. "As a man who's proud of his heritage, I don't want to be guilty of shoving others into a hole because of ethnicity."

"I see where you're going." She paused. "The call to Father Gabriel was in English."

His gut told him he was on to something. Investigators hadn't made any arrests that led to intel on the gang. The noise came from the gang, and law enforcement and media were swallowing it. He needed to look for the obscure, the ultimate moneymaker.

Jon whipped his truck behind a GPD cruiser parked in the Mendez driveway.

"Rachel likes you, and you made a good impression with her little girl. Why don't you ask the questions?" he said. "If it looks like she'd rather talk to me, I'll step in."

Leah stepped from the passenger side of Jon's truck and walked with him to the front of the home. The same officer from the previous day checked with Rachel before letting them inside.

Rachel stood in the foyer—red eyes and no makeup. "Come in." She led the way to the sunlit living area, where they'd spoken the previous day. She sat on a huge chair that swallowed her. Maybe it had been Judge Mendez's. An envelope was in her hand.

"We appreciate your seeing us this morning." Leah noted the children and grandmother were nowhere in sight.

She leaned forward and gave Leah the envelope. "The list I should have given you yesterday. There are only six criminals who vehemently threatened my husband over the past five years. These people were angry with his rulings. Four are currently incarcerated. If any of them are involved in my husband's death, they're working from inside a cell. Although my husband assured me he kept no secrets, I can't verify this is complete."

Leah scanned the list but didn't recognize any of the names. She handed it to Jon, but he obviously didn't have questions and returned the folded piece of paper. She tucked it into her shoulder bag. "Do you want to discuss the names?"

"There's nothing more for me to say. Have you found evidence for an arrest?"

"No more than what you've already heard from the media. Were you able to sleep last night?"

Rachel shook her head. "Thanks for asking. Even when my husband was only out of town, I rarely slept. Before my daughter went to bed, I told her Daddy was with the angels in heaven. She didn't take it well and crawled into bed with me. We comforted each other."

"I'm sincerely sorry. Agent Colbert and I won't take long. Please tell Ella I said hello."

"I will. How can I help you other than to give you my list?" Rachel's ragged voice hinted of a breakdown.

No one should experience lawless tragedy.

"You told us yesterday that your husband was acquainted with Officer Ian Greer, but it seems like they'd known each other since school days."

"Yes. I'm sorry." She sighed. "My mind wasn't functioning well yesterday. Still isn't. Ian and Nicolás had been good friends for years. His death devastated both of us."

To Leah, this confirmed the judge, Officer Greer, and Attorney Trevelle were killed for the same reason.

At Leah's nod, Jon switched the direction of the interview. "One of our leads is a young man who spent time in prison—Dylan Ortega. We understand he once worked for your husband as part of his community service. What can you tell us about him?"

Rachel swallowed hard. "I saw the FBI and police are looking for him. I've been thinking about Dylan—polite, kind. He did odd jobs, minor repair and landscaping needs around our property and at the judge's office. I remember he was shy and mannerly. My daughter talked to him sometimes, and whatever she said always made him laugh. We had no problems with his work. I never suspected him of misleading or deceptive conduct. While my husband believed in maximum sentencing, he wanted to see lives changed. Since Dylan belonged to our church, the judge gave him another chance by reducing his sentence and assigning community service work. His mother and I attend the same Mass, but I don't recall seeing Dylan with her often."

"Are you and Silvia Ortega friends?"

"Acquaintances. I think her son is innocent, but where is he? Please, find Dylan. He might have information about who killed my husband."

Compassion laced Jon's words. "We're doing our best, Mrs. Mendez."

"I know investigations take time."

"Father Gabriel spoke about his friendship with your husband, their golf outings and the community service link. Did your husband ever have reservations about Father Gabriel's position of forgiveness and second chances?"

Rachel hesitated. "While they chose not to discuss matters affecting their friendship, the judge was often frustrated with Father Gabriel's position regarding the various gangs and his desire to bring them to God. My husband preferred the spiritual aspect occur after the arrest."

"Did the difference of opinion create a wedge in their friendship?"

"Neither man would back down from his convictions."

"Judge Mendez still used St. Peter's for community service," Leah said.

"My husband believed in rehabilitation, and he was a man of faith. If the friendship looks complicated to you, note both men wanted the same thing. It was their methods of achieving it that caused disagreements but not at the cost of their friendship."

Leah thanked the woman for her candid response before switching gears. "Have you decided on a day and time for the funeral service?"

"Father Gabriel and I made arrangements last evening. The viewing will be on Friday evening with a prayer service, and the funeral Mass is scheduled for Saturday at 10 a.m. The wake will be at the parish."

Jon glanced at Leah. "Agent Riesel and I will be at both services."

Leah nodded.

Mrs. Mendez peered at them. "If I were you, I'd be looking for who's in attendance."

"We will," Leah said. Sometimes criminals returned to the scene of the crime—to gloat, satisfy some morbid curiosity, or make themselves look innocent.

Jon continued. "I have a question for you, a theory, but you may be able to confirm it."

"I'll do my best."

"Did Judge Mendez ever indicate the Veneno gang and the *reconquista* cry might be a facade for something else?"

Rachel fisted her hands. "I know he was determined to find out their means of making money, but he didn't tell me if he learned anything. He claimed the cartels from Mexico would not take over Galveston. But that's all."

18

SILVIA GREETED HER first dental cleaning of the day with a fake smile and kind words. Her heart ached, and her stomach rolled as though she'd be ill. Dylan must have lost his phone again because he still hadn't contacted her. She'd lain awake for two nights, thinking and praying while listening for the phone to ring.

Richard James asked her not to bother him or his wife again—Silvia was mistaken about his daughter and Dylan dating. Silvia wanted to scream at him. Mr. James thought Dylan wasn't good enough for his daughter, but Elena didn't look at Dylan's troubled past. She cared about his gentle heart, and she inspired him to be a better man.

Had Dylan and Elena run off together? They were in love, a sweet relationship made in heaven. Would they have gotten married? Dylan deserved happiness after all he'd been through. Although Elena wasn't Catholic, that mattered little at the moment.

But Dylan had been accused of a horrible crime. Where was he? What was stopping her son from contacting his mother, the woman who'd nurtured and loved him?

Silvia returned her attention to the dental patient and bade him good-bye. She had nearly twenty minutes until her next cleaning. Warren knew Dylan, and he didn't need to be at his store until 9:30. He'd pray with her, help her cope with the unknown. Sometimes he helped her understand the male side of life, totally foreign to her.

Warren answered on the first ring. "Silvia, has Dylan come home?"

"Not yet. I was hoping you might have heard from him."

"Not a thing. You and I have had our differences about Dylan's behavior, but I never saw any of this coming."

Such a dear man. "We can't expect to agree on everything."

"Have you contacted Elena?"

"She's not picking up, and her father doesn't appreciate my calls. He denies Elena even knows Dylan. Father Gabriel told me to pray, and I have. But I feel so helpless. I want to do something."

"Do you work all day?"

"Yes." And that was a good thing since her mind was consumed with the whole nightmare. "I did request Saturday off for Judge Mendez's funeral. Let's pray this will be straightened out by then."

"We can go to the funeral Mass together. I'll get someone to run the store for the day." He breathed in deeply, and she closed her eyes to envision his blue eyes and long lashes. "Honey, Dylan is a smart young man. No matter what's going on with him, he's resourceful and has a good head on his shoulders."

She treasured how Warren subtly kept her attention away from the police and FBI. "If he contacts you, will you persuade him to go to the police? I think it's the only way to prove his innocence."

"I'll do my best. How about dinner tonight? You don't need to be alone."

"I should stay home in case Dylan shows up." What if he was hurt or upset?

"Let me pick up dinner, and we can eat there. If Dylan arrives, I'll leave."

How thoughtful. "Then, yes, I'd love to share dinner with you."

"Be thinking about what you'd like. I'll search for some ideas, although no one can cook as well as you do," Warren said. "I'll text later. Keep praying for good to come of this. I love you, and I'm here for you."

Her heart warmed. "I love you, too." She ended the call and sank into a chair in the break room. Her phone rang, but the number was unfamiliar. Her pulse sped and she answered.

"Ms. Ortega, this is Agent Leah Riesel."

Silvia stiffened. "I'm at work."

"I won't take but a minute of your time. Honestly, I'm checking on you. You were right when we talked—I'm ignorant of how you feel. But I did cause my mother some heartache, and I regret my past actions. My fear is something will happen to Dylan before we find him. If you have any way to contact him, please let him know that Agent Colbert and I will do all we can to learn the truth. You have my number now. Let me be your friend and help you with your son."

Silvia's spirit crushed. She hadn't expected kindness from an agent who wanted Dylan in custody. "How can I trust you?"

"I give you my word."

19

JON STEERED HIS TRUCK TOWARD the Galveston County Justice Center. Leah sat beside him, navigating her phone. The county courthouse, post office, law enforcement facility, and an assortment of BBBs—bail bond businesses—covered Fifty-Fourth through Fifty-Ninth Streets, reminding him of a mall. It seemed like he and Leah were conducting busywork, and while necessary, Jon wanted to latch on to something.

Leah contacted Aaron Michaels and arranged an interview after their meeting with Chief Everson. She pulled Rachel's list from her purse and began typing the names into her phone. "I don't recognize the names Mrs. Mendez gave us. Shame on me."

"Maybe they appeared in his court before you arrived in H-town. What were the charges?"

"Drug dealers, assault and robbery, murder for hire . . . the typical. All swore to get even. Two are women." She touched her finger to her lips as though something had just occurred to her. "I've been thinking about the gang using women to carry messages. The girlfriends and wives of those who share the *reconquista* mantra could pass info at the grocery, Laundromat, nail salon, church. Anywhere."

Jon was impressed. He was the one who normally turned over every rock in an investigation. "We'd need specific women to tail. Our leads will keep us busy for a few days. I see tangible things for us to nail down first."

"Such as?" she said.

"A rattlesnake farm. The gang has to get their supply of venom somewhere."

"You mentioned wranglers before."

He swung a look her way, but Leah stared out the passenger side window. "You put me off before about this. Do I detect a problem with snakes?"

She kept her attention outside the truck. "I'd rather have a dog."

Was she admitting to a phobia or a dislike? "How bad?"

She turned his way. "I'm fine, and I agree it's a significant aspect of the case. I'll send a request for snake wrangler info."

Jon pulled into a parking area designated for the police department. Snakes sort of appealed to his wild nature, but Leah's fear could be a hindrance to working the case.

They exited his truck and walked to the law enforcement facility.

"Do you know Zachary Everson?" Leah said. "Because I don't."

"No. What are you thinking?"

"When we talked to Rachel Mendez, her body language hinted at a dislike for him. Maybe some history there, or I misread her. So I'll let you lead."

"All right. The judge openly criticized gang activities, and he could have tried a case involving a Veneno and not known the person was gang-related. And if Ian Greer made the arrest and Marcia Trevelle was prosecuting, then we have a solid link. I've requested the FIG to get us the data."

Chief of Police Zachary Everson, a wiry man with a military haircut, escorted Jon and Leah to his square office. A window faced the parking lot, allowing him to see those coming and going from the rear of the building.

Everson closed the door and sat behind his desk. Dark circles pitted beneath reddened eyes. "If we could drink, I'd pour us a double." He uttered an expletive.

"Not usually a drinking man myself," Jon said. "But I might change my mind when we've tossed the Venenos into jail."

"A Fed I like. First time for everything. When the time comes, I'll buy the bottle." He paused. "I did request your assistance for these murders, and together we can bring justice to grieving family and friends. What's new on your end?"

"Agent Riesel and I have conducted interviews since yesterday morning."

Leah gave her take on Silvia Ortega and Rachel Mendez. Then he relayed the pertinent info regarding Father Gabriel.

"We're on the same page," Everson said. "Father Gabriel is either a candidate for the next pope or looking for martyrdom. He's risking his life trying to reach gang members. Just hope his boldness for the faith doesn't get him killed."

"We've requested surveillance—for more than one reason." Jon wasn't ready to debate Father Gabriel further. "Whoever told the media we had a person of interest tossed a wrench into things."

Everson appeared taken aback. "Why?"

"I'd have liked an hour at least to run Ortega down before the media warned him." Jon studied him for a response.

"I contacted the media." He squeezed his fist. "I'm not backing down from any trail to find Ortega."

"Okay. I understand." Jon shoved aside his irritation. Three people who represented law and order had been killed on his watch. "Ortega's girlfriend claims she hasn't seen him."

"What's her name?"

"Elena James."

Everson wrote her name on a pad of paper. "He'll turn up—sooner than later. Silvia Ortega is one woman I don't trust."

"Why's that?" Jon replayed the phone conversation Leah had with Silvia.

"Seems odd she doesn't know where to find him."

"Unless he doesn't tell her everything. Do you have anyone watching the house?"

"Short on officers at the moment. Can you arrange it on your end?"

Jon studied Everson. His drawn facial muscles indicated more than one emotion. Definitely grief. Nervousness. Anger because three law enforcement officials were murdered on his watch. "Consider it done. Anything we should know about Rachel Mendez?"

"She'll not rest until the judge's killer is arrested, and she'll be on our tails until then."

Did Everson share the same dislike? "I understand you have the judge's phone. Any prints or leads?"

"Zero." Everson's features hardened. "I'll send you his phone records."

"What's there?"

"Last call was at 9 p.m. to his mother in Tampa. Judge Mendez was an icon around here. Good man. Respected the law and didn't mess around with offenders."

"Do you have intel on who's at the helm of the local Veneno gang?"

"Not yet. We have bad guys on the island, but none to my knowledge of this caliber. They've been questioned, and of course they have alibis. I suppose you want names?"

"We do. Have you heard anything about the gang enlisting members through coercion?"

"Coercion is an invention to commit violent crime. Too many kids are out there looking for ways to buck the system. Kids don't get the death penalty."

Leah jumped in. "What about the Venenos using women for communication?"

"Nothing's confirmed," Everson said. "Did Rachel Mendez give you a list of those who'd threatened the judge?" When Jon nodded, Everson continued. "How soon will you have backgrounds?"

"A couple of hours on basic info. Depends on what we learn. We'll make sure you receive the findings."

Everson settled back in his chair and took a long breath. He dragged his hand over his face. "The deaths have hit me and my officers real personal."

Leah nodded with obvious sympathy. "I'm sorry for your loss."

"Thank you. Ian Greer was a good officer, a notch above the rest. A friend." Everson hesitated. "Might as well tell you.

I dated Marcia Trevelle." He stared down at his desk before speaking. "More than dating. We were engaged. Supposed to be married in October."

The source of Everson's bad attitude surfaced. The unsolved murders were personal and professional, a mix of pride and emotions. "I'm sorry. You have a huge stake here, and I get it. We're all after the same thing."

Everson swallowed hard. "My officers are working on the other murders. I'll send you those reports. We're questioning and probing. Using our informants. It's obvious to me that when we find the judge's killer, we'll find Ian's and Marcia's."

"Any similarities noted?" Jon hadn't found anything other than the kill method and the staging of the bodies and dead rattlers, but maybe Everson had some insight. "Were the three victims working on the same case or cases? Greer made an arrest, Trevelle prosecuted, and Judge Mendez sentenced?"

Everson gazed out the window. A patrol car pulled in. "In theory, you make sense, and there are a couple cases with those parameters."

"Have you investigated them?"

"No connections to Venenos. Dead ends. We interviewed Judge Mendez's staff yesterday. I'll send you our initial report." He turned back. "Let me tell you what was going on leading up to the three murders. Last month, I started meeting with Ian, Marcia, and the judge. Ian believed the Venenos had moved into our area and were trafficking drugs, but he didn't have proof. At the second meeting, I insisted we form a task force with the FBI. I didn't want anyone killed. The others didn't agree. We had words, and I was booted out. They continued to meet, and when Ian was killed, I contacted the FBI, but it was too late to save Marcia and the judge.

To my knowledge, nothing was documented, and trust me, I've looked."

Leah spoke up. "When was the last time you spoke to any of them?"

"Last Friday afternoon, Ian told me to have a great weekend. Monday, I phoned Marcia after Ian's body was found and told her about my call to the FBI. She agreed. The Venenos took credit for the murder, and the FBI needed to be involved. I then contacted the judge, and he confirmed my decision. I was supposed to get back with him and Marcia after meeting with the FBI on Tuesday."

Instead of getting help, though, the police chief had seen wheels of justice move too slowly to protect these prominent Galveston citizens.

Everson took a glimpse of his watch. "I understand you're questioning Aaron Michaels here. Ready for me to show you where to conduct the interview?"

"Sure. Are you sitting in?"

"I'd rather watch. See if he changes his story. Appears lily-white." He handed Jon a file. "I want the gang stopped. Whatever it takes. I will not give up until arrests are made."

Revenge was not a police officer's best trait. Everson could be a problem if he was out to handle this himself.

20

LEAH SUGGESTED FLIPPING A QUARTER with Jon to see who'd question Aaron Michaels, and she won the toss.

The young man entered a small interview area provided by Everson. After Leah went through introductions, she invited Aaron to sit at a small table. Trembling, he eased onto a chair. Leah attempted to relax him, a narrow-shouldered, round-faced man, who questioned why the FBI wanted to see him after he'd previously spoken to the police.

"We're going over similar questions to see if you forgot to mention anything to Chief Everson." Leah spoke kindness into her words. "First, let me thank you for meeting with us."

"Okay." He gripped his hands on the tabletop. "But I don't think I left out anything."

"Aaron, your grades at the University of Houston are exemplary. Congratulations. Is this your senior year?"

"Yes, ma'am. Looking forward to my student teaching."

"A teacher? I thought about a career in education at one time. What's your major?"

"History. I plan to teach high school and coach track." He breathed in and out. "I'm ready to be a real adult. My parents will be glad to get me off their credit card debt."

Leah met his smile. "I'm sure they will. Any brothers or sisters?"

"Sister in high school. She'll be ready for college in two years."

"Your parents will have a break before she enters college. Dylan Ortega's mother, Silvia, gave us your name as one of her son's longtime friends. Yesterday you told police you hadn't seen Dylan for months. Was there a problem in the friendship?"

Aaron's knuckles bleached white. "We went different ways. Me with school and Dylan with his life."

"Had you attempted to contact him?" Leah said.

"A couple of times last Christmas and then once in February. He was busy."

"Work? School?"

Aaron rubbed his hands together. "He has a girlfriend. Wanted to spend time with her. He said she was good for him. I quit trying."

Leah looked to Jon for input.

"Sometimes we guys can't compete with a girl," Jon said. "Do you know her name?"

"I think Elena." Aaron paused. "Can't remember her last name. Saw her a couple of times. Hot. Dylan has good taste."

Jon turned to her, Leah's cue to jump back in. "Before February, what did you and Dylan do?"

"Grabbed a few beers. Hung out. We'd been friends since middle school."

"You're a member of St. Peter's?"

"Used to be. Don't go anymore. Not my thing."

Interesting link. "Do your parents and sister?"

"Yes. Like clockwork."

"Did Dylan change much after his conviction?"

"Dylan wanted to go straight. Get back into college and be successful, like start his own business."

"What interested him?"

"Owning a Mexican restaurant. His mom's a great cook, and she'd often told him that she'd like to own her own restaurant."

A point for Dylan's side. "Commendable."

Leah turned to Jon. "Had Dylan mentioned any new friends?" he said.

"No, sir. He and I were always the nerds—me with grades and him because he was shy and not interested in sports. We stuck together for years, and I'm still there for him."

"What happened for him to attempt a robbery?"

"Dylan was going through a rough time then." Aaron pressed his lips together. "I don't know what he was thinking. But he swore he'd never break the law again. I believed him. Still do. He's always been there for me. Even if I had a problem now, he'd find a way to help me. I'm giving him space so he can figure out this thing with Elena."

Leah filed Aaron's last response. "Thanks. You've given us much to think about," she said. "We all need good friends. I hope Dylan is aware of your loyalty."

Aaron scrubbed a hand down his face. "Look, I've told you all I know about him. I have no clue how his name got mixed up with the Venenos or Judge Mendez's murder. He's a great guy."

"If he does reach out, would you let me know?" Leah handed him her business card. "We need to ask him a few questions."

Aaron nodded. "I promise you, Dylan wouldn't do anything to mess up his life. He's on the right road."

21

LEAH AND JON WALKED the covered corridor from GPD to the county court building, where Judge Mendez maintained his office. They had a 1:45 appointment. Leah's thoughts focused on their discussion with Aaron Michaels.

"What Aaron implied bothers me," she said. "Wondering if he left the police department and immediately contacted Dylan."

"The ones who believe in Dylan will take the most risks."

Leah debated Dylan's personality . . . Was he a leader or a weak man whom others tried to protect?

Jon turned to her. "But if Aaron is as smart as his grades indicate, he wouldn't lead us to Dylan."

Leah's thoughts turned to their earlier interview with Everson. "Is Everson capable of working the case?"

Jon stopped until a young woman passed. "Everson is grieving and angry, a volatile meld."

"I can't imagine his loss of a fiancée and friends. In his line of work, personal stakes often create blind spots."

"His relationship with the victims combined with law enforcement skills is a plus—if he keeps his head. Hard for me to believe the three victims didn't document their findings. We're talking about professional people whose jobs required detailed notes."

"And they wouldn't have continued to meet if they hadn't found evidence. Neither, in my opinion, would they have been killed."

"Well, we're about to find out if Everson botched the interviews with the judge's staff or not." A text signaled her attention. A quick look showed the message was from Terri.

It's time we talked.

Leah's mind drifted to her best friend, an agent who worked the civil rights division in Houston. The last time she and Terri had talked, their friendship crumbled. Leah's fault, and she'd done nothing to rebuild the wall.

"Do we have new information?" Jon stood outside the entrance hallway to Judge Mendez's office.

"No." Leah struggled with ignoring or responding. Strange she had the courage to go after bad guys and risk her life but floundered when it came to interpersonal messes. "Give me a moment to answer this text."

"Go ahead. I'll check for updates."

She typed to Terri. **I agree. I'm in Galveston with Jon Colbert.** Terri responded immediately. **Working on the Venenos case? Yes. Will call when I can.**

Thanks. Miss us.

Me too.

Shoving aside her inner turmoil, she concentrated on the upcoming interview.

Jon opened the door. "The warrant came through for Judge Mendez's office, and a team will conduct the search late this afternoon. And the security footage for both his home and office is being analyzed."

Inside Judge Mendez's office, the receptionist, a young woman with large expressive green eyes, led them into a conference room. Leah sized up the four people who were well-acquainted with the judge's work habits, convictions, and cases. The receptionist had been friendly, but the iciness in the room had nothing to do with the air-conditioning's setting. The paralegal was in her midthirties, attractive, and used her French-manicured nails to address matters on her phone. She looked up from her device and cordially acknowledged Leah and Jon.

The law clerks had their impassive facade down to a science. Must be a course in law school.

The receptionist offered Leah and Jon beverages. Once they'd been served, she brought legal pads and pens and sat near the other woman.

How would Leah feel if her SWAT commander or SAC were killed? She'd be hit with paralyzing numbness and a brisk attitude. Angry and scared.

Jon thanked them for their time and introduced Leah and himself. "The FBI is assisting Galveston police in the investigation of not only the murder of Judge Mendez, but also of the deaths of Ian Greer and Marcia Trevelle. All three are suspected of being killed by a lethal injection of venom to the heart. The gang known as the Venenos have claimed responsibility."

One of the clerks, a distinguished-looking man with silver

hair and a matching mustache, cleared his throat. "My name's Ross Kempler. Judge Mendez and I worked closely together for over twenty-seven years on various levels. I can safely say I knew him better than anyone in this office. I called the judge a friend, and to say I'm angry is an understatement."

"Thank you," Jon said. "Agent Riesel and I appreciate any information you can provide. We will be interviewing each of you privately."

The two women had nothing substantial to say. The paralegal expressed a great deal of nervousness and said she feared for her life. The receptionist promised to keep her eyes and ears open.

Ross Kempler was the third interview. Leah believed his long-term friendship with Judge Mendez might offer work and personal habits.

"Mr. Kempler, what can you tell us about the judge?" Jon said.

"Loyal friend. Man of faith. Loved his family. He was a private person. What I can say is the judge had not disclosed any threats to me. If you were around him very long, then you understood he held a high regard for enforcing law. When he ruled on a case, he never backed down."

Kempler added that he knew Marcia Trevelle and had met Ian Greer a few times. "We all want those responsible to be arrested and tried in a court of law."

The younger clerk concluded the interview process. He avoided any pleasantries. "I have a family to protect, and I have nothing to add to your investigation."

"Have you been threatened?" Jon said.

He sat back in the plush leather chair. "I don't have to give a reason to exercise my rights."

As Jon and Leah walked to Jon's truck, Leah questioned the unwillingness of the judge's staff to offer much information. "I know they're frightened, but I wanted more."

"Maybe they're protecting their families and are simply being cautious," Jon said. "Or maybe they really don't know anything."

"Let's find out what Judge Mendez was working on and his ruling on cases during the last three years. Everson was vague about connection points between the three, but he could have assumed we'd be investigating that aspect with our resources."

"He's grieving and wanting to solve this himself, but he could be held for obstructing justice if he's concealing evidence."

"I'll make the request." Leah typed into her phone, then scrolled through emails. She saw intel on Father Gabriel. "We're on a roll. We have the background on Father Gabriel's nephew. Xavier Sanchez—must be a namesake—was his sister's son. In and out of juvie. Later convicted of selling drugs to a DEA agent. A member of the Texas mafia. Killed in a gang fight."

"Every gang member is his nephew, his weak spot," Jon said.

"A priest who failed at saving a member of his family. Big-time guilt." She stared up at the blue sky, her thoughts on Father Gabriel. "He sees his nephew in every face that breaks the law."

22

LEAH NEEDED THINK-TIME. Her stomach growled, but she wanted to talk through her and Jon's day before making inquiries at the Hotel Galvez about Dylan. She asked Jon to stop for cold drinks before driving to the eastern side of the island. She shed her professional jacket and left it in the truck, then kicked off her sensible shoes and rolled up the legs of her navy-blue slacks. The breeze off the ocean cooled their faces in the ninety-plus-degree temps.

"Too bad we're processing a murder." Jon slipped out of his shoes and socks. "If I have to take out after a bad guy in my bare feet, you're going with me." He shrugged off his jacket and tossed it on the truck seat.

"Yes, sir. But I'd outrun you."

"Fat chance. If you're lucky, you might taste my dust." He

tossed his shoes and socks into the truck alongside hers before shutting the door.

His words swirled through her. Made her sorta tingly. *Watch it, girl. Partners are hands off.* "I inherited fast-running genes. Did the whole track and basketball thing. You'd better hope I don't have to show you up."

"Check my stats." He adjusted his sunglasses.

The light bantering helped to unlock the tightness in her shoulders. With no one else around, she breathed in the salty air and listened to crying seagulls. Frothy waves gently lifted and fell. For a precious few moments, she let the hypnotizing rhythm flood her spirit before diving into a discussion about the investigation. She and Jon strolled along where the sea met the shore and lapped water onto their feet and ankles.

"We started the day with Father Gabriel," she said. "On to Rachel Mendez, Chief of Police Zachary Everson, Aaron Michaels, and Judge Mendez's staff."

"And the one person who could fill in a lot of the blanks is hiding out."

"As in guilty?"

"Haven't seen otherwise. Why would an innocent man evade the law?"

"Or are we headed in the wrong direction? Those closest to Dylan are unwavering in their support."

"Maybe he has them fooled," Jon said. "Somebody in the prison system could have educated him in the art of crime."

"Rachel Mendez had nothing derogatory to say." A question hit the surface of her thoughts. "Do we have the details on Dylan's original arrest?"

"I looked it up while you were texting earlier. The arresting officer is familiar: Ian Greer."

"Interesting to find out if Trevelle prosecuted."

"Anything's possible."

She watched three egrets tiptoe over the sand on spindly legs. They never roamed far from each other. "I agree with what you said earlier. Greer, Trevelle, and the judge were onto something that would bring the Venenos down." She stopped to wiggle her toes in the sand.

Leah and Jon spent the next fifteen minutes alongside the shore before heading back to his truck. At the truck, they wiped the sand from their bare feet and slipped into their shoes before climbing inside.

She grabbed her phone. "I'm calling Elena James again. A young woman sneaking around seeing a bad boy? You betcha she monitored what he was doing."

"Schedule an interview before leaving Galveston."

She pressed in Elena's number. The call went to voice mail, and Leah left a message. She checked the young woman's address while Jon started up the engine. "Elena lives with her parents. Shall we stop by later?"

"Put it on the list. While you have your phone out, why not talk to Lucinda Serrano? She's worked a long time for Father Gabriel."

Leah found the number for Father Gabriel's secretary. When the woman answered, Leah explained why she'd called.

"Oh, I can't believe the judge is gone. I've worked for St. Peter's for twenty-five years, and nothing this horrible has happened."

"How many of those years were for Father Gabriel?"

"All of them. He's been there close to thirty-two."

"Did you know any of the other victims?"

"Officer Ian Greer and his family used to live down the street from us. We were acquaintances. Marcia Trevelle was in the news because of being a prosecuting attorney. I never met her. Judge Mendez and his wife played an active role at St. Peter's."

Leah moved ahead. "Is Chief of Police Everson a member of St. Peter's?"

"Yes."

Father Gabriel claimed he didn't know Marcia Trevelle, but she and Everson were to be married in October. "What can you tell me about Father Gabriel?"

"Outstanding man. Cares about people to a fault." Lucinda hesitated before continuing. "I've been on vacation, but my husband is reluctant for me to return to work. He wants me to retire. He knows Father Gabriel will continue his crusade to rehabilitate lawbreakers."

"What do you mean?"

"Are you aware his nephew was in a gang and subsequently killed?"

"Yes. What's your take?"

"Father Gabriel thinks he has to bring every criminal into the church."

"Are you saying there are criminals at St. Peter's?"

"No! Of course not."

"What do you know about Dylan Ortega?"

Lucinda sighed. "I saw his name in the news, but I don't believe in his guilt. He's a good young man, despite his prior mistake that landed him in prison."

"What about others?"

"Agent Riesel, I'm done answering questions about the killings. I know nothing, and I'm honoring my husband's wishes. Talk to Chief of Police Everson or Father Gabriel. Good luck." The phone clicked.

Leah wondered why it felt like nearly everyone she and Jon had talked to had something to hide.

Jon commended the young manager of the Hotel Galvez for his confidence and professionalism. Papers were scattered over a wooden desk stained with coffee rings, but no apology from the young man. Jon liked that—the manager had a job to do and this was his method.

Jon led out the interview while Leah analyzed the conversation. They were a good team. Odd how two people synced well in such a short time. His previous experiences with partners were more about completing a mission and moving on to the next assignment. With Leah, he hoped they would work together again . . . though he wasn't ready to explore the reasons why.

"When was the last day Dylan Ortega reported to work?" Jon said.

The manager turned his attention to the computer. "Friday." He tapped his thumb on his desk. "I can't provide an alibi for him."

"What can you tell us about Dylan Ortega?"

The manager might not be old enough to shave, but no signs of deceit or apprehension crested his features. "He was a solid worker. Always on time until last week. Hated to fire him, but when an employee doesn't call in, I have no choice. He told me about his previous jail time."

"You took a chance on Dylan Ortega despite his record." Jon studied him. "I assume he gave you other references."

The manager opened a file drawer and pulled out what looked like a job application. "I meant to review this before you arrived. But I had a problem in the hotel that needed my attention." He glanced at the form and nodded. "I remember the interview with Dylan. He was well-mannered and confident in his skills. He listed Father Xavier Gabriel of St. Peter's church and Judge Nicolás Mendez as references. Both men backed him up. To me, if Judge Mendez had given him a job, I could too." He peered into Jon's face. "Now the judge is dead, and the FBI and police can't find Dylan. Hard for me to believe he's mixed up in a gang or murder."

"We're not saying he is. Dylan is a person of interest. We only want to talk to him."

"Are those FBI words for 'He's not guilty until a jury makes a decision, but we plan to arrest him'?"

"It means questioning." Jon pointed to the job application. "I'd like a copy of your document."

When the manager agreed, Jon snapped a pic. "Thanks. Okay for us to talk to his coworkers?"

"No problem. I'll introduce you to those who worked directly with him. Never had any complaints or reasons to question his work ethic."

Jon and Leah spent the next hour and a half posing the same questions and receiving the same answers—Dylan Ortega worked hard, no one phoned or visited him, and although quiet, he was friendly. No mention of criminal activity.

Afterward Jon and Leah talked in the parking lot of the hotel. Palm trees swayed beneath landscaping that mirrored the hotel's finery.

"We have two indicators of Dylan being a part of the murder," Leah said. "He's missing and Edgar Whitson ID'd him. However, I'm not totally convinced Dylan's a killer. Yet."

"You can play devil's advocate if you want. Edgar Whitson's

words are enough for me. I saw or heard nothing to doubt his testimony. If Dylan shows up with a solid alibi, I'll change my tune. In the meantime, I'm not nominating Dylan as the all-American citizen of the year."

"I'm glad you're my partner. If we agreed on everything, we'd miss a detail," she said.

"And I'm your fave as long as I bring you coffee."

She frowned. "I should have added a hamburger. Right now, I'm hungry. It's 7:30."

23

JON DROVE TO WILLIE G'S—a popular seafood restaurant on Harborside Drive. Neither had eaten since breakfast, and sharing dinner seemed like the perfect time to talk over more of the day's findings. Seafood ranked at the top of Leah's great foods list. Except catfish. She just couldn't develop a taste for it. Must be a Southern thing.

Jon pulled into a paid parking lot at Pier 21, and they exited his truck. Tourist attractions ranged from boat tours and exhibits about French pirate Jean Lafitte or the Great Storm of Galveston in 1900 to mouthwatering food and nightlife. Looked like fun if her attention hadn't been on the case.

By habit, she noted the area and people before she and Jon walked to the restaurant entrance. No one raised her suspicion. Inside, huge handblown glass fixtures in red, blue, yellow, white, and leopard hung from the ceiling like Christmas tree bulbs. The enticing aroma of fish swirled around them, and while her stomach growled, her mind sped with the unsolved case.

"I've been a sniper for too long," Leah said. "Just when I'm ready to enjoy a tasty meal, a sensation creeps over me like we're being watched through a rifle scope."

He huffed. "I'm right there with you."

"I'll hold a fork in one hand and my Glock in the other."

Jon greeted the hostess and requested a table by the windows where they could monitor who entered the restaurant. A young man with pinned-up dreadlocks took their drink and food orders. Leah selected crab-stuffed shrimp, and Jon opted for blackened snapper.

When they were alone again, she opened the conversation. "Where do we begin?"

"Zero in on the restaurant's guests who might be spying on us?"

"You go first," she said.

"Three minutes after we arrived, a couple was seated in the rear. They're real cozy."

"I saw them. They're completely absorbed in each other, only occasionally observing who's here." Oh, to have nothing on her mind but fabulous food and a good-looking guy. "She knows one of the waitstaff, a guy."

"I missed it."

"She acknowledged him when he escorted the couple to the table, a hint of a smile the guy with her didn't see. Could be history. A girl thing." She glanced around. "The others who've arrived have kids or are older." Her own words repeated in her mind. "Of course, members of the Venenos could have families."

"We're a distrustful lot." He leaned back in his chair.

Jon and Leah's waiter placed drinks before them. She took a sip of water, then sneaked a look behind her at the young couple. A bulge in the man's suit jacket pocket gave her pause. "Do you see indications of a gun?" Her left hand touched the Glock inside her pocket. If she believed in anything, it was her training.

"I'm watching." He stared while she studied his face. "We're good. He isn't packing. Looks like a rectangular box."

Jon had a definite charm about him and a steely determination she admired. But Leah needed to stop gawking at him like a schoolgirl. She grabbed her phone for new messages. Great, another disagreeable topic—snakes.

She refused to let the subject get in the way of their assignment. "Nothing's turned up on any rattlesnake farms in Houston, San Antonio, Austin, or Dallas areas. No purchase of rattlers or interest in the venom. Texas doesn't require a special permit to keep indigenous snakes."

"What about Tanitox, the laboratory in Austin?" he said.

"I assume they're regulated. Hold on while I check." She navigated to Tanitox's website. "Okay, they operate legally under a state wildlife dealer's license. After the venom is extracted and processed, it's still a raw material and therefore not regulated by the USDA or the FDA, but the manufacturers who use the venom have guidelines. Only two facilities in Texas extract venom regularly, Tanitox and a branch of A&M University."

"Someone's supplying venom."

She googled a video about milking snake venom. Her pulse raced.

The narrator's voice must have snatched Jon's interest. "What are you listening to?"

Her heart hammered. She swallowed the familiar panic. "Watching a video—how to milk a rattler. Looks like the venom has to be kept frozen or freeze-dried."

"I'm familiar with the process. When I was a kid in Oklahoma, I had an uncle who kept a pit of rattlers and milked them for sale. Dangerous job, but he kept the snakes sedated for easier handling. He sank a mint into lab equipment, thinking he'd hit a gold mine." Jon shook his head. "It's impossible to get rich from antivenom production. About a year later, he sold the business. It's worth looking deeper into private snake farms, but with a little guts and know-how, any person can extract venom."

Not her—ever. But Jon was right about finding the source of venom. "How can these guys ever hope to pull off a takeover of southwestern states with a few rattlers? Unless we're right about the gang using their battle cry as a cover for something else."

"The rapid spread to other cities likely means massive organization is in place—cells of Venenos recruiting other members. We haven't seen a rise in illegal drugs, prostitution, illegal weapons, gambling, money laundering, or any of the other violent crime methods of making money, only their mantra and eliminating those who take a position against them."

"Judge Mendez was one of those voices speaking strongly against the gang's illegal activities," she said. "But did he know his killer?"

"Another reason to have a list of those the judge sentenced in the last year, active cases on his desk, and the whereabouts of the six people on Rachel Mendez's list."

She wrapped her fingers around the glass of water. "Three people who were connected through law enforcement are dead because of the Venenos." Her thoughts lingered on Dylan. "How much did Elena know about Dylan?"

"Or how much did Dylan reveal about himself?"

Their food was served, and they ate in silence except for an occasional comment. Leah's phone rang.

She recognized Silvia's number and answered. "Ms. Ortega, this is Leah Riesel."

"I've talked to Dylan." Her voice quaked. "He's agreed to turn himself in to you and Agent Colbert."

"That is wonderful news. Very wise. Is he with you now?"

"No."

"Where would you like for us to meet?" Leah captured Jon's attention. "We're at Willy G's, but we can meet Dylan anywhere."

"I'll suggest the parking lot there in an hour. It's a busy spot, and he should be safe."

"Yes, ma'am." She described Jon's truck and where it was parked.

"Promise me you won't call the police."

"I promise. This will be between your son and us."

24

JON APPRECIATED THE RELATIONSHIP Leah had established with Silvia Ortega. Thanks to his partner's communication skills, the Veneno killings in Galveston could end tonight. Outside the restaurant, he and Leah walked to the corner and turned right toward the parking lot and his truck. A light flickered across the street between a Jimmy John's sandwich shop and a Starbucks, but Jon's gaze settled on the people standing close to him and Leah. He scanned the surroundings and obscure shadows, weighing, analyzing. From the intensity on Leah's face, she was probably doing the same. Somewhere Dylan waited for them.

Clusters of people talked and laughed—all ages, all cultures. Live music blared, blending a humid August night with a light Gulf breeze. A perfect evening for most. A light rain began to fall. When the narrow street cleared, they crossed to the busy parking lot.

Jon spoke in a hushed tone as they headed toward his truck in the third row. "Did Silvia say Dylan would turn state's evidence?"

"No, but a plea bargain is in his best interest."

The light rain quickly increased to a downpour. A group of teens hastened their pace across the lot toward the live music. Jon's sixth sense detected an ominous presence. Hanson used to tell him his premonitions were a gift from God.

Straight ahead, standing near the driver's side of his truck was a man, alone and concealed in the darkness. A streak of lightning illuminated the area, and Jon recognized it was Dylan.

A shot rang out from about fifty feet on their right. Dylan ducked. Then another shot. Weapons drawn, Jon and Leah raced from the first row of parked vehicles toward Dylan, moving between cars.

"FBI. Stop! Dylan, take cover." Jon then shouted for the crowd to stay back.

Screams rose through the rain. Dylan pulled a firearm and fired repeatedly at two men who made their way his direction. More could be waiting for an opportunity to pull the trigger.

Jon zigzagged through parked cars with the intent of stopping the shooters. Who were they? Leah bent and moved through another row of vehicles. Their unspoken goal was to approach Dylan from opposite sides and keep him alive. If given a clear shot at whoever was after him, he and Leah would take it. "Stay down," Jon said to Dylan.

"So you can kill me?" Dylan crouched low and stepped back. "I'm not a fool."

Another round of shots burst into the air.

Leah kept circling toward Dylan.

An SUV sped through the parking lot with its lights off.

Jon called out a warning, and Leah cleared the vehicle's path within seconds before it passed. Jon shouted again for bystanders to move out of the path of the oncoming SUV. But their presence hindered an immediate takedown of the two shooters.

Shots fired wildly from the two men and those inside the SUV. Screams erupted from the panic-stricken crowd. Leah raced after two teen girls and shoved them down beside a car.

The approaching SUV slammed on its brakes several feet past Jon and Leah, as though protecting the two shooters. The men emerged from the darkness and climbed inside. Shots continued to explode from the vehicle. Leah ran across the narrow pavement separating a row of parked vehicles from Jon's truck and took aim from the driver's side front tire. She shattered the SUV's rear window glass.

Dylan had disappeared in the melee. Jon joined Leah and tossed her his keys. "Start the truck. I'll cover you." He fired against a barrage of bullets. The shooters weren't getting away easily. He pelted the rear and side of the SUV's frame while it zoomed ahead.

Leah climbed inside his truck and slid it into reverse. The moment Jon opened the passenger door, she stepped on the gas and whipped around in pursuit of the SUV. Sirens pierced the night sky. A squad car fell in behind them after the SUV—headed east on Harborside Drive.

Those inside the SUV fired from the broken rear window. A bullet fractured Jon's windshield and zinged between him and Leah.

Close. Jon shot a glance at Leah. Her eyes were fixed on the street and the taillights of the SUV. Her foot pressed the gas pedal while the truck wove in and around traffic. Wiper blades swished over spidered glass.

"Do I make you nervous?" She veered around a motorcycle.

"I'd rather be at the wheel."

"You gave me the job." She sped through a red light in a protest of car horns and squealing brakes, holding the truck steady on the wet pavement. The SUV ran a second light as a car entered the intersection, forcing Leah to brake. She then zipped around the car and on through the red light. Ahead the SUV whirled right onto Eighteenth Street.

He wished for the hundredth time he was in control. "Forget my truck. Get these guys. They've done enough damage."

The SUV raced across the divided Broadway Avenue. The Gulf would soon be in view. She jammed the gas, closing the distance between the vehicles. The SUV swung left along Seawall Boulevard.

A man was walking across the busy boulevard. She whipped a sharp right to avoid hitting him and then yanked the truck back onto the street. The delay cost them ground.

Jon stole a look at multiple police cruisers behind them. "The only way these guys are getting away is to swim."

"Let them try."

He couldn't help but admire her tenacity. Tough gal. Then it hit him. "They have a boat." He made a quick call to Everson to relay that the SUV was heading toward the rocky end of the island.

"Don't be heroes," Everson said.

Leah kept pace.

Jon held his breath with his hand wrapped around his Glock. The road cleared, and he leveled three shots into the back of the SUV. A single bullet responded.

He hoped Everson had told the cops behind them he was one of the good guys.

The SUV hit the end of the road and spun sideways. Four figures emerged and scurried down the embankment to the rocky beach. Jon could see the outline of a speedboat bobbing in the water. He leaped from the truck after them before Leah stopped. She shone the headlights on the escaping men.

Gunfire erupted from the boat, breaking both truck headlights.

GPD officers pulled in. Red and blue lights painted the darkness. In the distance more sirens blared.

The four shooters from the SUV made it to the water and waded in with Jon gaining ground behind them. Through the haze of rain, Jon fired at the back of the man who trailed last. He fell. The second man whirled and aimed at Jon. Jon dropped to the rocks and brought down another man. Bullets whizzed over his head.

Gunfire burst from behind him. Jon jerked around. Another police car had arrived. Four officers headed down the rocky bluff with Leah. She sprayed bullets toward the fast-disappearing men.

"Two men down," Jon said.

"Got it—" The officer's last words before a bullet flew into his shoulder. He groaned and slid onto the rocks. A second officer raced with Jon to the water's edge. The speedboat jumped over waves. Jon fired repeatedly, but in the dark and rain, his sniper skills failed him.

Jon bent to the gunman facedown on the rocks. No pulse. An officer shone his flashlight on the man—Aaron Michaels.

25

LEAH STUDIED AARON MICHAELS'S BODY. A horrible waste of a life with no hope for rehabilitation. How very sad when the young man seemed excited about his future. Aaron had sworn Dylan was a good guy, an old friend, yet the young man lying in a pool of blood had tried to kill her and Jon. A 9mm lay beside his hand.

An officer approached her. "An ambulance will be here shortly."

"I'm afraid it's too late." She pointed to the weapon. "We interviewed him earlier today. Never had a clue."

"Another shooter bled out in the SUV," the officer said.

"Must have been five total." Leah stood and gazed out over the waves where the boat had disappeared.

Her attention settled back on Aaron Michaels. Leah

berated herself for not aggressively questioning him this morning. More questions, more pressure, and his true colors could have lit up like a neon light. He'd be alive if she'd done a better job.

Leah walked back to the truck with Jon. She remembered being nineteen years old and living on her own, working, and paying for college. A flash of repeated mistakes swept through her mind, ones she'd vowed never to make again. Failing to see Aaron Michaels's deception added to the list.

"We're beating ourselves up when there's not a thing we can do about him lying to us," Jon said.

"Except feel inept."

He opened his truck and pulled two flashlights from his glove box. Glass fragments littered the dashboard, seats, and floorboard.

"Sorry about your truck."

"It can be fixed." He handed her a flashlight and glanced around. "Aaron contacted Everson with an apparent good faith testimony, yet he was playing a role. Then Silvia tells us Dylan wants to turn himself in. I'd say he was out to get us, except the shooters were after him. Has he turned against the gang, and now they want him dead?"

"We'll never earn his trust or Silvia's again," she said.

"The Venenos will pay for this."

Leah agreed. Neither she nor Jon dealt well with defeat. Must be in their sniper DNA, part of why they were able to do what others couldn't or refused to do.

She and Jon walked the beach where the men had rushed into the water. Heavier rain pelted them, like punishment. An FBI team was on their way to sweep the scene as well as a helicopter in flight to search for the boat.

While Jon arranged for a twenty-four-hour car rental to deliver a vehicle to their site and AAA to pick up his truck, she ran the plates on the SUV. She verified the owner and shook her head.

She turned to Jon, fury mounting. "You've got to be kidding. The SUV belongs to Judge Nicolás Mendez. Rachel reported the vehicle stolen earlier in the day. Why weren't we notified?" She swiped at the rain soaking her face.

Jon's jaw rigid, he grabbed his phone, and she knew without asking he was calling Everson. She strained closer to listen, but he put the call on speaker.

"Everson, in case you haven't been updated, the owner of the SUV is Rachel Mendez," Jon said. "When were you told?"

"Exactly 7:45 p.m., when the officer protecting Mrs. Mendez and her family called it in. The same time you and Agent Riesel were engaged in a shoot-out and subsequent chase with said vehicle through the streets of my city."

Jon calmed. "What day and time was the vehicle last seen?"

"Yesterday afternoon. The grandmother discovered it missing from the garage this evening. The theft must have occurred during the night," Everson said. "I know what you're thinking. Why didn't the officer on duty hear or see what was going on?"

"Right."

"Said he never heard a thing."

"I want to talk to him."

"Hold on. Not like I'm sitting behind my desk."

Jon chuckled without any humor.

"Here's the officer's number."

Leah jotted it down.

Jon continued. "Dylan Ortega arranged to turn himself in, but he escaped during the chaos. We've got two dead men here—one of them Aaron Michaels. The second man hasn't been identified."

Everson swore. "Michaels squeaked when he walked."

"Not anymore." Jon wrapped up the call and turned to Leah. "Would you contact the officer on protection duty at the Mendez house? I might unload about him not doing his job and get written up."

"Funny you should ask the agent with the panther rep to be the pacifier here." The officer assigned to the Mendez home responded on the second ring. She introduced herself and informed him her partner was listening in. "I'll get straight to the point. How did thieves break into the garage and steal the SUV?"

"No sign of breaking and entering."

"Was anything else stolen?"

"She had a 9mm in the glove box. Registered. I reported it missing."

"You can tell her the SUV's been found and possibly the weapon. The vehicle was involved in a crime." She ended the call and laid the phone on the glass-crusted hood.

"I want a background on the officer. How do you not hear someone breaking and entering?"

"The interior of the house is monitored by security cameras. If he fell asleep, we'll find out." Leah wondered briefly if the officer had been bribed.

Jon opened his truck door and proceeded to pull out their possessions. "Unless the Venenos have an army behind them, coming after federal agents shows a lack of brains," he said.

Leah turned to him. "Are you thinking about the cover-up theory?"

"The magnitude of this operation. And Aaron Michaels

doesn't fit the Veneno profile. I'm convinced whatever's going on has nothing to do with a *reconquista* war cry. It's a front."

She wrapped her brain around the brewing concept. "If so, were Ian Greer, Marcia Trevelle, and Judge Mendez onto them?" She drew out a breath and picked up her phone. "I need to call Silvia." But the woman didn't answer. "Guess I'll text her."

Someone tried to stop Dylan from talking to us. Please tell him we want to talk.

"How far do you think that will get you?" Jon said, looking over her shoulder at the message.

Leah shook her head. "Who else knew about the meeting?"

26

IN A RENTAL CAR, Leah and Jon returned to the busy crime scene outside Willie G's, where police wove through the crowd asking questions and gathering intel on the firefight. Three ambulances flashed their lights, but she didn't see any paramedics in action. Good. The rain continued to assault them.

She spotted Everson by a cruiser under an umbrella. He reminded Leah of a football coach whose team was down in the fourth quarter.

They made their way through the crowd to Everson.

Water dripped off his poncho, and no eye contact. "The only good thing that came out of tonight was Aaron Michaels bleeding out," he said.

Leah resolved to be civil. "We're talking about a human being here, a young man whose life is gone."

"Doesn't change what he's done."

Leah fought to keep from punching him in the nose, which already looked like it had been placed out of joint a few times. "Here's the bottom line. When I get to the point a man's death doesn't affect me, then I'm no better than an animal."

Jon broke into the conversation. "Has Aaron Michaels's family been notified?"

"Officers are on their way there." Everson rubbed his jaw, but still no eye contact. "They'll get a statement."

"Send us a copy," Jon said. "A second man died in the firefight. Do you know his identity?"

"Landon Shaw." Everson stared into Jon's face. "Prescription drug theft in Dallas. Robbed a string of Walgreens on the same day. Tried to fence the drugs within three months and got caught. Now he's running with the Venenos. Or was."

Leah pulled her phone from her pocket. "I'll see what else we can find out about Shaw." She sent a request to the FIG for a background.

Without looking up from his notepad, Everson said, "I want Shaw's background on my desk first thing in the morning."

Leah bit her tongue. "Sure. How's the wounded officer?"

"Getting treated." He glanced up.

In that moment, Leah saw Everson's vulnerability. The hurt would devour him if he didn't deal with it soon. She was the poster child on that one.

As she and Jon walked back to the rental car, Jon pointed out what she'd been thinking since Everson mentioned Shaw's criminal record. "I'd be surprised if Shaw is part of the Venenos. *Reconquista* wouldn't have meant anything to him."

"So if we're not after this gang, maybe we should explore the drug angle." Leah sighed. "I wish we could have taken one of those men into custody."

"We have tomorrow."

Leah watched Jon walk around the front of the car. A lean man. Not an ounce of fat anywhere. She tried to tell herself she wasn't interested, only admiring.

Jon slid inside. "Partner, we made it through what was supposed to be our end. Thank God, we're alive for another day."

Her attitude hit bottom. "Why is it people thank God when life moves in a better light and curse the name when life stinks?" She stopped before her cynical views about a deity took over.

"I had a friend who thanked Him no matter what happened."

"What does your friend do for a living?"

A bit of sadness passed over him. "He died."

"I'm sorry. What was his name?"

"Hanson." He adjusted the air-conditioning. "Hanson's last words were for me to find God."

"You were with him when he died?"

"Yes."

He obviously didn't want to talk about it, and she wouldn't probe. "Have you found what you're looking for?"

"Yes and no."

"I don't believe in fairy tales," she said.

"What if God is real? And there's a chance at eternity?"

She believed in what she could see and touch. "I know faith gives many people comfort, and there are a lot of varieties to choose from. Religion's not for me." Leah needed to change the subject before she unloaded her nightmares. "Do you still want to stop by Elena James's home?" It was nearing 11:45 p.m.

"Yes. Let's be optimistic and believe Dylan is there ready to spill his guts."

"Don't hold your breath. I don't think her parents knew they were dating."

27

THE HOMES ON TIKI ISLAND were built straight up on narrow lots, leaving the low area for floodwaters that accompanied tropical storms and hurricanes. The James home had the elegance Leah had come to expect from many who lived in the coastal community surrounding Galveston. Three stories with lots of outdoor living space including a pool and a boat slip. Easily a million-dollar price tag.

"The Jameses must be doing well for themselves." Jon's observation echoed her own thoughts. He rang the doorbell of a double door. A yappy dog responded in its best watchdog voice. "If a woman answers, you lead out," he said.

"Got it."

He rang the bell a second time.

A light in the foyer flipped on, and a middle-aged woman with bare feet and dressed in white shorts opened the door.

Leah held up her credentials and introduced herself and Jon as members of Houston's FBI. "We'd like to talk to Elena James."

The woman's face blanched. "I'm Olivia James, her mother. Please wait while I get my husband." She closed the door and latched it.

"How long before you ring the doorbell again?"

"Twenty more seconds."

With four seconds remaining on Leah's countdown, the door opened. Olivia and a tall, tanned man appeared. Both were undeniably islanders with tanned skin, highlighted hair, and Botoxed faces.

"I'm Richard James. Explain to me why you're here at this hour. What's happened to our daughter?"

"Agent Colbert and I have questions regarding her friendship with Dylan Ortega," Jon said.

"Who?" He glared. "Are you referring to the man the police and FBI are looking for? The man wanted for questioning regarding the murder of Judge Mendez?"

"Yes, sir." Jon continued. "May we come in?"

He stiffened and for a moment Leah thought he'd slam the door in their faces. "I'm wondering if I should have my attorney present."

Lawyering up always delayed interviews, but it was the right of every citizen. Leah respected him for wanting to protect his daughter—she would do the same in his shoes. She picked up the conversation. "Legal counsel is your choice, Mr. James. But none of you are in any trouble. We just have a few questions for Elena that are important to our case."

"Then come in. We need to clear this up. Our daughter's reputation is at stake."

Leah and Jon were led to an open foyer with light oak floors. Mr. James pointed to a spacious living room facing the water. High ceilings gave the room an outdoor feel. Furnishings were black and white with accents in shades of turquoise, red, and yellow. Leah and Jon were seated on a white sofa, and Olivia James sat in a nearby chair.

Richard James paced the floor, hands in his cargo short pockets.

Jon started things off. "Dylan Ortega's mother, Silvia Ortega, gave us Elena's name, address, and cell phone number yesterday," he said. "Agent Riesel talked to your daughter then. Elena claimed she had no idea where Dylan could be found. Today when Agent Riesel phoned her with more questions, she didn't pick up. Is she here?"

"Not right now. She's out with friends," Mr. James said. "Where did this Ortega woman get Elena's information? Because she's harassing us."

Jon ignored the last half of the man's comment. "According to her, Dylan and Elena are dating."

Mr. James's face reddened. "Your source is a liar. He's never been here, and neither would our daughter associate with the likes of him."

"We can clear this up if we speak to Elena directly."

Mr. James addressed his wife. "When is Elena expected home?"

The woman touched her mouth before speaking. "Tomorrow."

Leah considered taking over the interview to calm Olivia. As if reading her thoughts, Jon glanced her way.

"Can you give us a number where we can reach her?" Leah lowered her voice. "All we need to do is ask a few questions."

Mrs. James trembled. "Elena apparently doesn't have additional information and chose to ignore you. I'll have her contact you when she returns. Richard, I don't like speaking to these people without our lawyer."

Jon faced Mr. James. "Sir, Agent Riesel and I are concerned about your daughter's safety. Dylan Ortega is missing, and he is a person of interest in Judge Mendez's murder."

"Are you insinuating our daughter is harboring a fugitive?"

"We'd feel better if we had confirmation she's all right."

Good one, Jon.

Mrs. James gasped. "You think they're together? Or he's holding her against her will?"

Another cue for Leah to soothe the woman's emotions. "We have nothing to indicate either scenario. When I talked to her, she said they'd broken up."

Mr. James yanked his phone from his pocket and dialed a number. "Elena, call home as soon as you get this." He turned to his wife. "What time did she leave?"

"Right after breakfast. She was getting her nails done, then meeting friends at Stewart Beach."

"Who is she with?" Richard's voice rose.

"She told me friends." His wife lingered on each word. The fear in her body language didn't match her words. "Maybe she has her phone off. I'm sure she'll call or text us soon."

"Soon? The FBI suspects our daughter is keeping company with a criminal or is in harm's way, and you want to wait until she feels like contacting us?" He stared at his wife. "You know where she is."

Her lips quivered and she peered into her husband's face.

"I'll try from my phone." She reached into her pocket for her phone.

The silence ticked by.

Mrs. James dialed. "Elena, this is an emergency. Please call me or your dad immediately." She laid the phone in her lap and looked up at her husband. Tears filled her eyes. "Richard, I'm frightened. She always picks up. Elena is a good girl—she makes good choices."

He knelt beside her. "I'm sorry I lost my temper." He turned to Jon and Leah. "I want Ortega picked up now."

"We're doing our best to locate him," Jon said. "Are you members of St. Peter's Catholic Church?"

He frowned. "We're not Catholic." Mr. James reached for his wife's hand, and she stood beside him. Both shared ashen faces. "Our daughter is missing. That's what we care about. Are you finished with the questions?"

Leah hated the desperation evident in these parents, and she wanted to help them find their daughter. "I think we're done until she's located," she said, getting to her feet. "We regret the turmoil. Please understand our concern for Elena."

Mr. James faced his wife. "I'm heading to Stewart Beach. I realize it's closed, but I can check the restaurants or businesses nearby."

Olivia dabbed beneath her right eye. "While you're gone, I'll contact some of her friends."

Mr. James wrapped his arm around his wife's waist. "We'll find her."

"We'd like to go with you." Jon captured Leah's attention, and she nodded.

Richard James clenched his fist. "Thanks."

28

SILVIA BELIEVED NOTHING GOOD happened after midnight. Her parents had instilled this in her as a teen when she wanted to stay out late. She'd repeated the same mantra to Dylan. When he turned thirteen, she'd worried he might follow a bad path, but he kept her rules. All went well until the year before the robbery. But that nightmare was over, and she didn't want him to ever experience prison again.

While a movie droned on and she snuggled next to Warren on the sofa, her thoughts hung like a huge question mark. As though feeling her distress, Warren squeezed her shoulders. Where was her son? What had happened tonight that stopped him from turning himself in? All she'd heard were news reports that a firefight had occurred. Had Dylan been hurt? Was he responsible?

Please, God. No. Dylan couldn't have broken the law again. The same worries repeated.

The past crept in unbidden, like a cold chill. When Dylan had been arrested for armed robbery and spent those nightmarish months in jail, she'd lit a candle for him every day. She'd visited him every Sunday afternoon and written countless letters. And when he returned to her, she saw her boy had matured into a strong man. He apologized for putting her through the humiliation of having a son in prison. He loved her, and he'd learned his lesson.

Silvia had believed him. Her heart sang with his change and growth. He'd enrolled in college and started classes and promised to always take care of her. That's when she told him about his trust, the hundred thousand dollars due him when he was twenty-five.

"Where did it come from?" he'd said. "My father?"

She'd touched his face. "What's important is the money is for your future."

"I'll be finished with college then." He didn't ask any more questions about the origin of the trust.

Warren stroked her shoulder and brought her back to the present. She attempted to concentrate on the TV. A heist/cop movie—Warren loved them.

Her phone rang, and she stared at it. The number wasn't familiar.

"Honey, answer it." Warren kissed her cheek. "It could be Dylan."

She obliged and heard her son's familiar voice. Choking back the emotion, she forged ahead. "Where are you? I've been so worried."

"I'm okay, Mom," Dylan said. "I wanted to let you know

I'm staying low until the cops realize I'm not guilty of killing Judge Mendez."

"Who opened fire tonight?" Silvia begged for Dylan to be innocent.

"Not me."

"Who then?"

"Doesn't matter. I'll handle it. After tonight, I'm finished with the law. I'm a man with a record. I'll do anything to make sure I'm never locked up again."

"All you need do is tell them where you were yesterday morning."

"I don't have an alibi."

"No one can vouch for you?" If only she hadn't already told the agents she hadn't seen Dylan at the time of the judge's murder.

"No. Look, I need to get a lawyer, but I can't afford a solid defense attorney."

A name entered her mind. "I'll see what I can do."

"I don't want you to put up your own money for a retainer." His voice sounded choked. "Did you hear about Aaron and Landon?"

A little bit of her died. "Yes. They were such nice young men." An alarm sounded in Silvia's head. "Did you know they were in a gang?"

"I talked to them about leaving. I mean Aaron only had a year of college left, but Landon wanted to get rich."

Why did he continue with them as friends? "Have you heard from Elena?" She held her breath, begging God for a yes.

"No. Why? Where is she?" He fired his words like a gun.

"I haven't been able to reach her."

"Never mind, Mom. I'll find her."

"Don't risk getting caught," she said.

"What if the gang has her? She might be hurt. Or worse. Elena means everything to me."

"How can I help?"

"I need cash."

"How much?"

"About five hundred."

She'd have to make a withdrawal from the bank. "Will you come to the house to get it?"

"Too risky. I'm sure GPD and the FBI are watching the house and following you."

"What do you suggest?"

"I'll send a friend by the dental office early tomorrow morning."

"I have a meeting at 7:30 and then back-to-back appointments. At lunch I can run by the bank."

"Okay, look for a pickup in the afternoon."

"Who?"

"I'm not giving you a name. That way you're innocent. The person will say, 'Dylan recommended you for a cleaning.' Then he'll ask to complete the paperwork. Wrap the money up in it."

Silvia's stomach soured. "This is hard, Dylan. You've been accused of murder. Police officers and the FBI won't leave me alone."

"I'm sorry. This will be over soon. Don't tell Warren anything. I don't like you seeing him."

"He's good to me." She refused to break down and cry. Too many tears had been shed and nothing resolved.

"You're too *good* for him. You can do a whole lot better than Warren Livingston."

He hung up, and she couldn't stop shaking.

"I assume you can't tell me anything," Warren said. "But I'm here for you. Always have been and always will be."

She buried her face in his chest. Dylan was jealous. Warren held her close, and she treasured his strong arms around her. "What would I do without you?"

"Marry me and let me take care of you."

29

JON HAD WALKED INTO TRAGEDIES in the past and hoped the search for Elena James didn't add another victim to the list. The probable danger hung heavy in his mind.

"This might not end well for the James family," Leah said. "I don't have a feel for Elena's personality because we've been given contradictory descriptions of her."

"In my opinion, Elena is a little more street-smart than her parents believe. But if she's naive and acting on emotion, we're looking at a dangerous situation." He started the engine and followed Richard James's silver Mercedes. "Let's just hope we find her or she shows up in the morning." But his gut told him otherwise.

They maneuvered through the soggy streets of Galveston to Stewart Beach, known for its family-friendly atmosphere. At

12:50 a.m., the area had been closed for hours. Richard James parked his car near the entrance and Jon pulled in behind him.

Jon stepped from the rental into the continuing downpour. He and Leah shut their doors.

Richard James panned the deserted beach. Even in the faint light, Jon saw his features were drawn. "Her red Nissan isn't here. She told her mother about spending the night with a girl-friend. But we don't know who." His attention moved across the street. "She likes the vegetarian pizza at Mario's. It's walking distance from here. I'm going to check."

"We'll come with you, sir," Jon said.

"Because you have questions for Elena?" He stepped closer to Jon, a challenge rooted in a father's fear.

"Our priority is your daughter's safety."

He ran his hand through rain-soaked hair. "I'm sorry." He hesitated, then stuck out his hand. "I appreciate your helping me find Elena."

Jon grasped it firmly. "Let's see if your daughter is nearby."

The three fell into step and crossed the street.

"Has this kind of disappearance occurred before?" Leah's question was soft, caring.

"No. We've always known where she was . . . until tonight. Even at college—she'll be a junior this fall at A&M—she keeps us informed of everything. Texts and phone calls to tell us about her day and what she's doing. She drives home most weekends. Says she misses us. Has never given us an ounce of trouble." He gazed around them. "Earlier in the summer she worked as a counselor at our church's youth camp."

Since the parents had been unaware of their daughter's relationship with Dylan, chances were she'd hidden other things from them. Poor decisions always caught up with people.

At the restaurant, several young people crowded around tables, but none were Elena. Richard didn't recognize any of them to ask about his daughter, and none of the staff had seen her. He phoned his wife and learned she hadn't heard from their daughter either.

With no other immediate leads to follow, there was no reason to remain in Galveston any longer.

"Richard—" Jon gave him his business card—"Leah and I need to drive back to Houston. Please contact one of us when you hear from your daughter. Never mind the hour. She may return home in the morning as she promised your wife."

They shook hands again, and Richard thanked them.

It was nearing 1:30 a.m. when Jon drove back to the Houston office, where Leah could pick up her car. Although tired, his mind sped with the day.

After twenty minutes of silence between them, he spoke up. "Can we make our list for tomorrow?"

"Good idea. I'm about to fall asleep while trying to figure out what we're missing." She reached for her phone. "First on the agenda?"

"Meet at the office at 8 a.m. Work through the mound of information and interviews on the drive to Galveston. What do you think? I'll bring coffee."

"Wonderful." She sounded like he'd given her a puppy.

"Good. Should have reports and backgrounds by then. The only thing I see interrupting our plans is if Dylan or Elena are found."

30

THURSDAY MORNING LEAH FOUND Jon outside Houston's FBI offices, leaning against a black Dodge pickup with a supersize coffee in each hand. When had he picked up the truck? Dressed in a gray sports jacket, he looked almost as good as he had in his camo pants and T-shirt, not that she'd tell him.

She grasped the offered cup, and their fingers brushed. Her heart flipped like a middle school girl's, but she had no time or interest in a relationship.

Get yourself focused on the murders in Galveston and off Jon.

Jon toasted her with the cup in his left hand. "Still your fave agent?"

"Today you outrank all the others." Why was she flirting?

He grinned, and she allowed a smile to meet his. "Got us a new ride. Picked it up a few minutes ago."

"What's wrong with my Camaro?"

"Consider what happened—"

"Never mind." She loved her car, and picturing it broken like Jon's truck didn't sit well, even if that meant he was going to drive. "How long until your truck is fixed?"

He huffed. "A couple of weeks. Are you ready to hit the road?"

She let the hot brew flow through her veins and fire up brain cells. "Ready to end this."

Within two minutes, they were driving south to Galveston.

"Did you see the ME's report about the blood on Judge Mendez's knuckles being his own?" Jon said. "I was hoping for a lead."

"Neither were there any hits on the trace DNA from the cigarette butts found at the crime scene. Do we have any good news?"

"Your coffee."

"You're right. I saw the FBI had cleared those on Rachel Mendez's list of any involvement in her husband's death. As well as those who'd completed community service at St. Peter's. Except Dylan Ortega."

"I requested an FBI follow-up for both lists. Hard to believe none of them were acquainted with Dylan."

She worked through reports on her laptop during the ride to Galveston. Nothing substantial to give an indication the case would unravel soon.

On the island, Jon pulled through a Chick-fil-A for more coffee and breakfast biscuits. He drove to the far eastern tip of the island and parked. Sort of a breakfast picnic while working. Once she stepped from the truck, a light breeze bathed her face.

"This is perfect." She breathed in the salty air.

"You mean being alone with me?"

She tossed him her best frown. "I mean our temporary office."

He held up a blanket. "I brought this."

She helped him spread out the blanket and then laid her laptop case and shoulder bag down. "Do we have an update on Elena?"

"Haven't heard a thing."

They opened their laptops and each grabbed a biscuit. "Jon, if the Jameses receive a ransom notice, they'd most likely be warned not to contact law enforcement."

"The Venenos haven't used kidnapping in the past. But if our theory is correct and we're not actually dealing with the real Veneno gang . . . anything's possible." He took a generous bite of his breakfast.

"I think we need another face-to-face with Olivia James."

He agreed and polished off one biscuit before she unwrapped hers.

Within forty-five minutes, she and Jon were standing in front of the Jameses' door. Olivia James answered the doorbell. At the sight of them, she paled. "Have you heard from Elena?"

"No, ma'am," Leah said. "Can we talk for a few minutes?"

"Yes. I'd hoped for better news. This isn't like Elena." Olivia motioned for them to come inside. Weariness etched lines at the corners of her eyes, and her face was puffy.

"We won't be long," Leah said. "Have you received a ransom call or note?"

Olivia startled. "No, not at all. Richard is filing a missing person report at the police station. Thank goodness Texas doesn't have a twenty-four-hour waiting period."

That meant Elena's name and photograph would be entered

into the National Crime Information Center, available to all law enforcement.

"Give Elena time. She's of age and may be with friends."

"I keep telling myself that, but I've called every person I can think of."

A knot twisted in Leah's stomach. The likelihood of finding the young girl alive dwindled by the hour. "You shouldn't be alone."

Olivia nodded. "This is the most difficult trial of my life."

Jon's phone chimed and he turned away to check it.

Leah reached out to lay a sympathetic hand on Olivia. "We'll stay in touch."

As Jon drove them back into Galveston, Leah downloaded the latest reports from the FIG. "We have Silvia Ortega's phone records."

"Two mothers grieving over their kids. Sad situation." Jon shook his head.

She shivered. Focusing on the data would be a welcome diversion. She pulled up the report listing numbers, dates, times, and if the call had been inbound or outbound. The FIG had matched up numbers with names and indicated three were burner phones. "Father Gabriel is listed. Rachel Mendez, Elena James, Silvia's work number, and a man by the name of Warren Livingston. His name is on the list of St. Peter's members."

"What's the point of sale for the burner phones?"

She read from her phone's screen. "A Walmart in Galveston. They were activated there too. One purchased in March, the second in May, and a third in July. Paid cash, so no credit card trail. Inbound and outbound calls and texts." She peered into the screen. "A call was made to Silvia at 12:10 this morning, lasting six minutes."

"Walmart security cameras might show us the buyer," Jon said.

"I'll make the request." She concentrated on her phone. "The second burner number is the one Silvia gave me for Dylan."

"Wanna bet the others are his too?" He pressed in a number and laid the phone between them. It rang once before Silvia answered. "This is Agent Colbert. Have you heard from Dylan?"

"No, sir."

Leah cringed at her quick response and the likelihood of a lie.

"After we spoke to you on Tuesday, we requested your cell phone records," Jon said. "Standard protocol. This morning we have a copy. Would you identify the names belonging to three numbers?"

"I'm at work."

"I'll be quick." He gave her the first number.

"Dylan."

Jon rattled off the second one.

"Both are his. I already told you he tends to lose them."

He gave her the third number from 12:10 this morning.

"No idea."

"You received a call from this number early this morning that lasted six minutes."

"You must be mistaken."

Jon glanced at Leah and shook his head before continuing. "How many phones has Dylan gone through in the last year?"

"I don't know."

"How many is he currently using?"

"No idea." Her voice rose. "I have a patient." The line went dead.

Leah fumed. "She's talked to him. But she wouldn't lead anyone to Dylan purposely."

"Let's head to our beach office and finish going through these reports."

Once set up again, Leah noted the temps had grown a few degrees warmer, but the ocean breeze was refreshing. Her thoughts zipped to how Jon's nearness affected her—and how she had to get past it. "I'm a visual gal, and I want to see the case on a relationship matrix spreadsheet. I know we have sophisticated software for analyzation, but this works for me." She pulled up a spreadsheet on her laptop and typed *Judge Nicolás Mendez*, *Ian Greer*, and *Marcia Trevelle* in three rows and again in three columns. "Who did Judge Mendez come into contact with recently?"

"Father Gabriel, Dylan Ortega, Chief of Police Everson, and Rachel Mendez."

She typed the additional names in rows below the victims' names and in the columns. "I'm adding Silvia Ortega, Aaron Michaels, Landon Shaw, and Elena James." She spoke while typing Xs in the rows. When finished, she turned the screen toward him.

He studied her spreadsheet. "Dylan is still our biggest suspect. Leah, this is a good bidirectional matrix of relationships."

Her face warmed. She typed *illegal drugs, prostitution, trafficking, alien smuggling, murder for hire, robbery*, and *kidnapping* into her computer. She thought about how each crime could link to the murders.

"Talk to me 'cause I hear the hum of wheels turning," Jon said.

"What information did Greer, Trevelle, and Judge Mendez die for?"

"It all points to them working on something private and undocumented." From the faraway look in his eyes, he was probing. "While it looks like Dylan Ortega might have murdered the judge, he's not working alone. Neither does he have a history that points to him playing a kingpin role." Jon rose to his feet and paced the beach. "What are we missing? Where do we go next?"

"Landon Shaw did time for prescription drug theft. I'd like to explore this further."

"Looking into his associates could help, but otherwise he seems like a dead end." Jon grimaced at the awful pun.

"So we circle back to the church connections," Leah said. "Looks like we've got more information about Father Gabriel." She read a report about the priest's community affiliations and accolades. "Nothing here indicates illegal activities. He's on a one-man crusade to better the world."

"Worst part is he's sincere. The Venenos—or whoever's behind this—have him in their sights too."

Leah nodded, still skimming the information. "Oh, my goodness. He lied to us. Says here he visited Dylan weekly the entire time he was in prison."

31

THE SERENITY JON HAD experienced at St. Peter's Tuesday had left the premises. He stopped in the hallway outside the priest's office and knocked on the door. "Father Gabriel, this is Agents Colbert and Riesel. We have questions."

The door opened to a weary-eyed priest. "I thought we'd covered everything. I'm extremely busy."

Jon expected the pushback. Right now, he didn't care. "This won't take long."

Father Gabriel hesitated, then stepped aside for Jon and Leah to enter. "Please, sit down. Good to see you, Agent Riesel."

"Thanks. We appreciate your carving out time for us."

Jon and Leah took their seats.

Father Gabriel sat behind his desk and eyed him. "You're angry, Agent Colbert."

"Frustrated."

"Obviously it's something about me. Bring it on."

Time for a few answers.

"Why did you claim to talk to Dylan only twice when, in fact, you visited him weekly in prison for eleven months?" Jon said.

"I visited him every Saturday, like I do for many incarcerated people. He refused to see me. I tried accompanying his mother on Sundays, but that didn't work either."

"If Dylan is devoted to his mother, why wouldn't he see you to oblige her?"

"His choice."

"And you never saw or spoke to him during the entire eleven months he sat in a cell?"

"No."

"Another question. Have you met Elena James?"

"Who is she?"

Jon took a deep breath. "Dylan's girlfriend or former girlfriend. She's missing."

Silence met him. "Dylan must still be missing too." Father Gabriel folded his hands. "Silvia came for prayer before going to work this morning. She's frantic."

"What about you?" Jon said. "You were threatened. We could arrange protection."

"No thanks."

"A dead man can't give absolution."

"I'm not a coward, Agent Colbert. And I have the assurance of eternal life."

"Will you at least consider locking your doors?"

"The church is where lost and hurting souls can find peace. People need easy entry to God's house. I'm not worried—God's looking after me."

It was pointless to insist on offering aid where it was so clearly being declined. Jon and Leah stood. "Be safe. Do not hesitate to contact GPD or us. God works through other people."

Father Gabriel smiled. "I get the message."

If the priest wasn't more careful, he'd be the next victim.

Jon chose to remain in St. Peter's parking lot for their temporary office.

"Father Gabriel's a fool," he said.

"Be that as it may, we can't force the man into protection." Leah peered at her phone. "The FIG dug up another connection between our three victims."

It was a case in which Greer had made the arrest, Trevelle prosecuted, and Judge Mendez ruled in favor of the prosecution.

Jon read over her shoulder. Will Rawlyns had been arrested for manslaughter at a local bar and was now serving time at the Wayne Scott Unit near Angleton. No gang affiliation, at least when he entered the system, but prison guards contended he'd joined the Texan Warlords. Recently he was diagnosed with stage 4 lung cancer. "He was sentenced to the same facility as Dylan."

"We need to talk to him today," Leah said. "He's definitely tangled with a few snakes, the two-legged kind."

"He could toss us a bone. What does he have to lose with cancer counting off his days?"

His phone alerted him to a call. He didn't recognize the number. "Colbert."

"FBI Agent Jon Colbert?"

"Yes, sir."

"My name's Warren Livingston. I own a souvenir shop along Seawall Boulevard in Galveston and a six-unit apartment building. Chief of Police Everson suggested contacting you and gave me your name and number. He said the FBI was working with them regarding the Venenos' crimes."

"How can I help?" Livingston had been on Silvia's cell phone records.

"I received a call from a man who said he was a Veneno. Told me I'd refused to rent an apartment to a gang member. The man accused me of working for the cops against the Venenos. Threatened to torch my apartment building, my shop, and my home unless I agreed to a $100,000 payoff." Livingston talked faster with each word.

This new crime diverged from past Veneno activity.

Livingston continued. "I told this guy I didn't cower to threats, and he told me I'd regret it. Now I realize I could be the next victim in this rage of murders."

Why pressure a landlord? "Mr. Livingston, where are you?"

"My store."

"Agent Riesel and I are in Galveston. We can be there within the hour. Can you give me an address?"

Livingston offered the addresses of the souvenir shop, apartment building, and his home, along with his cell phone number.

Jon touched End and explained the call. "The Venenos are expanding their crimes. I want to drive by his home and apartment building before stopping by his store."

"Why would they care about getting an apartment at that complex versus another place?"

He shook his head. "Looks like an excuse to extort money."

32

LEAH ADMIRED THE LIGHT-BLUE, white-shuttered, coastal-style apartment building belonging to Warren Livingston. Pink oleanders, Galveston's trademark blooming bush, lined both sides of the building. His home across the street was of similar style trimmed in darker-blue shutters, built to withstand the worst of winds and high enough to avoid flooding.

They exited the truck and walked around the apartment building and then Livingston's home. Quiet. No activity. Not even kids playing. They headed to Livingston's shop.

While Jon drove, Leah scrolled through her phone. "Livingston's a prominent businessman. No arrests. Community supporter. A member of St. Peter's—another link."

"Add him to your spreadsheet and his friendship with Silvia Ortega. We've seen quite a few calls back and forth between them."

Leah smiled at the thought that he liked her relationship matrix. *Too bad it hasn't shown us who is guilty.*

Jon and Leah walked into Livingston's Souvenir Shop between Sixth and Seventh Streets on Seawall Boulevard. Bustling with activity, the shop carried Galveston memorabilia—cups, pens, shells, candy, toys, T-shirts, boogie boards, and whatever else a tourist could want. A young woman with purple hair tied back in a ponytail stood behind the counter and prepared specialty coffee drinks for customers and sold locally made pastries.

Warren Livingston was a tall, white-haired man with an oceanfront tan and deep lines at the corners of his eyes. He introduced himself to Jon and Leah.

"Please give me a moment to take care of these customers," Livingston said.

When the shop emptied and the young barista took over the register, Livingston approached them. Jon shook his hand. "We're here to talk about the threat."

He drew in a breath. "I've cringed each time someone entered the shop. I'd like to think the threat was a prank since the gang has the island in panic mode. Kids could have done it."

"That could be the case," Jon said. "We stopped by your property and everything appeared to be in order."

"Thank you." Livingston dragged his hand over his face. "I need to be open here. I'm seeing Silvia Ortega, and I feel like I'm betraying her. But I don't trust Dylan, been thinking he could be behind the threat." He eyed the barista, who appeared to be listening. "Can we talk outside?"

"Of course," Jon said.

Livingston led them through a back room and closed the door behind them. The smell of spoiling food from a Chinese restaurant two doors down met her nose.

Leah pulled out her phone. "What is your barista's name?" When Livingston gave it to her, she typed it into her phone to check for a background later.

Jon resumed his questions. "Why do you suspect Dylan?"

"Rough boy. No boundaries. Silvia's given him everything he ever wanted. If she'd refused him a few times, he might not have wound up in prison. And he wouldn't live from one party to the next."

"Drinking? Drugs?"

"You name it. I'm surprised he's only been arrested once. Street smarts, I guess. I used to think Aaron Michaels was a good influence on him." Livingston shook his head. "Never saw that one coming."

"Were you acquainted with Landon Shaw?"

"Yes, sir. He's been by Silvia's when I was there. I saw he was killed in the same shooting as Aaron. He acted like an okay kid, but the news said he had a prison record." Livingston swallowed hard. "This keeps getting worse. I wish my gut instincts pointed to Dylan's innocence, but he doesn't like me. Told me to stay away from his mother. I think it's because I can read him better than she does. We'd be married if not for his objections."

Jon smiled at Leah to take over. She understood he wanted her to handle matters of the heart.

"Sir, have you tried talking to Dylan?" she said.

"He wouldn't listen to me." He paused. "He called Silvia last night while I was there . . . shortly after midnight. I heard a one-sided conversation. She encouraged him to give himself up. It sounds like he doesn't have an alibi. I heard her ask, 'How much?' and assumed he needed money."

"Do you think she'll help him?"

Livingston nodded, a bit reluctantly, Leah thought.

"Do you have any idea where Dylan is?"

"If I did, the police department would have arrested him." He drew in a ragged breath. "I don't want to obtain a concealed handgun license, but I'm concerned about Silvia and afraid for myself."

Leah added compassion to her gaze. "We won't stop you from legally carrying a weapon, but I do urge you to wait a little while longer. All law enforcement is committed to ending these tragedies. Please let us know anything you overhear or suspect."

"Trust me, I will."

The sound of breaking glass inside the shop reached them. The barista screamed.

The three rushed inside. A rock lay on the floor.

"Did you see anything?" Livingston said to the barista.

"No, sir."

Livingston whirled to Jon and Leah. "I'm telling you Dylan is behind this."

33

SILVIA PARKED HER CAR in the bank parking lot and locked it. Her gaze darted in every direction. Each bird in flight and scampering squirrel shook her resolve. Perspiration soaked her uniform. She dropped her keys and bent to pick them up, all the while praying she was doing the right thing. Dylan needed money. If he weren't an innocent man hiding from the law, he'd withdraw it himself. Even if a police officer questioned her, this was her bank and her money. She had a right to be here.

Silvia slowly rose from the pavement and placed her keys inside the side pocket of her purse. What if the chief of police had someone watching her? What if FBI agents peered at her through binoculars? Maybe Agents Riesel and Colbert, who kept pelting her with questions.

Taking a deep breath, she arched her shoulders and walked

toward the white-and-tan stone building housing her bank. Pain seared across the top of her head and down her back. Stress. Tension.

She'd help exonerate Dylan for the string of horrible crimes he hadn't committed. She could sell her house to pay for the best defense attorney money could buy. Mothers made sacrifices for their children. They hurt and cried, wiped away their tears only to face the same trauma again. Joy came with precious moments that overcame the bad ones.

Her mind swept to Aaron. Silvia had read that some boys looked for family in gangs and the promise of big money. She didn't understand what drove Aaron to the Venenos. What had changed him to choose a murderous gang? His parents were good people. She ached for them. Dylan and Aaron had played baseball and soccer, taken catechism, and gone on countless sleepovers. One Friday night when the boys were twelve, they decided to camp out in her backyard. She made a fire in the grill and let them make s'mores. As soon as the sun went down, Aaron flipped on the backyard light. Such big brave boys.

Landon behaved well too. He'd been at the house earlier on the night Dylan disappeared. Now they were both dead and only Dylan survived.

She approached the bank's entrance. As the door swung open, the air-conditioning bathed her face and dried the dampness. But the cooler temps didn't lift her burden.

A man was ahead of her, and Silvia was short on time. She glanced at the bank's security guard. Her knees wobbled. She decided to withdraw more than five hundred in case Dylan had underestimated his needs.

At the teller window, a young woman processed her completed withdrawal slip. Did the bank report sizable transactions?

She should have researched the law. Praying away her doubts, she resolved to have a stronger attitude. The money was hers to do with as she pleased.

"Would you like large bills for the seven hundred dollars?" The teller smiled.

"I prefer twenties."

Silvia left the bank, still shaking. Within ten minutes, she breathed the sterile air of Dr. Rios's dentist office. She was at the front, talking to his wife, Anna, who worked as a receptionist, when a man entered.

"Is Silvia Ortega here?" he said.

She studied him, dark-skinned and in his late twenties. His eyes were red, pupils enlarged. "I'm she."

"Dylan recommended you for a cleaning. I'm a little nervous about dentists and stuff."

Her heart beat so fast that it hurt. "You'll need to make an appointment and complete paperwork." Silvia opened the file drawer and pulled out the new-patient info sheet. "Since Dylan suggested I take care of your cleaning, why don't you come on back and I'll explain what's needed?"

"Appreciate the help, ma'am."

34

JON DROVE SOUTH ON ROUTE 288 to the working farm prison near Angleton that Will Rawlyns called home. Another steamy August day, clear blue sky, and not a hint of a breeze.

He and Leah passed a brick sign displaying "Wayne Scott Unit, Texas Department of Criminal Justice" and turned down a dead-end road, lined with live oaks. Rural and isolated. On the left side were one-story brick homes for prison employees.

Beyond grazing cows and horses in green pastures stood towering grain silos and huge barns. Wayne Scott Trusty buildings housed offenders who'd been convicted of lesser crimes. That's where Dylan had done his debt to society. The 5,766 acres provided plenty of farmwork to keep inmates busy.

"I checked Rawlyns's visitor list—a sister and Father Gabriel," Leah said as they exited Jon's truck.

"Our priest is everywhere."

They walked inside one of the buildings, where they waited for approval to see Rawlyns. The dank smell of discontent and greed seemed to permeate the air. These men were lifers, no parole and nothing to lose. Desperation spun their world on an axis reinforcing "Only the strong survive." How many were civil to family and friends? Usually the four walls and an open toilet plunged the inmates into a nasty attitude. For sure, chaplains and those committed to education and life skills had their hands full.

Rawlyns entered the air-conditioned interview room flaunting cuffs like armor. A scar from the corner of his left eye to his jawline swirled red and angry. The way his white inmate uniform draped his frame, cancer claimed weight loss.

Rawlyns slumped into a chair across from Leah and Jon. "I'm a busy man. What's this about?"

Jon introduced himself and Leah. "Mr. Rawlyns, we're looking for information on three murder cases in Galveston."

He leaned toward Jon, his dark eyes flaring like a lit match. "Sorta hard for me to do anyone in when I'm locked up. Why do you think I'd help you?"

"Because we can pull strings to make life easier."

Rawlyns snorted. "You aren't the first suit who's tried that approach."

"I'm thinking a once-a-week upgrade meal is better than the stuff served here."

Rawlyns hesitated. "I'm listening."

"Arresting officer Ian Greer, prosecuting attorney Marcia Trevelle, and Judge Nicolás Mendez are dead. We find it interesting since they were a part of your case."

"You askin' if I ordered the hits?"

"Did you?"

"I should have. But I didn't." He pointed to his chest where a tat identified his gang. "I'm a Texan Warlord, not a Veneno."

"But you're a smart man. You know what's going on inside and out." Obviously news about the three deaths being tied to the Veneno gang had reached this prison.

"I'd rather talk to the pretty lady." Rawlyns leered at her.

Leah smiled at the lifer, but it was a kind gesture, not a come-on. "You're saying the Venenos handled those murders?"

"Haven't they let everyone know it was them? You have interesting eyes. Full lips too. Real kissable."

Jon pinned Rawlyns with a stern look that said, *Back off.*

"Names?" Leah said.

"Can't help you there."

"What is the Galveston gang into? Drugs? Prostitution? Alien smuggling?"

"Not *reconquista.*"

Jon made a mental note. Solid hit.

She sighed. "What's their moneymaker?"

"No clue."

"Does the name Dylan Ortega mean anything to you?"

Jon watched Rawlyns—not a muscle twitch or a blink.

"Never heard of him."

"He did eleven months across the road," Leah said.

Rawlyns shook his head. "Now how would I know that?"

"Where would the gang get their supply of venom?"

"Ask one of them."

"Were Greer, Trevelle, or Judge Mendez getting too close?"

He laughed. "Meet my price—dinner, dancing, a bottle of tequila, and you in a short red dress—and maybe I'll tell you."

"Consider helping us," Jon said.

"I might be dying, but I'm not stupid. What are you thinking? Pain pills on demand? Smokes? A vacation in the Bahamas?"

Leah picked up the interview again. "I see you have a son. Leaving him an honorable legacy of a father—"

His features softened. "My son's twelve and already spent time in juvie. Doubt me giving up names to Feds would make a difference." A bit of wistfulness touched his words.

"Do you want him to end up like this?"

"Listen, no one deserves to be locked up like an animal." Rawlyns studied his cuffed hands for a moment. "A rattler can strike from any position. Some people think a rattler can't kill when its head is cut off. But they're wrong."

"What will you tell me?"

"I gotta have a couple of things first. Number one—let me see my son. Number two—yank him from his mother and put him in a place where he learns school is more important than the streets."

"I'll do my best."

"Bring him here with proof he won't be going back to her. Or don't come back."

"That will take time," she said. "It's impossible to remove a child from a home without due cause."

"Then I suggest you get busy. When you come again, wear that short red dress." He cocked his head at the guard. "I'm done."

Outside the prison walls en route to his truck, Jon deliberated the con's comments. "Rawlyns could have helped us if he wasn't so stubborn."

"True. I should have brought a change of clothes."

The image amused him. Leah's brown eyes bored into his, and he inwardly staggered with the intensity. She stirred a longing in him he didn't think possible—man to woman, soul to soul.

Jon shook away his thoughts. He didn't need someone who could get so close she would see through his control-guy facade.

"He gave us enough to move forward and promised us more," Jon said. "What he claimed about rattlers is true. If the leader is eliminated, the gang—Venenos or not—would continue to have lethal striking power."

"Two men are dead. How many more are they willing to lose or risk?"

"Depends on what's at stake."

35

SITTING IN THE VISITOR PARKING LOT at the Scott Unit, Leah
fought the rising irritation at not having more information. She
pulled out her phone to review the relationship matrix. "Jon,
Ian Greer's widow lives in Angleton. Looks like it's back up the
road a little. Shall I see if she's available?" When he nodded, she
phoned the woman and introduced herself. "Special Agent Jon
Colbert is with me. We're working with the Galveston Police
Department to find who killed your husband, Marcia Trevelle,
and Judge Mendez. We'd like to stop by and ask a few questions."

"Yes, of course. I'm home for the day, and my daughters are
with their grandparents."

"Thanks. We'll be there in about fifteen minutes."

Leah watched the countryside roll by. At a stop sign, she
rolled the window down and listened to the grasshoppers. "Love

the sound of nature," she said. "In Brooklyn, we have beautiful singing birds, but not nature's constant reminder. Neither do we have this stifling heat and humidity."

"Do you like Houston?"

"I do, especially the people." And it was far from the angst of family issues.

Jon's voice broke into her thoughts. "How about dinner when we're finished with Mrs. Greer's interview?"

She whipped her attention to him. "Are you asking me out?"

"Depends. Do you have a red dress?" He broke into a grin.

"Not funny." She attempted to smother a giggle, but a reminder of Rawlyns and his invitation bolted into her mind. "Yes to dinner but no to the outfit."

"Deal. Can't picture you in a dress anyway."

She widened her eyes. "As if I never wear one? Keep it up and I'll find the right moment to use you for target practice."

The teasing and the bantering relaxed her, and she needed a stress reliever. Would she grow tired of Jon's company? She shouldn't dwell on the other possibility. An update alerted her, and she read it aloud. "The barista at Warren Livingston's shop is clean."

"One more person to cross off our list." Jon pulled his truck into the driveway of the Greer home. A corner lot on a country road. A pasture with a few horses on one side of the property and thick woods on the other. The one-story home looked like it was built in the seventies with recent updates to incorporate a tin roof and front porch.

She and Jon greeted a dog of mixed variety and rang the doorbell. A slender woman with light-brown hair checked their identification and invited them inside to a living room that held a restored upright piano and family photos.

Once seated and past the pleasantries, Leah opened the conversation. "Our condolences in the loss of your husband."

Mrs. Greer pressed her lips together. "Thank you. Zachary, I mean Chief of Police Everson, told me you might call."

"Yes, ma'am. Agent Colbert and I have reviewed his report. Your husband and Judge Mendez had been friends for years."

"Since they were kids." A slight smile met them.

"Were you friends with Rachel Mendez?"

"Not really. We run in different circles. I'm more of the country type. Mrs. Mendez is a fine woman and has contributed much to the community."

"Were you friends with Marcia Trevelle?"

"Our mothers were close friends, and although I was older, she became a dear friend."

"I'm sorry for your losses."

"Some moments are harder than others. Zachary told me he didn't think our closeness had a thing to do with the murders. Anyway, you have a job to do, and I'm grateful, thankful to God, there are people like you to keep killers off the streets."

"Your husband was a courageous man. I'm sure you're proud of him." Leah stole a look at Jon. "I see you have two teenage daughters. How are they holding up?"

"Not well. Their father and Marcia were dear to them, too. We have a family reunion in October, and I can't bear the thought of going without Ian. Promise me you'll find who's killed good people."

"We won't give up until we do. Can you tell me if your husband, Ms. Trevelle, and the judge were investigating a case together?"

"They did work together and shared like interests. Give me a minute to think." She tapped her chin several times. "They used to meet for breakfast. For the past month or more, those breakfasts were more frequent, twice a week. I was thinking about it yesterday and wondered if there could be a thread that I needed to mention to Zachary. My Ian was restless, preoccupied."

"Did he mention what they'd been discussing?"

"Ian seldom told me about a case. I learned more from the media than my own husband. He didn't want to worry me."

"He must have cared for you very much."

On their way back to Houston, Jon cleared his throat, and Leah waited for him to speak. "So we've confirmed Ian Greer, Marcia Trevelle, and Judge Mendez met for breakfast periodically, no doubt to discuss whatever they were investigating."

"And apparently kept these meetings and what they might have discussed secret—even from their spouses. Do you think Everson knows anything more than what he's told us?"

"I think he would have shared it." Jon continued. "Will Rawlyns could have ordered a hit from his cell."

"He didn't strike me as the type to exact vengeance in this way." But Rawlyns's cryptic comment about rattlers lingered in Leah's mind.

"If he isn't responsible, we're back to square one: find Dylan Ortega."

36

JON UNLOCKED THE DOOR to his home, dark and empty. Some days he wished for a dog, but the animal would starve on Jon's schedule. His ten-acre gentleman's farm south of Houston held a stocked pond, thick woods, and lots of wildlife. The quietness usually soothed him, helped him unwind and think through critical information. Tonight, restlessness poured into his bloodstream. Dylan Ortega remained at large. Elena James was missing. Aaron Michaels was dead. Landon Shaw, a newly identified player, also lay in the morgue. A message on Jon's phone reported the speedboat from the Venenos' escape had been found in a vacant slip—and was reported stolen earlier in the week.

Jon's inability to make progress on the case reminded him of an out-of-control wildfire, and more people were bound to be hurt or killed. A mother who was frantic. A priest who wanted to save the world. Not good signs.

His mind rolled over methods of fighting fires. Remove the oxygen and starve the beast. How did he equate extinguishing a blaze to taking down a gang of killers? Was this even the work of a gang?

Jon opened the refrigerator door and pulled out a bottle of water. In this case, the oxygen could be the source of income, a hidden agenda the trio had stumbled upon. So what crime was feeding this blaze? Not one stinking bit of evidence pointed to arms dealing, prostitution, or illegal drugs.

But they *had* found strong indications of prescription drug theft.

He grabbed his laptop and sat on a barstool at the kitchen counter. After entering his secure password, he searched for unsolved gang-related activities in the Houston area with an emphasis on prescription drugs. Considering the Venenos' presence in Dallas, San Antonio, and Austin, he contacted the FIG to cross-reference related incidents in all four cities. They'd have an answer for him in a fraction of the time it would take him to make an analysis. In the meantime, he navigated to where his curiosity led him and learned that nine months ago, Molston Pharmaceuticals in Beyero, Texas, reported a theft with a street price of over sixty-five million dollars. Jon requested the details.

Closing the laptop, he leaned back against the stool. Transferring illegal goods in and out of Galveston wouldn't be a problem for someone determined to do so, but until they figured out what those things were and who, investigators were just spinning their wheels.

Clasping his hands behind his neck, he let his thoughts dwell on Leah . . . more than a great partner. He'd be a liar if he didn't admit her looks, brains, and personality had him in overdrive. Dark wavy hair and those incredible copper-colored eyes that softened in one breath and lit up with fire in the next. Working with her had taken his heart to a place he'd never been. She had a secret, and he sensed it when his comments touched on some pain disguised as sarcasm or teasing. Oddly enough, he didn't think it had a thing to do with snakes.

How would she feel about him if she knew his secret?

Hanson's and Chip's deaths were Jon's fault. His daredevil attitude. Poor judgment. Nightmares stalked him—the raging flames, crackling as though scoffing at all they devoured, shouting victory over every living thing. At times, he would swear he could hear Hanson speaking to him, calling for help.

A counselor told him he had survivor syndrome, a condition Jon had seen in others but not himself. The instructions were to accept the guilt, get involved with something constructive, and embrace his feelings—sounding like advice for a women's self-help group.

A Bible sat on the counter, a reminder of his promise to Hanson. Most days Jon read a few chapters. He'd gone through the book once and was now in the Gospel of John in the New Testament. Hanson said the answers to life's problems were in God's Word. Jon had doubts. But he owed it to Hanson to keep searching.

37

LEAH JARRED AWAKE AS her phone alarm blared. She and mornings were no longer friends—but with much to accomplish on her and Jon's list, she should start the day at 4 a.m. Should. She groaned. She wanted optimism to lace her thoughts, but the lack of progress on the murder cases made any positive thoughts difficult.

While whipping through her hair and light makeup routine, she scrolled on her phone and considered popping onto Facebook where she could catch a glimpse of her family.

Sixteen years had slipped by since she'd seen any member of her family, and not a day passed without a memory to prompt her to make contact. Sometimes she pressed in Mom and Dad's number, but she always lost her nerve after a few rings or one of them answered. A sniper and an agent who worked violent crime but didn't have the guts to call home. Sad.

For a moment, the idea once again tempted her. Dad used to

make a pot of coffee every morning at 5 a.m. He'd serve Mom a cup in bed to wake her up. But he was older now and habits changed. Waking him with a blast from the past might defeat her thoughts of reconciliation.

Why had they chosen not to tell her about her great-great-grandmother, her namesake? She'd escaped slavery in Alabama through the Underground Railroad and made her way to New York. There she'd started an orphanage and helped countless children find love, purpose, and an education. Leah learned this five years ago when she decided to examine her ancestry. The courage of the woman inspired Leah to be a better person, made her so proud she wanted to burst.

Years ago, her dad's brother suffered a childhood accident, leaving him to spend his days in a wheelchair. As a child, Leah thought her uncle's condition led her parents to adopting hard-to-place children. But they hadn't been honest, and if they'd taken the time to explain the family's heritage, life might have taken a different slant. She'd have better understood the chaos and craziness of her family.

Leave it alone.

Shouldering her bag with a change of clothes for the prayer service, she locked her apartment on the way out. This morning she'd buy the coffee. In the darkness on the way to her car, her phone rang. Terri.

Leah trembled. But still she didn't answer.

Her phone rang again.

She started the car engine.

Three times.

She missed Terri, a true sister-friend.

Four times.

The phone stopped ringing.

A moment later, she heard the ding of a voice mail.

She and Terri had met soon after she'd started at the Houston FBI office. Terri laughed easily, and other than putting cuffs on bad guys, she loved all things girlie from shoes to earrings. Leah learned more than she ever wanted to know about fashion and loved it. Yet, while Terri chatted on about her life, her goals, strengths, and challenges, Leah let little pass her lips about life in New York.

Leah's thoughts hammered against her brain. She could outshoot almost every man or woman in the state of Texas, but she couldn't talk to her best friend.

Before pulling out onto the street, she dialed Terri's number, pressed Speaker, and laid the phone in her lap. "Hey, I missed you earlier."

"Are you up or did I wake you?" The sweet sound of a good friend.

"Jon and I are heading to Galveston." Leah let her mind dwell on Jon for a moment. She liked him, the way he talked and carried himself. He had this little mannerism of lifting his chin when he differed in opinion with someone. Her heart tripped at the realization she'd be seeing him again in a short while.

Terri interrupted her musing. ". . . since the kids are still asleep. How's the case going?"

Her friend didn't expect details. "Slow. How are you and your family?" Leah managed not to choke on that last word.

"We're doing much better than I ever imagined. The kids are calling me *Mom*."

A hint of longing settled in Leah's heart, dousing the feelings of guilt and shame. "I'm happy for you."

"The last time we talked, you told me I was making a terrible mistake." Terri's tone held a note of wistfulness.

"I'm sorry." Leah hesitated. Could she unload her most

contemptible secret? She'd wanted to talk to Terri since her best friend had gotten married. This would be easier in person, but . . . "Do you have a few minutes?"

When Terri confirmed she did, Leah seized the invitation to share. "I was an only child until my parents adopted six children. My brothers and sisters have mental and physical challenges. The expectations for me to help care for my new siblings—and the fact that our parents' time was now so divided—caused me to resent them all. I felt unloved, so when I graduated from high school, I left home and never returned. The moment you told me about adopting children from Ethiopia, all I could think was what a demanding role you were accepting and how it might lead to the eventual breakup of your marriage." She managed to swallow the lump in her throat. "I'm sorry I didn't tell you the truth a long time ago."

"And I'm sorry for what you experienced."

"You're happy, right?" Leah wanted the marriage and children to work. She wanted her friend to feel loved and fulfilled.

"Extremely. We're settling in to family life, attending church."

Church? First Jon and now Terri. "If I'm allowed to indulge in any more selfishness, I want our friendship restored."

"Of course. We're good. Can we start fresh?"

"I'd love to. I need to come clean with a lot of garbage."

"We'll work through it together. What's first?"

"Can you send me pics of your children? I'd like to meet them and your husband."

"Perfect. How about Sunday for breakfast, about 9:00? We attend church on Saturday night."

"I'll be there as long as the case doesn't snatch my time."

"I understand," Terri said. "Then we must plan a shopping trip. I discovered a new boutique on my side of town . . ."

38

WHEN LEAH OPENED THE TRUCK DOOR, Jon saw her red-rimmed eyes. She handed him a supersize coffee.

"Need to talk?" he said.

She averted her attention to the cup holder. "I'm good."

Must be a happy-tears thing. "I woke up with a feeling today will be huge." He'd thought about the drug connection for a long time last night. "Landon Shaw got caught trying to sell stolen prescription drugs. Someone hacked into Molston Pharmaceuticals in Beyero and got away with drugs worth over sixty-five million dollars on the street."

"Open case?"

He nodded. "The drugs are coded and can be traced. I requested intel on Landon Shaw and learned he and Dylan did time together."

"Imagine that. Plenty of hours to form a plan. Neither of them seem smart enough to pull this off, but Landon could have introduced Dylan to the boss." She shrugged. "It's a theory, but how do the rattlesnakes fit?"

"A diversion while the gang slithers in and out of high-dollar ventures."

"We'll find out." She reached for her coffee. "For whatever it's worth, I like working with you."

"I'll remind you of that when we're being shot at again. Do you have a list of what's up for today and in what order?"

"Sure." She returned the coffee to the console and snatched her phone. "I know the prayer service is at 7 p.m. I think it's short. A lot of hours before then. Hold on while I check for updates."

"We are dynamic early in the morning."

"Or crazy." With her head bent over her phone, and her hair spilling over her face, she scrolled through her phone. "Landon Shaw had a partial pack of Marlboros on him. Silvia claimed the cigarettes at her house weren't Dylan's, but were they Landon's?" She tilted her head.

"Anything else?"

"Silvia made a withdrawal from the bank yesterday. One of the men on the surveillance team followed her inside and noted the teller gave her several hundred dollars in small bills. He wasn't able to count how much."

"Dylan needs money, and Mama's supplying. If this is what's going on, she has to get the money to him. Hard to avoid a surveillance team."

"He'd arrange a pickup. He's smart enough to cover up who and how." Leah gathered up her coffee. "But if he's really knee-deep in this, money shouldn't be an issue." She tapped her finger on her phone.

"What are you thinking?"

"We suspect the Venenos—or whoever this gang is—are dealing in prescription drugs. I want to find out if Silvia is taking any medications. The dental office is open. Let's see if there's a connection."

"Do you think she'd tell us the truth when she's lied about other things?"

"I have a plan."

"I'm sure you do." The faint scent of citrus invaded his senses. His mind trekked into unknown territory. Stopping himself before he made a fool of himself seemed wise, but his mouth seemed to take on a mind of its own. "Are you seeing anyone?"

She failed to look up from her phone. "With the hours I keep? What about you?"

"No. Same reason."

"Why ask?"

When he started this, he should have realized she'd toss it back at him like a fastball. "Just making conversation."

She glanced up. "Are you interested, Agent Colbert? You ventured toward this yesterday."

"If I am?"

"I'm a private person, a loner, and most of the rumors you've heard about me are true." She returned to her phone, her next words suggesting she was hiding a smile. "Maybe I'm a little interested too."

Maybe, as in she might go out with him? Or felt the same interest? Time to pull on the reins. For him to move forward in a relationship, he'd have to come clean.

"I brought donuts for the road," he said. "They're behind your seat."

"I've been smelling them and didn't know when to ask. Don't suppose you have blueberry?"

"Yep, they're listed on your background."

Jon seemed to inhale the last of the six glazed donuts as he and Leah entered a thriving professional community of upscale offices separated by walkways, courtyards, and parking on three sides. This held the dental practice of Dr. Pablo Rios, where Silvia had worked for the past twenty-four years. The receptionist informed them Silvia would be busy with a patient for the next fifteen minutes. They sat in matching chairs and chatted about baseball, one of Leah's favorite topics—the Yankees. Jon was an Astros fan.

When Silvia opened the door to the waiting room, her eyes widened at the sight of them. She positioned herself in a nearby chair and folded trembling hands in her lap.

"Have you found Dylan or Elena?" she whispered with an unsteady voice.

"No, ma'am," Leah said. "Have either of them contacted you?"

"Not yet."

"I know this has caused sleepless nights for you, but we're hoping to have the case resolved soon."

Silvia blinked back a tear. "I pray you discover my son's innocence." She sighed. "Sleep will come when he's home and free."

"Have you tried taking anything?"

Silvia shook her head. "I want to be alert in case he calls at night."

"Dylan is very fortunate to have a mother who cares so much." Leah invited kindness into her words.

"Someday you'll understand a love that means more than life."

"Being on your feet all day must be difficult."

"It is. I have problems with my back . . . a degenerative spine."

Leah had noted at times Silvia appeared to be uncomfortable. "How painful."

"The doctor prescribed medication for me to take." She stiffened, not as a sign of irritation, but more of discomfort.

"My grandmother had the same condition. What do you take?"

"OxyContin."

Strong stuff often sold on the streets. "Do you purchase it locally?" Leah said.

"Dylan gets the prescription for me at a discount pharmacy in Houston."

Doubts surfaced in Leah's mind. "Who's your doctor?"

"Why?"

Leah formed her words as graciously as possible. "Ms. Ortega, I can find out or you can tell me. I loathe what you're going through, but I'm not the enemy."

The receptionist stood from behind the counter. Gold jewelry hung in layers from her neck and wrist. "Silvia, you have a patient waiting." The woman turned to Leah. "This is a workplace, not an FBI office. In the future, I suggest you conduct your business elsewhere."

"My apologies for the interruption," Leah said. "Silvia, do you have the drugs with you?"

"They're at home."

"I'd like to stop by and pick up the prescription."

Silvia frowned. "Why?"

"It's important to our case."

She seemed to deliberate Leah's response. "In Dylan's defense?"

"Possibly."

"Silvia," the receptionist said, "you are putting us behind schedule."

Silvia opened the door to the patient area. "If you need anything else, you'll be talking to me through a lawyer."

39

OUTSIDE THE DENTIST OFFICE, Jon's cell rang, and he saw Father Gabriel's number. "Good morning, Father Gabriel."

"Agent Colbert, are you in Galveston?" The priest's breathless words made it sound like he'd been running.

"Yes. Are you in danger?"

"I was outside pulling weeds around the church when a bullet flew past my head, and someone yelled, 'You're a dead man.'"

Jon started hustling Leah toward his truck before Father Gabriel could say more.

"Where are you now?"

"In my office. I'd been warned enough. I ducked and rushed inside. From my window, I saw two men across the street with guns. That's when I called you."

"We're on our way. Lock the church doors. Call 911."

Jon veered the truck onto Thirty-Second Street and sped to St. Peter's. The shriek of sirens indicated police were also approaching the church.

"If they wanted Father Gabriel as their fourth victim, he'd be dead." He swung into the church parking lot, braked, and exited the truck. Two patrol cars pulled in beside him. He and Leah drew their Glocks and raced up the church back steps. The door flung open and Father Gabriel stood on the other side—pale, shaking.

"Thank you. If I hadn't moved to avoid a wasp, I'd be dead." He leaned against the side of the wooden door. "Two men ran toward the old Falstaff Brewery." He pointed toward Thirty-Third.

Jon raced toward the partially demolished building, Leah keeping pace. As Jon approached the massive, crumbling structure, it started to look more and more like something out of a horror movie, the perfect setting for drug deals, illegal parties, and the homeless. A figure was climbing up a pile of brick and debris, and Jon put on an extra burst of speed to leave Leah behind. His running days from high school to Quantico spun through his mind. The person disappeared inside a black window.

Jon leaped onto a fifty-foot hill of brick and plaster. He shouted back at Leah. "Look for an entrance seaside." He scrambled up, like he used to climb trees as a kid in Oklahoma, keeping his body close to the wall for cover.

His attention zeroed in on the window where the man had disappeared. The short steel barrel of a handgun jutted out from the side. He counted to three and whirled around the windowsill to fire into the open space. A grunt rose, and running footsteps sounded, quickly growing faint.

He fired again, then stepped inside the window and blinked several times to adjust his eyes to the shadows. Bending, he walked behind his Glock, moving toward a dim hallway. Footprints on the dusty concrete floor guided him farther into the structure.

He stole along graffiti-covered walls, past corroded doorways and even the rusted frame of an old Toyota stripped of its dignity.

A glimpse of light from the open roof picked up drops of blood on the floor. The groan heard earlier and now the blood indicated a wounded shooter.

Jon picked up his speed, moving swiftly past partially covered insulated pipes and up rusty metal stairs leading to the next level. At the landing, he listened before taking off after faint footsteps.

Darkness and trash made it difficult to trace the blood trail. Still he raced through a doorway and across a catwalk lined on one side with a metal railing. The other side would send him plunging to his death.

The corridor ended in a Y that led into darkness with no clear path. He bolted right. Tripped on something and fell facefirst. So much for being sure-footed.

He shook off the stun and continued until the patchy roof splashed light onto a brick wall showing obscenities in red and blue spray paint. No blood drops.

He rushed back the way he'd come, being careful to avoid whatever he'd tripped over the first time, and followed the other path to a window leading out onto a metal bridge, missing a few rungs and weaving in the faint breeze.

Leah . . . No shots had been fired. She must be okay. Father Gabriel claimed there were two men who'd headed toward the building. What happened to the second man?

No time to text or risk a ring signaling her location. He'd been guilty of sending partners to their death before. Never again.

He sprinted across the metal bridge and into a roofless, light-filled area. Signs that a segment of the homeless population in Galveston lived here—worn Army blankets hung for privacy, slashed mattresses, used syringes, and cigarette butts littered the space. He stepped down metal stairs to fallen pipes. These would stop a wounded man.

Then Jon saw a man dragging his leg, one hand on his thigh and the other wrapped around his gun. "Stop. FBI." His words echoed around him.

The man moved faster and disappeared around a corner with Jon closing the distance between them. An opening with a narrow beam for a bridge separated one part of the floor from the other. The man started across. He wobbled.

Could the metal beam hold both their weights?

If Jon chose to fire, he'd send the man to his death. The FBI never threatened. Besides, being able to question the shooter meant more. "Surrender now or I'll be forced to shoot."

The man stood midway on the rusty support. He straightened and stared at Jon.

"You don't have to jump." Jon stepped onto the beam. "Let's talk. Make it easy on yourself."

The man shook his head and glanced down. "I'll be a dead man."

"We can protect you. Someone has to end what's going on."

A shot fired from below knocked the man off the beam.

40

LEAH SEARCHED THROUGH one dirt-infested hole after another.
Once she saw a man scrambling up a flight of rickety metal stairs.
Perspiration dripped salty into her eyes, and she swiped with her
hand while hurrying up the stairs into an open area of birds and
humans inhabiting the same filth of rust and mold.

Gunfire echoed through the massive building. She stopped
to listen. The sound originated behind and to the right. Dare
she text Jon? Risk putting him in danger? She hid in the shadows
beneath metal steps and typed—OK?

Yes. U?

K. Call me.

Minutes later, her phone vibrated and she leaned against
foul-worded graffiti and a gang tag. "I heard gunfire."

"A shooter killed my man before he turned himself in."

"Did he offer any info?"

"No. Hoping his identity will give us a lead."

"I haven't found any signs of the second man," she whispered.

"Where are you?"

"East."

"Officers are inside and moving toward my location. Once I talk to them, they'll search the rest of the building."

"That will take hours."

"Head toward the seaside entrance."

"When I finish this area." She slipped the phone back into her pocket. She despised the apparent lack of value for human life. Had the man she'd been chasing killed his partner?

The building reminded her of a few spots in New York where the same type of crowd attempted survival. Through rubble and a scurrying of rats, she climbed to the top floor. Below, police officers threaded in and out of the building. If the bad guy was hiding inside, he could squirrel away for hours. She made her way to the farthest eastern point and peered out. Officers swarmed this section, too. One of them used a K-9.

Leah climbed down another level, always looking for obscure places, pockets beneath beams, under fallen pipes, and in dark corners. Evidence of those who'd roamed and used the building emerged like pop-ups on a website.

On the next lower level, she made her way to an open wall and walked carefully to the edge. A man raced down the street and disappeared between houses.

Jon learned the dead man's name was Brad Dixon. He had a record for burglaries. No gang affiliations or distinguishing tats.

Dixon carried a new burner phone, the same brand as the ones used by Aaron Michaels and Landon Shaw. Activated but no incoming or outgoing calls or texts.

Jon stopped in a grassy area midway between St. Peter's and the Falstaff building and watched Father Gabriel praying over Dixon's body. Did the priest realize he could have been the one receiving last rites? A puzzle, a commitment Jon failed to understand.

He shook his head and weighed what little they'd uncovered about the perpetrators. Who and what was behind all this? Dylan Ortega twisted in his mind like a key ready to unlock the who and why the gang existed.

Father Gabriel joined Jon and Leah and sighed. "Thanks for allowing me to finish my prayers. I recognize the deceased."

Jon's senses went on alert. "How do you know the man?"

"Mr. Dixon came to see me Monday afternoon. I'd never met him before. He asked to make confession."

"The day before Judge Mendez's death?" Jon said.

"Right. The confession never happened. We were interrupted. Chief Everson barged into my office without knocking and startled us. He demanded we talk immediately. I excused myself and left Mr. Dixon alone in my office. When I returned, he was gone." He paused. "Now he's dead. Perhaps I could have prevented this."

Questions bombarded Jon's mind, beginning with Father Gabriel and heading back to Everson. "I don't see how you could have prevented this. Did Dixon recognize Chief Everson?"

"I have no idea."

"What was Everson's urgency?" Jon said.

"He found out Marcia Trevelle had seen me earlier in the day. She was worried about him, asked for prayer."

"Let's talk in your office and see if we can figure out why Dixon came for confession and how it could be tied to today."

"All right."

Jon jogged with Leah to Father Gabriel's office but was unprepared for what they found inside. Desk drawers were thrown open and papers scattered on the floor. Books tossed into every conceivable place. Stacked boxes in a closet had been dumped upside down.

The priest remained in the doorway. He gasped. "What happened?"

"Were the shooters a diversion?" Jon directed his questions to Leah. "Why didn't Dixon and his bud walk into the church and forcibly take what they wanted? Or break in at night?"

"And did they find what they were looking for?" Leah stepped around the debris. "Father Gabriel, what do you have that they could possibly want?"

Father Gabriel shook his head. "I'll check to see what's missing, but I keep nothing of value here."

"You were nearly killed today," Jon said. "Do you see why you need a police officer to protect you? This could have been prevented."

"I kept thinking Chief Everson needs every uniformed officer until this is over." He drew in a deep breath. "They might not miss the next time. You're right. I need protection."

Leah pulled her phone from her pant pocket. "I'll contact Everson for an assigned officer, then Houston FBI. We need a team to sweep the area."

Jon glanced at Leah. "Have any gloves on you? I'd like to check the computer."

"We've used what I normally carry."

Father Gabriel spoke up. "I'll get a box from the nursery. Are you allergic to latex?" When Jon shook his head, Father Gabriel gave a rueful grin. "Still doubtful any would fit you."

"I can do it, and I'm fine with latex." Leah moved to the desk, but she kept her fingers away from the computer and keyboard until Father Gabriel returned with gloves. She wriggled them on.

"Thank goodness for babies' behinds." Jon chuckled.

She rolled her eyes at him. "Is the device locked?"

"Yes," Father Gabriel said. "The code's SaintPeter."

"When this is over, we're discussing password protection," she said.

Jon watched Leah quickly move over the keyboard.

"You'll find only church business. Emails to and from members and the diocese. Files of baptisms, marriages, and funerals. Earlier, I shut it down to cut a few roses from the front bushes before Judge Mendez's services. Then the shots were fired."

Jon wanted to ask more questions, but instead he focused on Leah. "What was accessed?"

"Nothing." She looked at the mess strewn over the floor. "Had to be a tangible item."

Yet someone seemed to believe Father Gabriel had something vital to the investigation. Jon formed his words to convey his thoughts without frustrating the man and causing him to shut down. "Who in your church has family who may not respect the law?"

The priest touched his white beard. "Family struggles bring many to the church regardless of the situation. I suppose you want the list."

"Yesterday."

"The prayer service will be in a couple of hours, and I need to prepare. Afterward, I'll go through the membership for the type of people you're looking for. This has to stop."

41

PRIOR TO JUDGE MENDEZ'S PRAYER SERVICE, Leah sat in the women's bridal area at St. Peter's and munched on a burger before showering and changing clothes. She'd been smart to add deodorant and makeup to her bag. The search through the Falstaff building had left her dripping in sweat. She sipped her Diet Coke and thought about the regrettable situation with Silvia Ortega.

Earlier this afternoon Leah and Jon had stopped by the woman's house to pick up her prescription bottle. A single pill inside had rattled as Silvia handed the bottle to Leah. A quick glance at the label told Leah all she needed to know.

Leah wrapped her fingers around the bottle. "Silvia, your prescription expired eight months ago. No pharmacy would fill OxyContin without a current prescription."

Silvia had stared at the wooden porch floor as though

looking at Leah pained her. "I told you Dylan buys them for me at a discount drugstore in Houston. The store reuses my old bottle to save money."

Did Silvia really believe that? "You're in the medical field and understand the strict laws guarding opioids. My job is to uphold the law. Where are you getting the OxyContin?"

Silvia hadn't responded, just closed the door with the click of two locks.

On their way back to the church, Leah had flipped open the bottle and read the identification on the tablet.

"It's a match," she told Jon. "These came from Molston Pharmaceuticals."

Silvia, have you lied to us since the beginning? Was the woman a part of gang activities? Or was she simply guilty of believing her son? The SAC had agreed to hold off on bringing Silvia in for now, confirming she had the potential to lead them to Dylan.

Her quick dinner at the church finished, Leah let a warm shower soothe her tired muscles. She changed clothes and redid her makeup. Her attention settled on Facebook. Perhaps it was the prayer service and people coming together for Judge Mendez that coaxed her into looking at familiar faces and learning about their lives.

Leah clicked on her mother's Facebook page and saw the family had gone to the Brooklyn Ice Cream Factory, and a whole album of photos resulted. Leah swiped at a tear. She was alone and hated it.

Tapping her finger on the side of her cell phone, she debated as she had many times before. What could Dad do but hang up?

She pressed in their landline number. In the past, she'd disconnected before the first ring or when he or Mom answered.

"Hello."

Her throat constricted. A myriad of memories of hearing Dad's voice swept over her.

"Hello?"

"Hey, Dad. It's Leah."

"Who?"

"Leah."

"Where are you?" He sounded kind and strong like the man she remembered.

"In Houston. I live here."

"Doing what?"

"I'm a special agent for the FBI." She hoped her career made him proud.

"It's been a long time."

"I'm sorry for what I did to all of you. I was selfish, didn't see how you and Mom wanted to help others less fortunate." There, she'd said it.

"Too—"

She heard a crash, and the phone went dead. Had he hung up? Leah trembled. She'd done this to herself. She'd sworn never to be rejected again. To keep her distance from her family. But she'd tried her best to become a better person. She'd taken the guilt and blame and pushed herself to expert marksmanship. Wore duty, priority, and responsibility like a shield. And for what? To one day make the call to Dad and hear him say he loved her? He forgave her? Please come home so they could begin to reconcile their differences? Start over? They'd talk about her brave great-great-grandmother Leah. She'd push a wheelchair, change a bedridden sister, have a conversation with an autistic brother, whatever was needed to make things right.

She and Silvia were in the same muddy waters, allowing those they loved to dictate their self-worth. And losing.

42

AS PEOPLE ENTERED St. Peter's sanctuary for Judge Mendez's prayer service, Jon monitored the right rear corner, and Leah handled the left corner.

Mrs. Mendez and her children and mother were the first to arrive. Even the children were dressed in black. Rachel Mendez carried the little boy and held her little girl's hand as she walked toward her husband's casket, facing the altar. She reflected her modeling career with grace and poise, her hair and makeup perfected. The little girl cried, and both Mrs. Mendez and her mother attempted to console her.

Other mourners trickled in—Silvia Ortega and Warren Livingston. The woman avoided Leah and Jon. Had Silvia told Warren about the drugs? Everson arrived in full regalia, all four of Judge Mendez's staff, and a man and woman whom Father

Gabriel greeted as Mr. and Mrs. Serrano. Good, he hoped to speak with Lucinda, the priest's secretary, when the service ended.

Jon glanced at Leah. Rachel Mendez had nothing on her. He believed he had the most gorgeous partner on the planet.

Whoa, back up.

Leah wore the typical navy-blue slacks, white silk blouse, gold earrings, and a simple necklace. Wavy dark hair touched her shoulders. She'd showered there at the church, and the damp curls were . . .

Stop it. Get back to business.

People moved to the middle of the pews to make room for others. Richard and Olivia James entered and seated themselves in a back pew. Olivia's eyes were red and swollen, and Richard sat ramrod straight. The couple gave anguish a new rung on the ladder of despair. If rebellion kept Elena separated from her parents, she wasn't the young woman other people described. Her school records showed a student who consistently made the dean's list and was active in community and church affairs. Jon wanted to find her alive.

When the people finished filing past the casket and speaking to Mrs. Mendez, Father Gabriel led the service of prayer and remembrances of Judge Nicolás Mendez. The priest recalled many of the judge's excellent contributions to the church and Galveston. He invited others to tell stories and reminisce about their experiences with him. A few comments met with laughter, and Jon learned the judge had a sense of humor.

Father Gabriel shared a few golf stories, as well as times the judge had met him at the church to pray for loved ones and upcoming trials. Others spoke about their experiences with Judge Mendez. Silvia spoke of how he visited the nursery before church and prayed over the babies and toddlers. Mrs. Mendez talked about his love for her and their family.

Jon scrutinized the two women to see if there was any spark of recognition between them. Nothing.

The silver-haired attorney, Ross Kempler, appeared to be spokesman for the judge's staff. Respect poured into his accountings of working alongside the judge for years. Jon studied each face, searching for malice or deceit. Although many were strangers, he observed prominent people in the community. If any of the mourners were glad the judge had been killed, none showed it.

Everson wore the stress of unsolved murders like a noose. Rightly so, as the victims were his friends and fiancée.

After a lengthy final prayer, Father Gabriel dismissed the people. Several chose to pay their respects one more time.

As the sanctuary slowly cleared, Jon approached Lucinda Serrano, a pale-blonde woman. "I'm FBI Special Agent Colbert. Can we talk for a few minutes?"

"You spoke with her on the phone." Mr. Serrano grasped his wife's waist. "She has nothing more to say."

Jon sensed Leah at his side, and he introduced her. "This won't take long." Jon pointed to a pew near the back of the sanctuary.

Mrs. Serrano turned to her husband. "Dear, these people are investigating the murders of three fine people."

He snorted his response, and the four were seated.

Jon recognized concern in the man's eyes while Mrs. Serrano grieved. "Father Gabriel told us you knew all the members of St. Peter's by name, young and old. And you never forgot a face."

She exchanged a look with her husband. "I want to help, and when the killers are found, I want to return to St. Peter's."

Mr. Serrano rubbed his face. "Lucinda, I know you want to return to work, and I realize you're fulfilled there. And while I don't want to live in fear for you, you have to decide if talking to the FBI is what's best."

Love wore many hats.

She patted her husband's hand. "Agent Colbert, you're after the wrong young man."

"I don't understand. We have a witness who puts Dylan Ortega at the church."

"Dylan called me the night before the judge's death. He was scared because the Venenos were after him. They'd tried to recruit him, and he'd said no. He thought he might need to hide and asked for advice." She drew in a breath. "I suggested getting as far away from Galveston as possible and to take his mother."

"Did you give him a specific place?"

"No. But what baffles me is he and Elena are both missing. Where are they, and why didn't they take Silvia?" She bit her lower lip. "I'm afraid the Venenos found them, and now they're dead." She covered her mouth.

"You and Dylan were close?"

She nodded. "I was his contact at church for his community service, and my son had gone to school with him. So we already had a connection. I became a mother figure who listened when his world took a confusing turn. Dylan talked to me about life, his dreams, and about a special young woman."

"Elena?" Leah said.

"Yes, ma'am. Not many were aware they were together. He was trying very hard to put the past behind him. Elena hadn't told her parents about them."

"Have you heard from Dylan or Elena?"

Lucinda shook her head. "If a witness saw Dylan at the

church's back door, then he must have been forced. It's impossible for him to be a Veneno or have anything to do with Judge Mendez's murder."

"Why?"

"He wouldn't want to hurt his mother or cause her any pain."

"Which is why you're questioning the fact that he left Silvia behind," Leah said.

"I meant emotional damage to his biological mother."

Jon's attention zeroed in on Lucinda. "What did you say?"

Lucinda blew out a sigh. "Silvia raised Dylan from a newborn, but she's not his birth mother. I witnessed the private adoption with Father Gabriel and a lawyer. Dylan learned the truth about three years ago while going through his mother's papers."

"Who is his mother?" Leah said.

"Rachel Mendez."

43

LEAH SHOULDN'T BE JOLTED BY TRUTH, any truth, but the identity of Dylan's biological mother delivered an incredulous moment. "Rachel Mendez is Dylan's mother, and you witnessed his private adoption?"

The secretary nodded. "The papers were signed at an attorney's office here in Galveston when Dylan was two days old," the woman said. "I never told anyone until this morning when I shared the secret with my husband and now you."

"Who was the attorney?"

"Ross Kempler."

The attorney who'd worked twenty-seven years for Judge Mendez. "Were Mrs. Mendez and Silvia friends before the adoption?"

"They met through Silvia's dental office. Rachel came to

Silvia with the adoption proposal, but I don't know why. Since then, they've worked together on church committees."

A picture formed in Leah's mind of two women developing an unusual bond, one knit together by circumstances. "I assume he wasn't supposed to find out about his adoption?"

"Silvia agreed to take him in under the stipulation he never learn the truth. Rachel had two more years of law school left. She modeled to pay bills, and a baby meant her future as she intended came to a halt. I know this sounds like Rachel was selfish, but adoption is a gift of love. She knew Silvia would be a better mother. They agreed in writing Rachel wouldn't later demand him back or insist upon visitation."

"The father?"

"Never mentioned. At least not to me."

"Money exchanged?"

"Not to my knowledge."

"Can you explain the circumstances around Dylan learning the truth?"

"He'd drifted into a bad crowd. Needed money and was looking through Silvia's things for a few dollars. Found a whole lot more. When Silvia got home from work one afternoon, he had the adoption papers in his hand. After the confrontation, Silvia contacted Rachel."

"Did Rachel and Dylan connect?"

"A couple of times. Dylan came to me, angry at both women. One woman had lied to him, and the other abandoned him. He no longer cared about either of them or himself. Soon after, he was arrested and served time. Dylan learned a lot about himself and life there. He was determined to be a better man. He reconciled with Silvia. Not sure if he ever had a meaningful conversation with Rachel."

"Did Judge Mendez know about Dylan?"

"No idea. You'd have to ask Rachel, but then she'd know where you learned about the adoption."

"Does it matter?" Leah said.

"I'm on Dylan's side. Always have been. Silvia and Rachel are fine women who love God. Silvia believes in Dylan, loves him unconditionally. I do too. He's the son I never had. With Rachel . . . she built a life without him, but experience is a wonderful teacher. Rachel serves the community, often guiding women to counseling and contributing to charities that help single mothers and their children." She rose to her feet. "I'm finished. I hope my information helps."

Adoption came full circle when Leah considered her parents, Terri, and now Silvia. She saw the struggles from all three scenarios. Why had these adoptions rolled into her life now? Dad used to say people grew to become productive members of society when they made mistakes, recovered, and moved forward.

Leah watched the Serranos walk away. She pulled up the Mendezes' phone records and turned to Jon. "We need to talk to Rachel."

"Now," he said, his tone flat in a way Leah had come to recognize as no more games. "You stand a better chance of making headway."

Rachel stood with her mother and children talking to Ross Kempler. Jon and Leah approached her.

"Can we talk privately?" Leah said.

Rachel's cheeks were stained with tears. "Tonight?"

"Yes, please." Leah gestured to the front pew.

Rachel made arrangements for her mother to take the children to the nursery area. She joined Leah and Jon at the front of the church. She dabbed at her eyes. "I'm sorry. This is incredibly difficult for me. Did you encounter any suspicious people tonight?"

"We learned new information that impacts the case."

"What kind of information?"

"Dylan Ortega's relationship to you." Leah offered compassion in her words.

"I see," Rachel said. "Lucinda must have told you. I suspected as much when I saw you talking to her. For the record, my husband knew the truth."

"Was he told before your marriage?"

"No. We had a discussion Sunday afternoon."

Why had Rachel waited so long? "How did he take the news?"

"Surprisingly well. He wanted to bring Dylan into our lives. We invited him to our house that evening and told him we were interested in being part of his life. Neither Nicolás nor I wanted to exclude Silvia. She was his mother."

"How did Dylan respond?"

"He wanted time to think about it and discuss things with Silvia. He'd never hurt her. She has his heart, gave him what he needed when I was too selfish."

"Then you talked to Dylan at 8:05 on Monday night."

"I was checking on him after Sunday's discussion, to find out if he'd made any decisions."

"Rachel, did Dylan in any way indicate he was angry with you or the judge? Would he have retaliated against your family for hurting him?"

"I can't imagine Dylan betraying our family in that way. My husband wouldn't have initiated a relationship with Dylan if he believed my son was a criminal." Rachel paused. "Neither my husband nor I would be foolish enough to risk our children's lives."

"I know Dylan is your son. I've seen your grief, and I understand you're confused and shaken about him and the tragedies this week. But if you know where he is, we need that information."

Rachel broke into a sob. "I wish I could help you, but I can't."

44

ALONE WITH FATHER GABRIEL in the huge sanctuary, the atmosphere felt spooky, as though the three of them were sharing the space with a paranormal being. Leah stifled the urge to shudder.

"The prayer service would have pleased the judge." Father Gabriel broke the spell and glanced at Jon. "Is there something you needed? I have preparations to make for tomorrow's funeral Mass and that list of names to finish compiling for you."

"We'll keep this brief," Jon said. He got straight to the heart of the matter. "Mrs. Serrano shared a bit of history with us tonight."

Father Gabriel gazed up at the statue of the suffering Jesus. "What kind of history?"

"Before Rachel left tonight, she confirmed Silvia Ortega's adoption of Dylan."

"His adoption has nothing to do with his alleged involvement with the judge's murder."

Jon frowned. "He was seen carrying the body of a man who's married to his biological mother!"

"Look," Father Gabriel said, "neither Rachel nor Silvia asked me to keep the adoption secret. I believe they assumed I would, but I kept the matter confidential for Dylan's sake."

Leah recalled his words at their first meeting. *Dylan needs someone to champion him.*

"What concerns me are a few important issues. Did he despise the judge because he was a father to Dylan's half brother and sister? Did he loathe Rachel and want to destroy what she loved? Either of those scenarios implicate him in murder."

"Agent Colbert, I'm finished discussing Dylan Ortega tonight."

"Are you covering for him?"

"No. Emphatically. My desire is for all to come to love Jesus Christ. No sacrifice is too great. None."

Leah could practically feel the heat of Jon's simmering anger. She wasn't going to rescue him. If he lost his temper with the priest, she'd stand by and listen.

"Are you sure? When you're saying tonight's prayers, ask God if you're obeying His commands or nursing your pride."

Jon drove toward Houston with Leah while his mind focused on a stubborn priest. Trying to get information out of Father Gabriel was like stumbling through a cornfield blindfolded. Once the funeral was over in the morning, he'd talk to the priest again and attempt to be civil. God might have shaken Father Gabriel into cooperating with law enforcement.

Calm down.

A statement from Hanson rolled through Jon's mind. *"Let God have His way with us. Choose to surrender."*

Father Gabriel said he was willing to sacrifice everything to bring others to Jesus Christ. Jon appreciated the priest's commitment and passion, but not his foolhardiness. The priest shoved caution aside, putting his life in danger so others might find faith. But Jon saw the similarities in his own life in how he felt about keeping people safe from crime. As strange as it sounded, watching Father Gabriel respond to the turmoil around him was inching Jon closer to allowing God to rule his life—the sovereignty thing, as Hanson called it. Jon wanted a God who knew everything—the good, the bad, the ugly . . . and all the secret stuff in between.

"Are you okay?" Leah said.

"Will be. Analyzing Father Gabriel's beliefs with my own. Respecting his faith in God is not the same as agreeing with him."

"Do you think a lot about God?"

He thought more about Hanson and why his friend believed right up to his last breath. "I want to find out where I fit in the universe."

"I grew up with morals, not about God but about the value of contributing positively to society. My grandmother took me to the Brooklyn Tabernacle, a church in New York, a few times, but it never really took for me. When I think about Silvia's faith and what Father Gabriel hasn't told us, I have to wonder if these people just like to think they're good."

"People aren't perfect. Just because they have faith doesn't mean they don't make mistakes." He shrugged. "But since I'm not sure about the God thing either, I'm only quoting an old friend."

"Let's talk again when we're finished with this case. I sound like I'm putting you off, but honestly Rachel has me analyzing everything she's said. Do you suppose something happened between the judge and his wife after she revealed this information?"

"That would definitely be a motive if Judge Mendez refused to allow him to be a part of his own children's lives. Was Rachel forced to choose between her son and her husband, and Dylan just cleaned up his mother's mess?" He considered the complexity of the relationships involved. "What about Silvia Ortega? She never indicated friendship with Rachel Mendez. Would she be angry enough to retaliate against the judge for violating the adoption agreement?"

"Find Dylan and we can fill in the blanks."

In the darkness, he shook his head. "You make this sound easy."

"I'm doing the encourage-my-partner thing. We keep bumping against those who offer half-truths, those who value their feelings and priorities above solving three murder cases."

Jon needed a break to clear his head. "Want to stop for dinner? I'm hungry."

"If it's quick. I'm exhausted with no resolution in sight."

"What will it be? Burger and fries? Pizza?"

"Not pizza unless it's authentic New York style. I'm terribly picky about hometown foods. But a grilled cheese from Sonic with tater tots is pure comfort food."

"Good choice. There's one at the next exit. Who's buying?"

"Depends on how much you order."

"I need a huge milk shake, two chicken sandwiches, and a cheeseburger. Large fries."

"We'll go dutch."

He enjoyed their bantering, but would it last? "Before we do a date thing in the future, I need to discuss a few issues from my past."

"If you knew mine, you'd run."

"I'm not afraid."

Back at home, as the clock neared 11 p.m., Jon's mind couldn't stop churning over how he'd lost his temper with Father Gabriel. He grabbed his Bible from the kitchen counter and turned to read more in the Gospel of John. He read the account of Jesus' betrayal and arrest and the magnitude of love demonstrated at the cross. Sacrifice that knew no boundaries.

Jon's gut burned, and not because he'd eaten so much. *I messed up tonight.* He snatched his phone and contacted Father Gabriel. The priest answered on the first ring. "This is Jon Colbert. I owe you an apology for tonight's outburst. I was way out of line."

"You were forgiven the moment you unleashed your feelings."

Jon closed his eyes and bit his tongue. "Then we're good."

"You're the better man. I should have taken the initiative since I'm guilty of the same offense. I should have told you about Dylan's adoption. Kindly accept my apology."

"Sure."

"A few minutes ago, I read a quote from Mother Teresa about putting our foot in our mouth. 'Follow the path of serenity. Why lose your temper if by losing it you offend God, trouble your neighbor, give yourself a bad time, and in the end have to set things aright anyway?'"

Jon smiled. "Truth."

As he wrapped up the call, Peter's denial of Jesus wouldn't leave him alone. Jon reread the text, concentrating on how Peter had sworn allegiance, then lied through his teeth. Peter lived. Jesus died. Good old Peter must have faced a heavy dose of survivor guilt. Too bad the two of them couldn't sit down and talk about sending good people to their deaths.

If Jon believed the Bible, Jesus came back to life and forgave Peter. Hanson and Chip weren't afforded that kind of miracle. Would his friends have held a grudge against him for leading them to their deaths? How many times had Jon gone over the past and how he'd failed his friends? Hanson claimed Jon could have a new identity in Christ.

Jon scooted back the chair and walked outside onto the front porch. He shoved his hands into his jean pockets and looked up at the millions of stars. Somebody designed the universe and put them into place, a Being much smarter than Jon.

"Truth," Jon said again, coming to a point of surrender in himself.

He would have to email Claire and tell her the good news. Hanson now had a brother-partner in faith.

45

EARLY THE NEXT MORNING, Leah crawled into Jon's rental truck. She moaned the hour. "We're consistently in the dark, either going to Galveston or coming home. And today's a funeral."

"Someone needs her coffee." Jon pointed to the large cups in the console, the smell of the brew wafting her way.

"Don't placate me." She scowled, but a smile crept through.

"But I'm right."

"This time. Thanks for the coffee. It's exactly what I need this morning to get my mind in gear. Any updates other than Elena and Dylan haven't been found?"

"One, but it's personal and has nothing to do with the case."

"Don't turn all Father Gabriel on me. Will it help make arrests?"

He patted the steering wheel. "Only in the eternal perspective."

"What?"

"Never mind. I'm in a weird mood. First off this morning, we need to fuel up for the day."

After a quick breakfast at the Sunflower Cafe, Jon and Leah made their way to the church. As the hour for Judge Mendez's service approached, several FBI agents and GPD officers stationed themselves as part of a security perimeter around St. Peter's. Only a fool would attempt a violent crime here today. And with three of the perpetrators dead, how many were left?

By 9:30, the sanctuary was at capacity, standing room only. While Leah devoted her attention to her assigned location, the same corner as the previous night, the number of people made her nervous. The heat index outside soared in the mid-nineties, and all the people inside the church caused the AC to work harder.

Father Gabriel emerged from a side room with Mrs. Mendez and her family. The children had changed from one black outfit to another. Poor kids. Losing their daddy and enduring the hours in church.

Isn't this the best place for children?

Where did the random thought come from?

She kept her stance, earbud in place, with Jon and the other FBI agents in strategic locations. Beneath her jacket was her Glock. Leah scrutinized the people, all ages and races. The sermon seemed short, Father Gabriel talking about the death and resurrection of Jesus and how His death meant Judge Mendez would live forever in heaven.

Leah was puzzled when the priest performed some bread

and wine rites. Had no idea what it meant, but she'd ask Jon later or look it up.

But her attention was immediately seized when a young man seated on an aisle stood and waved both arms. "This isn't over. More people will die."

46

WITH ONE HAND WRAPPED around his Glock, Jon rushed up the aisle from the rear of the church. Innocent people shoved together in pews on both sides of the aisle, their sobs of grief shifting to fear.

"Hey, man, is there a problem?" Jon said, noting the man had a recent bruise to the left side of his face and the wild light of a drug high emanating from his eyes. No visible weapon. "I can help."

Agents and officers quickly moved to avoid panic and lead people out of the church.

"No one can help me. It's gone too far."

"I'd like to try." He poured sincerity into his words. "Let's talk outside where we can have privacy."

"Who are you?" His crazed gaze darted about. "Why the gun?"

"FBI."

"I haven't done anything wrong. Just warning people. But I'm afraid."

"I appreciate your concern," Jon said. "Are you packing?"

"I'm not the one these people need to be afraid of."

"I get it. What's your name?"

"Henry Kantore."

"I'm Jon." He pointed to the aisle on his left. "Walk with me to the front, and we'll talk in Father Gabriel's office. No one is going to hurt you."

The young man wrapped his arms around his chest. "Okay."

Jon escorted him to the front of the church and cuffed him. No resistance. He caught Everson's attention and silently let him know the situation was handled. Jon and Henry exited the sanctuary and walked down the hall to Father Gabriel's office. The man smelled of days-old sweat. Jon heard the service continue with Father Gabriel's booming voice and organ music. He assumed people were allowed to file back into the pews.

Inside the office, Jon seated himself across from Henry and opened the conversation. "You said you're afraid. What's going on?"

"The Venenos are after me."

"Why?"

Henry sniffled and stared at the floor. "I refused to kill someone. Can't do it."

"Who?"

"Father Gabriel."

"So then why are you here?"

"To warn people about what happens when they get in the Venenos' way."

"I see. Where did you meet up with the Venenos?"

"Four guys showed up at the body-repair garage where I work."

"When was this?"

Henry scratched the back of his neck. "About a year ago."

"Did you know any of them?"

"Nope."

"They showed up at your work. Then what happened?"

"One of them asked if I'd look at his car. The battery wouldn't keep a charge, and he thought it needed to be replaced."

"What kind of car?"

"Mustang. Black. Newer model."

"Do you remember the plates?"

"Never looked at 'em. If he'd left the car, then I'd have written it down."

"Sorry I interrupted you," Jon said. "Keep going."

"The guy popped the hood. As I was looking at the battery and the wires, three of them got real close. One of the other guys said he had an invitation for me to join the Venenos. He told me I'd make 2K a week to start and be my own boss. I wasn't interested and told him so. The guy reminded me about my cousin in prison who got into trouble for hacking computers, and could I do the same thing? I knew where he was headed, so I told him I gave up those ways. No more jail time for me. No thanks."

When Henry paused, Jon pressed him to continue. "What happened then?"

"They threatened to kill me if I didn't do what they said. I told 'em if they wanted me to kill people, then we were finished talking. But one of them said I'd help them get into computers and find stuff for them. I gave in." He sniffed.

"Whose computers?"

"I forgot."

"You had to have names to get into systems."

Henry only shook his head.

"For a man who wants to help and be protected, you're not cooperating," Jon said.

"My mind isn't good."

"Try leaving the drugs alone." Jon swallowed his aggravation. "What kind of information did you access?"

"Personal stuff mostly."

"Like what?"

Henry shrugged. "Don't remember."

"Do the names Ian Greer and Marcia Trevelle sound familiar?"

"Nope."

"Did you get into any computers belonging to Officer Ian Greer, Attorney Marcia Trevelle, or Judge Nicolás Mendez?"

"I don't remember." Henry coughed.

"Do you need some water?" Jon said.

"Yeah, thanks."

Jon turned to the water cooler in Father Gabriel's office and pulled a cup from the dispenser. He flipped up the lever.

Henry rushed the door.

Jon dropped the cup and raced after him. Midway down the hall, he grabbed Henry by the shoulder and flipped him around. The man struggled but couldn't throw a punch with his wrists cuffed. Jon tossed him to the floor onto his stomach. He searched his pockets and wrapped his fingers around a syringe.

"What's in this?"

"I'm a diabetic." Henry groaned as Jon pressed him into the floor.

"If this is insulin, then I'm Frosty the Snowman."

"Please," Henry whimpered. "You're hurting me."

Jon let him see the syringe with the yellowish substance. "What is this?"

"None of your business."

Jon tightened his hold. "I made it my business."

"Rattler venom."

"Who were you going to use it on?"

"Father Gabriel. But I couldn't do it."

Jon huffed. "In front of all these people, cops, and FBI agents?"

"I was supposed to wait around until it was over and ask to make confession."

Like Brad Dixon. "Who else is with you?"

"Nobody."

"Attempted murder puts you under arrest." Jon radioed for officer assistance and alerted Leah and the other agents inside the sanctuary to look for others who might be waiting for the service to close.

"You said you'd help me," Henry said.

Jon eyed the syringe in his hand. "Can't help you unless you give me names and information."

"Anything. Whatever you need."

"Here's a word of advice, Henry. Don't break the law. Ever. The consequences are never small."

47

LEAH MET UP WITH JON as he ordered Henry to be held in protective custody at the Galveston Police Department until he and Leah could question him further. No one was to enter the cell.

The service ended and Judge Mendez's body was transported to the cemetery. After a brief prayer time, the body was lowered into the grave. Jon and Leah stayed at the grave site until the mourners left.

Rachel approached them while her mother escorted the children to the car. Two police officers and Chief of Police Everson awaited the small procession.

"Agent Riesel, do you have time to talk?" Rachel said.

"Yes, of course."

The two women made their way to a bench, leaving Jon and Father Gabriel alone. Rachel took a deep breath. "I apologize for not telling you the truth about Dylan. I'd like to explain a few things about me, my past, and how Nicolás helped mold me into a better woman."

Leah questioned if Rachel's explanation was the truth.

"I was a selfish younger woman. More narcissistic than I'd like to believe, and nothing I'm proud of. My modeling and law school were more important than anyone or anything. At least I had the sense not to abort Dylan. Silvia is a godly woman. She loved my son and became the mother I never could have been." Rachel swallowed hard.

"Take your time." Leah patted her arm. "This week has been a nightmare for you."

"Thank you." She glanced at her children and mother in the distance. "My mother is my best friend. Dad died of a heart attack shortly after Nicolás and I were married. She and Dad knew I had given up my baby for adoption, but they thought the family lived in Dallas. Last night I told Mom the truth, and she cried with me. I watched my son grow up and kept my word not to interfere. The only thing I've done for Dylan is establish a trust account for him when he's twenty-five.

"After graduating from law school, I went to work at a law firm and became friends with Marcia Trevelle. She introduced me to Nicolás. I'd never met a man so complex before. He believed in God and the law in that order. His faith in action moved me to place God foremost in my life too. While he had a reputation of little leniency with offenders, he had a gentle side. He laughed freely and loved life. I fell in love, so deeply that the emotions frightened me. He acted as though I were a queen, and when he told me he loved me, I knew I didn't deserve it. I wanted to be the woman who helped him serve the community. I confessed my past, but I couldn't bring myself to tell him

about Dylan. Last Sunday after church, he asked me about a
son I'd given up for adoption. I have no idea how he learned
the truth. Perhaps Lucinda told him or the lawyer who handled
the adoption, but it doesn't matter. It was hard, but he didn't
condemn me." She peered into Leah's face. "I believed I could
finally establish a relationship with my son. Then Monday
came. We were devastated about Ian and Marcia."

"And your husband didn't say a word about something they
were working on together?"

"No. When I questioned him, he said he'd tell me what was
happening on Tuesday after he talked to the FBI."

Father Gabriel told Jon he'd never heard of Henry Kantore.
Another person linked to the crimes, but where did Kantore fit?

Everson waited until Rachel and her family left the cemetery before approaching Jon and Leah. What the man lacked
in height, he carried in command and wide shoulders. Not an
ounce of waste on him.

"Tell me about the guy sitting in my jail," he said to Jon.

"His name's Henry Kantore. He confessed to being a
Veneno. Hired to hack into computers. Says he was supposed
to get Father Gabriel alone and use rattler venom on him. Tried
to make a run for it during questioning. Had a syringe full of
something in his pocket. We'll test it."

Everson huffed. "I want five minutes."

"He's in FBI custody."

"In my jail."

Jon gave him a stern look. "Not happening."

"How'd he get in with the Venenos?"

"Claims he was approached by four men who wanted his computer skills. Threatened him if he didn't agree. He said he hacked into systems but never had a name. Seemed clueless about Ian Greer or Marcia Trevelle."

Everson's face reddened. "Did he hold Marcia down when they injected her with rattler venom?"

"Agent Riesel and I are ready to question him."

"I'm sitting in."

Any problems with Everson's personal involvement with the victims, and Jon would have him removed.

Two hours had passed since Jon arrested Henry Kantore. His dilated pupils and the track marks on his arm indicated cocaine use.

"You had a fix this morning." Everson stated the obvious.

Henry ignored him and focused on Jon. "Who are these people?"

Jon introduced Leah and Everson. "We need information. Unless we get it, you'll be tried for three counts of murder and an attempt on a fourth. Not to mention the illegal drug use."

"How do you figure?"

Jon had heard pathetic whining before. Back a criminal against a wall, and he still thought he had bargaining power. In this case, Henry had a little leverage if he'd provide names. "You cooperate, and I'll see about reducing your sentence to violent street gang involvement and hacking—by your admittance. Three people might be alive if you hadn't given the killers a way into their computers."

"But I know some bad stuff going down. I expect a better deal—"

Everson bellowed out a swear. "Like your hands slapped so you can walk the street again, free to murder?"

Jon bored his attention into Everson. "We have this."

Everson dragged his tongue over his lower lip and glared at Jon.

At Jon's nod, Leah resumed questioning with the gentleness he'd come to expect. "Nasty bruise on your face. How'd it happen?"

"I fell yesterday."

"Where were you?"

"Don't remember."

"Could it have been the Falstaff building?"

Jon inwardly startled. Could Henry have been Brad Dixon's partner?

Henry hung his head and nodded. "I want out of this mess."

"So you were with Brad Dixon," she said. "What were you planning to do?"

"He'd left something in the priest's office from another time. He wanted out of the gang—we both did. But before he left the island, he wanted to make confession. When he was ready to talk to Father Gabriel, Everson walked in. Dixon got scared 'cause he had school bus on him."

Jon recognized the slang for Xanax. "What happened then?"

"When the priest left with the cop, Dixon hid the pills on a closet shelf. The boss got real mad and told him to get the drugs or he'd kill 'im. I went with Dixon 'cause he asked me. Then we planned to leave for Mexico."

"Did you kill him?"

Henry shook his head wildly. "I don't know who fired the shot."

"Were the drugs recovered?"

He nodded. "There were three of us. The other guy gave them to me later, and I made the drop."

"Who?"

"Not going there."

"Really? I thought you wanted to help. Where did you take the drugs?"

"I'm not saying anything else unless I get a better deal."

Leah sighed. "Like Agent Colbert, I want to help. But you've got to give me info and names."

"I'm a dead man!"

"We want to keep you safe," she said. "But think about the families of victims who are crying for justice. If Dixon left the drugs in Father Gabriel's office, why ransack it?"

"We were high. The boss wanted Dixon to leave syringes in the priest's office and look for anything to implicate him in the judge's death. Neither of us wanted to go to hell for planting evidence on a priest."

"Where are the syringes now?"

"Tossed them in the Falstaff building." Henry sighed. "I'll tell you what I can, but I need protection."

"Question one." Leah spoke barely above a whisper. "Who told you to attack Father Gabriel at this morning's funeral?"

"I don't know his name."

"How did he contact you?"

"My phone."

They had his cell phone. Running down numbers was part of the process.

"You told Agent Colbert about four Venenos who showed up at your garage," she said. "I need their names."

"I can give you two." Henry stared at his cuffed wrists.

"They're dead—Aaron Michaels and Landon Shaw. They also stole Judge Mendez's SUV."

That answered another question. "Is Dylan Ortega someone you know?"

He shifted and twisted in the chair.

"I'm waiting," she said.

"Never heard of him."

"Marcia Trevelle?"

He shook his head.

"Ian Greer?"

Henry flinched. "Nah."

"Elena James?" Leah said.

"No."

She turned to Jon. "He hasn't given us anything solid but who stole the Mendez SUV."

Everson broke into the conversation. "Our man here forgot another detail. Hey, Henry, according to your record, Officer Ian Greer arrested you for possession."

"I'm not good with names."

The lack of memory came with fried brains and a tendency to lie.

Everson rose from his chair and clamped his hands on Henry's shoulders. "Tell me about Marcia Trevelle."

"I've never heard of her."

Everson dug his hands deeper and Henry winced.

"Chief Everson," Jon said, not wanting to intervene further unless Everson got out of hand. "We are conducting the interview. Henry, you're lying. We're tired of hearing it."

"Told you, my memory's bad."

"One more question." Everson applied more pressure to

Henry's shoulders. "Did you witness the gang committing murder?"

He glared. "No."

Everson jerked him to his feet and went nose to nose. "What about watching them die?" His hands went for the throat.

Jon pulled him off. "Let him go, Everson. He's not worth it. His confession seals his guilt."

"I have my rights." Henry sputtered his words.

Everson released him and stepped back. He trembled with visible rage. "My jail."

"But you don't make the laws." Jon turned to Henry. "A word of warning while you're a guest of Galveston's finest. Chief Everson's fiancée was Marcia Trevelle. Officer Ian Greer was his good friend, like a brother. He's an angry and grieving man."

Henry's widened pupils sparked fear.

Jon looked from Everson to Henry. "I suggest helping us find the killers."

"Okay." Henry licked his lips. "I know a little about the rattlers."

48

LEAH KEPT A STOIC FACE while Jon faced Henry, but she wanted to believe they'd made progress. The suspect had sobered a bit, and she had an idea to press him on before he lawyered up.

"Henry," Leah said, "Agent Colbert and Chief Everson have lost patience. They don't understand you're frightened and want to help. Would you rather I ask them to leave the room so we can talk?"

"Yes, ma'am."

Jon and Everson protested, then left her alone. She'd nominate them for an Oscar. They'd be viewing from the one-way glass.

She gave Henry her full attention. "The truth now, or I might have to leave you alone with the chief of police and Agent Colbert. You haven't seen my partner in action, but I wouldn't cross either of them. They both scare me."

"Okay. The rattlesnake farm is not far from here. If there are others, I don't know about it." He stared at his cuffed wrists. "Alvin area. I can show you on a map."

She navigated on her phone to a map surrounding Alvin and zoomed in. Henry pointed to a rural spot and gave county road intersections. Jon would have local authorities notified of the location before she finished questioning him.

"Is the rattlesnake farm owned by Venenos?" she said.

"I suppose. Never asked."

"Who's the big boss?"

"How many times are y'all going to toss that question at me? No one has a name. It's the truth, and the honest truth."

"How many Venenos are there?"

"We aren't together at the same time."

Pulling answers from Henry was like deciding to diet with a candy bar in her mouth. "But you have names of some of them."

"So do you." He glanced at the window to his left. "Since one of 'em might be a cop, I'm not giving you any more than you already have."

She'd pose the question again at the Houston office. "Tell me about *reconquista*."

"It's something we're supposed to say to make the boss happy. I guess it matters to him."

"How does the gang make money?" She paused for the question to sink into Henry's head.

He squinted. "I work at the garage."

"Wrong. Try again."

He shuffled his feet. "We sell drugs."

"Cocaine?"

He shook his head. "Mostly prescription drugs."

"What kind?" she said.

"OxyContin, Percocet, Ambien."

"Have you sold to Dylan Ortega?"

"No idea."

"Where's your stash?"

"Sold 'em. You won't find a thing in my apartment."

She moved on. "How does your boss contact the gang?"

"Texts. He's smart. He gets me a new phone regularly. I think we all get new ones."

"How often?"

"Depends on how many texts we get."

"How does the phone transfer take place?"

"I get a text to leave my phone at a spot and how to pick up a new one."

"Where?"

"Never the same place. Sometimes in Galveston and other times in or around Houston."

"I'll need the locations of where you've dropped off or received a phone."

"What I've told you is good."

"I'm going to need more, Henry. Names, places. You know the charges without them."

"I'm a dead man if I give you a single name. I'd rather take my chances with the cop and a jury."

She shook her head. "Chief Everson and Agent Colbert won't like this. What if they choose to put the word out on the streets that you leaked names? Then cut you loose?"

He pointed at her with his cuffed hands. "I said I know about the rattlers. I told you where the farm is. I deserve a break for risking my neck."

★ ★ ★

Jon drove his rental truck behind an Alvin police squad car to the location Henry Kantore had given for the rattlesnake farm. Everson drove a pickup behind him.

Leah had been quiet, and he recognized her fear of snakes had surfaced like oil on water. How bad was her phobia?

Her phone alerted her to a text. "Everson sent info about the owner of the property. The man lives in Iowa and inherited the land from his father. Clean record. Everson wants us to contact him now."

He placed his phone on the dashboard and pressed Speaker. When a man answered, Jon introduced himself. "The section we're checking is on the northwest side."

"I haven't been down there for years," the man said. "The neighbor runs cows on part of the property. Would you call me if you find a rattler pit?"

"Yes, sir. Do you have a caretaker for the property?"

"If there's a problem, the neighbor would let me know."

"I'd like his name and number."

Leah had her fingers poised over her phone's keypad.

"Sure." The man relayed the neighbor's information.

"Has anyone contacted you about selling your property?" Jon said.

"A man phoned me about a year ago wanting to know if I'd sell a hundred acres from the northwest section, but I refused. It's been in my family a long time."

"Did he give you a name?"

"I didn't ask because I wasn't interested. He did offer quite a bit. Told him there isn't a public road access to the northwest acreage, but he was insistent. I think I kept his number.

Anyway, I'm in Seattle and won't be home until Wednesday. Want me to text it to you then?"

"Yes, please." Jon gave him his number. Could be something. Could be nothing.

They drove down a dirt road, then turned onto a rutted lane bordered on both sides by waist-high weeds. The lane soon ended, and they bumped over pastureland to a weather-beaten shack. Trodden-down weeds indicated other vehicles had been there. He parked the truck and together with Leah, Everson, and the officers, followed a path around dense woods. Jon noted Leah lingered at a patch of yellow black-eyed Susans and silverleaf nightshade. The harsh caw of a crow and the hum of insects reminded him of the hours spent as a boy exploring the land surrounding his home in Oklahoma.

A massive live oak to the west with its arching branches marked the direction of the pit, twenty feet north of the tree. According to Henry, the milking was done here, in the shack, and the equipment needed was brought to the site. The area was clean of any signs, only the bent weeds and scraping rake marks.

Jon found the pit. A metal grate held in place by heavy stones kept the snakes inside. Leah moved to his right, and he studied her face. Her flattened lips failed to mask her fear.

He lowered his tone. "No need to put yourself through this. Why not wait in the truck?"

She stared at the pit. Her gaze flew to his, liquid fire. "Stand down, Jon. This is my private war. I'm no coward."

Stand down?

"Agent Riesel," an officer said.

She swung toward the man who'd spoken her name. To her right, a four-foot rattler uncoiled, its head directed at her ankle, well within striking distance, just a yard away.

Jon pulled his gun. "Easy, Leah. I've got this."

"No. I'll kill it." With shaking hands she slowly pulled her Glock from her back waistband.

Her face paled.

The snake rattled its warning.

How long should he wait? If he jumped in to save her, she'd probably shoot him.

"Jon." Her voice trembled.

He fired, blowing off the rattler's head. "Stay away from its head. It can still bite."

"I know that!" Leah turned and walked back to the truck.

Jon ached for her. He'd experienced gut-wrenching terror, the paralysis of despising yet protecting yourself.

Jon and the officers removed the stones and used a dead branch to slide the grate and expose the pit.

One of the officers swore. Jon snapped a couple of pics. He estimated it contained a couple hundred rattlers.

"The Venenos won't be getting their venom here anymore." Everson peered over the lip at the poisonous snakes in the pit.

"We could contact the Sweetwater Rattler Wranglers," Jon said. "But it'll take time for them to get here."

"Forget that." Everson pulled his Sig.

Jon held up his hand. "There's a legal way to get rid of them. It's up to the property owner."

"He's not here." Everson turned to one of his officers. "Bring me the gas can on my truck bed. In my glove box are matches."

Before Jon could phone the owner and explain the situation, Everson fired repeatedly into the pit, like each one of them was a Veneno. Jon made the call anyway.

"I'm asking you to kill them," the owner said.

Everson added another magazine to his weapon and resumed firing.

The deputy returned. Everson grabbed the gas can and poured what was left into the pit. "Stand back. I'm sending these snakes where they belong," Everson said.

Jon texted Leah. Asking if she was okay might embarrass her. Talking to her might unleash venom she'd rather no one saw.

Everson eliminating the problem. Will scout the area. Be there in a few.

K. I'm a wimp. This is not who I want to be. I'd rather face a dozen armed bad guys than one snake.

He understood Leah more than she realized or might want him to know. She overcompensated as a sniper and agent to make up for the uncontrollable phobia. He wished he had a solution because he'd sign up for the program. But if he thought about it, there was much to learn about life, himself, and God while attempting to solve a problem.

You are human. On the way back to Houston, I'll tell you how my friends died.

But he wasn't sure spilling his guts would solve anything for her or him.

49

WHEN JON RETURNED TO THE TRUCK, Leah had news for him.

"Some additional background information came in on our good buddy Henry Kantore. Guess who he used to work for."

"I give. Who?"

"Will Rawlyns. Do you think he'll talk to us this time?"

"He likes you. Got a red dress? Dance music?" He swung her a grin.

She shot him a look. "I'll check on where things stand with CPS before we walk in." She tapped in the number.

At the Wayne Scott Unit, in the same interview room as their previous conversation, Will Rawlyns slowly lowered himself onto a chair. Lines across his forehead indicated pain. He frowned at Jon. "You're not here to chitchat, and you know my terms. You get nothing without my boy."

"Agent Riesel would like a few words," Jon said.

He gave Leah a sideways glance. "Good to see you again, pretty lady. Where is my son?" He plopped his cuffed hands onto the table with a clang.

"Young Will's school requested CPS look into his home life."

"Isn't she sending him to school?"

"Truancy is a problem. But he's getting into trouble—fighting."

Rawlyns jutted his jaw. "I want him away from her . . . permanently."

"Then you'll like what we've learned," Leah said. "Will Jr. was escorted from school yesterday afternoon to a foster home. The situation is under investigation."

"I still need to see him."

"We're working on visitation, but we can't promise anything." Leah paused. "Because of your health, I'm doing my best to make this happen. Do you have many visitors?"

"My sister occasionally. She never knows what to say. Not like I have this lifestyle of the rich and famous. Father Gabriel from St. Peter's church in Galveston. He's working on getting me to make confession. Ain't happening."

Jon took over. "We're looking for information about Henry Kantore," Jon said. "A friend of yours?"

Rawlyns snorted. "I know who he is. What's he done?"

"Claimed to be a Veneno."

"He's a skinny fish in a big pond. Tell you what, he ain't smart enough to pull off three murders." Rawlyns drew in a sharp breath that appeared to pain him.

Stage 4 had a way of taking the fight out of a man.

"He had a loaded syringe on him," Jon went on. "Said he'd been ordered to inject it in Father Gabriel."

"He ain't smart enough to fill a syringe with rattler juice either."

"But you know who is."

Rawlyns appeared to wrestle with how much to say. They needed to get his son to the prison.

Jon pressed on. "What can you tell us about Kantore?"

"I'll give you his record. You could learn these things from his file anyway. He started back in 2013 with Houston cocktail."

Jon was familiar with the Texas-based drug, a mix of Norco, Xanax, and Soma. "And?"

"Ecstasy, blow, oxy, some cheese."

The latter was another Texas-based drug, heroin with cold meds and an antihistamine.

"Henry snorted his profits," Rawlyns said before abruptly leaning back and calling an end to the interview. "Been a nice visit, but I'm done here. Don't come back without my boy. Best hurry 'cause I'm dying, and you want to know who's doing the murderin'."

The guard escorted Rawlyns from the interview room, leaving the stench of an unwashed body, laden with bitterness and unmanaged pain.

As Leah and Jon left the prison, Leah looked back at the closed doors. "I'm finding a way to get his son here. Rawlyns has nothing to live for but hope Will Jr. won't travel the same road as his father."

Jon drove them back to Houston, his thoughts lingering on Rawlyns. When this was over, he'd make a trip to visit the man again, try to offer some comfort. Maybe Father Gabriel was rubbing off on him. Speaking of priests . . . he needed to find a church for tomorrow, which meant research. He'd be visiting a lot of them in the weeks ahead until he found the right one.

His dry mouth was due to only one thing—baring his soul. In the early hours of this morning, he'd turned his life over to Christ, and now he planned to tell Leah about his last jump? What next?

"You have a strange look on your face. Angry?" she said.

"Thinking about what I wanted to tell you."

"I'm listening, Jon."

"My ego tells me I'm about to look like a coward." His forced bravado fell flat.

"Doubt it. You couldn't look any worse than I did today, failing to confront my snake fear. Someone could have been hurt out there. Never understood how I can be okay on a sniper mission where they're usually located."

"Every person on the planet has secrets, some worse than others. I think you're braver than I am." He glanced at Leah, who graced him with a wide smile.

Time for honesty. Truth. He waded through how to begin. "Ever feel stalked or haunted? Just plain scared?"

"I assume you're not talking about our job." She paused. "You mean the kind of fear like being around you?"

Okay, he'd take this segue. Might make his confession easier. "What are we going to do about this crazy attraction?"

"I'd like to run, but I'm stuck on the passenger side of this truck, traveling sixty miles an hour. Your secret's safe with me."

He chuckled to ease his nerves. "I used to be a smoke jumper." What had he gotten himself into?

"I had no idea. Were you a hotshot? Daredevil? No fire too huge kind of guy?"

He tossed her a feigned scowl. "I was the spotter. I had two close friends, partners—Hanson and Chip. We were like brothers. We came from different places, different backgrounds, but we shared the drive to stop wildfires. I led out, the jumper in charge. My job was to calculate wind, topography, ground hazards, and the beast's behavior."

Vivid scenes from that final fire played like a movie montage. "In Utah, we learned a man had hiked into the mountains, fell, and was trapped. A fire was sweeping toward him. He requested a rescue before the battery on his cell phone died. The three of us went after him. We choppered over the fire. It was an inferno. No place to jump." He could practically feel the heat of the flames, taste the smoke in his mouth. "I should have turned them around. Instead, I believed we were invincible. Thought I'd found a decent jump spot on a slope. Thick timber, but not far from the fire. I parachuted first. Chip and Hanson followed." Jon swallowed hard. "The smoke and flames got to Hanson and Chip. They didn't make it. I carried the injured man out."

She moaned softly. "I'm really sorry."

"I walked away." He swiped at the sweat on his forehead. "After six weeks, I went out again to lead a team into a wildfire in California. Thought I was ready. When it came time to jump, I froze. A coward." Stating his weakness cut deep. "That's when I resigned. Floated around for eight months before applying to the FBI. Being a sniper suits me. I'm still helping people, doing what most people fear. Different kind of fire."

She reached across the truck and touched his arm. "I don't see how your friends' deaths are your fault. The three of you were trained smoke jumpers." She stroked the top of his hand. "We're quite a pair. Two snipers who wrestle with strange fears. And scared to death of each other."

He liked the feel of her hand atop his. "What I've discovered is our strengths will overcome the junk holding us back from being better people. Faith, too."

"I have a part two to my story." She pulled back her hand, and he wondered briefly if the remark about faith was too much. "More personal than snakes."

"Want to unload?"

"Not tonight. But I will if you're going to ask me out," she said.

"Already confirmed. Dinner, dancing, and a short red dress."

"I don't own a red dress, partner. Should we talk about the case?"

"I suppose. Want to have lunch tomorrow and work on it?" An idea struck him. "I'll pick you up at noon, we can have lunch, and I'll show you my little acreage. I have a stocked pond, and the fishing's great."

She hesitated. "Okay, but I'll drive myself."

"Don't trust yourself with me or is it the control thing?"

"What do you think?"

He laughed. "Both."

"Spot-on," she said. "I've never been fishing in my life."

"First time for everything."

"Any snakes?"

"On occasion."

She glanced at the road ahead. "Got to start somewhere on all counts."

"I'll text you the address." Once he found a church, he'd invite her along. For both, one step at a time.

50

LEAH DROVE TO TERRI'S ADDRESS, a brick two-story in a solid neighborhood in west Houston. She parked her Camaro at the curb and breathed in and out.

I can do this. Be a friend. Put my past where it belongs.

Grabbing a dozen assorted muffins and another dozen mixed scones and pastries, she shouldered her purse and made her way up the front walk. The landscaping framed the home perfectly, as though guiding her to a house filled with love. She rang the doorbell and hoped the shakes stopped before Terri answered.

They didn't.

Terri opened the door, and both burst into tears. "We've officially become junior high girls," Terri said.

"I've missed you so much." Leah offered the breakfast treats. Terri tucked a long brown lock behind her ear and took the boxes. "Come in. Boys, I have someone special I want you to meet."

The aroma of bacon greeted her. A tall auburn-haired man wearing an apron and a huge smile walked down the hallway.

He stuck out his hand. "I'm Chris, and you must be Leah."

She shook his hand. "Yes. It's a pleasure to meet you. You're so tall."

"I think my height is the only reason Terri ever went out with me."

The stairway rumbled with the sound of footsteps, and two wide-eyed boys grinned. They introduced themselves as Caleb and Asher. "You're Mom's friend, right?" Caleb, the taller one, said. "You fight bad guys too."

Their candor put Leah right at ease. "I am. I've been looking forward to meeting you."

"Mom's got a big breakfast made." Caleb pointed down the hall. "My brother's kinda shy, but I'm not."

Leah bent to Asher, who looked to be about five years old. "I brought some dessert treats. Do you like muffins?"

He turned his head to look at Terri. "Mom and Dad say I have a sweet tooth."

"I do too. After breakfast would you and Caleb help me bring in a wedding gift for your mom and dad?"

"Yes, ma'am," the boys echoed.

"Wonderful. There might be something for each of you."

Leah straightened as the boys dashed off to the kitchen. "Your family is beautiful," she said to Terri and Chris, and for a moment she feared her eyes would drip again.

"And complete." Chris wrapped his arm around Terri's waist. "Food's about ready. Let's eat."

After breakfast, and the delivery of a mammoth basket

FATAL STRIKE

filled with sheets, pillowcases, towels, and scented soaps for the newlyweds, and a Marvel action figure for each of the boys, Leah toured their home.

"Your bedroom is so clean," Leah said to the boys, eyeing their bunk beds.

"We cleaned it for you," Caleb said. "But don't look under the bed or in the closet."

Leah held up a hand as if swearing a solemn oath. "I won't." She wished she hadn't made a fishing date with Jon. The boys seemed to have unlocked a padlock on her heart. Good memories gushed in about her siblings. "Hey, guys. Can I have a few minutes with your mom? Then we could play a quick game of basketball before I have to leave."

"Dad says we're the best he's ever seen," Caleb said.

"Maybe so, but I was pretty good in high school."

They bounded off, leaving her with the best friend she'd ever known. They walked back to the kitchen, where Chris was loading the dishwasher. "Outside, you two. This is my job."

On the rear patio, with the hum and gentle breeze of an overhead fan, Leah and Terri sank into cushioned chairs.

"I see why you're so very happy," Leah said. "Chris and the boys are amazing. You simply beam."

"Thank you. I never realized how good you are with kids."

Leah allowed another sweet memory with her siblings to warm her. "I enjoy their minds and uninhibited creativity."

"We've had a great new beginning this morning, haven't we?"

"Perfect in my book. But once I let the boys beat me in basketball, I need to get going. I promised Jon I'd let him show me how to fish."

Terri's blue eyes sparkled. "In all the years I've known you, I've never seen you get so serious about a guy."

"Jon's a good guy. A friend. And we're working together." Leah paused to figure out what else she could say to emphasize the professional relationship. "We'll most likely talk about the case."

Terri waved away the comment. "Of course. What else is there?" She grinned mischievously. "But, Leah, Jon Colbert is super cute. I can see you two together."

"We've only known each other since Tuesday."

"Maybe so, but something's put a spark in your eyes."

Leah sensed heat rising to her face. "He is fun."

51

SUNDAY AFTER EARLY MASS, Silvia fingered the business card belonging to Special Agent Leah Riesel. Warren wrapped his arm around her waist, comfort when she needed it. She looked at the card for the third time. Not knowing the truth left her grappling in a way that felt worse than what she might face.

Dylan hadn't been completely honest with her when he phoned her for money. The medication he'd been getting for her had likely come from illegal means. Her head throbbed. She'd suspected as much. Now the media said the FBI had arrested a man who claimed to be a Veneno, but his name hadn't been released. He'd been arrested at Judge Mendez's funeral, but from where she and Warren had been sitting, she hadn't seen his face.

Silvia needed to be sure he wasn't one of Dylan's friends, one who'd stopped by the house or the man who'd picked up the cash at the dental office, the young man who'd done drugs before he arrived. She tried to relax, but until she was assured the man in custody had no connection to Dylan, her efforts were useless. Aaron Michaels and Landon Shaw had spent time in her home, and she'd lied to the FBI about them. But if she acknowledged their friendship with Dylan, then he looked like a gang member too.

Dear God, I'm sinning for Dylan. I hate myself, but what choice do I have? Father Gabriel told me to sin no more and be honest. I can't betray my own son.

"Honey," Warren said, "the truth can be hard to take, but you're a strong woman."

He understood her. The one thing she held back from him was Dylan's adoption. Agents Riesel and Colbert had heard the truth about her son. Why keep it from Warren? Except not this morning. Her heart and mind ached for her precious boy. Before she agreed to Warren's marriage proposal, she'd tell him about the adoption, including the truth about Dylan's birth mother. She believed married couples shouldn't have secrets.

She tightened her fist. "I'll call Agent Riesel."

Warren kissed her cheek. "We're in this together."

She pressed in the number. The agent had been kind, gentle, and Silvia wanted to believe she could trust her. It rang once, twice, three times—

"Agent Riesel here."

Silvia weighed hanging up. She'd never been a coward, only naive at times, and she'd promised herself to be strong. "This is Silvia Ortega."

"Yes, ma'am. How can I help you?"

"The news said the FBI had arrested a man who confessed

to being a Veneno. I'd like to see if he's one of Dylan's friends." The words tumbled out much easier than Silvia had expected.

"Are you having second thoughts about your son's involvement?"

"I believe in his innocence, but I want to make sure the man you have under arrest is . . . a stranger."

"He's being held at the Galveston jail."

"If I come tomorrow, can I talk to him?"

Warren mouthed he'd drive.

"I'll arrange to meet you there," Agent Riesel said. "Can we tentatively schedule around nine?"

"Yes. Thank you."

Silvia wrapped up the call, Warren offering moral support in his tender gaze. She thanked God for sending the dear man to her. If only Dylan saw his remarkable qualities . . . Where had she gone wrong in mothering him?

Warren gathered her into his arms. "You need to be prepared if the man in custody is someone you recognize."

"I believe in my son." She closed her eyes to avoid unwanted tears. "He'd never do those terrible things." But the doubts wouldn't leave her alone.

52

FISHING? WAS LEAH OUT OF HER MIND? The word *tackle* meant nothing to her, except to bring down somebody she was chasing. But she'd done a lot worse than hooking a slimy worm.

Jon gripped the worn cork handle of his pole like the hand of a friend. He wound white line around a wheel and threaded it out to the end of the pole. He reminded her of a kid, so she'd try to emulate his enthusiasm in the stifling heat. New York's summer temps never melted her like this.

He nodded at a bucket filled with rich brown dirt and worms. "Caught these fellas right after breakfast," he said. "With last night's rain, they were easy to find."

"I need instructions."

He picked up a second pole, a little less worn, and handed it to her. "Reach into the bucket and pull out a worm. Then stick the hook through its fat little belly."

"Okay." She grasped a wiggly worm. If she'd dug bullets out of a man's flesh, she could hook a worm. And she did.

"Now stand up and throw the line into the water. I'll show you." He anchored his feet firmly and lifted the pole and line over his right shoulder and tossed it out over the water.

She rose to her feet and glanced at the worm dangling from the end of her line. Poor thing. She followed Jon's example and tossed the line close to his.

"Good one."

"What's under the box and newspaper?"

"Grasshoppers. Perfect for summer fishing."

At least he wasn't asking her to eat them. Been there. Done that.

"Half the fun of fishing is who you're with," he said.

She adored the peacefulness on his face, confirming he loved what he was doing. "Tell me about the art of fishing."

"Well, Agent Riesel, it's like working a case. Fish eyes are located on the sides of their heads, which means their blind spot is straight in front of them. That's why more than one agent works a case. Fish can see bright colors, the same way a pretty girl or a vulnerable person gets a bad guy's attention. Fish sense temperature changes and hear vibrations in the water." He nodded. "While we're fishing, we'll stand or sit. We won't make a lot of movement or noise. That's like waiting for a sniper shot. We want to keep our shadows out of the water."

"As we don't discuss a case where someone might hear. And we use our senses when we're headed to a sniper spot."

He gave her a thumbs-up. "Fish smell but rarely take bait because of it, except catfish. So we fishermen use different methods to attract fish. They aren't all drawn to the same type of lure. And I usually carry extra hooks in this case for the same reason."

Jon opened his tackle box beside them. "Most of these aren't needed in my pond, but when I'm doing serious fishing in other waters. Extra hooks could be compared to our proficiency with different weapons or hand-to-hand combat." He gestured to other items in the box. "A fisherman always has an extra line. Invariably your fishing line will get tangled or broken. Think of this as your backup, like the SWAT team." He picked up a little red-and-white ball. "This is a bobber. It floats on the water until a fish takes the bait and drags it down, showing the fisherman there's something on the line. Just like we gather evidence and follow the leads."

She'd seen a bobber before and wondered what it was used for.

He picked up what looked like a small rock. "You're looking at a sinker. It sends the hook and bait deep into the water. Consider it your informant or an agent working undercover."

Leah smiled from the inside out, ignoring the heat and humidity to concentrate on Jon's explanation. "All these things sound like good reminders, lessons for me to learn."

"Fishing is quality think-time about what we know and what we're missing."

Were her feelings showing? "How many times have you given this lecture to other agents?"

"This is the first."

"It's outstanding." She motioned for him to keep talking.

"This is veering into overkill." He laughed. "My lures imitate what the fish are after, like setting up a sting operation." He grabbed needle-nose pliers. "These are sometimes used to get the hook out of the fish."

"I can't decide if the pliers act like a good cop in bringing the fish some relief from the pain of the hook or if it's more of a bad cop, 'I'll get a confession out of you one way or another' thing."

He feigned a shocked look. "Like our chief of police friend? Would we stoop to intimidate a suspect?"

"Never. What's wrong with me?"

"I also have a line cutter. Can't think how to compare it, except in the most direct way: cutting a suspect loose. Oh, and a first aid kit."

"For us or the fish?"

"Whoever needs it."

For several minutes, they sat on the bank in silence. Her mind eased in and out of the case, her family, and Jon. Spending time with Caleb and Asher created a longing for her brothers and sisters. She didn't have problems with them, but with the way her parents had expected her to be like a parent too.

A robin caught her attention and flew toward Jon's farmhouse. The home reflected a type of comfort she enjoyed. Neatly kept flower beds, a kitchen that made her want to learn how to cook. *Jon Colbert, what would you think of me if you knew my past?*

While they enjoyed the shelter of a live oak, insects hummed and birds sang, creating a whimsical and peaceful setting. The sun glistening off the pond and an accompanying hint of a breeze had no similarities to her previous home in New York or her Houston apartment.

She picked up her phone when it dinged with a text message.

"No work this afternoon," he whispered.

"This is an agent who has connections with CPS. Her sister-in-law is a social worker. I talked to her yesterday."

"Right. We need info for Rawlyns."

She sent the reply text and slipped her phone back into her purse. "Is meeting with Silvia at the Galveston jail in the morning okay? She wants to see if Henry is one of Dylan's friends."

"The first time we met her, you said she was guilty of loving Dylan. Now we know more about her history." He shook his head. "Breaking the law to protect him only makes the consequences worse."

Leah's sympathy for Silvia deepened each time they talked. "For her sake, I hope she and Dylan are innocent, and he's alive."

Her phone alerted her to a text. Leah had a confirmed time to contact a social worker that evening.

Twenty minutes later, sweat dripping down her back, her line dipped. Then jerked slightly. "Do I have a fish?" she whispered.

"Stay cool," Jon said.

Her heart pounded like she'd just gotten a SWAT call.

"Take your time and reel it in. When it gets close to the bank, lift it out of the water."

Leah concentrated on landing her first fish—a perch, according to Jon. The fish wiggled in desperation. "It's very small." She watched Jon unhook it for her, then she tossed it back in. "When it grows, I'll catch it again."

"Celebration time." Jon reached into a cooler and handed her a cold bottle of water.

She twisted off the lid and drank deeply. "Tastes wonderful." She recapped it. "Ever swim here?" She remembered to whisper.

"Sometimes." Before she could protest, he gathered her into his arms.

"Jon, I'm drenched."

"Me too. But we're celebrating." His lips met hers, and despite the heat, the fish, and her misgivings about a relationship with him, she returned the kiss.

The temps grew hotter. She leaned back and reached for her pole.

"Rather be facing an army of armed terrorists?" he said.

She drew in the truth. Jon was exactly what she wanted, needed, in a man. The fright of reality made her want to run.

"Where do we go from here?" he said.

"Time for this lady to head back to Houston and shower. I'll have to drive with the windows down." She stepped back and kept her distance.

"Are you afraid of being kissed again?"

Before she could think of something clever, he'd reached out and reeled her in again . . . like a fish. His lips on hers stole her breath, leaving her dizzy. When it was over, she didn't attempt to escape his arms. "Thanks for teaching me how to fish, the analogy, and the lovely afternoon."

"The kiss?"

"Get over it, partner."

Their first real kiss, actually kisses, and she smelled worse than the fish.

53

FOR THE FIRST TIME IN DAYS, Leah unlocked her apartment door before the sun had gone down. She set a grilled chicken salad and her phone on the kitchen counter. The familiar sight of her clock collection in a corner antique curio cabinet gave her strange comfort as though time held the answers to her problems. What would Jon think of her steampunk decor—an old framed map of Europe combined with a Victorian sofa and lamps made from salvaged metal? Logic scolded her for allowing Jon to sink into her thoughts when her focus needed to be on the Venenos.

She had a call arranged later with the social worker from CPS. Confirmed updates for Will Jr. would help gather intel from his dad.

A whiff of her hot and ripe body sent her straight to the

bedroom to unload her backpack and step into the shower. Family pics downloaded from Facebook and lined up on her dresser made her feel not so alone. The smiling faces created a sense of belonging. She inhaled the freshness of potpourri, scents of vanilla, mint, and lime. Home.

She lingered in the shower to let the warm water cleanse and massage her. When the afternoon's dirt and grime flowed down the shower drain, she dried off and slid into yoga pants and a T-shirt.

Since Tuesday, her world had moved from one crisis to another, and it wasn't over yet. This evening she'd enjoy every moment alone. Her bed looked far too comfy. Later, after eating her salad, she'd crawl beneath the sheets, phone the social worker, and watch a Hallmark movie.

The doorbell rang.

Leah groaned. Dare she ignore it? She sighed. What if the visitor had a critical message? She trudged to the door. A quick peek through the security hole showed a deliveryman holding a long box.

Flowers? She opened the door.

"Leah Riesel?" When she nodded, the young man handed her the box. "These are for you."

"Who sent them?"

"There's a card, miss."

She thanked him before closing the door and locking it behind her. No one had sent her flowers in years. She carried the box to the reclaimed-metal table in her dining area. It was heavier than she expected. Must have a vase included. A square envelope with her name in gold script looked incredibly formal and sweet. Maybe Dad had a change of heart and sent them? She flipped on the brass-and-leather chandelier.

She loosened the envelope and carefully lifted the flap to read the card.

Leah,

    To my gorgeous partner. Looking forward to time alone with you.

Jon

A fishing lesson and two kisses prompted him to send these? They'd grown close as friends over the week and a definite attraction had drawn them together, but . . . A hint of anger settled on her.

She stepped back and crossed her arms over her chest. If she'd had the foresight, she would have learned who sent the flowers before the deliveryman left and instructed him to give them—probably roses from the size of the box—to his significant other.

Jon Colbert was about to get a piece of her mind. They barely knew each other. No more relationship stuff until the bad guys wore cuffs—and maybe not even then. She snatched her phone from the kitchen counter.

But curiosity tugged at her. She wanted to see the flowers before calling him, at least be gracious while being firm. Laying the phone aside, she lifted the lid.

In a flash a snake's head snapped up and fangs sank into the top of her left hand. Screaming, she jumped back. Fiery pain shot up her arm. A rattler crawled from the box and slithered across the table. Her worst fear lay a few feet from her. Her throat tightened. Heart hammered. Memories of the rattler pit flashed across her mind. She'd failed then, but this rattler had bitten her.

Her first instinct was to get her gun, but firing it had the potential to pierce the floor or wall, and an older couple lived next door.

A knife.

She flung open a kitchen utility drawer. Blinding agony in her hand stole her breath. Gulping for air, she snatched a chef's knife with her right hand. Panic seized control.

The rattler wriggled across the table, down a chair, and onto the floor toward her.

God, if You're real, I need help.

The rattler slithered across the hardwood floor onto the tiled kitchen three feet from her. Like yesterday.

She must recover from the paralysis of watching the rattler move closer, or it would strike her again. Leah clutched the knife. She raised it above her head and down, slicing its head off.

She kicked the open-fanged mouth across the room. With a flood of anger, fear, and pain, she cut the rest of the snake into pieces. All the years of snake phobia unleashed. Her breath came in spurts. Releasing the knife, she tapped 911 into her phone.

"I've been bitten by a rattlesnake," she said between shoots of pain. After reciting her address, she fought nausea and stumbled to unlock the door in case she fainted.

Her mind ran through first aid training. *Remain calm so as not to increase blood circulation and risk the spread of poison.*

Few people died from rattler bites.

Wash the area. She stepped over snake parts and ran warm water in the sink. After pumping soap onto her hands, she gingerly washed her swollen hand and used handfuls of water to rinse. Thank goodness she seldom wore rings or bracelets. She tossed a glance back at the snake's severed head, fangs still ready to unleash venom.

Acid rose in her throat. She craved water and reached into the cabinet for a glass. Dizziness attacked her. Thirst and low blood pressure were some of the symptoms. After she downed the water, her stomach revolted and the contents came back up with a vengeance.

She lifted her injured hand and immediately dropped it back into the sink. Must keep the injury below the heart level. No ice.

What had she forgotten?

Where were the paramedics?

What if the hospital had depleted their supply of antivenom?

She struggled to keep her eyes open and slid to the floor. The snake's open mouth seemed to move forward.

54

JON HEARD HIS PHONE RING while hot water from the shower flowed over his tired body. After Leah had left, he'd spent two more hours outside cleaning up around his home. Time to take more interest in his home. He'd walked an area behind his back porch for a potential pool location.

His phone rang a second and third time. Reaching for the towel, he dried his hands and grabbed the device. "Jon Colbert."

"Jon, this is SAC Thomas. Leah's at Houston Methodist Hospital, the Fannin location. Rattlesnake bite."

Chills swept over him. The Venenos. "What happened?"

"Not sure. She called 911 for help from her home. When the paramedics arrived, she'd passed out. She's regained conscious—"

"Was she bitten or injected with venom?"

"Bitten."

"How did a rattler get inside her apartment? Never mind. I'm on my way." He held the phone between his chin and shoulder while using the towel to finish drying his body. Leah's fear of snakes had risen a hundred notches.

"She's in a private room with agent protection. The hospital and the agents guarding her room are expecting you. Contact me after you see her," SAC Thomas said. "I'm sending a team to sweep her apartment and find the snake. I've checked and her complex has security cameras."

Jon laid the phone on the bathroom counter. Who found out where Leah lived and put a rattler inside her apartment?

Within five minutes, Jon was backing his truck out of his garage and heading into town. Sunday evening traffic had dwindled, and he'd make good time to the medical center.

She'd told him this week, *"I'd rather face a dozen armed bad guys than one snake."*

Poisonous snakebites were dangerous, but most people recovered if antivenom was administered within two hours. How long had she lain there before the paramedics arrived? How many times had she been bitten?

Slow down. Doctors were handling her care. There was nothing he could do now anyway. Hanson's words whispered in his mind—*"No need to feel helpless when God is guiding your way."*

God, I haven't felt this scared since the fire. Take care of Leah, okay?

At the hospital, he approached the nurses' station, and a pleasant young woman led him to Leah's room, where two plainclothes agents guarded her door. Jon presented his ID to the agents and they verified his information. Jon shook hands with each man and thanked them for protecting his partner. Jon turned to the nurse.

"She's going to be fine," the nurse said. "But the side effects of the antivenom have made her nauseous."

"Will she be released soon?"

"The doctor wants to watch her for the next few hours to make sure the vomiting stops and there are no allergic reactions to the medication."

Relief flooded his veins. He'd sit with her until the doctor gave the all clear and offer his rental truck as taxi service. Given her snake phobia, she might prefer a hotel rather than returning to her apartment. Jon opened the door and stepped inside the room. Leah's bluish lips startled him.

"Hey, partner." He stared into her pale face. Thank God, she was alive. And he told Him so.

"Who gave up my hideaway?"

Weak but alert. Good. "SAC Thomas." An IV trickled into a vein.

She nodded with half-mast eyes. "He's listed as an ER contact."

"I'm supposed to phone him after I hear your story." He wrapped his hand around hers.

"Why did you send flowers with a cheesy note?"

Had they drugged her? "I didn't send you anything."

"I know." She opened her copper-colored eyes. "Found out too late."

He shook his head. "Back up. What do flowers have to do with a rattler in your apartment?"

She closed her eyes.

"Are you going to be sick?" He slid a look at the metal emesis basin.

264

"I hope not. How disgusting." She frowned. "The snake was in the flower box." She told him about the delivery and what happened after she was bitten. "I didn't get a name from the deliveryman. About your height, young, blond hair."

"Your apartment complex has security cameras. We'll get him."

She reached for a cup of ice, and he helped her.

His thoughts raced over her story. "You killed the snake with a knife?"

"It's in pieces on my kitchen floor. I imagine my apartment looks gruesome." She paused. "I'll never be afraid of snakes again. Respect and caution but not fear."

He wanted to shout if not for the hospital. "You destroyed your phobia." He bent and brushed a kiss across her lips. "This is a congratulations kiss."

"Nice." Her face softened, and he wished he knew what she was thinking. "I suppose SAC Thomas has agents on this," she said.

"As we speak, they're sweeping your apartment."

"It's gruesome. But what about your place? A lot more areas to stick a rattler."

"Those guys don't want to mess with me."

She bit her lip but a smile still escaped. "Those guys have no idea what a snakebit sniper can do." She breathed in deeply. "I'm miserable company. Why don't you head on home? Once this IV finishes, the doctor will release me."

"Nope." He drew up a chair to her bedside. "I'm staying until the doctor says you can go home."

"It'll be a while."

"I sleep best in a chair." He studied her. "What did the note with the flower box say?"

She huffed. "It wasn't worth a rattler's bite." She glanced at the dripping IV. "If you're going to stay, then I guess it's my turn to spill my guts."

"Slicing up a rattler has given you courage."

"Or paralyzed my mind." She breathed deeply in and out. "I'll do my best."

He squeezed her hand lightly and held it.

"I'm the oldest of seven siblings, six adopted brothers and sisters."

"Impressive. Are the adopted siblings related?"

"Some."

"Your parents must have big hearts," he said.

"They're great people."

Her dry comment hinted at family issues. "Are you close?"

"They live in Brooklyn."

"I bet holidays and family get-togethers are loud and fun."

"Yes to the loud part, but it's been years since I've been home." She tilted her head. "My fault. I think because I never understood the adoptions or many of their actions."

"Families have their problems, Leah. I'm listening."

She told him how her parents had chosen to adopt hard-to-place children, their expectations for her, and how she'd resented and rebelled against them when life seemed unfair. "Looking back, I can see my faults more clearly . . . and have a better understanding of what they were thinking." She glanced away, then back to him. "But the night I graduated from high school, I packed my suitcase and made sure my parents knew I hated them for adopting my siblings. I left and never returned. Worked hard to do well in college, applied to Quantico, and here I am, a loner filled with regret."

"Ever try to contact them?"

"Many times, but I always hung up instead of talking. Except the day of Judge Mendez's prayer service. I talked to my dad. Apologized." She sighed. "It ended badly."

"That took guts." His new faith mere hours old, Jon had experienced only a small taste of the power of prayer. He didn't have the credentials to speak about God until he had a little more experience. But a nudging pushed him forward anyway. "God helps."

"If I thought so, I'd have a room full of preachers."

His phone summoned him with an incoming call, an unfamiliar number. "Jon Colbert."

"This is Ross Kempler. We need to talk."

55

JON SENSED LEAH STUDYING HIM. "Sure, Mr. Kempler. We can talk now." He tossed his attention to Leah, who'd obviously picked up on the name by her focus.

"I would prefer a face-to-face meeting."

"I'll be in Galveston in the morning."

"Is it possible to meet tonight? At your office?"

"I'm at Houston Methodist with Agent Riesel." Jon kept his eyes on Leah. At her go-ahead, he explained the situation. "She's receiving treatment for a rattler bite."

"Veneno attack?" His voice rose.

Jon touched her cheek. His partner's encounter with a rattler had scared him. "Something like that. But they underestimated her."

Kempler blew out air. "Agent Colbert, I'm able to provide

insight into this case. This is about my relationship with Judge Mendez."

"Let me know when you arrive. Agent Riesel is here under an assumed name."

"Look for me in about an hour." Kempler clicked off.

Jon moved to the window and gazed at the lit parking lot.

"What's going on?" Leah said.

"The tides are turning." He turned to her. "Kempler's driving here to talk about Judge Mendez."

"To the hospital?" She appeared to roll the thought around in her head. "Interesting. His conscience must be bothering him."

He studied her as she seemed to grimace in pain.

"Don't frown, Agent Colbert. I'm okay. I remembered I was supposed to call a social worker about Will Rawlyns's son. Would you hand me my phone?"

"Is that necessary?"

She glared, and he reached for her device. The call lasted all of two minutes. The social worker would do all she could to expedite the situation with Will Rawlyns Jr.

An hour and ten minutes later, Ross Kempler arrived at the hospital. Jon met him in the foyer and escorted him to Leah's room. Once inside, Jon closed the door.

"I'm grateful you were willing to see me tonight." Kempler walked to Leah's bedside. "I'm sorry to hear about your unfortunate encounter with a rattler."

"Let's just say this case got a whole lot more personal now."

Kempler nodded, then got quickly to the point of his visit. "As you two remember, I claimed ignorance of information about Judge Mendez's death. I've discussed things with my family, and we've decided I should share what I know about the private investigation that Judge Mendez, Ian Greer, and

Marcia Trevelle were conducting. Since the judge's funeral, I've wrestled with bringing criminals to justice and gut-wrenching fear for my family. This morning in church I was convicted to help you."

Jon pointed to a lone chair. "Would you like to sit down?"

"I'm a lawyer. Do my best work on my feet."

Jon chuckled to rid the room of stress. "Can I record our conversation?"

"No. This information is a means to run with the investigation. When it comes to a court of law, I'll be the first witness." He rubbed his face, lined with wisdom and experience. "If the Venenos have any indication of what I'm about to say, I'll be the next victim."

"Your family's safety is a priority. Should you require protection, don't hesitate to inform either of us," Jon said.

"Appreciate it. Last month, Officer Ian Greer stopped a man for running a red light. He discovered a stash of OxyContin, Percocet, and Ambien in the front seat. Real stupid. The man confessed to dealing but didn't know the name of the guy who supplied the drugs. Communication went through texts on a burner phone that he didn't have with him. Greer arrested the man. Next day he paid bail and a day later, he was found dead. By the time Greer gained access to the man's apartment, it had been ransacked. But Greer was able to trace the drugs he confiscated to a warehouse near Dallas. They'd been stolen nine months before the arrest."

"Molston Pharmaceuticals in Beyero, Texas?"

"The same."

"We have a man in custody under similar charges, only we weren't able to confiscate any drugs, and none were found in his apartment. He claims to be a Veneno."

"The one you arrested at Judge Mendez's funeral?" When Jon nodded in confirmation, Kempler sighed. "He didn't look familiar to me. Anyway, Greer discussed the situation with Judge Mendez and Marcia Trevelle. Both men were determined to get to the bottom of the murder. Trust me, the judge received his reputation honestly. When he chased a criminal or a situation, he stayed on the path until he resolved it. And Trevelle had the same dogged personality as Greer and the judge. But they came up essentially empty. The three learned Galveston was the second place the confiscated drugs had shown up, and a lot more were missing—to the tune of several million dollars on the street."

That lined up with what Jon had learned.

Kempler paced the floor. "After Officer Greer's body was found, the judge got worried. He told me Chief Everson had contacted the FBI for assistance, and the judge supported the decision. He said he had evidence in a safe place but not enough for law enforcement to make arrests."

"Do you have the evidence? Know where it is?"

He shook his head. "I've looked."

The FBI had swept Judge Mendez's home and office. "Was Judge Mendez a paper kind of guy or flash drive?"

"Both."

"If you haven't found the proof, it's unlikely the killers have either."

"Whatever those three discovered went to their graves."

Jon needed to think through this. "Why keep the details between the three of them? The stolen drugs had been reported to law enforcement. Everson would have known about them."

Kempler maintained an impassive look.

A thought punched Jon in the gut. "There's a dirty cop on the force."

Kempler held up his hand as if to forestall the question he knew was coming next. "All I've heard is a rumor."

Jon wrapped his arms around his chest. "Is Everson protecting one of his guys?" He yanked his phone from his pocket and pressed in Everson's number. The police chief answered on the first ring. "Jon Colbert here. I need information."

"Depends on what you're asking."

The response didn't ease Jon's mind about Everson's withholding information. "Do you have any reason to suspect that one of your officers might be behind the murders?"

"What?"

"You heard me. We think someone in your department might be involved with these gang hits."

Everson swore, and Jon could practically hear the man's blood boiling. "You can't believe everything you hear, Colbert, and especially not the lies of a junkie like Kantore."

"Are you certain? Do you know more about the off-the-books case than you've shared with the FBI?"

"Yes, I'm certain. Those three had no proof of anything or they'd have brought it to me."

Jon lowered his voice. "Then why were they killed?"

"Listen," Everson said, fury evident in his tone, "I'm going to find who killed Marcia. And it won't be one of my guys."

"You're not a one-man army."

"Watch me." Everson disconnected.

Jon slid his phone back inside his pocket and relayed the conversation.

Leah spoke up. "It's probably a long shot, but Mrs. Greer might have insight."

Jon searched through his contacts and soon had Mrs. Greer on the line.

"No, Ian never confided in me about his job," Mrs. Greer said. "He wouldn't have told me if he suspected a fellow officer."

"Do you think Chief Everson might be protecting someone on the force?"

"Absolutely not. If what you're saying is true, and a GPD officer is involved in my husband's death, Zachary would be the first in line to take him down."

"Thanks for the information." Once again, Jon pocketed his phone and told Leah and Kempler the conversation.

"So it all comes down to this evidence the judge had." Leah attempted to sit up, but Jon was instantly at her side.

"You can talk and rest at the same time."

"My partner's a helicopter." She gave him what he would classify as an irritated glare, but he ignored it. She spoke to Kempler. "You're still looking for it, right?"

He nodded. "Somewhere there's documentation, or he wouldn't have said so."

Jon deliberated the info. "The number of people Judge Mendez might trust is small, but I imagine it would probably include his wife and Father Gabriel. But if he refused to confide in you, then he certainly wouldn't risk their lives."

"I agree. We need to search where we least expect." Kempler drew in a breath. "The Venenos will be after the next person who might have the evidence. Maybe even me."

"Rachel Mendez," Leah said. "Everson already has officers assigned 24-7. Can we replace them with agents until this is settled? I'm not suggesting any of GPD are crooked, but I'd like to insist she take more precautions."

"Good move." Kempler turned to Jon. "I'm also requesting protection for my family."

56

LEAH DETESTED the endless slow drip of time—in her veins and in the hospital. Once Ross Kempler left, she considered ordering Jon out of the room so she could dress and go home. Closing her eyes, she replayed the moment she lifted the lid on the flower box and was bitten. Raising the knife and lowering it over the snake, severing its head and hacking away like a madwoman until it lay in pieces . . . cleaning her wound and contacting 911.

Her reaction to the rattler and victory over her fear filled her with relief. No more ophidiophobia. No more nightmarish jeers from her demons to echo in her mind.

You're a sniper for the FBI?

You're one of the top three marksmen in the US?

And you're afraid of snakes?

Leah had killed it. Literally. In a few hours she'd step inside her apartment and see the remains of what had stalked her for years. She could handle it. She basked in the satisfaction of being an overcomer. This victory also felt like a win on the case battlefront, and if those responsible for the Galveston murders had lost one fight, they'd lose another and another.

When she opened her eyes, Jon was examining her face as though it were beneath a microscope.

"Are you okay?" she said.

"Aren't I supposed to be asking you that?"

"I'm great. The nausea is wearing off."

"I'm sleeping on your couch tonight."

"No, you're not."

"Everything I've read says you shouldn't be left alone. If you're refusing my company, then who?"

She thought of Terri, but she didn't want to bother her. "I'll be fine."

"If you're worried about propriety—"

"Jon, it's not that. I don't want to impose."

"You're not. I need my partner."

She moaned. "Tell you what. I'll set my phone to go off every two hours and give you the times. When I'm alerted, I'll text you."

He frowned. "Forget to text me, and I'll be at your front door."

"I have no doubt. Would you hand me my phone? I want to check with the agents at the Mendez home."

He picked up her phone from the hospital stand and gave it to her. "They're in place. You had dozed off when I received a text. One of the agents reported Rachel Mendez has a bucket of questions. She wants to talk to you. The hour doesn't matter."

She pressed in Rachel Mendez's number. "It's probably a woman thing. I'll let you listen in."

Rachel picked up on the first ring.

"This is Agent Riesel. I understand you wanted me to call you."

"At whose request were the police officers replaced by FBI agents? I'm not upset, just concerned for my children and mother."

"We initiated the replacement after a new development."

"Has there been another murder?" Rachel's voice rose.

"No. We've been told your husband documented evidence identifying the likely perpetrators. We felt precaution made sense."

"If my husband had evidence like that, I'd have known about it. Nicolás and I employed an open relationship."

But she'd kept Dylan's connection to her from him for years. "What if he kept the evidence secret to protect you?"

Silence lingered on the other end of the phone. Finally, "He loved me very much, and his children were his treasure. Please accept my apologies. I want the killers found and prosecuted."

"I understand. But if you're holding back additional information, now is the time to tell me."

Rachel sighed. "The idea of Dylan being a part of these horrible crimes makes me physically ill. Nothing in my limited conversations with him indicated any criminal intent. Silvia Ortega raised my son with good values. Find him and help prove his innocence."

How much of what Rachel said was truth?

57

MONDAY MORNING, Silvia and Warren entered the building housing Galveston County Jail. Warren held her hand, giving her the strength she needed to endure what lay ahead.

"I'm going to wait out here," Warren said. "There are things you may need to say without my presence."

Silvia had counted on having Warren beside her during the ordeal. He had insight and wisdom, but she wouldn't protest. They had a bit of a wait anyway, since Agents Riesel and Colbert hadn't arrived yet.

Guilt threatened her resolve. Was she betraying her precious boy? Did he understand he'd been born of her heart if not of her womb? Fear for his safety mounted. A gang member or law enforcement officer could kill him.

Silvia thought about Rachel, the young woman who'd given

her baby boy up for adoption to focus on a career. The conversations were etched in Silvia's heart, beginning at the dental office when she'd cleaned Rachel's teeth over twenty-one years ago.

"No X-rays," Rachel had whispered. "I'm pregnant." A tear trickled down her cheek. "I should abort, but I don't want to kill my baby. Neither can I keep it when I have two more years of law school."

Silvia leaned into her. "Your words tell me your baby is dear to you."

"I don't know what to do." She blinked back more tears. "My parents would be so disappointed. Murder is sin, and I'm old-fashioned and believe in the church's stand on abortion. Father Gabriel would excommunicate me."

"There is a solution," Silvia said. "Adoption is a gift to someone who desperately wants a child."

"I've wondered about it, even considered various options." She peered into Silvia's face, her huge blue eyes filled with despair.

"Who else knows?"

"Only you."

"Do you want me to help you find a home for your baby through the church?"

"Yes, I need help. I can hide the pregnancy until mid-May when school is out. Then I can disappear until my due date of September 20."

Thinking back on how her friendship with Rachel began, Silvia wondered if she'd been naive, the one who'd been used. As their conversations continued, Rachel begged her to take the baby, claimed God had planned it. Father Gabriel assisted with the adoption, arranging for Ross Kempler to complete the legal paperwork. Rachel watched her son grow while Silvia threw her heart and soul into raising the boy.

She didn't understand then or now why she'd been the one selected to love Rachel's baby. Every day since then, she'd thanked God for His gift.

God, help me trust You for Dylan's innocence.

Warren broke the silence between them. "Remember we asked God to bless whatever happens and use it for His good."

She pushed aside her emotion. No reason to hide the truth any longer. She must tell Warren about the adoption without mentioning Rachel's name. "Warren, there's something I need to tell you about Dylan . . ."

☆ ★ ☆

When Agent Riesel entered the room, Silvia swallowed a lump in her throat and promised herself she'd not panic. The agent's left hand and wrist were bandaged. Silvia and Warren rose to greet her. Agent Riesel welcomed Silvia before giving Warren her attention.

"We meet again, Mr. Livingston," Agent Riesel said.

"You two know each other?" Silvia stared at him.

"I didn't want to alarm you." He seemed to sense her concern. "My shop and property were threatened. Chief Everson referred me to these agents."

"Is everything all right?"

"Oh yes. It may have been a hoax."

A twist of betrayal rose in Silvia, and she tried to choke it back. But she'd held information from him. "I'm not upset, but I wish you'd have told me."

"In the future, I won't keep anything from you. I promise." Sincerity laced his words.

"Neither will I." How wonderful of God to put a good man in her life.

"Agent Colbert is waiting for us," Agent Riesel said. "Are you ready?"

Warren squeezed Silvia's hand, and she followed the agent. Once inside the locked doors, Silvia pointed to Agent Riesel's left hand. "Did you have an accident?"

"Not exactly. A delivery boy brought me what I thought were roses. When I lifted the lid, I was bit by a rattler."

Silvia gasped and covered her mouth. "How dreadful."

"One more reason why I want these people stopped."

"Shouldn't you be home resting?"

Agent Riesel smiled, but Silvia thought it was forced. "I'm okay, and thanks for asking." She opened the door to a small, windowless room.

Agent Colbert rose and greeted Silvia. He'd always made her suspicious of his motives, as though Dylan were guilty without evidence. "Please, have a seat," he said. "The man in custody is being escorted to us."

She sat opposite the agents. Silvia feared she'd be ill. What was worse? Learning Dylan was a Veneno or him finding out she doubted his innocence? Long minutes passed before a brisk knock brought Agent Colbert to his feet and to the door.

The prisoner was brought inside, his hands in cuffs. Silvia's face grew hot. She peered into dark-brown eyes, studied the long nose and telltale signs of cocaine use on the insides of his arms. He nodded his recognition. This was the man who'd picked up the seven hundred dollars for Dylan.

"Ms. Ortega, do you recognize this man?" Agent Riesel said.

Her stomach whirled. "Yes."

Was this man receiving protection or getting some sort of deal for cooperating with the authorities? If Dylan were guilty of a crime, would he agree to help the FBI or the police in

exchange for a lesser sentence? She desperately needed to talk
to her son and drew in a prayer for strength. "I need to know if
my son, Dylan Ortega, is a member of the Veneno gang."

Moments ticked by. Why wasn't the man—whatever his
name was—giving her a simple answer?

"The agents showed me his picture, but he ain't nobody
I've seen."

Relief rushed through her, mingled with confusion. "Then
why did you come to where I work? I thought you were helping him, you might be his friend." Silvia regretted revealing her
role in aiding Dylan, but her desperation to know the truth
was too great.

"I got a call to pick up money from you. The man on the
phone told me where to get it and the place to drop it off. I—"

"Where was the drop-off site?" Agent Colbert said.

The man paused before answering. "A trash can outside
Moody Gardens."

Agent Colbert pushed paper and pen toward the man.
"That tourist site is expansive. We need a map like you gave us
previously for the rattler pit."

The man wrote with his cuffed hands and slid the paper
back to the agent.

Silvia couldn't see what was written, but she wasn't finished
with her questions. "What's your name?"

"Henry."

"What were you paid for picking up the money?"

"Another day to live."

Any other questions escaped her, so a police officer escorted
the man out of the room. "Agent Riesel, thank you," she said.
"You've closed a door for me. Since that man doesn't know
Dylan, I'm sure you've concluded he's a victim and not guilty

of any wrongdoing." There, she'd successfully repeated her rehearsed words.

Agent Riesel's eyes were gentle, kind. "Ms. Ortega, we must talk to your son. Henry Kantore's statement doesn't exonerate Dylan. Truthfully, it adds more weight to his involvement, tying Dylan to other members of the group responsible for these crimes. And we still have an eyewitness who is sure he saw Dylan the morning of Judge Mendez's death."

"You will find out my son is a good man." How many times had she spoken a form of those words? Dylan was innocent of the horrible crimes, and somehow she'd prove it.

58

AFTER SILVIA LEFT THE JAIL, Leah knew it was time to chat with Chief of Police Zachary Everson about his volatile temper.

"I want the full story of his relationships with Marcia Trevelle, Greer, and the judge," Leah said.

"You feel up to it?"

"If you don't let up on the hovering, I might have to show you how well I can shoot." She was only half-teasing. Seriously, Jon needed to drop the overprotective syndrome. Her hand ached, but she wasn't about to tell him that or let it keep her out of the game. "If you're busy looking out for me, we're lining ourselves up for a mistake."

"You're right," Jon said.

"Can I record that?"

He smiled. "I suggest we balance the questioning instead of one of us leading out."

They needed to be viewed as a team seeking the truth, not the FBI ganging up on Everson.

Within minutes, the three sat in Everson's office drinking cold bottles of water. They'd gotten past the rattlesnake bite story. Leah didn't believe in waiting out the inevitable but facing it. Everson seemed squeaky clean. Looked and acted the part of a man dedicated to saving and protecting lives.

"What's going on?" He crossed his arms over his chest.

Jon led out. "Chief—"

"Zachary. This case puts us on a first-name basis. Despite our differences."

"We need to confirm a few things," Jon said. "Are you telling us everything?"

The cords in his neck knotted. "If I had a lead on the Venenos, there'd be a few less of them." His jaw tightened. "I think I know where this is going. It's why you replaced GPD officers with agents for Rachel." His gaze drilled into Jon. "Who questioned my integrity?"

"Doesn't matter, Zachary."

He reached for a nearly empty bottle of water. "So what do you want, then?"

"We believe there's documentation of the investigation the three were conducting."

"I figured so. I've searched through Marcia's things but haven't found anything in the way of a notebook, computer file, flash drive, or slips of paper with information pertaining to their investigation."

Leah wrestled with the inconsistencies from those they'd interviewed since Tuesday. "Our teams who swept the judge's home and office also haven't turned up anything."

Zachary shook his head. "The judge wouldn't have

endangered her or the kids. I had tremendous respect for the man. His family meant more to him than his commitment to justice."

"What if I told you Dylan Ortega is Rachel's biological son?"

Zachary released his arms and blew out a breath. "Didn't see that coming."

"The judge was aware and was willing to welcome Dylan into the family." Leah let her words sink in. "It's highly unlikely he would have extended an invitation like that if he suspected his wife's son was in a gang or involved with the drug theft."

"Do you think any of your GPD officers had anything to do with this?" Jon said.

Everson snorted. "They know if there's even a hint of stepping over the line, they're outta here. Look, we must figure this out before there's another murder."

Leah exchanged a long look with Jon. Should they trust Everson with more details of the investigation? His personality might rub some people the wrong way, but she still believed he was grieving the loss of his fiancée and his officer. It hadn't been an easy week for the man.

Jon nodded and turned back to the police chief. "Those three believed the in-game was prescription drugs. There are at least three connection points to drugs stolen from Molston Pharmaceuticals."

Zachary ducked his head. "Landon Shaw got caught trying to hawk stolen drugs from that company. Ian Greer arrested a man in possession of prescription pills from there too. What's the third connection?"

Leah sighed. "Dylan Ortega."

59

AT THE RATE THEY WERE GOING, Leah believed she and Jon might as well establish residency in Galveston. Sitting in Zachary Everson's office, they tossed around all the possibilities connected to the investigation into the stolen prescription drugs.

Jon's phone rang, and he glanced at the number. "It's Richard James."

Leah's gaze flew to his. "Maybe he has word about Elena." She wanted the young woman to be safe and innocent from the chaos.

Jon answered the call. "Hello, Richard." He listened for a moment. "Wonderful news. Glad Elena is okay. Leah and I will be there in about twenty minutes." He slipped the phone into his pocket. "Elena showed up at home around 11 a.m. She says the Venenos nabbed her Wednesday evening. She's with her

DIANN MILLS

parents being treated at a medical clinic. She wants to talk to Leah." He stood. "They'll be home by the time we get there."

Zachary snatched his phone. "I'll send officers to the clinic and another squad car to the home. GPD will take care of 24-7 protection." He rose to his feet and held out his hand. "We are on the same side."

Jon shook his hand. "Appreciate it. I'm taking Elena's safety as a sign we're about to end this gang's terror streak."

Leah's thoughts spun. Was Dylan working with Elena's kidnappers? Had the girl seen or heard from him? "I want to know how she got away."

Jon headed for the door with her on his heels. "We're about to find out."

"Keep me posted," Zachary said.

At the Jameses' home, Jon parked at the curb. Zachary had worked fast because a GPD officer was already guarding the front door. After Leah and Jon displayed IDs, the officer gestured them inside.

Richard James met them in the foyer. His flushed face and red eyes spoke fathoms of his rattled emotions. "Thanks for coming. We arrived home about ten minutes ago. Elena is in the shower. Her mother is close by." He ran his fingers through light-colored hair. "My daughter is dehydrated, exhausted, dizzy. We've gotten a smoothie down her, but it will take time for her to recover."

Leah could only imagine the girl's ordeal. "Should she be hospitalized?"

"We tried to persuade her, but she refused. We filled a prescription for an antidepressant that should help her sleep, and our regular doctor is stopping by later. She's begged us not to leave her alone." He swiped beneath his eyes and regained his composure. "You have supported us throughout this nightmare.

287

We don't want her in danger ever again. What do you suggest other than the officers posted outside our home?"

"GPD twenty-four-hour protection is one solution. The other is to leave town until arrests are made."

"We have a cabin near Estes Park in Colorado. Olivia and I spoke briefly about going there." He pointed to the living area where Leah and Jon had spoken with him and Olivia on their first visit. "Elena hasn't said much about her ordeal other than what I told you. She's expecting you, so I don't imagine she'll be much longer."

"That's fine." Leah looked to Jon for the lead, and he didn't disappoint her.

"How were you reunited with your daughter?"

Richard paced as he'd done previously. "Olivia and I were having coffee before I drove to work. I've been going in later and later because I didn't like leaving my wife alone. We heard the alarm system chime that the back door had opened, and Elena walks in." He closed his eyes. "God answered our prayers. She fell into our arms and cried. She said the men holding her had gotten drunk and passed out. She managed to get away, and a woman at a farmhouse drove her home. I rushed out to the woman and thanked her. She gave me her contact information. My guess is she's in her late eighties." He pressed his quivering lips together. "Elena's wrists are rubbed raw from whatever they used to tie her up."

Elena emerged in the doorway. "Dad, I can take it from here." Her weak voice came out barely above a whisper.

Richard moved swiftly to his daughter's side, asking her if she needed anything.

"I'm okay. Haven't taken the medicine yet. It's more important I talk to the FBI people."

He helped his daughter into the room and onto the sofa, Olivia following close behind. The young woman's gaunt condition was evidence of her ill-treatment. No visible bruises, but the inner scars would likely linger for a long time. Leah dreaded asking her tough questions. The heart-wrenching concern for Elena and her parents brought a lump to her throat. And that was okay . . . Emotions made her human.

This was the first time Leah had seen Elena other than a photo. Even in her condition with wet hair dangling on her shoulders, her large blue eyes and flawless skin showed a beautiful young woman.

Leah moved to the sofa beside the girl. "Elena, I'm Leah Riesel. We talked on the phone before your disappearance."

"I remember," she said. "You're the FBI agent looking for Dylan. Is he still missing?"

"We're working hard to locate him." Leah pointed to Jon. "This is Agent Jon Colbert." He reached out to shake her hand. "We need to ask you some hard questions. Can you help us?"

Elena searched her mother's face before responding. "If I don't, someone else may go through the same nightmare."

60

LEAH STUDIED ELENA JAMES. She'd have to approach this interview with caution, taking care not to upset the girl or cause her more trauma. Elena had clearly been through an ordeal—and survived—but Leah didn't want to push her past her breaking point.

"We can do this at your pace," Leah said. "I'd like to record your statement. Do you mind?" When Elena and her parents agreed, Jon pressed Record on his phone. "Start at the beginning. Take your time. Don't be afraid of tears. We're here to help, and we understand this is painful for you."

Elena clung to her mother's hand. "First, I lied about Dylan when you called. The day before Judge Mendez's death, Dylan asked me to say we'd broken up because he was afraid something horrible might happen to me." She breathed in and out.

"He wouldn't explain why. Dylan had been careful about where we went, what we did. We were keeping our relationship quiet. The next day, I learned about Judge Mendez's death and how Dylan was a suspect." She shook her head. "I didn't believe it. Judge Mendez was more than a judge to him. His wife is . . ." Elena looked at Leah, a question in her eyes.

Leah squeezed her hand. "We know."

"Good. You understand then that I wanted to protect him. Help him find the evidence to prove his innocence. I tried phoning him, but he must have gotten a new phone."

"And you haven't heard from him since?"

Elena glanced at the floor. "No. Not long before this happened—before those men took me—Dylan came to me and said he'd done something stupid to help his mom. He refused to tell me what it was, but he did say he didn't know how to make it right. I never questioned him. I thought he'd talk about it when he was ready."

"Did you recognize any of your abductors?"

"Only one—Aaron Michaels." She broke into sobs. "Tell me you'll find him and put him in prison."

"You don't have to worry about him, Elena. He's dead," Leah said.

She startled. "How?"

"Take a deep breath." Leah hoped the words sounded as sympathetic as she sincerely intended them to be.

Elena swallowed a few times before resuming. "Wednesday afternoon, I had a manicure and pedicure, then met three friends at the beach. We'd be heading back to college soon, and this was going to be our last time to relax together. We planned to have dinner and spend the night at a friend's beach house. Dylan texted me. I mean I thought it was him. He wanted to talk." She looked at her dad. "I'm sorry I kept this from you. He wanted to meet you, but he was afraid you'd turn him away because of his past and not being farther along in his college education." She bit her lower lip and focused on her dad. "I love him."

Instantly Richard was on his knees in front of Elena. He drew her into his arms, and she cried on his shoulder. "I'm so sorry, Daddy. Sorry for everything."

Leah glanced away at the intimate tenderness. One day she wanted a close-knit family where love and honesty ruled. She'd felt it between Terri and Chris. She looked at Jon, and he gave her a reassuring smile. They were good together, and right this very minute, she wanted him in her life.

Elena pulled away from her dad, and he returned to his seat. She resumed her story. "I agreed to meet Dylan at Pocket Beach, and I'd catch up with my friends later. When I got there, he wasn't around. I walked up and down the beach but couldn't find him. He didn't answer his phone or the number from the text." She hesitated. "I went back to my car, and three guys were there. One was Aaron Michaels. Since he's a friend of Dylan's, I thought they'd know where to find him. Instead, Aaron dragged me to a black Mustang parked close by. Shoved me face-first onto the rear floorboard. He put his feet on my back, tied my hands, and blindfolded me." Elena lowered her head, and her mother stroked her hair.

"You can do this," Olivia said. "Your dad and I are not abandoning you."

"I feel stupid and ashamed."

"You're smart and wonderful. Nothing, absolutely nothing, will change our love for you," her mother said.

"God's love or ours," Richard said.

This family had faith going for them. Was she experiencing what she'd missed the years growing up without God?

Elena raised her head. "Thank you," she whispered. "I know you guys love me, but I still needed to hear that. And I love you so much."

Olivia put her arm around her daughter's shoulders and pulled her in tight.

Despite her watery eyes, Elena smiled. "I can go on now. In the back of the car, on that long ride to wherever we were going, I thought about how much I'd disappointed my parents." She lifted tearstained eyes to her father, who gave her an encouraging nod. "I'm not sure how long we were in the car. Aaron called someone and said they had me and were on their way. I tried to keep track of time. Perhaps an hour before we stopped. Someone pulled me from the car and led me over bare ground, like we were on a dirt road in the country. I could hear crickets chirping, but nothing else stands out, except we definitely weren't near the shore—I didn't hear any waves crashing. They took me inside a building and tied me to a chair, then removed the blindfold. When morning came, I realized I was inside a shed. Once a day they brought me a bottle of water and a banana."

Olivia sobbed.

Richard's face hardened. "I would have killed them."

"Did they tell you why they'd taken you?" Leah's question was gentle, intended to keep the conversation on track.

"I'm not sure. But I remember something I overheard Aaron saying: 'If Dylan finds out what we've done, he'll tell the cops about us.' He also said Dylan had this coming for not cooperating."

The girl had been used by this gang to intimidate Dylan,

coerce him into cooperating. Leah lightly squeezed Elena's hand in hers, sending courage through her touch. "Tell us how you got away."

"Last night I heard two of them talking about getting high and drunk. I kept listening for the worst, and then early in the morning their noises stopped. I assumed they passed out. I'd noticed a nail sticking out from the wall and scooted the chair to it. Using the nail, I managed to weaken the rope. When it broke, I untied myself and opened the door. No one was in sight. I started running. Sunrise looked incredibly beautiful, like a promise that I could get away." Her face lifted as though remembering the joy of freedom. "It was as though God was telling me I'd be okay. I made it to a road and kept going. Seemed like one field after another, and I had no idea where to go, except to run east toward the sun. At a farmhouse, I knocked on a door. An older woman answered, and she gave me water. I told her I'd gotten away from kidnappers. She wanted to call the police, but I told her I had to see my parents first. I feared one of the Venenos could have hacked your phones." She closed her eyes. "I just wanted to go home."

Elena's story was essentially over, but Leah had more questions for her. "Besides Aaron and the other two guys who abducted you, did you see any others?"

She shook her head.

"Do you remember any names mentioned?"

"No, ma'am."

"Would you help me reconstruct what the two men look like? I have a face-sketching app on my phone to help us."

Elena sat up straighter, seemed to gather her strength. "I'll do whatever it takes. I won't forget them."

The abductors intended to kill her, or they'd not have

allowed her to identify them. "Was anything said we should know?"

"Most of the time they talked about waiting on the next job and what they planned to do with their money. I never heard how or who gave it to them." She looked at her dad. "I want to call Silvia Ortega and tell her I'm okay. Maybe she'll tell me if she's heard from Dylan."

"Are you sure?" Leah said. "What if she unknowingly tells the wrong person that you've escaped?"

"Please."

"Baby, I'll contact her later when the authorities say it's okay," Richard said. "When Dylan's found, I want to meet the young man who stole my daughter's heart."

Leah hoped he was still alive.

61

SILVIA'S PHONE VIBRATED for the third time since she'd started this patient's cleaning. She turned to check the number but didn't recognize it. A text flew in: **Mom, call me @ this # ASAP.**

"Excuse me. I'll be right back," she said to the older woman in her chair. "You mentioned you were tired. Close your eyes until I return."

Silvia escaped to the bathroom, turned on the water, and tapped in the number, praying Dylan was okay.

He had to be safe.

He must have found proof of his innocence.

The moment he answered, the sound of his voice pierced her heart. "I'm here."

"Mom, I'm leaving the country today, and I want to meet you somewhere and say good-bye."

Her stomach twisted as the hope of a normal life for them dissolved. "Where are you going?"

"I'm not saying. That way you don't have to lie. Mom, the cops and FBI are hot on me, and I'm afraid they'll shoot first and discover I'm not a killer later. I'll be safe."

"Running doesn't solve the problem, Son. It only makes you look guilty."

"My mind's made up. Will you take the ferry to the Bolivar about six tonight?"

"I'll be there. Do you need anything?"

He sighed. "Hate to ask, but I could use money until I find a job."

She wouldn't mention the cash she'd given to the courier Dylan had sent to her office last week. Her son had to eat and pay for a place to live. "I have around ten thousand dollars in savings, but I'm not sure how much I can withdraw in one day."

"I'll pay you back—I promise. If only I had my trust fund."

She forbade herself to cry. "I'm not concerned about the money. Is Elena with you?"

"Mom, she's disappeared. I can't find her anywhere. I'm afraid she's been kidnapped. Or worse. Her father's a rich man, and he loves her. I'm sure he's doing more to help the law find her than I ever could." He choked on his words. "I have to believe she's okay. Hard to think of the next minute without her."

What a tangled mess this had become. Love had bitten her son, but instead of happiness, he was filled with heartache. "I'm praying for both of you. When this is over, we'll be stronger people for the suffering."

Dylan said nothing, but she didn't expect him to. "I'll withdraw as much as I can and meet you on the Bolivar Peninsula."

"Thanks, Mom. I love you. I'm buying a new phone and

tossing this one. Afraid the law is tracking your calls." The phone clicked off.

She'd go to the bank after her last appointment this afternoon.

She shut off the faucet and stared at her image in the mirror. What if she never saw Dylan again? She'd not be able to survive. She longed to go with him, protect him as she'd always done. Was she being foolish for such a thought? Would he allow her to join him?

Dear God, what am I supposed to do for mi hijo?

If Dylan refused to let her join him, she'd be okay with his decision. She and Warren cared for each other, and she'd marry him when the crimes against Dylan were dismissed. God might have given her Warren so she wouldn't have to face the future alone.

62

BEFORE THEY LEFT THE JAMESES' HOME, Leah and Jon formed a plan to ensure Elena was protected. A GPD officer would remain in place until the FBI could relieve them. Despite the police chief's assurances, neither Jon nor Leah were ready to fully trust Everson's force.

Elena pleaded with her parents to stay in Galveston. "If Dylan is alive, I want to be here for him. If he's dead, his mother will need me."

One of the agents working surveillance for Silvia contacted Leah. She and Jon stepped outside onto the patio, where they could both listen.

"Between 2:50 and 3:10 p.m., Ms. Ortega received three texts and returned a call to the same number. The call wasn't long enough to trace. She left the dentist office at 4:55. Made a stop at the bank. We are currently tailing her. Hold on, Agent Riesel." A moment later, he was back on the line. "She's heading east on the island."

"Stay on her, but keep your distance." She seized Jon's attention. "We're on our way." Leah dropped her phone into her bag, went back into the house, and quickly explained the need for them to leave. In less than sixty seconds, Jon was speeding toward the eastern side of the island while she tried calling Silvia's number.

"Get ahold of Warren Livingston," Jon said when her third effort yielded only the woman's voice mail. "See if he's heard from her."

She contacted Warren and asked if he knew why Silvia wouldn't be picking up her phone.

"She wouldn't answer if she's with a patient," he said. "At this hour, it may have been an emergency."

"If you hear from her, kindly let us know." Leah ended the conversation. "Nothing there." She swung to Jon. "I like Silvia, admire her values and the way she stands up for her beliefs. But she's naive about Dylan—he can't be innocent in this or Aaron Michaels wouldn't have targeted Elena."

"And you'd like to shield Silvia and Elena from additional hurt."

She nodded. He understood her on many levels, a little scary but in a comforting way. "Crazy, huh? Don't let my marshmallow attitude get out, or I'll lose my Panther nickname."

"No way, Agent Riesel. It's one more intriguing part of you."

The man had the knack of making her feel special. "I'm in good company."

The agent ahead of them called. "Ms. Ortega is nearing the Bolivar ferry dock. The next ferry leaves in fifteen minutes."

She repeated the agent's words to Jon. "Can we make it?"

Jon pressed on the gas and wove the truck in and out of traffic.

Horns blared. Brakes squealed. Leah held her breath as he missed one bumper and nearly scraped the fender of an SUV. "I feel like I'm on a movie set, and you're a stuntman."

"How do you think I felt when you drove my truck?"

"I'm lousy with empathy."

He grinned, but his eyes stayed glued to the road. "I used to race on the Oklahoma back roads. Picked up a few tricks before I got to Quantico."

They neared the ferry. Cars were boarding, and Silvia's blue Toyota had already secured a spot. Jon broke the line between a battered Honda and a red Chevy pickup. Both drivers laid on their horns, but he was now only three vehicles behind Silvia.

Leah stared over the other vehicles. "I think we're far enough behind for her not to suspect anything, and your truck's in the body shop."

"Hope she's leading us to Dylan. No coincidence she was at the bank."

"She might have withdrawn all she had."

Once they had their own spot on the ferry, they just needed to wait and watch. Jon pressed the automatic button and the windows rolled down. The salty air and sound of lapping waves and crying seagulls had become a large part of their days. Leah peered at the white foam and spotted a dolphin leaping grace-fully in the water. Any other time, she'd snap a pic, except her thoughts were focused on trying to take Dylan into custody. Doing so could secure answers to stop the violence, ending the wave of murders and panic on the island. And dissuade other gangs from spreading crime.

The agent ahead of them confirmed Silvia was seated in her car and not on her phone.

Eighteen minutes later, the ferry docked. Slow and orderly. Agitation seared her nerves. Finally Jon drove off the ramp onto Bolivar Peninsula. Silvia remained several vehicles ahead. She pulled into a parking area, and the surveillance agents drove past and into a new strip center on the opposite side of the street. All had eyes on Silvia's car. Jon chose a parking area three rows back from where Silvia sat with her car's engine running. Leah grabbed binoculars from her shoulder bag, and Jon reached for the same on the seat between them.

Leah studied the surrounding area. A young man strode across the parking lot toward Silvia's Toyota and opened the passenger door. "Dylan," she said.

"Let's go."

Leah and Jon drew their weapons and raced toward Silvia's vehicle. The two agents on surveillance rushed several feet behind them as backup. Jon raised his hand to slow them.

Dylan must have seen them because he bolted around the Toyota to the driver's side and jerked the car door open. He heaved Silvia out. His left hand gripped her lower neck, and he held a gun to her head. "I will shoot," he said.

The woman who'd raised him, loved him like no other? How could he be so callous? Silvia whimpered.

"Dylan, let your mother go." Leah spoke compassion into her words. "You don't want to hurt her. She loves you."

"I'm no fool. You're not taking me in for a crime I didn't commit."

Leah crept ahead, making eye contact with him and avoiding the distraction of Silvia's trembling. "Like your mother, I want to help. I've always wanted to help."

He glanced around and said something to Silvia, but Leah couldn't hear what. None of them had a clear shot at Dylan. Had the other agents requested more backup?

"You've run from the police and FBI," Leah said. "Now you're holding your mother at gunpoint. Explain this to me. I want to understand. Because right now your actions are not those of an innocent man."

"Please, Dylan." Silvia's tears streamed down her face. "We can work this out."

Leah stepped closer. Jon moved to her far right.

Dylan said something to his mother, then shoved her aside. Silvia tripped on the rough pavement as Dylan climbed into the driver's seat. The car charged in reverse.

Leah dove onto the pavement out of the way, grabbed her weapon, rolled, and came up firing. Jon dashed after the car, unloading bullets into the back window.

Silvia shrieked.

Dylan squealed tires around the corner of the parking lot toward the departing ferry.

Leah raced to Jon's truck, where the keys sat in the cup holder. Pressing the ignition button, she brought the engine to life and stomped the gas. Dylan would not get on the ferry alone. She had her own driving tricks. She palmed the steering wheel.

He drove onto the ferry.

Three more vehicles slid in behind him.

Leah entered the ramp, and it closed behind her. Dylan slid into place five vehicles ahead. He exited the car and bounded toward the upper deck, where people milled about. She bolted from the truck and zigzagged around cars and people up the metal stairs toward him.

No point in shouting for him to stop. He'd successfully placed men, women, and children around him. She wouldn't risk anyone's life to capture this young man. Pushing past them, she shortened the distance.

He ran along the deck railing, stopped, and aimed his weapon into the crowd. "Drop your gun, or I'll unload mine."

A woman screamed. Shouts rose, and the crowd struggled to clear themselves from danger.

Leah laid her Glock on the deck and held up her hands. "Turn yourself in, Dylan. You can't keep running. But you can help us arrest those responsible. My original deal still stands. I'll speak to the judge on your behalf."

He shook his head and escaped down another nearby staircase to the lower car level. In the distance, a speedboat was moving their way. Leah snatched her gun and pursued him while shouting for people to stay down.

"Dylan, this is a mistake."

He climbed over the rail and jumped.

Leah rushed to the railing. Waves crashed against the side of the ferry. Dylan surfaced and swam toward the speedboat. A driver and an armed man came into view. The gunman raised an automatic and took aim at her.

Leah fired first, sending the armed man overboard. The driver raised his own weapon.

Bullets pelted the ferry. More screams.

The speedboat jumped over the wake.

Leah directed a shot at Dylan and pulled the trigger.

63

SILVIA'S RIGHT ARM AND LEG stung from her tumble to the pavement. Blood seeped through the right leg of her green scrubs, and her arm and elbow fared the same. Her son had caused this? The last few moments with Dylan squeezed her heart as though she'd met a stranger.

Agent Colbert jogged to her. "Are you okay? Do I need to call an ambulance?" He eyed her bleeding leg. "You might need stitches."

Be strong. No reason for him to see your distress. "I'll be okay. A little hydrogen peroxide will clean me up. Are you okay? And the other men who were with you. Are they hurt?"

"They're fine."

She was afraid to ask, afraid to voice her fear, as if doing so would cause it to come true. "And Dylan? What's going to happen now with him?"

"I've texted Agent Riesel to contact me as soon as possible." She braved forward. "You'll tell me the truth, no matter how bad it is?"

Agent Colbert hesitated for a fraction of a second and then nodded. "Ms. Ortega, I know you want answers. I feel the same. We'll see what Agent Riesel learns." His phone rang, and he moved away to answer. Silvia studied him, but his facial expressions gave no indication of the conversation. The evening heat bore down, increasing the sick feeling in the pit of her stomach.

What possessed her boy to hold a gun to her? She didn't know he owned one. She'd never permitted a weapon in their home and denied Dylan access to toy guns. Had she instilled an unhealthy attitude? Or had his time in jail changed him, turned him against her though he promised he'd learned his lesson? He'd been forced to live with bad people, and their habits had woven into the fabric of her son. Had he panicked when he saw she'd been followed?

She touched her temple, where he'd pressed the barrel against her head. No. Silvia drew in her shattered emotions. She couldn't believe that, wouldn't believe her boy had substituted his upbringing for greed.

He told me he was sorry for causing me grief. He asked me to forgive him for what he was about to do. When I fell, he told me, "I love you, Mom. I'd rather die an innocent man than live as a guilty one."

Mi hijo. *My precious boy. I'd give my life to erase this evening.*

"You're not taking me in for a crime I didn't commit." Words of innocence. He might believe she'd set him up. But betrayal of her son wasn't a part of her thoughts. She'd always be on his side.

Agent Riesel was on the ferry now with Dylan. She'd attempt to talk to him, just like she'd promised when he'd agreed to meet with the agents near Willy G's. Silvia rubbed her scraped arm. Was she kidding herself? If Dylan pulled a gun on Agent Riesel, she'd have no choice but to fire at him. Were the people on the ferry in danger?

Dear God, what have I done wrong for Dylan to act this way?

She should call Father Gabriel to ask for prayers. Silvia shook her head. Her cell phone was in the car with Dylan. She desperately wanted to hear Warren's strong and reassuring voice.

Agent Colbert walked her way. The closer he came, the more his eyes shone with kindness.

"Any word?" she said.

"Yes, ma'am. Dylan jumped from the ferry. A speedboat picked him up."

A sharp breath cut across her chest. "You mean police officers?"

"The men who picked him up were armed."

This meant Dylan had planned an escape. All he wanted was the money? She stared at her scraped arm. It was time to acknowledge the truth: Her son was a Veneno. He knew who'd murdered those people. Threatened Warren? Killed his stepfather?

Jon smiled sadly and she knew there was more.

"Dylan was wounded."

She felt nauseous. Dylan had gotten away, but he'd been shot. *God, no. Please.* This kept getting worse.

64

JON WALKED ON BOARD the next ferry with Silvia. He considered requesting the woman join him and the other two agents in the car, but Silvia was suffering not only with physical pain but also emotional. She'd refused an ambulance or first aid, and her injuries required attention.

"If you want to talk, I'm here," he said. He had already asked her to explain what led to her meeting with Dylan on the peninsula.

She held her right arm. "I'd rather be alone with my thoughts. Thanks anyway."

"Sure?"

She nodded. "This is the most difficult ordeal of my life. I hope you never face the heartache of a child's actions." Her face tightened. "Dylan promised me he hadn't killed anyone. Then he saw you and everything changed."

"Silvia—" his tone rang with disbelief—"he tried to—"

"I know my son, and there's more to this than what you saw or I experienced."

"I'm sorry." Life had no guarantees. "I need to check for updates."

She looked out over the water. "Go right ahead, Agent Colbert."

"Jon. The name's Jon, short for Jonathan."

"Like in the Bible."

"Yes, ma'am." He moved several feet away to a secluded spot. He pressed in Zachary Everson's number and quickly briefed him about the last hour. "Appreciate it if you'd alert the local hospitals and clinics. Dylan has to get treatment somewhere."

"On it," Everson said. "So he had a backup plan in case the money transfer went south."

Jon's thoughts mirrored Everson's. "I'll ask Leah to escort Silvia for medical treatment before bringing her to your office. Based on what's transpired, it's clear Dylan did a 180 on his mother." He glanced back at Silvia. Pity washed over him.

"See you at police headquarters," Everson said.

Jon made arrangements with Leah, then phoned Rachel Mendez. He was convinced she was concealing information, but what would it take for her to open up? "We have reason to believe Dylan is working with those responsible for your husband's death. Have you spoken to him?"

"No, sir," Rachel said. "I'm having a difficult time accepting this. Is Silvia aware?"

"Yes, I'm with her."

"What does she have to say about Dylan's involvement?"

"She's still in denial." Jon took a harder tone with the widow.

"Listen, Mrs. Mendez, the time's come for you to tell us what you know."

"I'm afraid I can't say anything more, Agent Colbert." Rachel sighed. "You can call off the agents guarding my house. I'm sending my mother and my children to California. But I'm staying here until my husband's killer is found."

While leaving town could be the best way for the Mendez family to remain safe until arrests were made, Jon still needed answers. And he heard another emotion besides control in her voice. "What are you afraid of?"

"Nothing, sir, except my son could be a murderer, and his victim was a man I loved. Excuse me. I have things to do." She ended the call.

Frustrated, Jon dialed a number he'd memorized in the last few days.

"How can I help you?" Father Gabriel's tone dripped with exhaustion and rightfully so. They all were tired.

Jon told Father Gabriel about the incident on Bolivar Peninsula, omitting the part about a surveillance team keeping an eye on Silvia. "As expected, she's upset. May need your counsel."

Father Gabriel groaned. "Poor woman. She's always done her best for Dylan, believed in him when no one else did. I'll wrap up things here and drive to the police department."

"She seems to be eaten up with shame."

"Shame is a very powerful psychological theme. It gets in the way of forgiveness. Weave it with rejection, and we get misery."

Jon understood exactly what Father Gabriel meant. "One more thing: Dylan was shot during the firefight on board the ferry. I have no idea how badly."

"It's hard for me to believe Dylan would take money and treat Silvia with such disrespect. He didn't learn a thing in prison."

That was the most condemning word Jon had heard from Father Gabriel. "Reminds me of what my granddad used to say. 'Son, when you learn a tough lesson, keep the receipt, because some lessons are too hard to repeat.'"

Father Gabriel chuckled lightly. "I'll be using your granddad's line. Appreciate your contacting me."

Jon pocketed his phone and returned to Silvia's side. Her eyes were red, her face puffy, and she radiated a grief that came from a source far beyond the physical fall. Taking her hand in his, he spoke silent comfort into the woman who was guilty of loving a son who'd broken her heart.

Leah sat with Silvia in the chilly emergency room. Silvia had nothing to say, a nasty brew of fear and grief. She'd received three stitches to her lower right leg and multiple scrapes due to the rough tumble—in far too many ways. Silvia contacted Warren and downplayed her injuries. She told him what happened, then asked him to wait for her call.

"I need time to think," she'd said. "We can talk later."

While they waited for a nurse to deliver and administer a tetanus shot, Leah tried to engage Silvia in a conversation. "Would you like to talk about this afternoon?"

"Jon asked the same thing. My son disappointed me." Her chin trembled. "Somewhere he's hurt, and I ache for him."

Leah formed the words she needed to convey. "Silvia, I'm the one who shot Dylan."

She buried her face in her hands. Sobs rose from what

appeared to be her soul. "I assumed you had. Did he shoot anyone?"

"He threatened the people on the ferry, but he didn't open fire. The gunfire erupted from the speedboat that rescued him. When Dylan jumped, I shot him."

"It's all a nightmare, and I can't wake up." Silvia grasped her middle. "I'm going to be sick." She walked to the sink and emptied the contents of her stomach.

Leah wet a paper towel and wordlessly handed it to her. Had her own mother reacted to Leah's behavior like this? Had her mother regretted leaving her alone in a dressing room at the mall when her emotionally upset sister demanded she come home immediately?

Leah felt a sense of shame wash over her. Perhaps she had been justified in feeling hurt and abandoned in the moment. But hadn't she done the same thing to her family, leaving them and cutting off all communication? And hadn't she been miserable as a result?

As Silvia returned to her chair from rinsing out her mouth, Leah wondered what Father Gabriel would say to the hurting mother . . . and to herself. She faced the distraught woman. "What is your faith, your God, saying to you?" An unusual subject for Leah, but the woman might share her feelings.

A tear trickled over her cheek, and she whisked it away with a bandaged hand. "I learned the value of faith from my parents. They moved here from Mexico when I was a young girl. My father was a dentist, and he opened his practice here in Galveston. My mother worked as his receptionist. They instilled in me the power of God and His sacrifice for us. Everything they earned above paying for basic needs went to the church. From them I learned no matter what life brings, He is always there."

"Even now? In the midst of so much pain?"

"I trust God for His provision. And He's telling me to forgive Dylan." Silvia paused. "Do you know our heavenly Father?"

"Let's say I'm researching Him."

Silvia gave her a weak smile. "Faith isn't about something you can see or document on a report. We're human and clinging to God isn't easy. It's a choice, one we have to make on a daily basis, sometimes even minute to minute."

Silvia had effectively reversed the conversation. Leah thought about Terri and how easily her friend had been able to forgive her for the silence she imposed on their relationship. Had Terri's faith helped her find the strength to do so?

"And what about you?" Silvia said. "Are you allowing the poison of disbelief to stand in the way of your relationship with God?"

"When I see horrible crimes and compare them to a deity who's supposed to be in control, I'm skeptical. Angry."

"People aren't perfect—" Leah smiled at that as Silvia continued—"and God gives us freedom to make our own decisions. I'm doing my best to hold on even though I want to sink into a pit of fear and despair." Silvia touched her nose, and Leah gave her a tissue from the counter. "I must have made mistakes with Dylan to push him into breaking the law."

Leah envisioned how Silvia must have nurtured her son. "I don't think you taught him how to use a gun or rob a convenience store. He did those things on his own. You took him to church and taught him how to live life according to your beliefs."

"No matter how many times I tell myself I did the right things, the guilt is still there. When you're a mother, you'll understand. We mothers can be illogical about our children and blame ourselves when they go astray."

Did Mom and Dad blame themselves for her mistakes?

"What I'm saying is I can't take another breath without God. And I'm going to cling to Him even when I don't understand why bad things happen. Because I believe good can come out of bad things. I may not see the good right away, but I trust God for it."

A concept so foreign to Leah that she refused to ask for clarification. "I'm sorry Dylan put you through this. Did he say where he was going?"

Silvia shook her head. "Where was he shot?"

"The left shoulder area."

She stiffened her shoulders. "The water could cause an infection. Maybe he'll decide the running's over and choose to turn himself in at a medical facility." While Silvia's words carried a theme of hopefulness, her tone sounded flat.

"That would be wise, a positive step forward," Leah said.

"Are you going to take me home?"

"First we'll drive to the police department. Agent Colbert and Chief of Police Everson have some questions."

"I hate the thought of it."

"I'll be with you. Do you want me to contact your dental office?"

"It's not necessary. I don't want to miss tomorrow and have Dr. Rios and Anna scrambling."

The nurse entered the room with the injection. Too bad she didn't have a vial to help Silvia discern the truth about Dylan.

If there was a God, Leah hoped He comforted Silvia.

65

JON HAD SUGGESTED fried rattlesnake for dinner at Leah's apartment, but she nixed that idea. Her hand ached from the snakebite as she and Jon packed up the remains of their carry-out Greek food from dinner, but the reminder wasn't a bad thing.

"What style do you call this?" He ran his fingers over the polished steel countertop and examined the brass beads at the edges.

"Steampunk."

He stared at the table and settled on the chandelier. "I'll need to read up on it. It's different. All you."

She laughed at his fumbling over her unusual tastes. "I'm not touching that." She wiped off her dining room table and spoke her mind. "Have we been looking at this case all wrong?"

He snapped a lid on a huge plastic container of tzatziki sauce. "If we were sailing on the right waters, we'd have hit shore."

She feigned a frown. "How long did it take you to come up with that metaphor?"

"Instantly. But I'm right there with you. Smart people with a lot of money seem to have devised a plan to send us in the wrong direction."

She returned to the table and closed a Styrofoam container of pita bread. Her mind couldn't wrap around what they were missing. "Since we haven't heard from any local hospitals, Dylan's in a lot of pain somewhere. Or dead. What are you thinking?"

Jon grabbed up the throwaways and carried them to the trash under the sink. "Remember *The Godfather*? 'Keep your friends close and your enemies closer.' What if we've met the kingpin, talked to him or her? Let's run through the list: Rachel Mendez is afraid, and she's not the type of woman who scares easily. Zachary Everson is led by vengeance. Father Gabriel would sacrifice his own life for a bad guy. Silvia Ortega would do anything for Dylan, and I put Elena James in that category too. Dylan nearly got himself killed during his getaway today, but he probably knows who's running the show."

A thought hit Leah. "We're chasing Dylan. Could it be he's the fall guy, and the boss man is banking on us killing him? The man I shot from the ferry was a known felon, bad all the way through but not a member of a gang. His background shows a steady stream of arrests from breaking and entering to assault." Leah tapped her fingernail on the table. "Could our kingpin have stolen the drugs from Molston Pharmaceuticals and rigged up a Veneno gang with a fake battle cry to cover up the theft? Ian Greer, Marcia Trevelle, and Judge Mendez found the evidence?"

"Well, there is someone we've met we haven't considered closely."

Leah faced him. "Who?"

"Warren Livingston."

She shook her head. "Jon, our desperation is showing through. Warren is one of the good guys. Remember he was threatened and—"

"Perfect cover."

Her thoughts froze because Jon made sense. "Seems impossible."

"While you were at the hospital with Silvia, I started digging into his background. Warren stocks his souvenir shop from Mexico. No big deal, right? Until I looked for his vendors. He doesn't use any. He fills his shelves personally by making frequent trips to Mexico City. Why, when he can pick up the phone or order online?"

"Did you notify agents in Mexico City?"

"Sure."

"Go on," she said. "I know there's more."

"I gained access to the Galveston security cams around Warren's properties. Want to guess who visited his shop three times in the last three months?"

"Dylan?"

"Good one, but wrong. Aaron Michaels. We have footage of him entering and leaving the shop, staying around ten minutes each time."

Aaron?

Leah sank into a chair. "Dylan's a low crawl, but he may have more than one legitimate reason for despising Warren. What's the rest?"

"Thought you'd never ask." He scrolled on his phone and handed it to her.

She skimmed the notes he'd compiled. "Warren attended the University of Arizona for three years. College records show more than one infraction for assault, and that eventually led to his leaving school. Arrested twenty-two years ago in Phoenix for embezzlement, but charges were dropped. Possible overseas accounts. Has a home in Mexico City worth over two million dollars." She'd thought his apartment building and home were a scale above a souvenir shop. "Have you requested agents in Phoenix investigate Warren's family there?" The man's parents and a sister still lived in Arizona.

"Yep."

She handed Jon's phone back to him. "Have you run this past anyone else?"

"Only you."

Her thoughts spun. "Warren's a good-looking man, dresses well. Silvia has a heart of gold, but she's not . . . How do I say it? The woman I'd expect him to be with? What does she have that he needs to make his plan work? She's a dental hygienist with an adopted son who's bad news."

Jon paced her small kitchen and dining room. "Link it to Dylan and prescription drugs."

What would attract a striking and wealthy man with criminal connections to a modest woman? Jon's comment played and replayed in Leah's mind. "Silvia is in the medical field, which equates to prescription drugs. She's taking stolen OxyContin that Dylan got for her." She lifted her chin. "Have we researched the dentist she works for? His name's Pablo Rios."

He lifted his phone from his pocket and typed. "I'm requesting a background."

"If Warren is involved, he has his bases covered."

"I'm sure of it." He finished and set his phone on the counter. "There's always a weak spot. We keep digging." He downed his iced tea. "It will take a while for Rios's background check to be completed. I sure could use a kiss."

Leah stood and wrapped her arms around his neck. "Not sure it's in your future." The man had the most gorgeous brown eyes.

His lips lowered. "I'll make up your mind for you."

Jon's kiss, warm and sweet, left her tingly. He backed up and gathered her hands into his. "Being alone with you is dangerous. I don't want to mess us up."

She trembled at his nearness, and she valued what he meant, what she felt. "Me either. I'm happy and scared at the same time."

"I want this case wrapped up, but I don't want to give up working with you."

"Is it possible to have both?"

"We'll figure it out. The future's never certain, but I want to see if there's an us in it."

66

TUESDAY MORNING, Jon joined Leah at the FBI office, eager to see her again and to get back to work on the case. Rios's background had come in late last night, and he'd spent several hours combing through the dentist's information.

Pablo Rios, originally from Mexico, became a US citizen twenty-five years ago and purchased his dental practice a year later. Fifteen years ago, the DEA put him under surveillance for suspected prescription drug trafficking, but nothing was proven. Rios's practice was small: his wife served as the receptionist—from their visit to the office Jon remembered her as a taskmaster—and Silvia Ortega worked as the sole hygienist.

Jon was planning to file a search warrant for the dentist office later this morning and question both Rios and Warren Livingston. But first he and Leah had an 8 a.m. meeting with

Amanda Barton, the woman who was taken hostage in her own home last week. Ms. Barton wanted to thank the SWAT team for saving her and her family's lives.

The commander waved at Jon and Leah as they entered the conference room, then gestured for them to join him and Ms. Barton at the table. "Agents Riesel and Colbert, an appreciative lady would like to meet you." He made introductions.

Ms. Barton graciously responded. "Thank you will never be enough to express my gratitude. When I think about what those men planned to do and how you saved my family, I shake all over again." She tapped her heart. "One minute please." When she regained her composure, she continued. "I would have given those men anything they wanted. But you ended our fears. Neither my sister nor I will ever forget how you saved our children. Someday I want to make it up to you."

Leah stepped forward. "We are just a part of a powerful SWAT team. Everyone worked together. We're glad to have helped."

"My sister blames herself for the tragedy."

Another case of survivor guilt. "I'm sorry."

"Last night I learned her ex-boyfriend must have told those two about the money I keep at the house."

An alarm sounded in Jon's mind. "Did she mention this to the police?"

Amanda shook her head. "She was afraid for her child and herself—he or one of his no-good friends might hurt them. But he's dead now."

"What was his name?" Jon said.

"Aaron Michaels."

Jon hid his reaction. He recalled the men who'd held the women and children captive. Neither of their names had surfaced in the three Galveston homicides or the FBI investigation.

"Where is your sister now?"

"Why?" Ms. Barton's face paled.

Jon nodded at Leah, and he listened to her push concern into her words. "Ms. Barton, your sister may have important information that's connected to another case we're working on. Can we speak to her now?"

Tears filled her eyes. "Is she in danger? My phone's in my car or I'd call her now."

"You could use my phone," Leah said.

Ms. Barton responded without hesitation. "Yes, I will."

The other SWAT team members filed out of the room to give the woman some privacy.

Ms. Barton pressed in numbers. "Hey, Cecelia, it's me. I'm at the FBI office. I know you were hesitant about saying anything, but I told them about Aaron. One of the agents wants to talk to you. Can you excuse yourself and go somewhere private?" She gave Leah the phone.

Jon remembered the young woman from the SWAT mission.

Leah thanked Cecelia for her time. "We'd appreciate any information about Aaron Michaels. I'd like to put my phone on speaker. Agent Colbert is with me, and we'd like to record our conversation."

"No recording until you have the entire gang in jail." The young woman's voice weakened. "I don't mind if the other agent is listening."

"Okay. Tell me about Aaron."

"I met him on the college campus. Hired him as an advanced algebra tutor. He was nice and extremely intelligent. We became friends and started dating. He was good with my two-year-old daughter, and everything went well for about three months. Then he changed."

"How?"

"He showed up drunk at my sister's house, where I live. Amanda had taken her kids to dinner. I asked Aaron to leave and told him we were finished. He grabbed me and smacked me in the face." Cecelia's voice cracked as she continued. "He said if I wanted my daughter to stay alive, I had to do whatever he wanted, whenever he wanted. At times, he'd just show up. He must have watched for Amanda to leave, because my daughter and I were always alone. Sometimes he held a gun on us." She sniffed. "The last time was a week before the break-in. He told me about some friends of his who needed money."

"I'm sorry to put you through remembering the whole nightmare," Leah said.

"It's okay," Cecelia said, though Leah could tell it really wasn't. "It's been a secret so long, it helps to finally talk about it."

"Do you have someone you trust you can share these things with?" After enduring Aaron's abuse for so long, to have also experienced the trauma of being held hostage . . .

"I've started talking to a priest."

"Who?"

Jon guessed the name before Leah asked.

"Father Xavier Gabriel. A friend recommended him. My sister went with me to the first session."

"Can you give us the name of the friend who recommended Father Gabriel?"

"Rachel Mendez. She and Amanda have been good friends for years."

67

RACHEL MENDEZ? Was she a friend or foe? After watching Amanda Barton leave the FBI offices, Leah slipped into the chair at her desk.

"So we're adding Rachel Mendez to the list of those we need to talk to this morning," Jon said. "Warren Livingston still has my attention."

"Why didn't she tell us Aaron Michaels had abused Cecelia or that she'd recommended Father Gabriel for counseling? Rachel is not stupid. She had to suspect the men who broke into the Barton home were linked to Aaron and possibly the death of Judge Mendez. That falls under withholding information, and she can't plead ignorant when she's a lawyer."

"I think she's protecting Dylan any way she can," he said.

Leah checked the status of search warrants they'd filed this morning for Livingston's properties and Rios's dental practice. No go yet. "Silvia Ortega is linked to all three parties. Do you think she's been inadvertently aiding this drug trafficking effort?"

"Why don't you give her a call, try to probe her for more information? I'll ask agents to bring in Rachel, Warren, and Pablo Rios."

"Good idea." She grabbed her phone and pressed in the woman's number. "Hi, Silvia, how are you feeling?"

"I appreciate your asking. I'm sore. Advil is helping."

"Are you alone or do you have someone looking after you?"

"You actually caught me on the way to the office. But Warren came over last night. Like a couple of kids, we watched some movies. He was trying to keep my mind off Dylan."

Leah seized the opening. "Warren's a good friend. I imagine it's hard to find time to get together when he's so busy with his store."

"We manage. At least once a week, he stops by the office."

"Wonderful. You're lucky Dr. Rios doesn't mind."

"They're friends, so it's an opportunity for them to talk. Warren does mission work in Mexico City, and Dr. Rios sends toothbrushes, toothpaste, and floss."

A means to smuggle drugs? "How generous."

"Yes, I'm blessed with a great boss and Warren."

"I won't keep you any longer. I'm glad you're feeling better today." Leah waited for the line to disconnect before relaying the conversation and her suspicions to Jon.

He rubbed his chin. "She's as much a victim as those grieving the loss of a loved one."

"We're used to working our own division or staring down a rifle scope, using technology, stats, wind calculations, not dealing with people we care about."

Jon nodded, then excused himself to take care of some things at his desk.

Sitting back in her chair, Leah lifted the mug of lukewarm coffee to her lips. If their theory proved correct, Warren's relationship with Silvia was in place to launder money and drugs through Dr. Rios's dental practice. But they needed evidence to make arrests.

Leah sighed. She had a few minutes to get caught up on paperwork, though she'd rather clean toilets than shuffle papers. No way around it but to dive into the least favorite part of her job.

Ten minutes later, she received a call from the reception area—a welcome diversion. "Agent Riesel? There's an older gentleman here to see you. Says it's important."

Edgar Whitson? "Who is he?"

"Roy Riesel."

Leah's pulse sped. Dad? In Houston? Had something happened to Mom or one of her siblings? "I'll be right there." She rose from her chair on wobbly legs, then sat again.

She reached for her phone and texted Jon.

My dad's in the reception area. Wants to see me.

You can do this. I'm praying.

With no time to deliberate what prayer meant for her, she placed her phone in her jacket pocket and walked to the reception area. She felt like a soldier heading to the front lines. Was this meeting a good thing or a not-so-good thing? She pushed through the double doors to where Dad stood staring out the window facing Highway 290. His hands were stuck in his pockets, a trait she remembered when he had many things on his mind. His thick hair had turned white, but his shoulders were still erect.

She drew in a deep breath. "Dad."

He turned and took long strides to her. His nut-brown eyes moistened. Three feet in front of her, he stopped as though an invisible wall separated them, a wall of miscommunication, one she wanted to demolish. She needed courage outside herself to make the step.

Leah opened her arms. "Dad, I've missed you. I'm sorry for the problems I caused."

He wrapped his arms around her, and she fell into his embrace, the same firm hands that had comforted and strengthened her when she was a little girl. His soft sobs brought on her own remorse. Her tears flowed with his, a river of regret. After several long moments, he put her at arm's length. "You're grown up and incredibly beautiful."

She wiped her eyes. "Thank you. We can talk in a conference room." She spied his visitor badge.

"Alone with my girl? Good."

The New York accent, spun with the familiar voice, filled her with longing.

In an interview room, they sat across from each other. Father and daughter. Years apart. She reached over the table, and he lifted her hand into his. Firm. Strong. Lines around his eyes and across his brow had aged him.

"I'm ashamed of how our call ended last week," he said. "I was nervous and dropped my phone. It shattered. I started to call you back on your mother's phone, but your number was on mine. Leah, I love you and I've never stopped missing you." He pressed his lips together before beginning again. "I researched you online. My little girl puts her life in danger to keep people safe."

His words sounded proud, and she relished the thought.

"I've been well trained. And I work with a great team of people in violent crime and SWAT. Currently I'm on a homicide case."

He sucked in a breath. "I didn't realize."

Confession time. "Protecting others is a way for me to make up for the foolish years."

"And I blame myself. Too many shoulds." He stared wordlessly into her face and blinked. "You've changed. Your eyes are calm."

"It took a while for me to figure out some of life. My work experiences along with a heavy dose of reality have a way of molding a person into a better human being." She sealed their time together in memory, never to be forgotten.

He glanced down at their hands, knit together. "I used to hold your hand like this when you were a little girl."

"I remember. When I'd lose a basketball game, you'd have to talk me down off the cliff. The perfectionist in me still has a habit of surfacing."

"We have a lot of catching up to do."

"I look forward to it. Tell me about Mom and my brothers and sisters."

"Before I dive into the whole family thing, I want to apologize for all the poor decisions your mother and I made raising you and your siblings. We never included you in the conversations, never asked you how you felt about it." He blew out a sigh. "We expected far too much. All the times we let you down, disappointed you, missed important events."

"It's okay, Dad."

He shook his head. "No, it's not. Will you forgive your mother and me?"

She swallowed a lump. "Yes. A million times yes. I was horrible, so please forgive me."

Tears filled his eyes and he nodded. "We're a pair, aren't we? Your mother is the one who insisted I fly here. She wanted to come, and she will the next time."

A catch in her throat forced control. Next time? "Can we put the ugliness behind us and start fresh? I understand rough waters are ahead, but I want my family back. Not on holidays and an occasional email, but permanently."

"Absolutely." Dad grinned. "If the guard out front hadn't ordered me to leave my phone in the car, I'd show you photos."

"Protocol, Dad. Know what? I've followed my family on Facebook for years."

He studied her. "There's something else you're holding back. What is it?"

Dare she ruin the reunion? "I have this question burning inside me." She gazed at his lined face. "Why did you keep my great-great-grandmother's identity a secret, and yet you named me after her?"

"What?" He startled. "Her name was Leah?" When she affirmed it, he breathed in deeply. "I never heard about her."

"She escaped slavery in Alabama through the Underground Railroad. Settled in New York City and started an orphanage for children. It's a powerful story. I'm so very proud of her."

Dad tilted his head. "My grandmother never talked about her family. Your mother named you Leah because we liked it. Neither of us had a clue, except my grandmother wasn't happy with the choice."

"I thought she was why you and Mom opted for adoption."

"Your uncle's tragic accident prompted us. When did you find out about your ancestry?" Dad said.

"About five years ago. On a whim, I did a DNA test and

decided to dig deeper. A book's been written about Grandma Leah. I have it."

"Wow. That's amazing. Got to read it, and your mom will love the family history."

"She was stubborn and fought for the orphans' rights."

"Now I know where our strong wills came from." He swiped beneath his eye. "Thank you for telling me the story. Thanks more for seeing me."

"I've dreamed of this, of us talking. How long are you in town?"

"Until tomorrow. Can we have dinner tonight?"

"I'd love it. I can look at your photos then."

"Maybe a FaceTime with your mom too."

His words brought her longtime dream to the surface. She'd relive this reunion time and time again.

A knock on the door broke the sweet reunion, and Jon stepped in. "Leah, I'm sorry to bother you. We have a signed search warrant for the Galveston site. Chopper's picking us up in ten."

She rose from her chair. "Dad, this is my partner, Agent Jon Colbert."

Jon reached out to shake his hand. "It's a pleasure, sir. Working alongside your daughter has made me a better man."

"I'd expect nothing less," Dad said.

She sensed the warmth rising up her neck and into her cheeks. She hugged her dad and promised to call him about dinner. "Dad, stay here. Another agent will have to escort you to the front."

"I understand." His face clouded. "Be careful. I don't need a hero, just my daughter."

68

BOARDING A CHOPPER ALWAYS gave Jon a twinge of appre-hension. Not the flying so much as memories of hovering over a wildfire. Maybe one day, they'd vanish. With noise-canceling headphones in place to block the sound of whirling blades, he filled Leah in on what had transpired over the last thirty minutes.

"No one could raise the agents assigned to Rachel Mendez's protection detail this morning, so when a couple guys drove to her house to pick her up, they found the two agents dead, execution-style. She's missing."

Leah's gaze flew to his. "And her mother and children?"

"Unclear. It's possible Rachel sent them out of town already, maybe went with them. But there's more. Richard James called me—Elena's gone. No note. Neither is anything missing. Her bedroom has a balcony, and they assume she left or was taken from there. They haven't seen her since she went to bed last night. I tried Silvia's cell phone and the dentist office. No answer there. The surveillance team said she went to work this morning and hasn't left the office. I asked them to check inside, but the front and back doors are locked. No signs on either door about closing. They forced entry. Nothing indicated a problem, but no one's there. It's possible Silvia and the Rioses left through a side door that provides access to a community courtyard and adjoining offices."

"What about Warren?"

"He isn't picking up at his shop or on his cell. The only person who responded was Father Gabriel."

"Tell me the missing people are at St. Peter's."

"I wish. Father Gabriel received a call warning him the Venenos were doing a roundup. He informed the officer assigned to him, and they're at GPD headquarters."

"Rachel, Elena, and Silvia, the three women important to Dylan," Leah said. "Warren and possibly the Rioses. They're together somewhere."

As if timed to precision with his recap, Jon's phone alerted him to an incoming call. He plugged his phone into the head-phones. It was Zachary Everson. "A neighbor to the Mendezes saw a man matching Warren Livingston's description enter the home about 7 a.m."

"Any gunfire?" He wished Leah were listening in.

"No," Everson said. "But the home's security cam isn't show-ing anything. My conclusion is the system's been hacked—probably was done before their SUV was stolen."

"Leah and I discovered he's not the savory guy we thought. We were waiting on search warrants this morning and for him and Rachel to be brought in. We also have a search warrant for Dr. Pablo Rios's office." Jon explained the previous DEA investigation and the possible link to Warren Livingston.

"Officers checked Silvia's home and Warren's," Everson said. "No one answered at either home. I'll send officers to the Rioses' residence."

"As soon as we land, Leah and I will join our agents at the dentist office." Jon ended the call, still gripping his phone, his thoughts spinning. He told Leah about the findings. "People are missing, and we have no clue if they're dead or alive or who's responsible."

God, I pray not one more victim.

Galveston came into view, and Leah spoke. "I'm thinking this is what they want—GPD and the FBI in one location to distract us. The rattlesnake scare diverted law enforcement. We need to work smarter, Jon. What's on the island worth the risk? Moving a shipment of prescription drugs?" She stared at her injured left hand. "Do they need to transport drugs to another location while we're occupied on the opposite end of the island?"

The chopper descended for landing, and Jon's phone signaled a text, an unknown number.

Flew home a day early. Here's the number for the man who wanted to buy acreage.

Jon leaned back and closed his eyes. The man who owned the farm where they found the rattlesnake pit had come through. This was the break they needed. *Thank You.*

"Everything okay?" Leah said.

"Better than okay. The man who wanted to buy the land where we found the rattler pit used a burner. It's a number we've seen on Aaron Michaels's phone."

Once the chopper landed, Leah and Jon raced to an awaiting car. Jon drove, but she didn't care. Her thoughts zeroed in on missing people and those suspected of masterminding the crimes.

Jon's phone sounded, and he glanced at the caller. "It's Kempler. Can you take it?"

She snatched it and hit Speaker. "Mr. Kempler, this is Agent Riesel. Jon and I are in a time-sensitive situation."

"I'll make it quick. I found the evidence."

She swung a look at Jon. "Where?"

"The judge gave me a Bible years ago. I kept it in my desk. Never thought to look inside. But I was moving it aside to get something else and dropped it. A note fell out addressed to me. It said, 'What you are looking for is in the family frame on my wall.' Took a while to examine what he'd written, but it's all documented. He believed Dr. Pablo Rios and Warren Livingston were dealing in prescription drugs. The judge didn't have enough proof."

Confirmation. "Are you sure the evidence you have isn't enough proof?" Jon wondered if they should pick up the judge's notes before doing anything else.

"I'll bring everything to GPD—will that work?"

Jon exchanged a look with Leah. Was Everson trustworthy enough? "Yes. We're on our way with a search warrant to Rios's office now. We'll call when we're done."

As Kempler ended the call, Jon turned to Leah. "I feel like I smacked the piñata and it broke. Now to find out where all these people are."

As Pablo Rios's dental office came into view, Leah recognized the vehicle of the agent assigned to Silvia's surveillance. "Jon, I'm requesting the agent's car. Ross Kempler has the documentation to help make arrests, and I want to get my hands on it."

"Hey, you can't take off without me. I'm your partner."

She exited the rental car. "Timing is too important."

69

LEAH FOUND ROSS KEMPLER and Father Gabriel sitting in
Everson's office. Ross produced Judge Mendez's notes in his own
handwriting and the documented evidence. While Greer, Trevelle,
and the judge believed their findings were inconclusive, their private investigation had uncovered substantial information to bring
in Warren Livingston and Dr. Pablo Rios for questioning.

Leah was concerned about Father Gabriel's and Ross's safety
and persuaded them to stay with Everson until Jon finished with
the sweep of the dental office. She received a call from Silvia and
took it outside Everson's office.

"Are you all right?" Leah said. "The police were at your home,
but you didn't answer the door."

"I must have been in the shower." Her voice quivered. She
must be in pain. "Are you in Galveston?"

"Yes."

"Can you and Agent Colbert come by the house? I need to tell you something important about Dylan as soon as possible."

"Is he with you?"

"No. Just come, please."

"Jon's busy, but I'll be there in a few minutes." Leah told Everson where she was going and left the building. She texted Jon and drove to the Ortega address.

After ringing Silvia's bell and pounding on the door, Leah walked around to the back of the house with her gun drawn. Neat and clean. Perfect flower beds. The back door was locked.

She peered through windows. Nothing.

A gun barrel pressed against the back of her head. "Drop it," a man said.

Leah obliged, and he pulled her wounded hand behind her back. She winced. Someone swung her around.

Two men. Both with weapons. One man grabbed her phone and tossed it into the flower bed.

"We're taking a little drive." The man who held her spoke with a thick Hispanic accent.

"Where?"

"You'll find out."

Jon had worked alongside the agents sweeping the rooms of Dr. Rios's dental facility for the past several minutes, and they hadn't found anything suspicious. Whoever had left there did so in a hurry. The computers had been erased of data, and that had to have been initiated before leaving the office. The tech guys in Houston should be able to recover the data.

"The reception area looks clean," an agent said. "Finger-printing will take time."

Jon nodded. "I'll continue searching for a little longer, then I'm heading to Chief Everson's office."

"Agent Riesel has my car."

"I'll make sure it's returned."

While the agents checked out Dr. Rios's desk, closet, and credenza, Jon headed for the back room where supplies were stored. Clean. Orderly. Then a locked closet in the break room caught his attention. He snatched a tiny dental instrument from a nearby tray and picked the lock. Inside the closet, he flipped on a light. Stacks of small plastic, zippered cases marked *Dental Supplies for Mexico Missions*. The cases were clear except for a bright-blue bottom about an inch thick. Why the extra padding?

He unzipped a case and removed a toothbrush, regular-size toothpaste, and dental floss. The bottom appeared to be glued and stitched. Grabbing a corner and slicing it with the dental pick, he pulled back the bottom.

Two layers of pills . . . Prescription drugs with the same iden-tifying codes as those missing from Molston Pharmaceuticals.

Jon ripped open enough dental aid containers to discover thousands of dollars of prescription drugs. Some of the drugs were not from Molston Pharmaceuticals. With the number of trips Warren made to Mexico, no doubt much of the stolen shipment had been transported under the guise of a mission project.

Why had they left the drugs behind? No time? Who'd alerted them?

70

HER HANDS TIED AND a sweaty blindfold applied, Leah was shoved into the rear seat of a dark-colored Mustang matching Mr. Whitson's and Elena's descriptions of the vehicle involved in the crimes.

Four times the car came to a halt, and Leah assumed they were at stop signs or traffic lights. She calculated about twenty minutes before the driver shut off the engine. One of the men pulled her from the car. Waves slapped against the shore and seagulls cried out. Nothing more to distinguish where she'd been taken. Someone opened a creaky door and told her to climb the stairs. She counted twelve steps. The second floor? Her blindfold was removed but not the bindings around her wrists. She blinked. The two men who'd abducted her blocked the only doorway she could see as if she'd make a run for it. The room reeked of grease and marijuana.

Warren Livingston faced her. "Well, look who we have here."

"The FBI has evidence to convict you," she said.

He slapped her face, staggering her, but she stayed on her feet. "I'm smarter than they are," he boasted.

Resolve rose inside her. She ignored the stinging and eyed him. "Doubt it."

Dr. Rios and his wife walked into the room. "Looks like you're taking care of our problem," Dr. Rios said. "Where's her partner?"

"We'll get him." Warren turned to one of the men who'd nabbed Leah. "Put her in with the others, then get out of here. I'll call when I need you."

In a small living room, Dylan lay on a blood-soaked sofa. An even bloodier shirt was wrapped around his left shoulder, where Leah had shot him. Fever clouded his eyes. His face was pale. Looked like he needed immediate medical help or he'd die. Silvia blanched at the sight of Leah. She sat on the edge of the sofa, holding Dylan's hand.

On the opposite wall, Rachel and Elena were tied back to back, their ankles bound with ropes.

The man forced Leah to the tiled floor and tied her ankles. She'd been roughed up before, and Warren's men were no exception. Livingston and Dr. Rios and his wife entered the area.

"Dylan, you brought this on yourself," Warren said. "You were told to behave, or your girlfriend and mother would be harmed. Problem is, I didn't say which mother." He laughed, a spine-chilling sound. "I have all three women and an FBI agent as a bonus."

Dylan attempted to speak. "Told you," he whispered. "I delivered the drugs like you said."

"My man says he didn't get them."

He spoke haltingly, pain evident in his voice. "Then he stole them from you, not me."

"You're a stupid coward. All you had to do was deliver the goods and dump Mendez's body. And you managed to botch up both. I've given you plenty of chances to comply. I even picked you up when the Feds had you trapped on a ferry. Lost a man doing it. Now you're going to face the consequences."

Mrs. Rios stomped across the room and held a gun to Silvia's head. Dylan attempted to rise from the sofa but fell back.

"Where are the drugs? Tell me or this time she bleeds."

"Stop," Rachel said. "How much money do you need?"

Mrs. Rios jutted her chin at Rachel. "More than you have."

"My husband left me wealthy. If you'll give me a phone, I'll make a transfer now."

Warren towered over Rachel. "It's the principle of the thing. You steal from me and the doc here, we recoup. Dylan either spills his guts, or he watches us kill all of you, one at a time. Slowly. Trust me, I know how it's done."

"Warren, why?" Silvia stood, the only person not tied. "You have plenty of money. The FBI and the police must know we're missing. Leave before you're caught."

"Is sweet Silvia looking out for me?" Warren sneered. "I put up with you for one reason: keeping Dylan in line after he decided to get your pills from one of my dealers. I admit I didn't expect him to escape my men when he got shot." He glared at her. "Do you think I'd choose a woman like you? A dumpy, cross-carrying fool?"

Silvia rushed him from the sofa and hammered her fists into his chest until he grabbed her hands. She spat in his face. "You worthless piece of trash. You'll rot in hell for what you've done."

He grabbed her by the throat and pushed her onto the floor.

He tied her hands and feet. "Don't say another word, or you'll die first."

Warren wasn't bluffing. "Silvia, easy," Leah said. "The FBI and Chief Everson are looking for us."

"We'll be long gone before they find you." Warren laughed again, the same guttural sound Leah had heard a few moments before. "Hey, Agent Riesel, what did you think of the *reconquista* slogan? That kept you guessing, I bet. As well as the time I reported being threatened and had a rock tossed through my window. Did you enjoy the box of roses?"

If Leah could stall him, Jon might be able to locate her. "Who killed Brad Dixon?"

Warren ignored the question. He seemed to be interested only in continuing to outline his accomplishments. "Using the real Venenos to mask our actions was my idea. Helped us recruit guys into our little gang. Kept the law scrambling," Warren said. "The rattler venom is a nice touch. No weapons. No bullet casings. Pure genius."

"We've put the pieces together, Warren. We will stop you."

"You're out of time, Agent Riesel. We're heading out of the country. Dylan, I'll be back in ten minutes. If you have something to confess then, I just might spare Silvia's life."

71

JON PHONED EVERSON AND relayed what he'd found at the dental office.

"Sounds like that's the evidence we've been looking for. I'm sending out a BOLO and media alert for Livingston and the Rioses," Everson said. "Father Gabriel told me Pablo Rios and his wife have recently joined St. Peter's. They'd been guests of Silvia Ortega and Warren Livingston."

No surprise there. "He's there, right? Let me talk to him."

"Hang on."

Father Gabriel greeted him. "Just learned about the drugs found at the dental office. Hard for me to believe it's true."

"What can you tell me about the couple?"

"Dr. Rios has been my dentist for years. Gracious, kind. This makes me feel like a fool. Warren Livingston is a part of this? Poor Silvia, to think I endorsed her and Warren seeing each other. Do you think she's involved? Coaxed Dylan to join them?"

"Right now, we don't have those answers," Jon said.

"I played right into the whole mess. About three years ago, Dr. Rios and his wife talked to me about changing membership to St. Peter's. Said they'd found a church they'd decided to call home. I welcomed them."

"You aren't the first person to be used in illegal activities."

"Jon, I received exactly what I prayed for—criminals to find peace and forgiveness within the walls of St. Peter's. Ironic. I could still have a positive impact."

Jon wasn't sure how to comment, when his idea of a positive impact was a lengthy prison sentence. "Were they friends of Rachel and Judge Mendez?"

"You'd have to ask Rachel. The family used the dental practice."

"Thanks. Can I talk to Everson again?" When Everson responded, Jon continued. "Do you know if Ian Greer and Marcia Trevelle were Rios's patients?"

"Yes. Me too. It's no coincidence the three victims went to the same dentist. They figured it out."

"You could be next on the list. Seriously, watch your back," Jon said. "We need to cross-check Rios's patients with St. Peter's members. In the meantime, is Ross Kempler still with you?"

"Yes. Leah wanted both men to stay here. Why? Wait, hold on a minute. Looks like a call has come in regarding the BOLO."

Jon waited while his mind shoved pieces into place. An established dental practice laundering drugs into Mexico. Silvia taking stolen OxyContin. How had the victims put it together? Or had they simply gotten close enough to make the killers nervous? What role did Silvia play? Everson came back online. "An officer from the Jamaica Beach Police Department spotted Rios's vehicle turning onto a dirt road on the west side of the island. He must think law enforcement has seawater for brains. GPD officers are on their way."

Jon texted Leah to join him, then headed out to the intersection Everson gave him.

Leah glanced around the room to see if there was anything they could use to get free. She scooted toward Silvia until they were back-to-back. "Untie me," she whispered. "And tell me how you ended up here."

Silvia fumbled with the knots. "Warren's men picked up Dylan in the water. Somehow he got away." Silvia's voice dropped to a whisper. "Dylan called me this morning. He needed help—he was hurt badly. I tried to call Rachel, but there was no answer. So I called Warren and he promised to pick up medical supplies. He met me at the dental office and we snuck out the side door. I'm sorry, Agent Riesel. After the shooting on the ferry, I knew I was being watched and I couldn't take the chance that I might lead the FBI to Dylan." Silvia sobbed. "But when I got into Warren's car, he pulled a gun and drove me here. He forced me to call you."

Leah felt the knots begin to loosen a bit.

"Dylan, Elena, and Rachel had already been abducted."

"Mom, I didn't steal his drugs." Dylan's weak voice indicated his body was losing the battle to survive. "I bought OxyContin from Aaron." He sucked in a breath. "He's the one who told me about Warren."

"He blackmailed you," Silvia said.

"I'm sorry. Never killed anyone."

"Don't worry. God will save us."

"I'm not sure that's going to be possible," he whispered. "If I don't make it, know that I love you."

Warren and the Rioses came back into the room before Silvia could untie Leah. Warren's phone rang. He listened and swore, then texted someone. "We have to get out of here. Cops are headed this way."

"We're way ahead of them." Dr. Rios reached for a gun in his waistband.

"Hold off," Warren said. "I have a better idea."

72

AS JON DROVE WEST ON THE ISLAND, a billowing cloud of gray rose in the distance. Fire? He wove in and out of traffic to where Rios's vehicle had been seen. Sirens blared. Red and blue lights flashed.

He swerved left around a motorcycle.

An ambulance passed him at breakneck speed on the opposite side of the road, a white cargo van close behind. Everyone was in a hurry to save a life.

Jon swung onto a dirt-and-sand road leading straight toward the burning beach house. Flames leaped through the structure mounted on twelve-foot-high beams. He sprinted from the car with his gun drawn. Screams of help rose above the crackling fire.

The old fear jolted his senses.

If he waited for firefighters to arrive, it could be too late. Heat from the mounting inferno caused a window to explode.

He heard Leah's voice scream for help above the others.

"Leah!"

Coward. You'd rather watch them die in the fickle beast.

Jon stared at the blue sky being colored by choking gray smoke. The pungent smell of burning timber brought back a surge of vivid memories—his demons, ones he desperately wanted to overcome. The cries inside the house contrasted with watching Hanson and Chip suffer. He refused to let history repeat itself.

He raced to the stairway that led inside and up to the central area of the house. "Leah, I'm on my way."

Was he telling her or himself?

He doused himself with a nearby hose and ripped off his shirt, using it to cover his mouth while moving toward the cries for help. Each step increased the heat. Dread seared his gut.

The door leading into the kitchen was flung wide. Not good. Oxygen was feeding the blazing monster, helping it grow faster. Thick smoke met him. He dropped to his knees and crawled toward the voices he heard. Rachel Mendez and Elena James were tied on the floor nearest the doorway. They coughed as the beast stole their oxygen. He untied Rachel, nearest him. "Free Elena and get out of here."

He hurried to Leah in the fog of smoke, untying her, then Silvia, and handed them his wet shirt. "Go, now. Use this to cover your mouth."

"Not without Dylan," Silvia said.

If Dylan were alive, he wouldn't survive much longer in the smoke and flames, but neither would the women. "I'll carry him out. You won't do him any good if you collapse."

"He's hurt." Silvia gasped for breath.

Elena and Rachel coughed their pleas for Jon to help Dylan. He swung to Leah. "Get these women out of here. I have Dylan."

Leah shouted above the fire's roar for the women to hurry, but Silvia refused to leave until Jon lifted Dylan into his arms. The three women shadowed Leah through mounting flames and a blinding fog of smoke. Jon believed the kid had passed out or was dead.

Jon's eyes stung, blinding him. He stumbled toward the flame-ringed doorway, the impressive heat sending him staggering backward. Was this how his life was going to end? Like Hanson and Chip in the mouth of the fire?

Sparks rained from above them, and a creak sounded. The roof was collapsing. He searched for another way out, but the smoke blinded him. He hoped the women had made it down the stairs and clear of the burning structure.

The ceiling crashed on and around him.

Jon stumbled, regained his balance, and held his breath. He steadied Dylan in his arms before plowing through the flames to the stairway. His body ached. Fire scorched his bare back and shoulders. Smoke filled his lungs. His mind focused on one thing—getting Dylan and himself to safety.

At the stairway, he hoisted Dylan into his arms and started the descent. Flames lapped at his head and trailed down his back. For certain, the steps wouldn't hold his weight. He placed a foot on brittle wood and stepped through it and on through another and another while holding on to Dylan.

Hands reached for him. "We got you, sir." A firefighter took Dylan.

Jon coughed and sputtered. He thought his lungs would burst. On safe ground, another firefighter and Everson escorted him to an awaiting paramedic. Leah rushed forward, yanking off her oxygen mask. Her gaze examined every inch of him.

"I'm all right," he said between burning breaths. Silvia, Rachel, and Elena breathed through oxygen masks while staring at the paramedics treating Dylan. Their faces were streaked black with soot.

"Dr. Rios, his wife, and Warren responsible for this?" Jon bent to his knees to breathe.

Leah nodded. "They left a few minutes before you showed up."

"I passed a white cargo van on the road." Jon coughed hard again. He straightened and shrugged off a paramedic's attempt to give him oxygen while another wanted to examine his burns. Instead, Jon grabbed a bottle of water and his dirty shirt from Leah. "Where were they headed?" His voice held the raspy hoarseness of smoke inhalation.

Everson had pulled out his phone. "I'll check to see if a van's been reported missing." Within moments, Everson had a hit.

"It's heading north on I-45," Everson said. He gave orders for his officers to pursue the vehicle.

Jon moved toward the car. He gulped more water. "Are you coming with me?"

She raced ahead of him with two more bottles of water in her hands. "I'm driving. Got the keys?"

He patted his pocket and tossed them to her.

"I'm behind you," Everson called.

Jon's raw skin stung as though the flames still licked at his flesh.

"You look awful," she said while opening the car door. "Sure you want to do this?"

"Don't even go there."

She roared the engine to life and whipped the car around, throwing sand and dirt in their wake. Within seconds, they were on Seawall, heading toward the Galveston bridge. "Thank God you're okay."

"Be careful what you say, or I might think you really believe that." He coughed, his lungs threatening to explode.

"I think I do." She pressed the gas pedal. "Thought I'd lost you."

"Disappointed?"

"I'd like to punch you." She coughed and reached for water. "But you're in bad shape."

"Take a look in the mirror."

"Jon, you overcame your fear of fire."

He leaned over, fighting the agony in his chest. "I wasn't alone. Do I have any hair left?"

"Patches, but it will grow back. Not sure about the condition of your shoulders and back."

His lungs felt like a torch had ignited them. "Did you get anything from Livingston or the women?"

"I heard all we need," Leah said. "Dylan was involved with the prescription drugs but no murders. Warren blackmailed him."

Jon had questions, but he needed to give his throat a break.

"There's a whole lot more we don't know," she said. "If Dylan survives, we'll have a better understanding of the drug operation and what Ross Kempler found." She shot him a quick look. "Conversation's over. Close your eyes until we catch up."

"Fat chance."

Six minutes later, a text landed in his phone. Jon snatched his device. He forced strength into his body and read the update with a raspy voice. "The van is surrounded by police in the middle of a parking lot in Seabrook." He paused. "Shootings reported. I have the address."

His cough shook the vehicle.

"We need SWAT on this." She took Jon's phone and tapped in a number at a traffic light.

His thoughts raced faster. SWAT would take too long to mobilize.

73

JON WAS READY TO JUMP OUT of the car as soon as Leah stopped beside a barricade of Seabrook police cars, all with lights flashing. Everson pulled in and raced toward Jon and Leah. They joined the Seabrook police and learned Warren was still inside the stolen van.

Too many times a showdown caused those holed up to panic and come out shooting. Jon feared Everson might be just as caustic. A potential problem when the chief of police's emotions veered toward revenge on many levels. Jon quickly asserted the FBI's authority in the jurisdictional soup.

Jon glanced at Leah and whispered, "We've got to keep Everson away from the scene before someone is killed."

"I'll handle this," Everson said.

"You'll get yourself killed." Jon coughed, his chest seared raw.

"You're in no shape to do anything but head to the hospital." He touched his sidearm. "Livingston and Rios are mine."

"To gun down?" Leah said. "How would Marcia feel about it?"

"I'd be doing it for her."

Jon shook his head. "Everson, an angry man can't reason with a criminal. SWAT is on its way, and we can barricade the area."

Jon's words were barely uttered before Everson jogged toward the van. He raised his hands. "Warren, let's end this before anyone else gets hurt. We can talk. No need for any more bloodshed."

Jon's shouts were drowned out by the sound of gunfire erupting from a broken window.

Zachary Everson went down, blood spreading across his chest.

Jon and Leah ran toward him, firing into the van. Seabrook police rushed forward, providing cover and shooting out the van's tires while Jon and Leah pulled Everson back to the line of police cars.

Jon prayed it wasn't too late.

Leah checked Everson's pulse. "He's alive." She stepped aside for the paramedics, who bent to administer emergency treatment.

"They will never surrender," Jon said.

"I'm thinking the same thing," Leah said.

"Can you negotiate?" He broke into a burning cough. "My voice is—"

"Worthless. Sure, I can bullhorn."

"I have an idea. I'll retrieve a flash-bang and work my way around the van." He handed her his phone and looked behind him to an officer who matched his stature and had the same dark hair. Jon bent low and made his way to the man. He explained the need to change clothes and for the officer to appear as though paramedics were treating him.

Leah grabbed a bullhorn and went into action. "Warren, this is Agent Leah Riesel. Everyone in there okay?"

"Leah, good to hear your sweet voice. I see you survived the fire. But let's spare the chitchat."

"We have proof of your crimes, Warren. This is going to go one of two ways. If I were you, I'd opt for a peaceful solution."

He snorted. "I'll take my chances right here. Got me plenty of ammo and a plan."

Jon ducked and moved around the cruisers. He needed to get to the passenger side of the van undetected, shoot out a window, and toss in the flash-bang. Guaranteed to deafen and disorient those inside. Between the ringing of their ears and the temporary blindness, Warren and his cohorts could be overpowered.

"Warren, we need to work this out before these police officers turn their weapons on you."

"Look where that got Everson."

Jon was close enough to the van now to see that Warren was holding a gun to Mrs. Rios's head. There was no sign of the dentist, and Jon feared the man was already dead.

"Shooting at cops will only add to your crimes," Leah said to Warren.

He swore. "Listen, if you get everyone to back off, including Agent Colbert, I might be open to negotiating. I've got a grenade in my pocket. Don't make me toss it."

Jon valued Leah's delay tactics. *Keep talking, Warren. Your pride is showing through.*

She ordered the officers to clear the scene. Those in the parking lot drove away, except for a few cars and a Ford F-350 truck parked twenty feet from the van.

Jon forced air into his lungs. He needed to take Warren out. He took advantage of the distraction the retreating officers provided to creep to the front of the van.

"Now I'm ready to talk," Warren said to Leah. "I'll swap Anna Rios for you. You and I will take a little vacation."

Jon's heart skipped a beat. *Over his dead body.*

"What about Dr. Rios?"

"He's dead. Lay your gun down, nice and easy. Walk toward me. I'll tell you when to stop. You'd better hope no one goes near that truck parked to your right."

"Whatever you need." She obeyed and walked toward the van, holding her arms away from her sides.

Jon heard the van's door open and assumed Warren was preparing to make the exchange. Anna whimpered.

Jon's training kicked in. He stilled his spirit. Concentrated on the target. Tuned out what was going on around him. Prayed for accuracy—and for his coughing to abate while his lungs craved release from the smoke.

He peered around the front of the van. Warren held a gun in his right hand. The grenade was in his left, which was wrapped around Anna Rios's throat. But his finger was not on the pin. He pushed the woman several feet away from him and grabbed Leah.

Jon positioned his finger on the trigger. Leah twisted out of Warren's grasp. The man stumbled.

Jon aimed.

His stomach revolted.

His vision blurred.

He fired.

The hour was approaching 1:30 a.m. when Leah and Jon sat in the emergency room at Memorial Hermann Hospital at the Texas Medical Center. Leah held Jon's hand firmly in hers. Or was it the other way around? For sure, they were a team. She had no intentions of leaving him.

The nurse had disappeared to get his discharge papers and a prescription. Jon argued that he knew how to treat smoke inhalation and refused to be admitted.

Zachary Everson lay in serious condition at the same hospital, after being life-flighted from Galveston. He'd undergone surgery for a pierced lung. Anna Rios had been taken into custody. Pablo Rios and Warren Livingston were dead. Dylan was in a Galveston hospital, showing signs of improvement, much to Silvia's relief. Leah felt confident Dylan would accept a plea bargain and tell authorities everything he knew about Livingston's operation. Between his testimony and the evidence Jon and Ross Kempler had found, she was hopeful the FBI could tie up the loose ends of this case.

Father Gabriel had brought Rachel Mendez to the hospital to meet with them. Leah still wasn't sure why the woman had deliberately withheld information pertinent to the case, but the former attorney had come to make amends and promise her full cooperation. She was no exception to how love and fear often did strange things to those cuffed with emotion. After she left with the priest, Jon said it would be interesting to see what Rachel testified to under oath. As for Father Gabriel . . .

"I decided I like the guy," Jon had said.

"Me too. He looks at life differently than I do, and I realize it's about his priestly vows."

The curtain separating her and Jon from the next patient swung open, and Leah's dad walked in.

Her heart took a leap. Dad looked old and frightened. She rushed to him. "Dad, I'm fine. Jon's going to be okay too."

He drew her into his arms, the sound of his sobs bringing on her own, like their reunion this morning. "Leah, all I could think of was losing you again."

"How did you find out?"

"The news of the firefight popped on my phone's alert. I drove here as soon as I learned where the injured had been taken."

"I haven't even washed my face."

"It's a beautiful face."

She wanted to spare him any more anxiety.

Dad turned to Jon. "How are you doing?" He grimaced at Jon's exposed raw flesh.

"I'll heal," Jon said. "Looks worse than it is."

"You're being admitted?"

"I can handle this better at home. We're waiting on a nurse to bring the discharge papers."

Dad smiled, a sweet, loving gesture she remembered from years ago. "I'll take a seat in the waiting area until I know everything's okay. Been through a few emergency ordeals with my kids. The doctor may pressure you to stay." He kissed Leah's cheek and left the two alone.

"Close one, Agent Colbert," Leah said.

"For you or me?" His hoarse voice continued.

In her concern over him, she'd forgotten he'd saved her life.

"Both of us. You saved my life twice, and I owe you. But I'm glad this case is over."

"Now you hurt my feelings."

She squeezed his hand. "Except for us."

"Seriously." He breathed in deeply. "I don't want us to walk away and label our time together as a solved case."

She needed to be honest. "We could label the case as how we met?"

"And?"

He was making this hard. "The beginning of a meaningful relationship?"

He coughed. "You got me choked up."

She hesitated, more truth time. "You've shown me a lot about life and created a desire in me to learn more about God. Thank you." She lightly kissed his raw lips. "Hope that didn't hurt."

"Bring it on."

"Good, 'cause I think we're stuck with each other."

His phone chirped with a text. "Would you mind checking my message?" He closed his eyes.

Jon was weaker than he realized. "It's from Richard James. He says, 'Thank you for saving Elena's life and helping to end the deaths. Olivia and I are forever grateful.' What would you like for me to say?"

"Thanks, and treasure your family."

Her eyes watered. "Oh, that's so sweet."

"Are you turning girlie on me?"

"It's not impossible."

"Do you have a red dress?"

If Jon was teasing her, he'd be okay. "I'm going to stop worrying about you." Leah touched his lips. "Enough talking. You need your rest."

"You're a nurse now?" He frowned but she ignored him.

"Remember I carry a gun too."

"Will you always be this bossy?"

"Count on it. Can I have another smoky kiss?"

"If you insist." And he was glad she did . . . before he broke into a spluttering of coughs. "We need practice."

Something they agreed on.

EPILOGUE

Leah picked up her pace to baggage claim. Home at last in humid Houston, and she loved it. She'd spent three days with her family in New York, her second visit. A treasured time filled with rekindled love and tears. They'd made a strong start to place family as a priority.

The night of the takedown, Dad had been overwhelmed at the sight of her and Jon at the hospital. His concern and her reassurance that she was okay cemented the father-daughter relationship. He'd followed her to Jon's house. She'd slept in a chair in Jon's bedroom, and Dad had slept on the couch. The next day, she showed him Great-Great-Grandma's book and he took pics of her steampunk decor to share with her siblings.

In the weeks following the Livingston case, Leah had kept in touch with Silvia. Dylan had been sentenced to twelve months in prison for his role. When he'd accepted Aaron Michaels's offer of cheap OxyContin, Warren had coerced Dylan into joining his band of hoodlums, threatening to harm his mother and girlfriend if he didn't comply. Aaron had forced him at gunpoint to deliver Judge Mendez's body to St. Peter's. Dylan's second stint in prison seemed to have changed him, though. He was taking online college courses, moving ahead with his goal of finishing a degree in social work. And this time he was willing to meet with Father Gabriel, who visited Dylan weekly as part of his commitment to minister to those incarcerated.

Among others on the priest's list had been Will Rawlyns. Father Gabriel had stepped in to help address the domestic concerns Rawlyns had for his son and managed to arrange for the boy to visit the prison before Senior passed away from cancer.

According to Silvia, the priest had also been spending a lot of time with Zachary Everson, who decided to resign as police chief since his recuperation would take months.

All thoughts of the tumultuous week she'd first met Jon faded as she stepped onto the escalator to take her to baggage claim. There. There was the sweet man who'd taken aim at her heart and hit the bull's-eye. Some of the scars from the fire might never heal, others would fade in time. She referred to them as his sacrifice of love. If not for looking like a crazy girl, she'd run down the steps to grab a kiss.

Restrain yourself, Leah.

In one week's time, she'd taken the journey of a lifetime, one filled with acceptance and forgiveness of herself, the gift of love, and the knowledge of a God who loved her unconditionally. In four months, her life had taken a direction toward eternal hope.

As Leah stepped off the escalator, Jon opened his arms, and she fell into his embrace.

"Missed you," he said. "A good trip?"

She nodded. Later she'd tell him about what a special time she'd had with her parents and her brothers and sisters. He was invited on the next trip. "You told your parents about your decision?" she said.

"Yep. Can't tell what they're more excited about, seeing you again next weekend or our transfer to the Dallas office."

"For sure, it's you. I'm your tagalong."

He squeezed her waist. "Dad has already expressed how he feels about you—and how I'm not allowed to mess up our relationship."

She'd found an apartment in Dallas with a three-month lease, and Jon had purchased a fifty-acre farm north of the city, a two-hour drive to his parents in Oklahoma. Their relationship was moving ahead with the speed of a jet, but she was ready. "And you're positive about this. About us?"

"Is this the gal who has to be in the driver's seat?"

"For sure."

He brushed a kiss across her lips. "Does that answer your question?"

"Oh yes."

"I have reservations for dinner."

"Wonderful. Where?"

"It's a surprise."

"Do I need a dress?"

"I didn't think you owned one."

Leah had bought a tasteful red dress in New York. And she'd wear it tonight. She knew what the dinner meant. She'd say yes and welcome the future ahead.

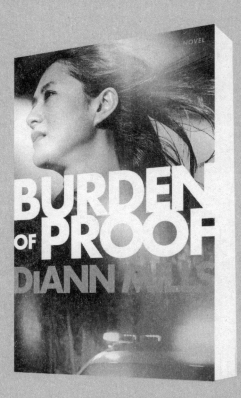

APRIL'S STOMACH RUMBLED, and her fridge at home looked like she'd hung a Vacancy sign on it. Donuts were the last thing she needed after the earlier emotional trauma, as though filling her body with sugar and grease might reduce the overwhelming guilt, but her car still swung into the busy parking lot of a popular donut shop a few blocks from her home.

How sad she also looked for something sweet to soothe the ache of loneliness. The idea of calling someone special, sharing her miserable past hours, and doing the same for him tugged on her heartstrings. Maybe her future held the possibility, but right now no one stood backstage, waving.

A slight chill blew in from the north, and she grabbed her FBI jacket from the backseat, slipping it over her blouse. Inside the shop, she took a place in line behind four other customers.

What drove a man to give up on himself and life? Benson had invited her onto the roof with him . . . so she could watch him commit suicide? For a while, she believed she'd gained his trust. Then an absent wallet destroyed his confidence and hers.

A young woman behind her scolded a crying baby. "I told you to hush. All this way, you've whined and screamed. I'm hungry, so deal with it. Should have left you alongside the road."

The insensitive words irritated April, especially on the heels of the earlier incident. Loving mothers treated their children with tenderness, not like they were liabilities. They protected them from a world that was often harsh. April turned to the young woman who held the crying baby in pink pajamas. Tears stained the child's cheeks, and mucus flowed over her lips.

"Are you a real FBI agent?" The mother looked to be in her early twenties, long ponytail, taller than average.

"Yes."

The young woman shoved the baby into April's arms. "Take her for a few minutes, please. I need to breathe."

April attempted to return the baby, but the mother stepped back. "She's making me crazy."

"I see you're upset. We can talk." April patted the baby's back, but the child only cried louder.

"I'm done with her." The young woman rushed toward the entrance and disappeared into a mass of parked vehicles.

"Hey—" What just happened? April held the baby close to comfort her and detected a dirty diaper. She was shivering, too. Shrugging off her jacket, April stepped out of line to wrap the baby—who wailed louder than before.

The mother might have gone to her car for a diaper bag.

Seven minutes ticked by. April pushed through the entrance of the shop into the cold air, cradling the crying baby girl. At least the jacket kept her warm. April scanned the parking lot and walked to the rear. The young woman had disappeared.

"Well, little one, looks like it's just you and me," she whispered and walked toward the front of the shop with the intention of calling Child Protective Services. "Wish I knew how to ease your tears."

A man jogged her way. "Stop! You have my daughter."

What had she been hit with now? April sized him up for a potential struggle. Trim build. Wore a brown leather jacket and a cap pulled down over his forehead. And a distinct frown.

"Why did you kidnap my daughter?" Despite the cool air, sweat beaded his brow. Before April could respond, the baby whirled to him with open arms. "Isabella, Daddy's here for you." He attempted to take the baby, but April stepped back.

"You can't take this child. A woman gave her to me, and I'm sure she'll return in just a minute." He was close enough to inflict harm.

His face reddened. "Just give me my daughter, and we'll be going." He grabbed April's arm.

She kicked him in the shin, and he winced but didn't release his hold. She held the baby tighter and kept her away from the man's grasp. "Stand down. I'm FBI." April couldn't protect Benson, but she could keep this child from potential harm. The baby's tears settled into a sob.

He looked at the jacket and released her arm as though he'd been burned. "This is yours?"

"Yes. I'm Agent April Ramos. This baby is under my care until I find her legal guardian."

"I'm Isabella's father." He reached into his pocket. "She was kidnapped last night, and I followed the car here. My driver's license—"

"Only proves your name."

"I'm asking you for the last time to give me my daughter."

"Or you'll do what?" She made eye contact.

He rubbed his hand over a stubbly chin. He trembled. "What if she were your daughter? How would you react?"

"I certainly wouldn't accost an FBI agent."

He hesitated. "I need help with a serious situation."

The moment the words were uttered, April's instincts kicked in. "Is this about the woman who left me with the baby?"

He glanced around the parking lot as though he planned to grab the baby and bolt. "Can we talk? The diaper bag is in my truck, and Isabella needs to be changed. I smell her."

Fat chance of that happening. "Why don't you get the bag, and I'll change her inside the donut shop while you tell me your problem."

He shook his head and opened the inside of his jacket just enough for her to see a Beretta. He closed his jacket, covering the weapon. Her Glock was tucked in her shoulder bag. "Don't reach for your gun," he whispered. "I don't want to hurt you."

"Sir, it's difficult for me to be sympathetic when you've pulled a gun on a federal officer. What about endangering your daughter?"

A muscle twitched below his eye, and he patted the gun inside his jacket. "Follow me to my truck, and I'll explain."

"No."

"You have no choice."

She always had a choice, but not when an innocent child was placed in danger. She'd fight for this baby when the only risks were her own. He gestured for her to take the lead and pointed to a 2018 green Chevy pickup, extended cab. He slid her shoulder bag down her arm and placed it in his opposite hand. There went her Glock and phone. All she needed was an opportunity to seize control. They passed a woman with two small children. No point calling out to them when the man beside her had a gun.

They neared the truck, and out of habit, she memorized the plates. He clicked a key fob. "Open the rear driver's-side door," he said. "A diaper bag's inside with everything you need to change Isabella. And a clean sweatshirt and pants." He looked into the baby's face, and his facade saddened. "Sweetie, I know it's cold, but that diaper has to come off." The baby jabbered some unintelligible language.

April obeyed him, and he backed up six feet, eliminating the opportunity for hand-to-hand combat. She laid the baby with her head nearly touching the car seat midway across. Her diaper-changing skills were at ground zero, but she managed and used a wet wipe to wash the baby's face. "She is beautiful."

"Thank you." His voice shook. Maybe he was second-guessing his actions.

She needed him to trust her. "I'm ready to hear your explanation."

"Not yet. Put Isabella in the car seat." He kept his distance.

No one was in sight to even question the crime taking place. Once the baby was secure, he pressed the barrel of the gun against her back.

She sighed. Was he reading her mind or had she left all logic at the office with Benson's suicide? "Let's talk about what's bothering you and get this straightened out."

"Open the driver's door and scoot over to the other side. Don't try a thing, or I'll use the gun."

She obeyed and crawled over the console. As soon as her

feet hit the floorboard on the passenger side, he was seated and locked the doors. No way to kick him with the console . . .

"Don't forget the seat belt," he said.

"Sir, your actions will have serious consequences."

His brown eyes bored hard into her face. "I'm a desperate man."

This must be a domestic or custody dispute. The baby no longer cried, a blessing since April questioned what kind of insanity she'd met for the second time today. Images of the early morning death slammed into her brain. In truth, the memory would never leave her.

"Do you live alone?" her abductor said.

"Yes."

"Address?"

She gave him one.

He typed into his phone. "That belongs to the FBI." He pulled the Beretta from his jacket and aimed it at her. "This is a life-and-death matter. I hate pulling you into my circumstances. But I have no choice when my daughter is threatened."

Definitely a troubled man. She'd gain the upper hand at her home. With that reassurance, she gave him the correct address.

"We'll talk there." He typed into his phone and placed the truck in reverse.

While Jason drove to Agent Ramos's home through heavy traffic, he worried the cops were on his tail. Emotion for what he'd experienced over the last several hours threatened to break loose. He'd shed nearly as many tears as when Lily died. Now Russell . . . And he'd almost lost his baby girl. Jason stared at

Isabella through the rearview mirror. "Daddy is so sorry for what you went through." She'd been the victim of his worst nightmare: an abduction.

"Are you ready to talk?" the agent said.

"Not yet." The tiny woman beside him probably had hand-to-hand combat skills beyond his imagination. He'd done his best to avoid a flying fist or foot. At least he had her purse, most likely containing a cell phone and a weapon. A huge risk. But her influence in law enforcement could right a terrible wrong. Several of them. "I'm thinking through how to present my story."

She nodded. "Okay."

"I'm Jason, and you've met my daughter, Isabella."

April nodded. "I'm glad I was there. Would you like for me to call Isabella's mother and let her know her daughter's safe?"

"Isabella's mother died a year ago, giving birth to our daughter." He'd disappointed Lily too. She'd kissed Isabella at two hours old, just before saying good-bye to them forever. What had he just done? "Nabbing a federal agent was an impulsive decision. Not my normal way of handling a problem."

"I won't deny you're in a lot of trouble. Let's talk this out."

He swallowed hard. "No amount of talk can fix the tragedy affecting my life."

"Then I need to hear what you have to say."

After two more turns, he pulled into a driveway in front of a cottage-style home. A risky plan formed, one of justice and a way to solve a murder.

DISCUSSION QUESTIONS

1. When Agents Jon Colbert and Leah Riesel are asked to team up in a high-pressure situation, Leah wonders how well their partnership will work. What preconceptions does she have about him? What does he know about her? When you meet someone new, what might color your impression of that person? What can you do to overcome negative preconceptions?

2. As an FBI sniper, Leah often finds herself in deadly situations: taking the lives of other people before they can do more harm. What makes her pause before she pulls the trigger? Is this approach to law enforcement the best, even only, option at times? Why or why not?

3. Silvia Ortega remains adamant that her son, Dylan, is not responsible for the recent murders in Galveston. Which side did you land on at the beginning of *Fatal Strike*: Dylan's guilt or innocence? What factors do you consider when you hear an eyewitness account like Edgar Whitson's? How much weight do you give possible motives and past behavior?

4. Father Gabriel tells Jon and Leah that he believes in "second, third, and as many chances as it takes to help a person find the way to righteousness." Is he being too naive, as Jon fears? Where do you fall on the spectrum between the priest's and the FBI agents' approaches to handling crime? When is it appropriate to show mercy and grace and when should justice be meted out?

5. Why is Jon reluctant to share certain details of his past with his colleagues at the FBI? How is he coping with the deaths of his friends? What counsel would you give someone dealing with survivor's guilt?

6. Like Jon, Leah is carrying a heavy burden from her past and has cut off communication with her family and, recently, even one of her good friends. What led to Leah's decision to sever these ties? What might cause a person to dissociate from their family? What prompts Leah to reach out? What advice or support could you give to help bring about reconciliation (if appropriate)?

7. Police Chief Zachary Everson has a major stake in solving the recent Galveston murders, but Jon fears some of his methods may be problematic. Which of Everson's actions seem to be motivated by revenge or anger and not a search for truth? How do you respond when you've been hurt or wronged?

8. Silvia tries to justify her quest to aid Dylan as just part of what mothers do for their children. But what do the physical clues reveal about how she might really feel? How does the body's response indicate truth, even when we try to deny it?

9. Leah's fear of snakes reaches a tipping point when one is delivered to her apartment. What are you afraid of? Describe a time when you've faced your fear head-on.

10. Several people in *Fatal Strike* withhold critical information from the FBI, but two who stand out are Rachel Mendez and Ross Kempler. Why do you think they were reluctant to share certain details about Dylan and the judge with Jon and Leah?

ABOUT THE AUTHOR

DiANN MILLS is a bestselling author who believes her readers should expect an adventure. She combines unforgettable characters with unpredictable plots to create action-packed romantic suspense novels.

Her titles have appeared on the CBA and ECPA bestseller lists; won two Christy Awards; and been finalists for the RITA, Daphne du Maurier, Inspirational Reader's Choice, and Carol Award contests. *Firewall*, the first book in her Houston: FBI series, was listed by *Library Journal* as one of the best Christian fiction books of 2014.

DiAnn is a founding board member of the American Christian Fiction Writers and a member of Advanced Writers and Speakers Association, Sisters in Crime, and International Thriller Writers. She is codirector of the Blue Ridge Mountains Christian Writers Conference, where she continues her passion of helping other writers be successful. She speaks to various groups and teaches writing workshops around the country.

DiAnn has been termed a coffee snob and roasts her own coffee beans. She's an avid reader, loves to cook, and believes her grandchildren are the smartest kids in the universe. She and her husband live in sunny Houston, Texas.

DiAnn is very active online and would love to connect with readers through her website at www.diannmills.com or on Facebook (www.facebook.com/diann.mills.5), Twitter (@ DiAnnMills), Pinterest (www.pinterest.com/DiAnnMills), and Goodreads (www.goodreads.com/DiAnnMills).